African Adventures: 1

African Adventures: 1

Swallow

★

Benita

H. Rider Haggard

LEONAUR

African Adventures: 1—Swallow & Benita
by H. Rider Haggard

Leonaur is an imprint of Oakpast Ltd

Material original to this edition and
presentation of text in this form
copyright © 2009 Oakpast Ltd

ISBN: 978-1-84677-794-3 (hardcover)
ISBN: 978-1-84677-793-6 (softcover)

http://www.leonaur.com

Publisher's Notes

Contents

Swallow

Ditchingham, 20th May, 1898

My Dear Clarke, Over twenty years have passed since we found some unique opportunities of observing Boer and Kaffir character in company; therefore it is not perhaps out of place that I should ask you to allow me to put your name upon a book which deals more or less with the peculiarities of those races—a tale of the great Trek of 1836.

You, as I know, entertain both for Dutchman and Bantu that regard tempered by a sense of respectful superiority which we are apt to feel for those who on sundry occasions have but just failed in bringing our earthly career to an end. The latter of these admirations I share to the full; and in the case of the first of them, as I hope that the dour but not unkindly character of *Vrouw* Botmar will prove to you, time softens a man's judgment. Nor have I ever questioned, as the worthy *Vrouw* tells us, that in the beginning of the trouble the Boers met with much of which to complain at the hands of English Governments. Their maltreatment was not intentional indeed, but rather a result of systematic neglect—to use a mild word—of colonies and their inhabitants, which has culminated within our own experience, only, thanks to a merciful change in public opinion, to pass away for ever. Sympathy with the *Voortrekkers* of 1836 is easy; whether it remains so in the case of their descendants, the present masters of the Transvaal, is a matter that admits of many opinions. At the least, allowance should always be made for the susceptibilities of a race that finds its individuality and national life sinking slowly, but without hope of resurrection, beneath an invading flood of Anglo-Saxons.

But these are issues of today with which this story has little to do.

Without further explanation, then, I hope that you will accept these pages in memory of past time and friendship, and more especially of the providential events connected with a night-long ride which once we took on duty together among the "*schanzes*" and across the moon-lit paths of Secocoeni's mountain.

Believe me, my dear Clarke,

Your sincere friend

H. Rider Haggard

To Lieut.-Colonel Sir Marshal Clarke, R.A., K.C.M.G.

CHAPTER 1
Why Vrouw Botmar Tells Her Tale

It is a strange thing that I, an old Boer *vrouw*, should even think of beginning to write a book when there are such numbers already in the world, most of them worthless, and many of the rest a scandal and offence in the face of the Lord. Notably is this so in the case of those called novels, which are stiff as *mealie*-pap with lies that fill the heads of silly girls with vain imaginings, causing them to neglect their household duties and to look out of the corners of their eyes at young men of whom their elders do not approve. In truth, my mother and those whom I knew in my youth, fifty years ago, when women were good and worthy and never had a thought beyond their husbands and their children, would laugh aloud could any whisper in their dead ears that Suzanne Naudé was about to write a book. Well might they laugh indeed, seeing that to this hour the most that I can do with men and ink is to sign my own name very large; in this matter alone, not being the equal of my husband Jan, who, before he became paralysed, had so much learning that he could read aloud from the Bible, leaving out the names and long words.

No, no, *I* am not going to write; it is my great-granddaughter, who is named Suzanne after me, who writes. And who that had not seen her at the work could even guess how she does it? I tell you that she has brought up from Durban a machine about the size of a pumpkin which goes tap-tap—like a woodpecker, and prints as it taps. Now, my husband Jan was always very fond of music in his youth, and when first the girl began to tap upon this strange instrument, he, being almost blind and not able to see it, thought that she was playing on a spinet such as stood in my grandfather's house away in the Old Colony. The noise pleases him and sends him to sleep, reminding him of the days when he courted me and I used to strum upon that spinet with one finger. Therefore I am dictating this history that he may have plenty of it, and that Suzanne may be kept out of mischief.

There, that is my joke. Still there is truth in it, for Jan Botmar, my husband, he who was the strongest man among the fathers of the great trek of 1836, when, like the Israelites of old, we escaped from the English, our masters, into the wilderness, crouches in the corner yonder a crippled giant with but one sense left to him, his hearing, and a little power of wandering speech. It is strange to look at him, his white hair hanging upon his shoulders, his eyes glazed, his chin sunk upon his breast, his great hands knotted and helpless, and to remember that at the battle of Vechtkop, when Moselikatse sent his regiments to crush us, I saw those same hands of his seize the only two Zulus who broke a way into our *laager* and shake and dash them together till they were dead.

Well, well, who am I that I should talk? For has not the dropsy got hold of my legs, and did not that doctor, who, though an Englishman, is no fool, tell me but yesterday that it was creeping up towards my heart? We are old and soon must die, for such is the will of God. Let us then thank God that it is our lot to pass thus easily and in age, and not to have perished in our youth, as did so many of our companions, the *Voortrekkers*, they and their children together, by the spear of the savage, or by starvation and fever and wild beasts in the wilderness. Ah! I think of them often, and in my sleep, which has grown light of late, I see them often, and hear those voices that none but I would know today. I think of them and I see them, and since Suzanne has the skill to set down my words, a desire comes upon me to tell of them and their deeds before God takes me by the hand and I am borne through the darkness by the wings of God.

Also there is another reason. The girl, Suzanne Kenzie, my great-granddaughter, who writes this, alone is left of my blood, since her father and grandfather, who was our adopted son, and the husband of our only child, fell in the Zulu war fighting with the English against Cetywayo. Now many have heard the strange story of Ralph Kenzie, the English castaway, and of how he was found by our daughter Suzanne. Many have heard also the still stranger story of how this child of ours, Suzanne, in her need, was sheltered by savages, and for more than two years lived with Sihamba, the little witch doctoress and ruler of the Tribe of the Mountains, till Ralph, her husband, who loved her, sought her out and rescued her, that by the mercy of the Lord during all this time had suffered neither harm nor violence. Yes, many have heard of these things, for in bygone years there was much talk of them as of events out of nature and marvellous, but few have heard them right. Therefore before I go, I, who remember and know them all,

12

would set them down that they may be a record for ever among my descendants and the descendants of Ralph Kenzie, my foster-son, who, having been brought up amongst us Boers, was the best and bravest Englishman that ever lived in Africa.

****

And now I will tell of the finding of Ralph Kenzie many years ago.

To begin at the beginning, my husband, Jan Botmar, is one of the well-known Boer family of that name, the most of whom lived in the Graafreinet district in the Old Colony till some of them trekked into the Transkei, when I was still a young girl, to be as far as they could from the heart of the British power. Nor did they trek for a little reason. Listen and judge.

One of the Bezuidenhouts, Frederick, was accused of treating some black slave of his cruelly, and a body of the accursed *Pandours*, the Hottentots whom the English had made into a regiment, were sent to arrest him. He would not suffer that these black creatures should lay hands upon a Boer, so he fled to a cave and fought there till he was shot dead. Over his open grave his brethren and friends swore to take vengeance for his murder, and fifty of them raised an insurrection. They were pursued by the *Pandours* and by burghers more law abiding or more cautious, till Jan Bezuidenhout, the brother of Frederick, was shot also, fighting to the last while his wife and little son loaded the rifles. Then the rest were captured and put upon their trial, and to the rage and horror of all their countrymen the brutal British governor of that day, who was named Somerset, ordered five of them to be hanged, among them my husband's father and uncle. Petitions for mercy availed nothing, and these five were tied to a beam like Kaffir dogs yonder at Slagter's Nek, they who had shed the blood of no man. Yes, yes, it is true, for Jan, my man, saw it; he saw his father and his uncle hanged like dogs. When they pushed them from the beam four of the ropes broke—perhaps they had been tampered with, I know not—but still the devils who murdered them would show no mercy. Jan ran to his father and cast his arms about him, but they tore him away.

"Do not forget, my son," he gasped as he lay there on the ground with the broken rope about his neck, nor did Jan ever forget.

It was after this that the Botmars trekked into the Transkei, and with them some other families, amongst whom were the Naudes, my parents. Here in the Transkei the widow Botmar and my father were near neighbours, their steads being at a distance from each other of about three hours upon horseback, or something over twenty miles.

In those days, I may say it without shame now, I was the prettiest girl in the Transkei, a great deal prettier than my granddaughter Suzanne there, although some think well of her looks, but not so well as she thinks of them herself, for that would be impossible. I have been told that I have noble French blood in my veins, though I care little for this, being quite content to be one of the Boers, who are all of noble blood. At least I believe that my great-grandfather was a French Huguenot Count who fled from his country to escape massacre because of his religion. From him and his wife Suzanne, so it is said, we women of the Naudes get our beauty, for we have always been beautiful; but the loveliest of the race by far was my daughter Suzanne who married the Englishman, Ralph Kenzie, from which time our good looks have begun to fall off, though it is true that he was no ill-favoured man.

Whatever the cause, in my youth, I was not like the other Boer girls, who for the most part are stout, heavy, and slow of speech, even before they are married, nor did I need to wear a *kapje* to keep a pink and white face from burning in the sun. I was not tall, but my figure was rounded and my movements were as quick as my tongue. Also I had brown hair that curled and brown eyes beneath it, and full red lips, which all the young men of that district—and there were six of them who can be counted—would have given their best horse to kiss, with the saddle and bridle thrown in. But remember this, Suzanne, I never suffered them to do so, for in my time girls knew better what was right.

Well, among all these suitors I favoured Jan Botmar, the old cripple who sits yonder, though in those days he was no cripple but the properest man a girl could wish to see. My father was against such a match, for he had the old French pride of race in him, and thought little of the Botmar family, as though we were not all the children of one God—except the black Kaffirs, who are the children of the devil. But in the end he gave way, for Jan was well-to-do; so after we had "*opsitted*" together several times according to our customs, and burnt many very long candles,[1] we were married and went to live on a farm of our own at a distance. For my part I have never regretted it, although doubtless I might have done much better for myself; and if Jan did, he has been wise enough not to say so to me. In this country most of us women must choose a man to look after—it is a burden that Heaven

---

1. It is customary among the Boers for the suitor to sit up alone at night with the object of his choice. Should the lady favour him, she lights long candles, but if he does not please her she produces "ends," signifying thereby that she prefers his room to his company.—Author.

lays upon us—so one may as well choose him one fancies, and Jan was my fancy, though why he should have been I am sure I do not know. Well, if he had any wits left he would speak up and tell what a blessing I have been to him, and how often my good sense has supplied the lack of his, and how I forgave him, yes, and helped him out of the scrape when he made a fool of himself with—but I will not write of that, for it makes me angry, and as likely as not I should throw something at him before I had finished, which he would not understand.

No, no; I do not regret it, and, what is more, when my man dies I shall not be long behind him. Ah! they may talk, all these wise young people; but, after all, what is there better for a woman than to love some man, the good and the bad of him together, to bear his children and to share his sorrows, and to try to make him a little better and a little less selfish and unfortunate than he would have been alone? Poor men! Without us women their lot would be hard indeed, and how they will get on in heaven, where they are not allowed to marry, is more than I can guess.

So we married, and within a year our daughter was born and christened by the family name of Suzanne after me, though almost from her cradle the Kaffirs called her "Swallow," I am not sure why. She was a very beautiful child from the first, and she was the only one, for I was ill at her birth and never had any more children. The other women with their coveys of eight and ten and twelve used to condole with me about this, and get a sharp answer for their pains. I had one which always shut their mouths, but I won't ask the girl here to set it down. An only daughter was enough for me, I said, and if it wasn't I shouldn't have told them so, for the truth is that it is best to take these things as we find them, and whether it be one or ten, to declare that that is just as we would wish it. I know that when we were on the great trek and I saw the *kinderchies* of others dying of starvation, or massacred in dozens by the Kaffir devils, ah! then I was glad that we had no more children. Heartaches enough my ewe lamb Suzanne gave me during those bitter years when she was lost. And when she died, having lived out her life just before her husband, Ralph Kenzie, went on commando with his son to the Zulu war, whither her death drove him, ah! then it ached for the last time. When next my heart aches it shall be with joy to find them both in Heaven.

CHAPTER 2

How Suzanne Found Ralph Kenzie

Our farm where we lived in the Transkei was not very far from the ocean; indeed, any one seated in the *kopje* or little hill at the back of the house, from the very top of which bubbles a spring of fresh water, can see the great rollers striking the straight cliffs of the shore and spouting into the air in clouds of white foam. Even in warm weather they spout thus, but when the south-easterly gales blow then the sight and the sound of them are terrible as they rush in from the black water one after another for days and nights together. Then the cliffs shiver beneath their blows, and the spray flies up as though it were driven from the nostrils of a thousand whales, and is swept inland in clouds, turning the grass and the leaves of the trees black in its breath. Woe to the ship that is caught in those breakers and ground against those rocks, for soon nothing is left of it save scattered timbers shivered as though by lightning.

One winter—it was when Suzanne was seven years old—such a south-east gale as this blew for four days, and on a certain evening after the wind had fallen, having finished my household work, I went to the top of the *kopje* to rest and look at the sea, which was still raging terrible, taking with me Suzanne. I had been sitting there ten minutes or more when Jan, my husband, joined me, and I wondered why he had come, for he, as brave a man as ever lived in all other things, was greatly afraid of the sea, and, indeed, of any water. So afraid was he that he did not like the sight of it in its anger, and would wake at nights at the sound of a storm—yes, he whom I have seen sleep through the trumpetings of frightened elephants and the shouting of a Zulu *impi*.

"You think that sight fine, wife," he said, pointing to the spouting foam; "but I call it the ugliest in the world. Almighty! it turns my blood cold to look at it and to think that Christian men, ay, and women and children too, may be pounding to pulp in those breakers."

"Without doubt the death is as good as another," I answered; "not that I would choose it, for I wish to die in my bed with the *predicant* saying prayers over me, and my husband weeping—or pretending to—at the foot of it."

"Choose it!" he said. "I had sooner be speared by savages or hanged by the English Government as my father was."

"What makes you think of death in the sea, Jan?" I asked.

"Nothing, wife, nothing; but there is that fool of a Pondo witch-doctoress down by the cattle *kraal*, and I heard her telling a story as I went by to look at the ox that the snake bit yesterday."

"What was the story?"

"Oh! a short one; she said she had it from the coast Kaffirs—that far away, up towards the mouth of the Umzimbubu, when the moon was young, great guns had been heard fired one after the other, minute by minute, and that then a ship was seen, a tall ship with three masts and many 'eyes' in it—I suppose she meant portholes with the light shining through them—drifting on to the coast before the wind, for a storm was raging, while streaks of fire like red and blue lightnings rushed up from her decks."

"Well, and then?"

"And then, nothing. Almighty! that is all the tale. Those waves which you love to watch can tell the rest."

"Most like it is some Kaffir lie, husband."

"May be, but amongst these people news travels faster than a good horse, and before now there have been wrecks upon this coast. Child, put down that gun. Do you want to shoot your mother? Have I not told you that you must never touch a gun?" and he pointed to Suzanne, who had picked up her father's *roer*—for in those days, when we lived among so many Kaffirs, every man went armed—and was playing at soldiers with it.

"I was shooting buck and Kaffirs, papa," she said, obeying him with a pout.

"Shooting Kaffirs, were you? Well, there will be a good deal of that to do before all is finished in this land, little one. But it is not work for girls; you should have been a boy, Suzanne."

"I can't; I am a girl," she answered; "and I haven't any brothers like other girls. Why haven't I any brothers?"

Jan shrugged his shoulders, and looked at me.

"Won't the sea bring me a brother?" went on the child, for she had been told that little children came out of the sea.

"Perhaps, if you look for one very hard," I answered with a sigh, little knowing what fruit would spring from this seed of a child's talk.

On the morrow there was a great to do about the place, for the black girl whose business it was to look after Suzanne came in at breakfast time and said that she had lost the child. It seemed that they had gone down to the shore in the early morning to gather big shells such as are washed up there after a heavy storm, and that Suzanne had taken with her a bag made of spring-buck hide in which to carry them. Well, the black girl sat down under the shadow of a rock, leaving Suzanne to wander to and fro looking for the shells, and not for an hour or more did she get up to find her. Then she searched in vain, for the spoor of the child's feet led from the sand between the rocks to the pebbly shore above, which was covered with tough sea grasses, and there was lost. Now at the girl's story I was frightened, and Jan was both frightened and so angry that he would have tied her up and flogged her if he had found time. But of this there was none to lose, so taking with him such Kaffirs as he could find he set off for the seashore to hunt for Suzanne. It was near sunset when he returned, and I, who was watching from the *stoep*, saw with a shiver of fear that he was alone.

"Wife," he said in a hollow voice, "the child is lost. We have searched far and wide and can find no trace of her. Make food ready to put in my saddle-bags, for should we discover her to-night or tomorrow, she will be starving."

"Be comforted," I said, "at least she will not starve, for the cook girl tells me that before Suzanne set out this morning she begged of her a bottle of milk and with it some biltong and meal cakes and put them in her bag."

"It is strange," he answered. "What could the little maid want with these unless she was minded to make a journey?"

"At times it comes into the thoughts of children to play truant, husband."

"Yes, yes, that is so, but pray God that we may find her before the moon sets."

Then while I filled the saddle-bags Jan swallowed some meat, and a fresh horse having been brought he kissed me and rode away in the twilight.

Oh! what hours were those that followed! All night long I sat there on the *stoep*, though the wind chilled me and the dew wet my clothes, watching and praying as, I think, I never prayed before. This I knew well—that our Suzanne, our only child, the light and joy of our home, was in danger so great that the Lord alone could save her. The country where we lived was lonely, savages still roamed about it who hated the white man, and might steal or kill her; also it was full of leopards, hyenas, and other beasts of prey which would devour her. Worst of all, the tides on the coast were swift and treacherous, and it well might happen that if she was wandering among the great rocks the sea would come in and drown her. Indeed, again and again it seemed to me that I could hear her death-cry in the sob of the wind.

At length the dawn broke, and with it came Jan. One glance at his face was enough for me. "She is not dead?" I gasped.

"I know not," he answered, "we have found nothing of her. Give me brandy and another horse, for the sun rises, and I return to the search. The tide is down, perhaps we shall discover her among the rocks," and he groaned and entered the house with me.

"Kneel down and let us pray, husband," I said, and we knelt down weeping and praying aloud to our God who, seated in the Heavens, yet sees and knows the needs and griefs of His servants upon the earth; prayed that He would pity our agony and give us back our only child. Nor, blessed be his name, did we pray vainly, for presently, while we still knelt, we heard the voice of that girl who had lost Suzanne, and who all night long had lain sobbing in the garden grounds, calling to us in wild accents to come forth and see. Then we rushed out, hope burning up suddenly in our hearts like a fire in dry grass.

In front of the house and not more than thirty paces from it, was the crest of a little wave of land upon which at this moment the rays of the rising sun struck brightly. There, yes, there, full in the glow of them, stood the child Suzanne, wet, disarrayed, her hair hanging about her face, but unharmed and smiling, and leaning on her shoulder another child, a white boy, somewhat taller and older than herself. With a cry of joy we rushed towards her, and reaching her the first, for my feet were the swiftest, I snatched her to my breast and kissed her, whereon the boy fell down, for it seemed that his foot was hurt and he could not stand alone.

"In the name of Heaven, what is the meaning of this?" gasped Jan.

"What should it mean," answered the little maid proudly, "save that I went to look for the brother whom you said I might find by the sea if I searched hard enough, and I found him, though I do not understand his words or he mine. Come, brother, let me help you up, for this is our home, and here are our father and mother."

Then, filled with wonder, we carried the children into the house, and took their wet clothes off them. It was I who undressed the boy, and noted that though his garments were in rags and foul, yet they were of a finer stuff than any that I had seen, and that his linen, which was soft as silk, was marked with the letters R. M. Also I noted other things: namely, that so swollen were his little feet that the boots must be cut off them, and that he was well-nigh dead of starvation, for his bones almost pierced his milk-white skin.

Well, we cleaned him, and having wrapped him in blankets and soft-tanned hides, I fed him with broth a spoonful at a time, for had I let him eat all he would, he was so famished that I feared lest he should kill himself. After he was somewhat satisfied, sad memories seemed to come back to him, for he cried and spoke in England, repeating the word "Mother," which I knew, again and again, till presently he dropped off to sleep, and for many hours slept without waking. Then, little by little, I drew all the tale from Suzanne.

It would seem that the child, who was very venturesome and full of imaginings, had dreamed a dream in her bed on the night of the day when she played with the gun and Jan and I had spoken together of the sea. She dreamed that in a certain *kloof*, an hour's ride and more away from the stead, she heard the voice of a child praying, and that although he prayed in a tongue unknown to her, she understood the words, which were: "O Father, my mother is dead, send some one to help me, for I am starving." Moreover, looking round her in her dream, though she could not see the child from whom the voice came, yet she knew the *kloof*, for as it chanced she had been there twice, once with me to gather white lilies for the burial of a neighbour who had died, and once with her father, who was searching for a lost ox. Now Suzanne, having lived so much with her elders, was very quick, and she was sure when she woke in the morning that if she said anything about her dream we should laugh at her and should not allow her to go to the place of which she had dreamt. Therefore it was that she made the plan of seeking for the shells upon the seashore, and of slipping away from the woman who was with her, and therefore also she begged the milk and the biltong.

Now before I go further I would ask, What was this dream of Suzanne's? Did she invent it after the things to which it pointed had come to pass, or was it verily a vision sent by God to the pure heart of a little child, as aforetime He sent a vision to the heart of the infant Samuel? Let each solve the riddle as he will, only, if it were nothing but an imagination, why did she take the milk and food? Because we had been talking on that evening of her finding a brother by the sea, you may answer. Well, perhaps so; let each solve the riddle as he will.

When Suzanne escaped from her nurse she struck inland, and thus it happened that her feet left no spoor upon the hard, dry *veldt*. Soon she found that the *kloof* she sought was further off than she thought for, or, perhaps, she lost her way to it, for the hillsides are scarred with such *kloofs*, and it might well chance that a child would mistake one for the other. Still she went on, though she grew frightened in the lonely wilderness, where great bucks sprang up at her feet and baboons barked at her as they clambered from rock to rock. On she went, stopping only once or twice to drink a little of the milk and eat some food, till, towards sunset, she found the *kloof* of which she had dreamed. For a while she wandered about in it, following the banks of a stream, till at length, as she passed a dense clump of mimosa bushes, she heard the faint sound of a child's voice—the very voice of her dream. Now she stopped, and turning to the right, pushed her way through the mimosas, and there beyond them was a dell, and in the centre of the dell a large flat rock, and on the rock a boy praying, the rays of the setting sun shining in his golden, tangled hair. She went to the child and spoke to him, but he could not understand our tongue, nor could she understand his. Then she drew out what was left of the bottle of milk and some meal cakes and gave them to him, and he ate and drank greedily.

By this time the sun was down, and as they did not dare to move in the dark, the children sat together on the rock, clasped in each other's arms for warmth, and as they sat they saw yellow eyes staring at them through the gloom, and heard strange snoring sounds, and were afraid. At length the moon rose, and in its first rays they perceived standing and walking within a few paces of them three tigers, as we call leopards, two of them big and one half-grown. But the tigers did them no harm, for God forbade them; they only looked at them a little and then slipped away, purring as they went.

Now Suzanne rose, and taking the boy by the hand she began to lead him homeward, very slowly, since he was footsore and exhausted, and for the last half of the way could only walk resting upon her shoulder. Still through the long night they crawled forward, for the *kopje* at the back of our stead was a guide to Suzanne, stopping from time to time to rest a while, till at the breaking of the dawn with their last strength they came to the house, as has been told.

Well it was that they did so, for it seems that the searchers had already sought them in the very *kloof* where they were hidden, without seeing anything of them behind the thick screen of the mimosas, and having once sought doubtless they would have returned there no more, for the hills are wide and the *kloofs* in them many.

CHAPTER 3

The Story of the Shipwreck

"What shall we do with this boy whom Suzanne has brought to us, wife?" asked Jan of me that day while both the children lay asleep.

"Do with him, husband!" I answered; "we shall keep him; he is the Lord's gift."

"He is English, and I hate the English," said Jan, looking down.

"English or Dutch, husband, he is of noble blood, and the Lord's gift, and to turn him away would be to turn away our luck."

"But how if his people come to seek him?"

"When they come we will talk of it, but I do not think that they will come; I think that the sea has swallowed them all."

After that Jan said no more of this matter for many years; indeed I believe that from the first he desired to keep the child, he who was sonless.

Now while the boy lay asleep Jan mounted his horse and rode for two hours to the stead of our neighbour, the *Heer* van Vooren. This Van Vooren was a very rich man, by far the richest of us outlying Boers, and he had come to live in these wilds because of some bad act that he had done; I think that it was the shooting of a coloured person when he was angry. He was a strange man and much feared, sullen in countenance, and silent by nature. It was said that his grandmother was a chieftainess among the red Kaffirs, but if so, the blood showed more in his son and only child than in himself. Of this son, who in after years was named Swart Piet, and his evil doings I shall have to tell later in my story, but even then his dark face and savage temper had earned for him the name of "the little Kaffir."

Now the wife of the *Heer* van Vooren was dead, and he had a tutor for his boy Piet, a poor Hollander body who could speak English. That man knew figures also, for once when, thinking that I should be too clever for him, I asked him how often the wheel of our big wagon would turn round travelling between our farm and Capetown Castle, he took a rule and measured the wheel, then having set down some figures on a bit of paper, and worked at them for a while, he told me the answer. Whether it was right or wrong I did not know, and said so, whereon the poor creature grew angry, and lied in his anger, for he swore that he could tell how often the wheel would turn in travelling from the earth to the sun or moon, and also how far we were from those great lamps, a thing that is known to God only, Who made them for our comfort. It is little wonder, therefore, that with such unholy teaching Swart Piet grew up so bad.

Well, Jan went to beg the loan of this tutor, thinking that he would be able to understand what the English boy said, and in due course the creature came in a pair of blue spectacles and riding on a mule, for he dared not trust himself to a horse. Afterwards, when the child woke up from his long sleep, and had been fed and dressed, the tutor spoke with him in that ugly English tongue of which I could never even bear the sound, and this was the story that he drew from him.

It seems that the boy, who gave his name as Ralph Kenzie, though I believe that really it was Ralph Mackenzie, was travelling with his father and mother and many others from a country called India, which is one of those places that the English have stolen in different parts of the world, as they stole the Cape and Natal and all the rest. They travelled for a long while in a big ship, for India is a long way off, till, when they were near this coast, a storm sprang up, and after the wind had blown for two days they were driven on rocks a hundred miles or more away from our stead. So fierce was the sea and so quickly did the ship break to pieces that only one boat was got out, which, except for a crew of six men, was filled with women and children. In this boat the boy Ralph and his mother were given a place, but his father did not come, although the captain begged him, for he was a man of some importance, whose life was of more value than those of common people. But he refused, for he said that he would stop and share the fate of the other men, which shows that this English lord, for I think he was a lord, had a high spirit. So he kissed his wife and child and blessed them, and the boat was lowered to the sea, but before another could be got ready the great ship slipped back from the rock upon which she hung and sank (for this we heard afterwards from some Kaffirs who saw it), and all aboard of her were drowned. May God have mercy upon them!

When it was near to the shore the boat was overturned, and some of those in it were drowned, but Ralph and his mother were cast safely on the beach, and with them others. Then one of the men looked at a compass and they began to walk southwards, hoping doubtless to reach country where white people lived. All that befell afterwards I cannot tell, for the poor child was too frightened and bewildered to remember, but it seems that the men were killed in a fight with natives, who, however, did not touch the women and children. After that the women and the little ones died one by one of hunger and weariness, or were taken by wild beasts, till at last none were left save Ralph and his mother. When they were alone they met a Kaffir woman, who gave them as much food as they could carry, and by the help of this food they struggled on southward for another five or six days, till at length one morning, after their food was gone, Ralph woke to find his mother cold and dead beside him.

When he was sure that she was dead he was much frightened, and ran away as fast as he could. All that day he staggered forward, till in the evening he came to the *kloof*, and being quite exhausted, knelt upon the flat stone to pray, as he had been taught to do, and there Suzanne found him. Such was the story, and so piteous it seemed to us that we wept as we listened, yes, even Jan wept, and the tutor snivelled and wiped his weak eyes.

That it was true in the main we learned afterwards from the Kaffirs, a bit here and a bit there. Indeed, one of our own people, while searching for Suzanne, found the body of Ralph's mother and buried it. He said that she was a tall and noble-looking lady, not much more than thirty years of age. We did not dig her up again to look at her, as perhaps we should have done, for the Kaffir declared that she had nothing on her except some rags and two rings, a plain gold one and another of emeralds, with a device carved upon it, and in the pocket of her gown a little book bound in red, that proved to be a Testament, on the fly leaf of which was written in English, "Flora Gordon, the gift of her mother, Agnes Janey Gordon, on her confirmation," and with it a date.

All these things the Kaffir brought home faithfully, also a lock of the lady's fair hair, which he had cut off with his *assegai*. That lock of hair labelled in writing—remember it, Suzanne, when I am gone—is in the wagon box which stands beneath my bed. The other articles Suzanne here has, as is her right, for her grandfather settled them on her by will, and with them one thing which I forgot to mention. When we undressed the boy Ralph, we found hanging by a gold chain to his neck, where he said his mother placed it the night before she died, a large locket, also of gold. This locket contained three little pictures painted on ivory, one in each half of it and one with the plain

24

gold back on a hinge between them. That to the right was of a handsome man in uniform, who, Ralph told me, was his father (and indeed he left all this in writing, together with his will); that to the left, of a lovely lady in a low dress, who, he said, was his mother; that in the middle a portrait of the boy himself, as anyone could see, which must have been painted not more than a year before we found him. This locket and the pictures my great-granddaughter Suzanne has also.

Now, as I have said, we let that unhappy lady lie in her rude grave yonder by the sea, but my husband took men and built a cairn of stones over it and a strong wall about it, and there it stands to this day, for not long ago I met one of the folk from the Old Colony who had seen it, and who told me that the people that live in those parts now reverence the spot, knowing its story. Also, when some months afterwards a minister came to visit us, we led him to the place and he read the Burial Service over the lady's bones, so that she did not lack for Christian Burial.

Well, this wreck made a great stir, for many were drowned in it, and the English Government sent a ship of war to visit the place where it happened, but none came to ask us what we knew of the matter; indeed, we never learned that the frigate had been till she was gone again. So it came about that the story died away, as such stories do in this sad world, and for many years we heard no more of it.

For a while the boy Ralph was like a haunted child. At night, and now and again even in the daytime, he would be seized with terror, and sob and cry in a way that was piteous to behold, though not to be wondered at by any who knew his history. When these fits took him, strange as it may seem, there was but one who could calm his heart, and that one Suzanne. I can see them now as I have seen them thrice that I remember, the boy sitting up in his bed, a stare of agony in his eyes, and the sweat running down his face, damping his yellow hair, and talking rapidly, half in English, half in Dutch, with a voice that at times would rise to a scream, and at times would sink to a whisper, of the shipwreck, of his lost parents, of the black Indian woman who nursed him, of the wilderness, the tigers, and the Kaffirs who fell on them, and many other things. By him sits Suzanne, a soft *kaross* of jackal skins wrapped over her nightgown, the dew of sleep still showing upon her childish face and in her large dark eyes. By him she sits, talking in some words which for us have little meaning, and in a voice now shrill, and now sinking to a croon, while with one hand she clasps his wrist, and with the other strokes his brow, till the shadow passes from his soul and, clinging close to her, he sinks back to sleep.

But as the years went by these fits grew rarer till at last they ceased altogether, since, thanks be to God, childhood can forget its grief. What did not cease, however, was the lad's love for Suzanne, or her love for him, which, if possible, was yet deeper. Brother may love sister, but that affection, however true, yet lacks something, since nature teaches that it can never be complete. But from the beginning—yes, even while they were children—these twain were brother and sister, friend and friend, lover and lover; and so they remained till life left them, and so they will remain for aye in whatever life they live. Their thought was one thought, their heart was one heart; in them was neither variableness nor shadow of turning; they were each of each, to each and for each, as one soul in their separate spirits, as one flesh in their separate bodies. I who write this am a very old woman, and though in many things I am most ignorant, I have seen much of the world and of the men who live in it, yet I say that never have I known any marvel to compare with the marvel and the beauty of the love between Ralph Kenzie, the castaway, and my sweet daughter, Suzanne. It was of heaven, not of earth; or, rather, like everything that is perfect, it partook both of earth and heaven. Yes, yes, it wandered up the mountain paths of earth to the pure heights of heaven, where now it dwells for ever.

The boy Ralph grew up fair and brave and strong, with keen grey eyes and a steady mouth, nor did I know any lad of his years who could equal him in strength and swiftness of foot; for, though in youth he was not over tall, he was broad in the breast and had muscles that never seemed to tire. Now, we Boers think little of book learning, holding, as we do, that if a man can read the Holy Word it is enough. Still Jan and I thought as Ralph was not of our blood, though otherwise in all ways a son to us, that it was our duty to educate him as much in the fashion of his own people as our circumstances would allow. Therefore, after he had been with us some two years, when one day the Hollander tutor man, with the blue spectacles, of whom I have spoken, rode up to our house upon his mule, telling us that he had fled from the Van Voorens because he could no longer bear witness to the things that were practised at their stead, we engaged him to teach Ralph and Suzanne. He remained with us six years, by which time both the children had got much learning from him; though how much it is not for me, who have none, to judge. They learnt history and reading and writing, and something of the English tongue, but I need scarcely say that I would not suffer him to teach them to pry into the mystery of God's stars, as he wished to do, for I hold that such lore is impious and akin to witchcraft of which I have seen enough from Sihamba and others.

I asked this Hollander more particularly why he had fled from the Van Voorens, but he would tell me little more than that it was because of the wizardries practised there. If I might believe him, the *Heer* Van Vooren made a custom of entertaining Kaffir witch doctors and doctoresses at his house, and of celebrating with them secret and devilish rites, to which his son, Swart Piet, was initiated in his presence. That this last story was true I have no doubt indeed, seeing that the events of after years prove it to have been so.

Well, at last the Hollander left us to marry a rich old *vrouw* twenty years his senior, and that is all I have to say about him, except that if possible I disliked him more when he walked out of the house than when he walked in; though why I should have done so I do not know, for he was a harmless body. Perhaps it was because he played the flute, which I have always thought contemptible in a man.

Chapter 4

The Shadow of the Englishmen

Now I will pass on to the time when Ralph was nineteen or thereabouts, and save for the lack of hair upon his face, a man grown, since in our climate young people ripen quickly in body if not in mind. I tell of that year with shame and sorrow, for it was then that Jan and I committed a great sin, for which afterwards we were punished heavily enough.

At the beginning of winter Jan trekked to the nearest *dorp*, some fifty miles away, with a wagon load of *mealies* and of buckskins which he and Ralph had shot, purposing to sell them and to attend the *Nachtmahl*, or Feast of the Lord's Supper. I was somewhat ailing just then and did not accompany him, nor did Suzanne, who stayed to nurse me, or Ralph, who was left to look after us both.

Fourteen days later Jan returned, and from his face I saw at once that something had gone wrong.

"What is it, husband?" I asked. "Did not the *mealies* sell well?"

"Yes, yes, they sold well," he answered, "for that fool of an English storekeeper bought them and the hides together for more than their value."

"Are the Kaffirs going to rise again, then?"

"No, they are quiet for the present, though the accursed missionaries of the London Society are doing their best to stir them up," and he made a sign to me to cease from asking questions, nor did I say any more till we had gone to bed and everybody else in the house was asleep.

"Now," I said, "tell me your bad news, for bad news you have had."

"Wife," he answered, "it is this. In the *dorp* yonder I met a man who had come from Port Elizabeth. He told me that there at the port were two Englishmen, who had recently arrived, a Scotch lord, and a lawyer with red hair. When the Englishmen heard that he was from this part of the country they fell into talk with him, saying that they came upon a strange errand. It seems that when the great ship was wrecked upon this coast ten years ago there was lost in her a certain little boy who, if he had lived, would today have been a very rich noble in Scotland. Wife, you may know who that little boy was without my telling you his name."

I nodded and turned cold all over my body, for I could guess what was coming.

"Now for a long while those who were interested in him supposed that this lad was certainly dead with all the others on board that ship, but a year or more ago, how I know not, a rumour reached them that one male child who answered to his description had been saved alive and adopted by some Boers living in the Transkei. By this time the property and the title that should be his had descended to a cousin of the child's, but this relation being a just man determined before he took them to come to Africa and find out the truth for himself, and there he is at Port Elizabeth, or rather by this time he is on his road to our place. Therefore it would seem that the day is at hand when we shall see the last of Ralph."

"Never!" I said, "he is a son to us and more than a son, and I will not give him up."

"Then they will take him, wife. Yes, even if he does not wish it, for he is a minor and they are armed with authority."

"Oh!" I cried, "it would break my heart, and, Jan, there is another heart that would break also," and I pointed towards the chamber where Suzanne slept.

He nodded, for none could live with them and not know that this youth and maiden loved each other dearly.

"It would break your heart," he answered, "and her heart; yes, and my own would be none the better for the wrench; yet how can we turn this evil from our door?"

"Jan," I said, "the winter is at hand; it is time that you and Ralph should take the cattle to the bush-*veldt* yonder, where they will lie warm and grow fat, for so large a herd cannot be trusted to the Kaffirs. Had you not better start tomorrow? If these English meddlers should come here I will talk with them. Did Suzanne save the boy for them? Did we rear him for them, although he was English? Think how you will feel when he has crossed the ridge yonder for the last time, you who are sonless, and you must go about your tasks alone, must ride alone and hunt alone, and, if need be, fight alone, except for his memory. Think, Jan, think."

"Do not tempt me, woman," he whispered back in a hoarse voice, for Ralph and he were more to each other than any father and son that I have known, since they were also the dearest of friends. "Do not tempt me," he went on; "the lad must himself be told of this, and he must judge; he is young, but among us at nineteen a youth is a burgher grown, with a right to take up land and marry. He must be told, I say, and at once."

"It is good," I said, "let him judge;" but in the wickedness of my heart I made up my mind that I would find means to help his judgment, for the thought of losing him filled me with blind terror, and all that night I lay awake thinking out the matter.

Early in the morning I rose and went to the *stoep*, where I found Suzanne drinking coffee and singing a little song that Ralph had taught her. I can see her now as she stood in her pretty tight-fitting dress, a flower wet with dew in her girdle, swinging her *kapje* by its strings while the first rays of the sun glistened on the waves of her brown and silk-like hair. She was near eighteen then, and so beautiful that my heart beat with pride at her loveliness, for never in my long life have I seen a girl of any nation who could compare with my daughter Suzanne in looks. Many women are sweet to behold in this way or in that; but Suzanne was beautiful every way, yes, and at all ages of her life; as a child, as a maiden, as a matron and as a woman drawing near to *eld*, she was always beautiful if, like that of the different seasons, her beauty varied. In shape she was straight and tall and rounded, light-footed as a buck, delicate in limb, wide-breasted and slender-necked. Her face was rich in hue as a *kloof* lily, and her eyes— ah! no antelope ever had eyes darker, tenderer, or more appealing than were the eyes of Suzanne. Moreover, she was sweet of nature, ready of wit and good-hearted—yes, even for the Kaffirs she had a smile.

"You are up betimes, Suzanne," I said when I had looked at her a little.

"Yes, mother; I rose to make Ralph his coffee, he does not like that the Kaffir women should boil it for him."

"You mean that you do not like it," I answered, for I knew that Ralph thought little of who made the coffee that he drank, or if he did it was mine that he held to be the best, and not Suzanne's, who in those days was a careless girl, thinking less of household matters than she should have done.

"Did Swart Piet come here yesterday?" I asked. "I thought that I saw his horse as I walked back from the sea."

"Yes, he came."

"What for?"

She shrugged her shoulders. "Oh! mother, why do you ask me? You know well that he is always troubling me, bringing me presents of flowers, and asking me to *opsit* with him and what not."

"Then you don't want to *opsit* with him?"

"The candle would be short that I should burn with Swart Piet," answered Suzanne, stamping her foot; "he is an evil man, full of dark words and ways, and I fear him, for I think that since his father's death he has become worse, and the most of the company he keeps is with those Kaffir witch-doctors."

"Ah! like father, like son. The mantle of Elijah has fallen upon Elisha, but inside out. Well, it is what I expected, for sin and wizardry were born in his blood. Had you any words with him?"

"Yes, some. I would not listen to his sweet talk, so he grew angry and began to threaten; but just then Ralph came back and he went away, for he is afraid of Ralph."

"Where has Ralph gone so early?" I asked, changing the subject.

"To the far cattle-*kraal* to look after the oxen which the Kaffir bargained to break into the yoke. They are choosing them this morning."

"So. He makes a good Boer for one of English blood, does he not? And yet I suppose that when he becomes English again he will soon forget that he was ever a Boer."

"When he becomes English again, mother! What do you mean by that saying?" she asked quickly.

"I mean that like will to like, and blood to blood; also that there may be a nest far away which this bird that we have caged should fill."

"A nest far away, mother? Then there is one here which would be left empty; in your heart and father's, I mean;" and dropping her sunbonnet she turned pale and pressed her hands upon her own, adding, "Oh! speak straight words to me. What do you mean by these hints?"

"I mean, Suzanne, that it is not well for any of us to let our love wrap itself too closely about a stranger. Ralph is an Englishman, not a Boer. He names me mother and your father, father; and you he names sister, but to us he is neither son nor brother. Well, a day may come when he learns to understand this, when he learns to understand also that he has other kindred, true kindred far away across the sea; and if those birds call, who will keep him in the strange nest?"

"Ah!" she echoed, all dismayed, "who will keep him then?"

"I do not know," I answered; "not a foster father or mother. But I forgot. Say, did he take his rifle with him to the *kraal*?"

"Surely, I saw it in his hand."

"Then, daughter, if you will, get on a horse, and if you can find Ralph, tell him that I shall be very glad if he can shoot a small buck and bring it back with him, as I need fresh meat."

"May I stay with him while he shoots the buck, mother?"

"Yes, if you are not in his way and do not stop too long."

Then, without more words, Suzanne left me, and presently I saw her cantering across the *veldt* upon her grey mare that Ralph had broken for her, and wondered if she would find him and what luck he would have with the hunt that day.

Now it seems that Suzanne found Ralph and gave him my message, and that they started together to look for buck on the strip of land which lies between the seashore and the foot of the hills, where sometimes the blesbok and springbok used to feed in thousands. But on this day there were none to be seen, for the dry grass had already been burnt off, so that there was nothing for them to eat.

"If mother is to get her meat today," said Ralph at length, "I think that we must try the hill side for a duiker or a bush-buck."

So they turned inland and rode towards that very *kloof* where years before Suzanne had discovered the shipwrecked boy. At the mouth of this *kloof* was a patch of marshy ground, where the reeds still stood thick, since being full of sap they had resisted the fire.

"That is a good place for a *riet*-buck," said Ralph, "if only one could beat him out of it, for the reeds are too tall to see to shoot in them."

"It can be managed," answered Suzanne. "Do you go and stand in the neck of the *kloof* while I ride through the reeds towards you."

"You might get bogged," he said doubtfully.

"No, no, brother; after all this drought the *pan* is nothing more than spongy, and if I should get into a soft spot I will call out."

To this plan Ralph at length agreed, and having ridden round the *pan*, which was not more than fifty yards across, he dismounted from his horse and hid himself behind a bush in the neck of the *kloof*. Then Suzanne rode in among the reeds, shouting and singing, and beating them with her *sjambock* in order to disturb anything that might be hidden there. Nor was her trouble in vain, for suddenly, with a shrill whistle of alarm by the sound of which this kind of antelope may be known even in the dark, up sprang two *riet*-buck and dashed away towards the neck of the *kloof*, looking large as donkeys and red as lions as they vanished into the thick cover. So close were they to Suzanne that her mare took fright and reared; but the girl was the best horsewoman in those parts, and kept her seat, calling the while to Ralph to make ready for the buck. Presently she heard a shot, and having quieted the mare, rode out of the reeds and galloped round the dry *pan* to find Ralph looking foolish with no *riet*-buck in sight.

"Have you missed them?" she asked.

"No, not so bad as that, for they passed within ten yards of me, but the old gun hung fire. I suppose that the powder in the *pan* was a little damp, and instead of hitting the buck in front I caught him somewhere behind. He fell down, but has gone on again, so we must follow him, for I don't think that he will get very far."

Accordingly, when Ralph had reloaded his gun, which took some time—for in those days we had scarcely anything but flintlocks—yes, it was with weapons like these that a handful of us beat the hosts of Dingaan and Moselikatse—they started to follow the blood spoor up the *kloof*, which was not difficult, as the animal had bled much. Near to the top of the *kloof* the trail led them through a thick clump of mimosas, and there in the dell beyond they found the *riet*-buck lying dead. Riding to it they dismounted and examined it.

"Poor beast," said Suzanne; "look how the tears have run down its face. Well, I am glad that it is dead and done with," and she sighed and turned away, for Suzanne was a silly and tender-hearted girl who never could understand that the animals—yes, and the heathen Kaffirs, too—were given to us by the Lord for our use and comfort.

Presently she started and said, "Ralph, do you remember this place?"

He glanced round and shook his head, for he was wondering whether he would be able to lift the buck on to the horse without asking Suzanne to help him.

"Look again," she said; "look at that flat stone and the mimosa tree lying on its side near it."

Ralph dropped the leg of the buck and obeyed her, for he would always do as Suzanne bade him, and this time it was his turn to start.

"Almighty!" he said, "I remember now. It was here that you found me, Suzanne, after I was shipwrecked, and the tigers stared at us through the boughs of that fallen tree," and he shivered a little, for the sight of the spot brought back to his heart some of the old terrors which had haunted his childhood.

"Yes, Ralph, it was here that I found you. I heard the sound of your voice as you knelt praying on this stone, and I followed it. God heard that prayer, Ralph."

"And sent an angel to save me in the shape of a little maid," he answered; adding, "Don't blush so red, dear, for it is true that ever since that day, whenever I think of angels, I think of you; and whenever I think of you I think of angels, which shows that you and the angels must be close together."

"Which shows that you are a wicked and silly lad to talk thus to a Boer girl," she answered, turning away with a smile on her lips and tears in her eyes, for his words had pleased her mind and touched her heart.

He looked at her, and she seemed so sweet and beautiful as she stood thus, smiling and weeping together as the sun shines through summer rain, that, so he told me afterwards, something stirred in his breast, something soft and strong and new, which caused him to feel as though of a sudden he had left his boyhood behind him and become a man, aye, and as though this fresh-faced manhood sought but one thing more from Heaven to make it perfect, the living love of the fair maiden who until this hour had been his sister in heart though not in blood.

"Suzanne," he said in a changed voice, "the horses are tired; let them rest, and let us sit upon this stone and talk a little, for though we have never visited it for many years the place is lucky for you and me since it was here that our lives first came together."

Now although Suzanne knew that the horses were not tired she did not think it needful to say him nay.

CHAPTER 5

A Love Scene and a Quarrel

Presently they were seated side by side upon a stone, Suzanne looking straight before her, for nature warned her that this talk of theirs was not to be as other talks, and Ralph looking at Suzanne.

"Suzanne," he said at length.

"Yes," she answered; "what is it?" But he made no answer, for though many words were bubbling in his brain, they choked in his throat, and would not come out of it.

"Suzanne," he stammered again presently, and again she asked him what it was, and again he made no answer. Now she laughed a little and said:

"Ralph, you remind me of the blue-jay in the cage upon the *stoep* which knows but one word and repeats it all day long."

"Yes," he replied, "it is true; I am like that jay, for the word I taught it is 'Suzanne,' and the word my heart teaches me is 'Suzanne,' and—Suzanne, I love you!"

Now she turned her head away and looked down and answered:

"I know, Ralph, that you have always loved me since we were children together, for are we not brother and sister?"

"No," he answered bluntly, "it is not true."

"Then that is bad news for me," she said, "who till today have thought otherwise."

"It is not true," he went on, and now his words came fast enough, "that I am your brother, or that I love you as a brother. We are no kin, and if I love you as a brother that is only one little grain of my love for you—yes, only as one little grain is to the whole sea-shore of sand. Suzanne, I love you as—as a man loves a maid—and if you will it, dear, all my hope is that one day you will be my wife," and he ceased suddenly and stood before her trembling, for he had risen from the stone.

For a few moments Suzanne covered her face with her hands, and when she let them fall again he saw that her beautiful eyes shone like the large stars at night, and that, although she was troubled, her trouble made her happy.

"Oh! Ralph," she said at length, speaking in a voice that was different from any he had ever heard her use, a voice very rich and low and full, "Oh! Ralph, this is new to me, and yet to speak the truth, it seems as old as—as that night when first I found you, a desolate, starving child, praying upon this stone. Ralph, I do will it with all my heart and soul and body, and I suppose that I have willed it ever since I was a woman, though until this hour I did not quite know what it was I willed. Nay, dear, do not touch me, or at the least, not yet. First hear what I have to say, and then if you desire it, you may kiss me—if only in farewell."

"If you will it and I will it, what more can you have to say?" he asked in a quick whisper, and looking at her with frightened eyes.

"This, Ralph; that our wills, who are young and unlearned, are not all the world; that there are other wills to be thought of; the wills of our parents, or of mine rather, and the will of God."

"For the first," he answered, "I do not think that they stand in our path, for they love you and wish you to be happy, although it is true that I, who am but a wanderer picked up upon the *veldt*, have no fortune to offer you—still fortune can be won," he added doggedly.

"They love you also, Ralph, nor do they care over much for wealth, either of them, and I am sure that they would not wish you to leave us to go in search of it."

"As for the will of God," he continued, "it was the will of God that I should be wrecked here, and that you should save me here, and that the life you saved should be given to you. Will it not, therefore, be the will of God also that we, who can never be happy apart, should be happy together and thank Him for our happiness every day till we die?"

"I trust so, Ralph; yet although I have read and seen little, I know that very often it has been His will that those who love each other should be separated by death or otherwise."

"Do not speak of it," he said with a groan.

"No, I will not speak of it, but there is one more thing of which I must speak. Strangely enough, only this morning my mother was talking of you; she said that you are English, and that soon or late blood will call to blood and you will leave us. She said that your nest is not here, but there, far away across the sea, among those English; that you are a swallow that has been fledged with sparrows, and that one day you will find the wings of a swallow. What put it in her mind to speak thus, I do not know, but I do know, Ralph, that her words filled me with fear, and now I understand why I was so much afraid."

He laughed aloud very scornfully. "Then, Suzanne," he said, "you may banish your fears, for this I swear to you, before the Almighty, that whoever may be my true kin, were a kingdom to be offered to me among them, unless you could share it, it would be refused. This I swear before the Almighty, and may He reject me if I forget the oath."

"You are very young to make such promises, Ralph," she answered doubtfully, "nor do I hold them binding on you. At nineteen, so I am told, a lad will swear anything to the girl who takes his fancy."

"I am young in years, Suzanne, but I grew old while I was yet a child, for sorrow aged me. You have heard my oath; let it be put to the test, and you shall learn whether or no I speak the truth. Do I look like one who does not know his mind?"

She glanced up at the steady, grey eyes and the stern, set mouth and answered, "Ralph, you look like one who knows his mind, and I believe you. Pray God I may not be deceived, for though we are but lad and girl, if it prove so I tell you that I shall live my life out with a broken heart."

"Do not fear, Suzanne. And now I have heard what you had to say, and I claim your promise. If it be your will I will kiss you, Suzanne, but not in farewell."

"Nay," she answered, "kiss me rather in greeting of the full and beautiful life that stretches before our feet. Whether the path be short or long, it will be good for us and ever better, but, Ralph, I think that the end will be best of all."

So he took her in his arms, and they kissed each other upon the lips, and, as they told me afterwards, in that embrace they found some joy. Why should they not indeed, for if anywhere upon the earth, if it be given and received in youth before the heart has been seared and tainted with bitterness and disillusion, surely in such a pledge as theirs true joy can be found. Yes, and they did more than this, for, kneeling there upon that rock where once the starving child had knelt in by-gone years, they prayed to Him who had brought them together, to Him who had given them hearts to love with and bodies to be loved, and the immortality of Heaven wherein to garner this seed of love thus sown upon the earth, that He would guide them, bless them, and protect them through all trials, terrors, sorrows, and separations. As shall be seen, this indeed He did.

Then they rose, and having, not without difficulty, lifted the *riet-*

buck ram upon Ralph's horse and made it fast there, as our hunters know how to do, they started homewards, walking the most part of the way, for the load was heavy and they were in no haste, so that they only reached the farm about noon.

Now I, watching them as we sat at our mid-day meal, grew sure that something out of the common had passed between them. Suzanne was very silent, and from time to time glanced at Ralph shyly, whereon, feeling her eyes, he would grow red as the sunset, and seeing his trouble, she would colour also, as though with the knowledge of some secret that made her both happy and ashamed.

"You were long this morning in finding a buck, Ralph," I said.

"Yes, mother," he answered; "there were none on the flats, for the grass is burnt off; and had not Suzanne beaten out a dry *pan* for me where the reeds were still green, I think that we should have found nothing. As it was I shot badly, hitting the ram in the flank, so that we were obliged to follow it a long way before I came up with it."

"And where did you find it at last?" I asked.

"In a strange place, mother; yes, in that very spot where many years ago Suzanne came upon me starving after the shipwreck. There in the glade and by the flat stone on which I had lain down to die was the buck, quite dead. We knew the dell again, though neither of us had visited it from that hour to this, and rested there awhile before we turned home."

I made no answer but sat thinking, and a silence fell on all of us. By this time the Kaffir girls had cleared away the meat and brought in coffee, which we drank while the men filled their pipes and lit them. I looked at Jan and saw that he was making up his mind to say something, for his honest face was troubled, and now he took up his pipe, and now he put it down, moving his hands restlessly till at length he upset the coffee over the table.

"Doubtless," I thought to myself, "he means to tell the tale of the Englishmen who have come to seek for Ralph. Well, I think that he may safely tell it now."

Then I looked at Ralph and saw that he also was very ill at ease, struggling with words which he did not know how to utter. I noted, moreover, that Suzanne touched his hand with hers beneath the shelter of the table as though to comfort and encourage him. Now watching these two men, at last I broke out laughing, and said, addressing them:

"You are like two fires of green weeds in a *mealie* patch, and I am wondering which of you will be the first to break into flame or whether you will both be choked by the reek of your own thoughts."

My gibe, harmless though it was, stung them into speech, and both at once, for I have noticed, however stupid they may be, that men never like to be laughed at.

"I have something to say," said each of them, as though with a single voice, and they paused, looking at one another angrily.

"Then, son, wait till I have finished. Almighty! for the last twenty minutes you have been sitting as silent as an ant-bear in a hole, and I tell you that it is my turn now; why, then, do you interrupt me?"

"I am very sorry, my father," said Ralph, looking much afraid, for he thought that Jan was going to scold him about Suzanne, and his conscience being guilty caused him to forget that it was not possible that he should know anything of the matter of his love-making.

"That is good," said Jan, still glaring at him; "but I am not your father."

"Then why do you call me son?" asked Ralph.

"Almighty! do you suppose that I sit here to answer riddles?" replied Jan, pulling at his great beard. "Why do I call you son, indeed? Ah!" he added in a different voice, a sorrowful voice, "why do I when I have no right? Listen, my boy, we are in sore trouble, I and your mother, or if she is not your mother at least she loves you as much as though she were, and I love you too, and you know it; so why do you seek to make a fool of me by asking me riddles?"

Now, Ralph was about to answer, but Suzanne held up her hand, and he was quiet.

"My son," went on Jan with a kind of sob, "they are coming to take you away from us."

"They! Who?" asked Ralph.

"Who? The English, damn them! Yes, I say, damn the English and the English Government."

"Peace, Jan," I broke in, "this is not a political meeting, where such talk is right and proper."

"The English Government is coming to take me away!" exclaimed Ralph bewildered. "What has the Government to do with me?"

"No," said Jan, "not the English Government, but two Scotchmen, which is much the same thing. I tell you that they are travelling to this place to take you away."

Now, Ralph leaned back in his chair and stared at him, for he saw that it was little use to ask him questions, and that he must leave him to tell the tale in his own fashion. At last it came out.

"Ralph," said my husband, "you know that you are not of our blood; we found you cast up on the beach like a storm-fish and took

39

you in, and you grew dear to us; yes, although you are English or Scotch, which is worse, for if the English bully us the Scotch bully us and cheat us into the bargain. Well, your parents were drowned, and have been in Heaven for a long time, but I am sorry to say that all your relations were not drowned with them. At first, however, they took no trouble to hunt for you when we should have been glad enough to give you up."

"No," broke in Suzanne and I with one voice, and I added, "How do you dare to tell such lies in the face of the Lord, Jan?"

"——When it would not have been so bad to give you up," he went on, correcting himself. "But now it seems that had you lived you would have inherited estates, or titles, or both."

"Is the boy dead then?" I asked.

"Be silent, wife, I mean—had he lived a Scotchman. Therefore, having made inquiries, and learned that a lad of your name and age had been rescued from a shipwreck and was still alive among the Boers in the Transkei, they have set to work to hunt you, and are coming here to take you way, for I tell you that I heard it in the *dorp* yonder."

"Is it so?" said Ralph, while Suzanne hung upon his words with white face and trembling lips. "Then I tell you that I will not go. I may be English, but my home is here. My own father and mother are dead, and these strangers are nothing to me, nor are the estates and titles far away anything to me. All that I hold dear on the earth is here in the Transkei," and he glanced at Suzanne, who seemed to bless him with her eyes.

"You talk like a fool," said Jan, but in a voice which was full of joy that he could not hide, "as is to be expected of an ignorant boy. Now I am a man who has seen the world, and I know better, and I tell you that although they are an accursed race, still it is a fine thing to be a lord among the English. Yes, yes, I know the English lords. I saw one once when I went to Capetown; he was the Governor there, and driving through the streets in state, dressed as bravely as a blue-jay in his spring plumage, while everybody took off their hats to him, except I, Jan Botmar, who would not humble myself thus. Yet to have such clothes as that to wear every day, while all the people salute you and make a path for you, is not a thing to be laughed at. See boy, it just comes to this: here you are poor and little, there you may be rich and much, and it is our duty not to stand in your road, though it may break our hearts to lose you. So you had best make up your mind to go away with the damned Scotchmen when they come, though I hope that you will think kindly of us when you get to your own country. Yes,

yes, you shall go, and what is more, you may take my best horse to ride away on, the thoroughbred *schimmel*, and my new black felt hat that I bought in the *dorp*. There, that is done with, praise be to God, and I am going out, for this place is so thick with smoke that I can't see my own hand," and he rose to go, adding that if the two Scotchmen did not want a bullet through them, it would be as well if they kept out of his way when they came upon the farm.

Now in saying that the room was thick with smoke Jan lied, for both the men's pipes went out when they began to talk. But as I knew why he lied I did not think so much of it. To tell the truth, at that moment I could see little better than he could, since, although I would have poisoned those two Scotchmen before I suffered them to take Ralph away, the very thought of his going was enough to fill my eyes with tears, and to cause Suzanne to weep aloud shamelessly.

"Wait a bit, father—I beg your pardon, Jan Botmar," said Ralph in a clear and angry voice; "it is my turn now, for you may remember that when we began to talk I had something to say, but you stopped me. Now, with your leave, as you have got off the horse I will get on."

Jan slowly sat down again and said:

"Speak. What is it?"

"This: that if you send me away you are likely to lose more than you bargain for."

Now Jan stared at him perplexedly, but I smiled, for I guessed what was to come.

"What am I likely to lose," he asked, "beyond my best horse and my felt hat? *Allemachter!* Do you want my span of black oxen also? Well, you shall have them if you like, for I should wish you to trek to your new home in England behind good cattle."

"No," answered Ralph coolly, "but I want your daughter, and if you send me away I think that she will come with me."

Chapter 6

The Coming of the Englishmen

Now on hearing this Suzanne said, "Oh!" and sank back in her chair as though she were going to faint; but I burst out laughing, half because Ralph's impertinence tickled me and half at the sight of my husband's face. Presently he turned upon me in a fine rage.

"Be silent, you silly woman," he said. "Do you hear what that mad boy says? He says that he wants my daughter."

"Well, what of it?" I answered. "Is there anything wonderful in that? Suzanne is of an age to be married and pretty enough for any young man to want her."

"Yes, yes; that is true now I come to think of it," said Jan, pulling his beard. "But, woman, he says that he wants to take her away with him."

"Ah!" I replied, "that is another matter. That he shall never do without my consent."

"No, indeed, he shall never do that," echoed Jan.

"Suzanne," said I in the pause that followed, "you have heard all this talk. Tell us, then, openly what is your mind in the matter."

"My mind is, mother," she answered very quietly, "that I wish to obey you and my father in all things, as is my duty, but that I have a deeper duty towards Ralph whom God gave me out of the sea. Therefore, if you send away Ralph without a cause, if he desires it I shall follow him as soon as I am of age and marry him, or if you keep me from him by force then I think that I shall die. That is all I have to say."

"And quite enough, too," I answered, though in my heart I liked the girl's spirit, and guessed that she was playing a part to prevent her father from sending away Ralph against his will.

"All this is pretty hearing," said Jan, staring from one to the other. "Why, now that I think of it, I never heard that you two were more than brother and sister to each other. Say, you shameless girl, when

42

did all this come about, and why do you dare to promise yourself in marriage without my consent?"

"Because there was no time to ask it, father," said Suzanne, looking down, "for Ralph and I only spoke together this morning."

"He spoke to you this morning, and now it seems that you are ready to forsake your father and your mother and to follow him across the world, you wicked and ungrateful child."

"I am not wicked and I am not ungrateful," answered Suzanne; "it is you who are wicked, who want to send Ralph away and break all our hearts."

"It is false, miss," shouted her father in answer, "for you know well that I do not want to send him away."

"Then why did you tell him that he must go and take your roan horse and new hat?"

"For his own good, girl."

"Is it for his own good that he should go away from all of us who love him and be lost across the sea?" and choking she burst into tears, while her father muttered:

"Why, the girl has become like a tiger, she who was milder than a sheep!"

"Hush, Suzanne," broke in Ralph, "and you who have been father and mother to me, listen I pray you. It is true that Suzanne and I love each other very dearly, as we have always loved each other, though how much we did not know till this morning. Now, I am a waif and a casta-way whom you have nurtured, and have neither lands nor goods of my own, therefore you may well think that I am no match for your daughter, who is so beautiful, and who, if she outlives you, will inherit all that you have. If you decide thus it is just, however hard it may be. But you tell me, though I have heard nothing of it till now, and I think that it may be but idle talk, that I have both lands and goods far away in England, and you bid me begone to them. Well, if you turn me out I must go, for I cannot stay alone in the *veldt* without a house, or a friend, or a hoof of cattle. But then I tell you that when Suzanne is of age I shall return and marry her, and take her away with me, as I have a right to do if she desires it, for I will not lose everything that I love in the world at one stroke. Indeed nothing but death shall part me from Suzanne. Therefore, it comes to this: either you must let me stay here and, poor as I am, be married to Suzanne when it shall please you, or, if you dismiss me, you must be ready to see me come back and take away Suzanne."

"Suzanne, Suzanne," I interrupted angrily, for I grew jealous of the girl; "have you no thought or word, Ralph, for any save Suzanne?"

"I have thoughts for all," he answered, "but Suzanne alone has thought for me, since it seems that your husband would send me away, and you, mother, sit still and say not a word to stop him."

"Learn to judge speech and not silence, lad," I answered. "Look you, all have been talking, and I have shammed dead like a stink-cat when dogs are about; now I am going to begin. First of all, you, Jan, are a fool, for in your thick head you think that rank and wealth are everything to a man, and therefore you would send Ralph away to seek rank and wealth that may or may not belong to him, although he does not wish to go. As for you, Ralph, you are a bigger fool, for you think that Jan Botmar, your foster-father here, desires to be rid of you when in truth he only seeks your good to his own sore loss. As for you, Suzanne, you are the biggest fool of all, for you wish to fly in everybody's face, like a cat with her first litter of kittens; but there, what is the use of arguing with a girl in love? Now listen, and I will ask you some questions, all of you. Jan, do you wish to send Ralph away with these strangers?"

"Almighty! *vrouw*," he answered, "you know well that I would as soon send away my right hand. I wish him to stop here for ever, and whatever I have is his; yes, even my daughter. But I seek what is best for him, and I would not have it said in after years that Jan Botmar had kept an English lad not old enough to judge for himself from his rank and wealth because he took pleasure in his company and wished to marry him to his girl."

"Good," I said. "And now for you, Suzanne; what have you to say?"

"I have nothing to add to my words," she replied; "you know all my heart."

"Good again. And you, Ralph?"

"I say, mother, that I will not budge from this place unless I am ordered to go, and if I do go, I will come back for Suzanne. I love you all, and with you I wish to live and nowhere else."

"Nay, Ralph," I answered sighing, "if once you go you will never come back, for out yonder you will find a new home, new interests, and, perchance, new loves. Well, though nobody has thought of me in this matter, I have a voice in it, and I will speak for myself. That lad yonder has been a son to me for many years, and I who have none love him as such. He is a man as we reckon in this country, and he does not wish to leave us any more than we wish him to go. Moreover, he loves Suzanne, and Suzanne loves him, and I believe that the God who brought them together at first means them to be husband and wife, and that such love as they bear to each other will give them more

44

together than any wealth or rank can bring to them apart. Therefore I say, husband, let our son, Ralph, say here with us and marry our daughter, Suzanne, decently and in due season, and let their children be our children, and their love our love."

"And how about the Scotchmen who are coming with power to take him away?"

"Do you and Ralph go to the bush-*veldt* with the cattle tomorrow," I answered, "and leave me to deal with the Scotchmen."

"Well," said Jan, "I consent, for who can stand up against so many words, and the Lord knows that to lose Ralph would have broken my heart as it would have broken that girl's, perhaps more so, since girls change their fancies, but I am too old to change. Come here, my children."

They came, and he laid one of his big hands upon the head of each of them, saying:—

"May the God in Heaven bless you both, who to me are one as dear as the other, making you happy with each other for many long years, and may He turn aside from you and from us the punishment that is due to all of us because, on account of our great love, we are holding you back, Ralph, from the home, the kin and the fortune to which you were born." Then he kissed each of them on the forehead and let them go.

"If there be any punishment for that which is no sin, on my head be it," said Ralph, "since never would I have gone from here by my own will."

"Aye, aye," answered Jan, "but who can take account of the talk of a lad in love? Well, we have committed the sin and we must bear the sorrow. Now I go out to see to the kraaling of the cattle, which we will drive off to the bush-*veldt* tomorrow at dawn, for I will have naught to do with these Scotchmen; your mother must settle with them as she wills, only I beg of her that she will tell me nothing of the bargain. Nay, do not come with me, Ralph; stop you with your dear, for tomorrow you will be parted for a while."

So he went, and did not return again till late, and we three sat together and made pretence to be very happy, but somehow were a little sad, for Jan's words about sin and sorrow stuck in our hearts, as the honest words of a stupid, upright man are apt to do.

****

Now on the morrow at dawn, as had been arranged, Jan and Ralph rode away to the warm *veldt* with the cattle, leaving me and Suzanne to look after the farm. Three days later the Scotchmen came, and then it was that for love of Ralph and for the sake of the happiness of my daughter I sinned the greatest sin of all my life—the sin that was destined to shape the fates of others yet unborn.

I was seated on the *stoep* in the afternoon when I saw three white men and some Cape boys, their servants, riding up to the house.

"Here come those who would steal my boy from me," I thought to myself, and, like Pharaoh, I hardened my heart.

Now in those days my sight was very good, and while the men were yet some way off I studied them all and made up my mind about them. First there was a large young man of five-and-twenty or thereabouts, and I noted with a sort of fear that he was not unlike to Ralph. The eyes were the same and the shape of the forehead, only this gentleman had a weak, uncertain mouth, and I judged that he was very good-humoured, but of an indolent mind. By his side rode another man of quite a different stamp, and middle-aged. "The lawyer," I said to myself as I looked at his weasel-like face, bushy eyebrows, and red hair. Indeed, that was an easy guess, for who can mistake a lawyer, whatever his race may be? That trade is stronger than any blood, and leaves the same seal on all who follow it. Doubtless if those lawyers of whom the Lord speaks hard things in the Testament were set side by side with the lawyers who draw mortgage bonds and practise usury here in South Africa, they would prove to be as like to each other as are the grains of corn upon one *mealie* cob. Yes, when, all dressed the same, they stand together among the goats on the last day few indeed will know them apart.

"A fool and a knave," said I to myself. "Well, perhaps I can deal with the knave and then the fool will not trouble me."

As for the third man, I took no pains to study him, for I saw at once that he was nothing but an interpreter.

Well, up they rode to the *stoep*, the two Englishmen taking off their hats to me, after their foolish fashion, while the interpreter, who called me "Aunt," although I was younger than he was, asked for leave to off-saddle, according to our custom. I nodded my head, and having given the horses to the Cape boys, they came up onto the *stoep* and shook hands with me as I sat. I was not going to rise to greet two Englishmen whom I already hated in my heart, first because they *were* Englishmen, and secondly because they were about to tempt me into sin, for such sooner or later we always learn to hate.

"Sit," I said, pointing to the yellow-wood bench which was seated with strips of *rimpi*, and the three of them squeezed themselves into the bench and sat there like white-breasted crows on a bough; the young man staring at me with a silly smile, the lawyer peering this way and that, and turning up his sharp nose at the place and all in it, and the interpreter doing nothing at all, for he was a sensible man, who knew the habits of well-bred people and how to behave in their presence. After five minutes or so the lawyer grew impatient, and said something in a sharp voice, to which the interpreter answered, "Wait."

So they waited till, just as the young man was beginning to go to sleep before my very eyes, Suzanne came onto the veranda, whereupon he woke up in a hurry, and, jumping off the bench, began to bow and scrape and to offer her his seat, for there was no other.

"Suzanne," I said, taking no notice of his bad manners, "get coffee," and she went, looking less displeased at his grimaces than I would have had her do.

In time the coffee came, and they drank it, or pretended to, after which the lawyer began to grow impatient once more, and spoke to the interpreter, who said to me that they had come to visit us on a matter of business.

"Then tell him that it can wait till after we have eaten," I answered. "It is not my habit to talk business in the afternoon. Why is the lawyer man so impatient, seeing that doubtless he is paid by the day?"

This was translated, and the lawyer asked how I knew his trade.

"In the same way that I know a weasel by its face and a stink-cat by its smell," I replied, for every minute I hated that advocate more.

At this answer the lawyer grew white with anger, and the young lord burst into a roar of laughter, for, as I have said, these English people have no manners. However, they settled themselves down again on the yellow-wood bench and looked at me; while I, folding my hands, sat opposite, and looked at them for somewhere about another hour, as the interpreter told them that if they moved I should be offended, and, for my part, I was determined that I would not speak to them of their business until Suzanne had gone to bed.

At last, when I saw that they would bear it no longer, for they were becoming very wrathful, and saying words that sounded like oaths, I called for supper and we went in and ate it. Here again I noticed the resemblance between the young man and Ralph, for he had the same tricks of eating and drinking, and I saw that when he had done his meat he turned himself a little sideways from the table, crossing his legs in a peculiar fashion just as it always had been Ralph's habit to do.

"The two had one grandfather, or one grandmother," I said to myself, and grew afraid at the thought.

CHAPTER 7

The Sin of Vrouw Botmar

When the meat was cleared away I bade Suzanne go to bed, which she did most unwillingly, for knowing the errand of these men she wished to hear our talk. As soon as she was gone I took a seat so that the light of the candles left my face in shadow and fell full on those of the three men—a wise thing to do if one is wicked enough to intend to tell lies about any matter—and said:

"Now, here I am at your service; be pleased to set out the business that you have in hand."

Then they began, the lawyer, speaking through the interpreter, asking, "Are you the *Vrouw* Botmar?"

"That is my name."

"Where is your husband, Jan Botmar?"

"Somewhere on the *veldt*; I do not know where."

"Will he be back tomorrow?"

"No."

"When will he be back?"

"Perhaps in two months, perhaps in three, I cannot tell."

At this they consulted together, and then went on:

"Have you living with you a young Englishman named Ralph Mackenzie?"

"One named Ralph Kenzie lives with us."

"Where is he?"

"With my husband on the *veldt*. I do not know where."

"Can you find him?"

"No, the *veldt* is very wide. If you wish to see him you must wait till he comes back."

"When will that be?"

"I am not his nurse and cannot tell; perhaps in three months, perhaps six."

Now again they consulted, and once more went on:

"Was the boy, Ralph Mackenzie, or Kenzie, shipwrecked in the *India* in the year 1824?"

"Dear Lord!" I cried, affecting to lose my patience, "am I an old Kaffir wife up before the *Landdrost* for stealing hens that I should be cross-questioned in this fashion? Set out all your tale at once, man, and I will answer it."

Thereon, shrugging his shoulders, the lawyer produced a paper which the interpreter translated to me. In it were written down the names of the passengers who were upon the vessel *India* when she sailed from a place called Bombay, and among the names those of Lord and Lady Glenthirsk and of their son, the Honourable Ralph Mackenzie, aged nine. Then followed the evidence of one or two survivors of the shipwreck, which stated that Lady Glenthirsk and her son were seen to reach the shore in safety in the boat that was launched from the sinking ship. After this came a paragraph from an English newspaper published in Capetown, dated not two years before, and headed "Strange Tale of the Sea," which paragraph, with some few errors, told the story of the finding of Ralph—though how the writing man knew it I know not, unless it was through the tutor with the blue spectacles of whom I have spoken—and said that he was still living on the farm of Jan Botmar in the Transkei. This was all that was in the paper. I asked to look at it and kept it, saying in the morning that the Kaffir girl seeing it lying about the kitchen had used it to light the fire; but to this day it is with the other things in the wagon chest under my bed.

When the paper was done with, the lawyer took up the tale and told me that it was believed in England that Lord Glenthirsk had been drowned in the sea, as indeed he was, and that Lady Glenthirsk and her son perished on the shore with the other women and children, for so those sent by the English Government to search out the facts had reported. Thus it came about that after a while Lord Glenthirsk's younger brother was admitted by law to his title and estates, which he enjoyed for some eight years, that is, until his death. About a year before he died, however, someone sent him the paragraph headed "Strange Tale of the Sea," and he was much disturbed by it, though to himself he argued that it was nothing but an idle story, such as it seems are often put into newspapers. The end of the matter was that he took no steps to discover whether the tale were true or false, and none knew of it save himself, and he was not minded to go fishing in that ugly water. So it came about that he kept silent as the grave, till at length, when the grave yawned at his feet, and when the rank and the lands and the wealth were of no more use to him, he opened his mouth to his son and to his lawyer, the two men who sat before me, and to them only, bidding them seek out the beginning of the tale, and if it were true, to make restitution to his nephew.

Now—for all this, listening with my ears wide open, and sometimes filling in what was not told me in words, I gathered from the men before they left the house—as it chanced the dying lord could not have chosen two worse people for such an errand, seeing that although the son was honest, both of them were interested in proving the tale to be false. Since that time, however, often I have thought that he knew this himself, and trusted by the choice both to cheat his own conscience and to preserve the wealth and dignity for his son. God, to whom he has gone, alone knows the truth of it, but with such a man it may very well have been as I think. I say that both were interested, for it seems, as he told me afterwards, that the lawyer was to receive a great sum—ten thousand pounds—under the will of the dead lord for whom he had done much during his lifetime. But if Ralph were proved to be the heir this sum would have been his and not the lawyer's, for the money was part of his father's inheritance; therefore it was worth just ten thousand pounds to that lawyer to convince himself and the false lord that Ralph was not the man, and therefore it was that I found him so easy to deal with.

Now after his father was dead the lawyer tried to persuade the son to take no notice of his dying words, and to let the matter rest where it was, seeing that he had nothing to gain and much to lose. But this he would not consent to, for, as I have said, he was honest, declaring that he could not be easy in his mind till he knew the truth, and that if he did not go to find it out himself he would send others to do so for him. As the lawyer desired this least of anything, he gave way, and they set out upon their journey—which in those days was a very great journey indeed—arriving at last in safety at our stead in the Transkei; for, whether he liked it or not, his companion—who now was called Lord Glenthirsk—would not be turned aside from the search or suffer him to prosecute it alone.

At length, when all the tale was told, the lawyer looked at me with his sharp eyes and said, through the interpreter:

"*Vrouw* Botmar, you have heard the story, tell us what you know. Is the young man who lives with you he whom we seek?"

Now I thought for a second, though that second seemed like a year. All doubt had left me, there was no room for it. Ralph and no other was the man, and on my answer might hang his future. But I had argued the thing out before and made up my mind to lie, though, so far as I know, it is the only lie I ever told, and I am not a woman who often changes her mind. Therefore I lied.

"It is not he," I said, "though for his sake I might wish that it were, and this I can prove to you."

Now, when I had told this great falsehood, prompted to it by my love for the lad and my love for Suzanne, his affianced wife, my mind grew as it were empty for a moment, and I remember that in the emptiness I seemed to hear a sound of laughter echoing in the air somewhere above the roof of the house. Very swiftly I recovered myself, and looking at the men I saw that my words rejoiced them, except the interpreter indeed, who being a paid servant coming from far away, from the neighbourhood of Capetown I believe, had no interest in the matter one way or the other beyond that of earning his money with as little trouble as possible. Yes, they smiled at each other, looking as though a great weight had been lifted off their minds, till presently the lawyer checked himself and said:

"Be so good as to set out the proofs of which you speak, *Vrouw* Botmar."

"I will," I answered, "but tell me first, the ship *India* was wrecked in the year 1824, was she not?"

"Undoubtedly," answered the lawyer.

"Well, have you heard that another ship called the *Flora*, travelling from the Cape I know not whither, was lost on this coast in the same month of the following year, and that a few of her passengers escaped?"

"I have heard of it," he said.

"Good. Now look here," and going to a chest that stood beneath the window, I lifted from it the old Bible that belonged to my grandfather and father, on the white pages at the beginning of which are written the record of many births, marriages, deaths and other notable events that had happened in the family. Opening it I searched and pointed to a certain entry inscribed in the big writing of my husband Jan, and in ink which was somewhat faint, for the ink that the traders sold us in those days had little virtue in it. Beneath this entry were others made by Jan in later years, telling of things that had happened to us, such as the death of his great-aunt who left him money, the outbreak of small-pox on the farm, and the number of people who died from it, the attack of a band of the red Kaffirs upon our house, when by the mercy of God we beat them off, leaving twelve of their dead behind them, but taking as many of our best oxen, and so forth.

"Read," I said, and the interpreter read as follows:

"On the twelfth day of September in the year 1825 (the date being written in letters) our little daughter Suzanne found a starving English boy in a *kloof*, who had been shipwrecked on the coast. We have taken him in as a gift of the Lord. He says that his name is Rolf Kenzie."

"You see the date," I said.

"Yes," answered the lawyer, "and it has not been altered!"

"No," I added, "it has not been altered;" but I did not tell them that Jan had not written it down till afterwards, and then by mistake had recorded the year in which he wrote, refusing to change it, although I pointed out the error, because, he said, there was no room, and that it would make a mess in the book.

"There is one more thing," I went on; "you say the mother of him you seek was a great lady. Well, I saw the body of the mother of the boy who was found, and it was that of a common person very roughly clad with coarse underclothes and hands hard with labour, on which there was but one ring, and that of silver. Here it is," and going to a drawer I took from it a common silver ring which I once bought from a pedlar because he worried me into it. "Lastly, gentlemen, the father of our lad was no lord, unless in your country it is the custom of lords to herd sheep, for the boy told me that in his own land his father was a shepherd, and that he was travelling to some distant English colony to follow his trade. That is all I have to say about it, though I am sorry that the lad is not here to tell it you himself."

When he had heard this statement of mine, which I made in a cold and indifferent voice, the young lord, Ralph's cousin, rose and stretched himself, smiling happily.

"Well," he said, "there is the end of a very bad nightmare, and I am glad enough that we came here and found out the truth, for had we not done so I should never have been happy in my mind."

"Yes," answered the lawyer, the interpreter rendering their words all the while, "the *Vrouw* Botmar's evidence is conclusive, though I shall put her statement in writing and ask her to sign it. There is only one thing, and that is the strange resemblance of the names," and he glanced at him with his quick eyes.

"There are many Mackenzies in Scotland," answered Lord Glenthirsk, "and I have no doubt that this poor fellow was a shepherd emigrating with his wife and child to Australia or somewhere." Then he yawned and added, "I am going outside to get some air before I sleep. Perhaps you will draw up the paper for the good lady to sign."

"Certainly, my lord," answered the lawyer, and the young man went away quite convinced.

After he had gone the lawyer produced pen and ink and wrote out the statement, putting in it all the lies that I had told, and copying the extract from the fly-leaf of the Bible. When he had done the interpreter translated it to me, and then it was that the lawyer told me about the last wishes of the dying lord, and how it would have cost him ten thousand pounds and much business also had the tale proved true. Now at last he gave me the paper to sign. Besides the candles on the table, which being of mutton fat had burnt out, there was a lamp fed with whale's oil, but this also was dying, the oil being exhausted, so that its flame, which had sunk low, jumped from time to time with a little noise, giving out a blue light. In that unholy blue light, which turned our faces ghastly pale, the lawyer and I looked at each other as I sat before him, the pen in my hand, and in his eyes I read that he was certain that I was about to sign to a wicked lie, and in mine he read that I knew it to be a lie.

For a while we stared at each other thus, discovering each other's souls. "Sign," he said, shrugging his shoulders, "the light dies."

Then I signed, and as I wrote the lamp went out, leaving us in darkness, and through the darkness once more I heard that sound of laughter echoing in the air above the house.

CHAPTER 8

The Wisdom of Suzanne

Now, although Suzanne heard not a word of our talk, still she grasped its purport well enough, for she knew that I proposed to throw dust into the eyes of the Englishmen. This troubled her conscience sorely, for the more she thought of it the more did it seem to her to be wicked that just because we loved him and did not wish to part with him, Ralph should be cheated of his birthright. All night long she lay awake brooding, and before ever the dawn broke she had settled in her mind that she herself would speak to the Englishmen, telling them the truth, come what might of her words, for Suzanne, my daughter, was a determined girl with an upright heart. Now feeling happier because of her decision, at length she fell asleep and slept late, and as it happened this accident of fate was the cause of the miscarriage of her scheme.

It came about in this way. Quite early in the morning—at sunup, indeed—the Englishmen rose, and coming out of the little guest-chamber, drank the coffee that I had made ready for them, and talked together for a while. Then the young lord—Ralph's cousin—said that as they journeyed yesterday at a distance of about an hour on horseback from the farm he had noticed a large *vlei*, or *pan*, where were many ducks and also some antelope. To this *vlei* he proposed to ride forward with one servant only, and to stay there till the others overtook him, shooting the wild things which lived in the place, for to be happy these Englishmen must always be killing something. So he bade me farewell, making me a present of the gold chain which he took off his watch, which chain I still have. Then he rode away, smiling after his fashion; and as I watched him go I was glad to think that he was no knave but only an easy tool in the hands of others. We never met again, but I believe that death finished his story many years ago; indeed, all those of whom I tell are dead; only Jan and I survive, and our course is well-nigh run.

When Suzanne awoke at length, having heard from a Kaffir girl that the strangers had ordered their horses, but not that the young lord had ridden forward, she slipped from the house silently, fearing lest I should stay her, and hid herself in a little patch of bush at the corner of the big *mealie* field by which she knew the Englishmen must pass on their return journey. Presently she heard them coming, and when she saw that the young lord was not with them, she went to the lawyer, who pulled up his horse and waited for her, the rest of the party riding on, and asked where his master was, saying that she wished to talk with him. And here I must say, if I have not said it before, that Suzanne could speak English, though not well. The Hollander tutor had instructed her in that tongue, in which Ralph also would converse with her at times when he did not wish others to understand what they were saying, for he never forgot his mother language, though he mixed many Dutch words with it.

"He has ridden forward an hour or more ago. Can I take any message to him for you?" said the lawyer. "Or if you wish to talk of business, to speak to me is to speak to him."

"That may be so," answered Suzanne, "still I like to draw my water at the fountain itself. Yet, as he has gone, I beg you to listen to me, for when you have heard what I have to say I think that you will bring him back. You came here about Ralph Kenzie, did you not, and my mother told you that he is not the man whom you seek, did she not?"

The lawyer nodded.

"Well, I tell you that all this tale is false, for he is the very man," and she poured out the true story of Ralph and of the plot that had been made to deceive them about him.

Now, as I have said, Suzanne's English was none of the best and it is possible that the lawyer did not understand. For my part, however, I think that he understood well enough, for she told me afterwards that is face grew grey and anxious as he listened, and that at length he said:

"All this you tell me is very strange and weighty, so much so that I must bring my friend back to look more closely into the matter. Return now to the farm and say nothing of having met me, for by this evening, or tomorrow at the latest, we will come there again and sift out the truth of this question."

To this she agreed, being guileless, and the lawyer rode away after the other. All that day and all the next Suzanne scarcely spoke to me, but I saw that she was expecting something to happen, and that she glanced continually towards the path by which the Englishmen had journeyed, thinking to see them riding back to the farm. But they rode back no more, and I am sure that the cunning lawyer never breathed one word of his meeting with Suzanne and of what took place at it to the young lord. That book was shut and it did not please him to reopen it, since to do so might have cost him ten thousand pounds. On the third morning I found Suzanne still looking down the path, and my patience being exhausted by her silence, I spoke to her sharply.

"What are you doing, girl?" I asked. "Have we not had enough visitors of late that you must stand here all day awaiting more?"

"I seek no new visitors," Suzanne said, "but those who have been here only, and I see now that I seek in vain."

"What do you mean, Suzanne?"

Now of a sudden she seemed to make up her mind to speak, for she turned and faced me boldly, saying:

"I mean, mother, that I told the Englishman with the red hair, the agent, that all the fine tale you spun to him about Ralph was false, and that he *was* the man they came to find."

"You dared to do that, girl?" I said, then checked myself and added, "Well, what did the man say?"

"He said that he would ride on and bring the young lord back that I might talk with him, but they have not come."

"No, nor will they, Suzanne, for if they sought they did not wish to find, or at least the lawyer did not wish it, for he had too much at stake. Well, things have gone finely with you, seeing that your hands are clean from sin, and that Ralph still stays at your side."

"The sin of the parents is the sin of the child," she answered, and then of a sudden she took fire as it were, and fell upon me and beat me with her tongue; nor could I hold my own before this girl of eighteen, the truth being that she had right on her side, and I knew it. She told me that we were wicked plotters who, to pleasure ourselves, had stolen from Ralph everything except his life; and many other such hard sayings she threw at me till at last I could bear it no more, but gave her back word for word. Indeed, it would be difficult to say which had the best of that quarrel, for if Suzanne's tongue was the nimbler and her words were winged with truth, I had the weight of experience on my side and the custom of authority. At last, as she paused breathless, I cried out:

"And for whose sake was all this done, you ungrateful chit, if it was not for your own?"

"If that was so, which is not altogether true," she answered, "it would have pleased me better, if, rather than make me a partner in this crime, and set me as bait to snare Ralph, you had left me to look after my own welfare."

56

"What!" I exclaimed, "are you then so shallow hearted that you were ready to bid farewell to him who for many years has been as your brother, and is now your affianced husband? You know well whatever he might promise now, that if once he had gone across the sea to England, you would have seen him no more."

"No," she answered, growing calm of a sudden, "I was not so prepared, for sooner would I die than lose Ralph."

"How, then, do you square this with all your fine talk?" I asked, thinking that at length I had trapped her. "If he had gone you must have lost him."

"Not so," she answered, innocently, "for I should have married him before he went, and then I could have been certain that he would return here whenever I wished it."

Now when I heard this I gasped, partly because the girl's cleverness took the breath from me, and partly with mortification that I should have lived to learn wisdom from the mouth of a babe and a suckling. For there was no doubt of it, this plan, of which I had not even thought, was the answer to the riddle, since by means of it Ralph might have kept his own, and we, I doubt not, should have kept Ralph. Once married to Suzanne he would have returned to her, or if she had gone with him for a little while, which might have been better, she would certainly have brought him back, seeing that she loved us and her home too well to forsake them.

Yes, I gasped, and the only answer that I could make when I reflected how little need there had been for the sin which we had sinned, was to burst into weeping, whereon Suzanne ran to me and kissed me and we made friends again. But all the same, I do not think that she ever thought quite so well of me afterwards, and if I thought the more of her, still I made up my mind that the sooner she was married and had a husband of her own to preach to, the better it would be for all of us.

Thus ended the story of the coming of the Englishmen, and of how Ralph lost his wealth and rank. We never heard or saw more of them, seeing that in those days before the great Trek we did not write letters, and if we had we should not have known where to send them, nor did the post-cart pass the door twice a week as it does in this overcrowded land of Natal.

****

Now I must go on to tell of the doings of that devil upon earth, Swart Piet, and of how the little Kaffir witch-doctoress, Sihamba Ngenyanga, which means She-who-walks-by-the-moonlight, became the slave and saviour of Suzanne.

At this time the *Heer* van Vooren, Swart Piet's father, had been dead for two years, and there were strange stories as to the manner of his death which I do not think it necessary to set out here. Whether or no Swart Piet did or did not murder his father I cannot say, nor does it matter, for at the least he worked other crimes as bad. After the death of the *Heer* van Vooren, however he may have chanced to die, this is certain, that Swart Piet inherited great riches as we used to reckon riches in those days; that is, he had vast herds of cattle and goats and sleep, some of which were kept for him by native chiefs far away, as much land as he wanted, and, it was said, a good sum in English gold. But he was a strange man, not like to other men, for he married no wife and courted no misses, that is until he took to courting Suzanne, and his only pleasure was to keep the company of Kaffir chiefs and women and to mix himself up with the devilments of the witch-doctors. Still, as every man has his fate, at last he fell in love with Suzanne, and in love with her he remained during all his wicked life, if that can be love which seeks to persecute and bring misery upon its object. It was just before the coming of the Englishmen that this passion of his manifested itself, for whenever he met the girl—outside the house for the most part, since Jan did not like to have him in it—he made sweet speeches and passed foolish pleasantries which, to be just, I am sure Suzanne never encouraged, since all her heart was elsewhere.

Now Swart Piet had information of everything, for his Kaffir spies brought it to him; therefore he very soon learned that Jan and Ralph had gone away with the cattle to the warm *veldt*, and that we two women were alone in the house. This was his opportunity, and one of which he availed himself, for now two or three times a week he would ride over from his place, take supper and ask leave to sleep, which it was difficult to refuse, all this time wearying the poor girl with his attentions. At last I spoke my mind to him about it, though not without hesitation, for to tell truth Swart Piet was one of the few men of whom I have ever been afraid. He listened to me politely and answered:

"All this is very true, Aunt, but if you desire a fruit and it will not fall, then you must shake the tree."

"What if it sticks to the bough?" I asked.

"Then, Aunt, you must climb the tree and pluck it."

"And what if by that time it is in another man's pouch?"

"Then, Aunt," he answered with one of those dark smiles that turned my blood cold, "then, Aunt, the best thing which you can do is to kill the other man and take it out, for after that the fruit will taste all the sweeter."

"Get you gone, Swart Piet," I said in anger, "for no man who talks thus shall stay in my house, and it is very well for you that neither my husband nor Ralph Kenzie are here to put you out of it."

"Well," he answered, "they are not here, are they? And as for your house, it is a pretty place, but I only seek one thing in it, and that is not built into the walls. I thank you for your hospitality, Aunt, and now, good-day to you."

"Suzanne!" I called, "Suzanne!" for I thought that she was in her chamber; but the girl, knowing that Piet van Vooren was here, had slipped out, and of this he was aware. He knew, moreover, where she had gone, for I think that one of his Kaffir servants was watching outside and told him, and thither he followed her and made love to her.

In the end—for he would not be put off—he asked her for a kiss, whereat she grew angry. Then, for he was no shy wooer, he tried to take it by force; but she was strong and active and slipped from him. Instead of being ashamed, he only laughed after his uncanny fashion, and said:

"Well, missy, you have the best of me now, but I shall win that kiss yet. Oh! I know all about it; you love the English castaway, don't you? But there, a woman can love many men in her life, and when one is dead another will serve her turn."

"What do you mean, *myn Heer* van Vooren?" asked Suzanne, afraid.

"Mean? Nothing, but I shall win that kiss yet, yes, and before very long."

CHAPTER 9

How Suzanne Saved Sihamba

Now in a valley of the hills, something over an hour's ride from the farm, and not far from the road that ran to Swart Piet's place, lived the little Kaffir witch-doctoress, Sihamba Ngenyanga. This woman did not belong to any of the Transkei or neighbouring tribes, but had drifted down from the North; indeed, she was of Swazi or some such blood, though why she left her own people we did not know at that time. In appearance Sihamba was very strange, for, although healthy, perfectly shaped and copper-coloured rather than black, she was no taller than a child of twelve years old—a thing that made many people believe that she was a bush woman, which she most certainly was not. For a Kaffir also she was pretty, having fine small features, beautiful white teeth, and a fringe of wavy black hair that stood out stiffly round her head something after the fashion of the gold plates which the saints wear in the pictures in our old Bible.

This woman Sihamba, who might have been a little over thirty years of age, had been living in our neighbourhood for some three or four years and practising as a doctoress. Not that she was a "black" doctoress, for she never took part in the "smelling-out" of human beings for witchcraft or in the more evil sort of rites. Her trade was to sell charms and medicines to the sick, also to cure animals of their ailments, at which, indeed, she was very clever, though there was some who said that when she chose she could "throw the bones" and tell the future better than most, and this without dressing herself up in bladders and snake skins, or falling into fits, or trances, and such mummery. Lastly, amongst the natives about, and some of the Boers too, I am sorry to say, she had the reputation of being the best of rainmakers, and many were the head of cattle that she earned by prophesying the break-up of a drought, or the end of continual rains. Indeed, it is certain that no one whom I ever knew had so great a gift of insight into the omens of the weather at all seasons of the year, as this strange Sihamba Ngenyanga, a name that she got, by the way, because of her habit of wandering about in the moonlight to gather the herbs and the medicine roots which she used in her trade.

On several occasions Jan had sent animals to be doctored by this Sihamba, for she would not come out to attend to them whatever fee was offered to her. At first I did not approve of it, but as she always cured the animals, whatever their ailments might be, I gave in on the matter.

Now it happened that a few months before some travellers who had guested at our house gave Suzanne a little rough-haired dog bred of parents which had been brought from England. Of this dog Suzanne grew very fond, and when it fell sick of the distemper she was in much distress. So it came about that one afternoon Suzanne put the dog in a basket, and taking with her an old Hottentot to carry it, set out upon her grey mare for the valley where Sihamba lived. Now Sihamba had her hut and the huts of the few people in her service in a recess at the end of the valley, so placed that until you were quite on to them you would never have guessed that they were there. Down this valley Suzanne rode, the Hottentot with the basket on his head trotting by her side, till turning the corner she came upon a scene which she had very little expected. In one part of the open space beyond her, herded by some Kaffirs, were a number of cattle, sheep and goats. Opposite to them in the shadow under the hillside stood the huts of Sihamba, and in front of these grew a large tree. Beneath this tree was Sihamba herself with scarcely any clothing on her, for she had been stripped, her tiny wrists bound together behind her back and a rope about her neck, of which one end was thrown over a bough of the tree. In front of her, laughing brutally, stood none other than Swart Piet and with him a small crowd of men, mostly half-breed wanderers of the sort that trek from place to place claiming hospitality on the grounds of cousinship or poverty, until they are turned off as a nuisance. Also there were present a few Kaffirs, either headmen in Swart Piet's pay or some of his dark associates in witchcraft.

At first Suzanne was inclined to turn her horse and fly, but she was a brave girl, and the perilous state of the little doctoress moved her to pity, for where Swart Piet was there she suspected cruelty and wicked motive. So she rode on, yes, straight up to Swart Piet himself.

"In the name of Heaven what passes here, *myn Heer*?" she asked.

"Ah! Miss Suzanne, is it you?" he answered. "Well, you have not chosen a nice time for your visit, for we are about to—hang—this thief and witch, who has been duly convicted after a fair trial."

"A fair trial," said Suzanne, glancing scornfully at the rabble about her, "and were these friends of yours the jury? What is her offence?"

"Her offence is that she who lives here on my land has stolen my cattle and hid them away in a secret *kloof*. It has been proved against her by ample evidence. There are the cattle yonder mixed up with her own. I, as Veld-Cornet of the district, have tried the case according to law, and the woman having been found guilty must die according to law."

"Indeed, *myn Heer*," said Suzanne, "then if I understand you right, you are both accuser and judge, and the law which permits this is one that I never heard of. Oh!" she went on angrily, "no wonder that the English sing a loud song about us Boers and our cruelty to the natives when such a thing as this can happen. It is not justice, *myn Heer*, it is a crime for which, if you escape the hand of man, God will bring you to account."

Then for the first time Sihamba spoke in a very quiet voice, which showed no sign of fear.

"You are right, lady," she said; "it is not justice, it is a crime born of revenge, and my life must pay forfeit for his wickedness. I am a free woman, and I have harmed none and have bewitched none. I have cured sick people and sick creatures, that is all. The *Heer* says that I live upon his land, but I am not his slave; I pay him rent to live here. I never stole his cattle; they were mixed up with mine by his servants in a far-off *kloof* in order to trump up a charge against me, and he knows it, for he gave orders that the thing should be done, so that afterwards he might have the joy of hanging me to this tree, because he wishes to be avenged upon me for other matters, private matters between me and him. But, lady, do not trouble yourself about the fate of such a poor black creature as I am. Go away and tell the story if you will, but go quickly, for these sights of death are not fit for young eyes like yours to see."

"I will not go," exclaimed Suzanne, "or if I go, it shall be to bring down upon you, Swart Piet, the weight of the law which you have broken. Ah! would that my father were at home; he does not love Kaffirs but he does love justice."

Now when they heard Suzanne speaking such bold words and saw the fire in her eyes, Swart Piet and those with him began to grow afraid. The hanging of a witch-doctoress after a formal trial upon the charge of theft of cattle was no great matter in those days, for such thefts were common and a cause of much trouble to out-lying farmers, nor would anyone in these half-settled regions be likely to look too closely into the rights and wrongs of an execution on account of them. But if a white person who was present went away to proclaim to the authorities, perhaps even to the Governor of the Cape, whose ear could always be won through the missionaries of the London Society, that this pretended execution was nothing but a murder, then the thing became serious. From the moment that Suzanne began to speak on behalf of Sihamba, Swart Piet had seen that it would be impossible to hang her unless he wished to risk his own neck. But he guessed also that the girl could not know this, and therefore he determined to make terms by working on her pity, such terms as should put her to shame before all those gathered there; yes, and leave something of a stain upon her heart for so long as she should live.

"I do not argue law with young ladies," he said, with a little laugh, "but I am always ready to oblige young ladies, especially this young lady. Now, yonder witch and cattle-thief has richly earned her doom, yet, because you ask it, Suzanne Botmar, I am ready to withdraw the prosecution against her, and to destroy the written record of it in my hand, on two conditions, of which the first is that she pays over to me by way of compensation for what she has stolen, all her cattle and other belongings. Do you consent to that, witch?"

"How can I refuse?" said Sihamba, with a bitter laugh, "seeing that if I do you will take both life and goods. But what is the second condition?"

"I am coming to that, witch, but it has nothing to do with you. Suzanne, it is this: that here, before all these people, as the price of this thief's life, you give me the kiss which you refused to me the other day."

Now, before Suzanne could answer, Sihamba broke in eagerly, "Nay, lady, let not your lips be stained and your heart be shamed for the sake of such as I. Better that I should die than that you should suffer defilement at the hands of Swart Piet, who, born of white blood and black, is false to both and a disgrace to both."

"I cannot do it," gasped Suzanne, turning pale and not heeding her outburst, "and, Heer van Vooren, you are a coward to ask it of me."

"Can't you?" he sneered. "Well, you need not, unless you please, and it is true that young women like best to be kissed alone. Here, you Kaffirs, pull that little devil up; slowly now, that she may learn what a tight string feels like about her throat before it chokes her."

In obedience to his command three of the evil fellows with him caught hold of the end of the rope which hung over the bough, and began to pull, dragging the light form of Sihamba upwards till only the tips of her big toes touched the ground.

"Doesn't she dance prettily?" said Swart Piet with a brutal laugh, at the same time motioning to the men to keep her thus a while.

Now Suzanne looked at the blackening lips and the little form convulsed in its death struggle, and could bear the sight no more.

"Let her down!" she cried, and, springing from the saddle, for all this while she had been seated upon her horse, she walked up to Piet, saying, "Take what you seek, but oh! for your sake I wish to God that my lips were poison."

"No, no," gasped Sihamba, who now was lying half choked upon the ground.

"That is not our bargain, dear," said Piet; "it is that you should kiss me, not I you."

Again Suzanne shrank back, and again at his signal the men began to pull upon the rope. Then seeing it, with her face as pale as death, she learned forward and touched his lips with hers, whereon he seized her round the middle, and, drawing her to him, covered her with kisses till even the brutes with him called to him not to push his jest too far and to let the girl go. This he did, uttering words which I will not repeat, and so weak was Suzanne with shame that when his arms were taken from her she fell to the ground, and lay there till the old Hottentot, her servant, ran to her, cursing and weeping with rage, and helped her to her feet. For a while she stood saying nothing, only wiping her face, as though filth had bespattered it, with the sun *kapje* which had fallen from her head, and her face was whiter than the white cap. At last she spoke in a hoarse voice:

"Loose that woman," she said, "who has cost me my honour."

They obeyed her, and snatching up her skin rug Sihamba turned and fled swiftly down the valley. Then Suzanne went to her horse, but before she mounted it she looked Swart Piet straight in the eyes. At the time he was following her, begging her not to be angry at a joke, for his madness was satisfied for a while and had left him. But she only looked in answer, and there was something so terrible to him in the dark eyes of this young unfriended girl that he shrank back, seeing in them, perhaps, the shadow of fate to come. Then Suzanne rode away, and Swart Piet, having commanded his ruffians to fire the huts of Sihamba, and to collect her people, goods, and cattle, went away also.

Just at the mouth of the valley something stirred in a bush, causing the horse to start, so that Suzanne, who was thinking of other things, slipped from it to the ground. Next moment she saw that it was Sihamba, who knelt before her, kissing her feet and the hem of her robe.

"Rise," she said kindly; "what has been cannot be helped, and at least it was no fault of yours."

"Nay, Swallow," said Sihamba, for I think I have said that was the name which the natives had given to Suzanne from childhood, I believe, because of the grace of her movements and her habit of running swiftly hither and thither—"Nay, Swallow, in a way it was my fault."

"What do you mean, Sihamba?"

"I mean, Swallow, that although I am so small some have thought me pretty, and the real reason of Black Piet's hate for me is—but why should I defile your ears with the tale?"

"They would only match my face if you did," answered Suzanne grimly, "but there is no need; I can guess well enough."

"You can guess, Swallow; then you will see why it was my fault. Yes, yes, you will see that what I, a black woman, who am less than dirt in the eyes of your people, would not do to save my own life; you, a white chieftainess, and the fairest whom we know, have done of your own will to keep it in me."

"If the act was good," answered Suzanne, "may it go to my credit in the Book of the Great One who made us."

"It will go to your credit, Swallow," answered Sihamba with passion, "both in that Book and in the hearts of all who hear this story, but most of all in this heart of mine. Oh! listen, lady; sometimes a cloud comes over me, and in that cloud I who was born a doctoress see visions of things that are to happen, true visions. Among them I see this: that many moons hence and far away I shall live to save you as you have saved me, but between that day and this the cloud of the future is black to my eyes, black but living."

"It may be so," answered Suzanne, "for I have heard that you have the Sight. And now, farewell; you had best seek out some friends among your people and hide yourself."

"My people," said Sihamba; "then I must seek long, for they are very, very far away, nor do they desire to see me."

"Why not?"

"Because as it chances I am by blood their ruler, for I am the only child of my father's head-wife. But they would not have me set over them as chieftainess unless I married a man, and towards marriage I have no wish, for I am different from other women, both in body and heart. So having quarrelled with them on this and another matter of policy I set out to seek my fortune and left them to theirs."

"Your fortune was not a good one, Sihamba, for it led you to Swart Piet and the rope."

"Nay, lady, it led me to the Swallow and freedom; no, not to freedom but to slavery, for I am your slave, whose life you have bought at a great price. Now I have nothing left in the world; Swart Piet has taken my cattle which I earned cow by cow and bred up heifer by heifer, and save for the wit within my brain and this *kaross* upon my shoulders, I have nothing."

"What, then, will you do, Sihamba?"

"What you do, Swallow, that I shall do, for am I not your slave bought at a great price? I will go home with you and serve you, yes, to my life's end."

"That would please me well enough, Sihamba, but I do not know how it would please my father."

"What pleases you pleases him, Swallow; moreover, I can save my food twice over by curing his cattle and horses in sickness, for in such needs I have skill."

"Well," she said, "come, and when my father returns we will settle how it shall be."

CHAPTER 10

The Oath of Sihamba

Suzanne came home and told me her story, and when I heard it I was like a mad woman; indeed, it would have gone ill with Swart Piet's eyes and hair if I could have fallen in with him that night.

"Wait till your father returns, girl," I said.

"Yes, mother," she answered, "I wait for him—and Ralph."

"What is to be done with the little doctoress, Sihamba?" I asked, adding, "I do not like such people about the place."

"Let her bide also till the men come back, mother," she answered, "and then they will see to it. Meanwhile there is an empty hut down by the cattle *kraal* where she can live."

So Sihamba stopped on and became a body servant to Suzanne, the best I ever saw, though she would do no other work save that of attending to sick animals. Ten days afterwards Jan and Ralph returned safe and sound, leaving some Kaffirs in charge of the cattle in the bush-*veldt*. Very glad we were to see them, since, putting everything else aside, it was lonely work for two women upon the place with no neighbour at hand, and in those days to be lonely meant to be in danger.

When we were together Jan's first question to me was:

"Have those Englishmen been here?"

"They have been here," I answered, "and they have gone away."

Jan asked me nothing more of the matter, for he did not wish to know what had passed between us. Only he looked at me queerly, and, as I think, thought the worse of me afterwards, for he found out that Suzanne and I had quarrelled about the song I sang in the ears of the Englishmen, and what that song was he could guess very well. Yes, yes, although he had been a party to the fraud, in his heart Jan put all the blame of it upon me, for that is the way of men who are mean, and always love to say "The woman tempted me," a vile habit which has come down to them with their blood.

Meanwhile another talk was passing between Ralph and Suzanne. They had rushed to meet each other like two separated colts bred in the same meadow, but when they came together it was different. Ralph put out his arms to embrace her, but she pushed him back and said, "No, not until we have spoken together."

"This is a cold greeting," said Ralph, amazed and trembling, for he feared lest Suzanne should have changed her mind as to their marriage. "What is it that you have to tell me? Speak on, quickly."

"Two things, Ralph," she answered, and taking the least of them first, she plunged straightway into a full account of the coming of the Englishmen, of all that had passed then, and of her quarrel with me upon the matter.

"And now, Ralph," she ended, "you will understand that you have been cheated of your birthright, and this I think it just that you should know, so that, if you will, you may change your mind about staying here, for there is yet time, and follow these Englishmen to wherever it is they have gone, to claim from them your heritage."

Ralph laughed and answered, "Why, Sweet, I thought that we had settled all this long ago. That your mother did not tell the men quite the truth is possible, but if she played with it, it was for the sake of all of us and with my leave. Let them go and the fortune with them, for even if I could come to England and find it there, I should be but as a wild buck in a sheep *kraal*, out of place and unhappy. Moreover, we should be separated, dear, for even if you would all consent, I could never take you from your own people and the land where you were born. So now that there is an end to this, once and for ever, let me kiss you in greeting, Suzanne."

But she shook her head and denied him, saying, "No, for I have another tale to tell you, and an uglier—so ugly indeed that after the hearing of it I doubt much whether you will wish to kiss me any more."

"Be swift with it then," he answered, "for you torment me," and she began her story.

She told how that, after he had gone away, Swart Piet began to persecute her; how he had wished to kiss her and she had refused them, so that he left her with threats. Then she paused suddenly and said:

"And now, before I finish the story, you shall swear an oath to me. You shall swear that you will not attempt to kill Swart Piet because of it."

At first he would swear nothing, for already he was wild with anger against the man, whereupon she answered that she would tell him nothing.

At last, when they had wrangled for a while, he asked her in a hoarse voice, "Say now, Suzanne, have you come to any harm at the hands of this fellow?"

"No," she answered, turning her head away. "God be thanked! I have come to no harm of my body, but of my mind I have come to great harm."

Now he breathed more freely and said:

"Very well, then, on with your story, for I swear to you that I will not try to kill Swart Piet because of this offence, whatever it may be."

So she went on, setting out everything exactly as it had happened, and before she had finished Ralph was as one who is brain sick, for he ground his teeth and stamped upon the earth like an angry bull. At last, when Suzanne had told him all, she said:

"Now, Ralph, you will understand why I would not let you kiss me before you had heard my story. It was because I feared that after hearing it you would not wish to kiss me any more."

"You talk like a foolish girl," he answered, taking her into his arms and embracing her, "and though the insult can only be paid back in blood, I think no more of it than if some beast had splashed mud into your face, which you had washed away at the next stream."

"Ah!" she cried, "you swore that you would not try to kill him for this offence."

"Yes, Sweet, I swore, and I will keep my oath. This time I will not try to kill Swart Piet."

Then they went into the house, and Ralph spoke to Jan about this matter, of which indeed I had already told him something. Jan also was very angry, and said that if he could meet Piet van Vooren it would go hard with him. Afterwards he added, however, that this Piet was a very dangerous man, and one whom it might be well to leave alone, especially as Suzanne had taken no real hurt from him. Nowadays, and here in Natal, such a villain could be made to answer to the law, either for attempting the life of the Kaffir, or for the assault upon the girl, or for both, but in those times it was different. Then the Transkei had but few white people in it, living far apart, nor was there any law to speak of; indeed each man did what was right in his own eyes, according to the good or evil that was in his heart. Therefore, as Jan said, it was not well to make a deadly enemy of one who was restrained by the fear of neither God nor man, and who had great wealth and power, since it might come about that he would work murder in revenge or raise the Kaffirs on us, as he who had authority among them could do very easily. Indeed as will be seen he did both these things, or tried to do them.

When his anger had cooled a little Jan spoke to us in this sense and we women agreed with him; but Ralph, who was young, fearless, and full of rage, set his mouth and said nothing.

As for Sihamba Jan wished to send her away, but Suzanne, who had grown fond of her, begged him that he would not do so, at least until he had spoken with her. So he ordered one of the slaves to fetch her, and presently the little woman came, and having saluted him, sat herself down on the floor of the sitting room after the Kaffir fashion. She was a strange little creature to see in her fur *kaross* and bead broidered girdle, but for a native she was very clean and pretty, with her wise woman's face set upon a body that had it been less rounded might almost have been that of a child. Also she had adorned herself with great care, not in the cast-off clothes of white people but after her own manner, for her wavy hair which stood out from her head was powdered over with that sparkling blue dust which the Kaffir women use, and round her neck she wore a single string of large blue beads.

At first Jan spoke to her crossly, saying:

"You have brought trouble and disgrace upon my house, Sihamba, and I wish you to begone from it."

"It is true," she answered, "but not of my own will did I bring the trouble, O Father of Swallow," for so she always called Jan. Indeed, for Sihamba, Suzanne was the centre of all things, and thus in her mouth the three of us has no other names than "Father" or "Mother" or "Lover" of Swallow.

"That may be so," answered Jan, "but, doubtless, Black Piet, who hates you, will follow you here, and then we shall be called upon to defend you, and there will be more trouble."

"It is not I whom Black Piet will follow," she replied, "for he has stolen all I have, and as my life is safe there is nothing more to get from me," and she looked at Suzanne.

"What do you mean, Sihamba? Speak plain words," said Jan.

"I mean," she answered, "that it is not I who am now in danger, but my mistress, the Swallow, for he who has kissed her once will wish to kiss her again."

Now at this Ralph cursed the name of Swart Piet aloud, and Jan answered,

"It is a bullet from my *roer* that he shall kiss if he tries it, that I swear."

"I hope it may be so," said Sihamba; "yet, Father of Swallow, I pray you send me not away from her who bought me at a great price, and to whom my life belongs. Look; I cost you but little to keep, and that little I can earn by doctoring your horses and cattle, in which art I have some skill, as you know well. Moreover I have many eyes and ears that can see and hear things to which yours are deaf and blind, and I tell you that I think a time will come when I shall be able to do service to all of you who are of the nest of the Swallow. Now, if she bids me to go I will go—for am I not her servant to obey?—yet I beseech you do not so command her."

Sihamba had risen as she spoke, and now she stood before Jan, her head thrown back, looking up into his eyes with such strange power that, though he was great and strong and had no will to it, yet he found himself forced to look down into hers. More, as he told me afterwards, he saw many things in the eyes of Sihamba, or it may be that he thought that he saw them, for Jan was always somewhat superstitious. At least this is true that more than once during the terrible after years, when some great event had happened to us he would cry out, "I have seen this place, or thing, before, I know not where." Then if I bade him think he would answer, "Now I remember; it was in the eyes of Sihamba that I saw it, yonder in the Transkei before Ralph and Suzanne were married."

Presently she freed his eyes and turned her head, whereon Jan grew pale and swayed as though he were about to fall. Recovering himself, however, he said shortly,

"Stay if you will, Sihamba; you are welcome for so long as it shall please you."

She lifted her little hand and saluted him, and I noticed that it was after another fashion to that of the Kaffirs who lived thereabouts, after the Zulu fashion indeed.

"I hear your words, chief," she said, "and I stay. Though I be but a lizard in the thatch, yet the nest of the Swallow shall be my nest, and in the fangs of the lizard, Sihamba, there is poison and woe to the hawk of the air or the snake of the grass that would rob this nest wherein you dwell. Listen now to my oath—you whom she loves. Cold shall this heart be and stiff this hand, empty shall this head be of thoughts and these eyes of sight, before shame or death shall touch the swift wings of yonder Swallow who stained her breast for me. Remember this always, you whom she loves, that while I live, I, Sihamba Ngenyanga, Sihamba the walker by moonlight, she shall live, and if she dies I will die also."

Then once more she saluted and went, leaving us wondering, for we saw that this woman was not altogether as other Kaffirs are, and it came into our minds that in the time of need she would be as is a sharp spear in the hand of one who is beset with foes.

That night as we lay abed I talked with Jan, saying:

"Husband, I think there are clouds upon our sky, which for many years has been so blue. Trouble gathers round us because of the beauty of Suzanne, and I fear Swart Piet, for he is not a man to be stopped by a trifle. Now, Ralph loves Suzanne and Suzanne loves Ralph, and, though they are young, they are man and woman full grown, able to keep a house and bear its burdens. Why then should they not marry with as little delay as may be, for when once they are wed Van Vooren will cease from troubling them, knowing his suit to be hopeless?"

"As you will, wife, as you will," Jan answered, somewhat sharply, "but I doubt if we shall get rid of our danger thus, for with you I think that the tide of our lives has turned, and that it sets towards sorrow. Ay," he went on, sitting up in the bed, "and I will tell you when it turned; it turned upon the day that you lied to the Englishmen."

CHAPTER 11

A Fight and a Shot

Early the next morning I sought for Ralph to speak to him on the matter of his marriage, which, to tell truth, I longed to see safely accomplished. But I could not find him anywhere, or learn where he had gone, though one of the slaves told me that they had seen him mount his horse at the stable. I went down to the cattle *kraal* to look if he were there, and as I returned, I saw Sihamba seated by the door of her hut engaged in combing her hair and powdering it with the shining blue dust.

"Greeting, Mother of Swallow," she said. "Whom do you seek?"

"You know well," I answered.

"Yes, I know well. At the break of dawn he rode over yonder rise."

"Why?" I asked.

"How can I tell why? But Swart Piet lives out yonder."

"Had he his gun with him?" I asked again and anxiously.

"No, there was nothing but a *sjambock*, a very thick *sjambock*, in his hand."

Then I went back to the house with a heavy heart, for I was sure that Ralph had gone to seek Piet van Vooren, though I said nothing of it to the others. So it proved indeed. Ralph had sworn to Suzanne that he would not try to kill Piet, but here his oath ended, and therefore he felt himself free to beat him if he could find him, for he was altogether mad with hate of the man. Now he knew that when he was at home it was Swart Piet's habit to ride of a morning, accompanied by one Kaffir only, to visit a certain valley where he kept a large number of sheep. Thither Ralph made his way, and when he reached the place he saw that, although it was time for them to be feeding, the sheep were still in their *kraal*, *baa*-ing, stamping, and trying to climb the gate, for they were hungry to get at the green grass.

"So," thought Ralph, "Swart Piet means to count the flock out himself this morning. He will be here presently."

Half an hour afterwards he came sure enough, and with him the one Kaffir as was usual. Then the bars of the gate were let down, and the sheep suffered to escape through them, Swart Piet standing upon one side and the Kaffir upon the other, to take tale of their number. When all the sheep were out, and one of the herds had been brought before him and beaten by the Kaffir, because some lambs were missing, Swart Piet turned to ride homewards, and in a little gorge near by came face to face with Ralph, who was waiting for him. Now he started and looked to see if he could escape, but there was no way of doing it without shame, so he rode forward and bid Ralph good-day boldly, asking him if he had ever seen a finer flock of sheep.

"I did not come here to talk of sheep," answered Ralph, eyeing him.

"Is it of a lamb, then, that you come to talk, *Heer* Kenzie, a ewe lamb, the only one of your flock?" sneered Piet, for he had a gun in his hand and he saw that Ralph had none.

"Aye," said Ralph, "it is of a white ewe lamb whose fleece has been soiled by a bastard thief who would have stolen her," and he looked at him.

"I understand," said Piet coldly, for he was a bold man; "and now, *Heer* Kenzie, you had best let me ride by."

"Why should I let you ride by when I have come out to seek you?"

"For a very good reason, *Heer* Kenzie; because I have a gun in my hand and you have none, and if you do not clear the road presently it may go off."

"A good reason, indeed," said Ralph, "and one of which I admit the weight," and he drew to one side of the path as though to let Piet pass, which he began to do holding the muzzle of the gun in a line with the other's head. Ralph sat upon his horse staring moodily at the ground, as though he was trying to make up his mind to say something or other, but all the time he was watching out of the corner of his quick eye. Just as Swart Piet drew past him, and was shaking the reins to put his horse to a canter, Ralph slid from the saddle, and springing upon him like light, he slipped his strong arm round him and dragged him backwards to the ground over the crupper of the horse. As Piet fell he stretched out his hands to grip the saddle and save himself, so that the gun which he carried resting on his knees dropped upon the grass. Ralph seized it and fired it into the air; then he turned to face his enemy, who by this time had found his feet.

"Now we are more equally matched, *myn Heer* van Vooren," he said, "and can talk further about that ewe lamb, the only one of the flock. Nay, you need not look for the Kaffir to help you, for he has run

74

after your horse, and at the best he will hardly dare to thrust himself between two angry white men. Come, let us talk, *myn Heer.*"

Black Piet made no answer, so for a while the two stood facing each other, and they were a strange pair, as different as the light from the darkness. Ralph fair-haired, grey-eyed, stern-faced, with thin nostrils, that quivered like those of a well-bred horse, narrow-flanked, broad-chested, though somewhat slight of limb and body, for he was but young, and had scarcely come to a man's weight, but lithe and wiry as a tiger. Piet taller and more massive, for he had the age of him by five years, with round Kaffir eyes, black and cruel, coarse black hair that grew low upon his brow, full red lips, the lower drooping so that the large white teeth and a line of gums could be seen within. Great-limbed he was also, firm-footed and bull-strengthed, showing his face the cruelty and the cunning of a black race, mingled with the mind and mastery of the white; an evil and a terrible man, knowing no lord save his own passions, and no religion but black witchcraft and vile superstition; a foe to be feared indeed, but one who loved better to stab in the dark than to strike in the open day.

"Well, *myn Heer* van Vooren," mocked Ralph, "you could fling your arms about a helpless girl and put her to shame before the eyes of men, now do the same by me if you can," and he took one step towards him.

"What is this monkey's chatter?" asked Piet, in his slow voice. "Is it because I gave the girl a kiss that you would fix a quarrel upon me? Have you not done as much yourself many times, and for a less stake than the life of one who has been doomed to die?"

"If I have kissed her," answered Ralph, "it is with her consent, and because she will be my wife; but you worked upon her pity to put her to shame and now you shall pay the price of it. Do you see that whip?" and he nodded toward the *sjambock* that was lying on the grass. "Let him who proves the best man use it upon the other."

"Will be your wife——" sneered Piet, "the wife of the English castaway! She might have been, but now she never shall, unless she cares to wed a carcase cut into *rimpis*. You want a flogging, and you shall have it, yes, to the death, but Suzanne shall be—not your wife but——"

He got no further, for at that moment Ralph sprang at him like a wild cat, stopping his foul mouth with a fearful blow upon the lips. Then there followed a dreadful struggle between these two. Black Piet rushed again and again, striving to clasp his antagonist in his great arms and crush him, whereas Ralph, who, like all Englishmen, loved to use his fists, and knew that he was no match for Piet in strength, sought to avoid him and plant blow after blow upon his face and body. This, indeed, he did with such success that soon the Boer was covered with blood and bruises. Again and again he charged at him, roaring with pain and rage, and again and again Ralph first struck and then slipped to one side.

At length Piet's turn came, for Ralph in leaping back caught his foot against a stone and stumbled, and before he could recover himself the iron arms were round his middle, and they were wrestling for the mastery.

Still, at the first it was Ralph who had the best of it, for he was skilful at the game, and before Swart Piet could put out his full strength he tripped him so that he fell heavily upon his back, Ralph still locked in his arms. But he could not keep him there, for the Boer was the stronger; moreover, as they fought they had worked their way up the steep side of the *kloof* so that the ground was against him. Thus it came about that soon they began to roll down hill fixed to each other as though by ropes, and gathering speed at every turn. Doubtless, the end of this would have been Ralph's defeat, and perhaps his death, for I think that, furious as he was, Black Piet would certainly have killed him had he found himself the master. But it chanced that his hand was stayed, and thus. Near the bottom of the slope lay a sharp stone, and as they rolled in their fierce struggle, Piet's head struck against this stone so that for a few moments he was rendered helpless. Feeling the grip of his arms loosen, Ralph freed himself, and running to the *sjambock* snatched it from the ground. Now Piet sat up and stared at him stupidly, but he made no effort to renew the fight, whereon Ralph gasped:

"I promised you a flogging, but since it is chance that has conquered you more than I, I will take no advantage of it, save this——" and he struck him once or twice across the face with the whip, but not so as to draw blood, and added, "Now, at least, I am free from a certain promise that I made—that I would not kill you—and should you attempt further harm or insult towards Suzanne Botmar, kill you I will, Piet van Vooren."

At first Swart Piet did not seem to feel the blows, but presently he awoke, as it were, and touched his cheeks where the *sjambock* had struck him as though to assure himself that he was not dreaming some evil dream. Then he spoke in a hollow, unnatural voice. "You have won for this time, Ralph Kenzie," he said, "or, rather, Fate fighting for you has won. But it would have been better for you and your dear also, if you had never struck those blows, for I tell you, Ralph Kenzie, that as your whip touched me something broke in my brain, and now I think that I am mad."

"Mad or bad, it is all one to me," replied Ralph. "You have had your warning, and you had best keep sane enough to remember it." Then turning he went to his horse, which was standing close by, mounted and rode away, the other answering him nothing.

Still Ralph did not get home without another adventure, for when he had gone a little way he came to a stream that ran from a hillside which was thick with trees, and here he stopped to doctor his hurts and bruises, since he did not wish to appear at the house covered with blood. Now this was a foolish enough thing to do, seeing the sort of man with whom he had to deal, and that there was bush where anyone could hide to within a hundred and twenty yards of his washing place. So it proved indeed, for just as Ralph had mounted his horse and was about to ride on, he felt a sharp stinging pain across his shoulders, as though someone had hit him on the back with a stick, and heard the sound of a gunshot fired from the cover of the bush, for there above the green leaves hung a cloud of smoke.

"That is Swart Piet who has crept round to cut me off," Ralph thought to himself, and for a moment was minded to ride to the smoke to seek him. Then he remembered that he had no gun, and that that of his enemy might be loaded again before he found him, and judged it wisest to canter into the open plain and so homewards. Of the hurt which he had taken from the bullet he thought little, yet when he reached the house it was seen that his escape had been narrow indeed, for the great ball had cut through his clothes beneath his shoulders, so that they hung down leaving his back naked. Also it had furrowed the skin, causing the blood to flow copiously, and making so horrible a sight of him that Suzanne nearly fainted when she saw it. For my part I made certain that the lad was shot through the body, although, as it turned out, in a week, except for some soreness he was as well as ever.

Now this matter caused no little stir among us, and Jan was so angry that, without saying a word to anyone, he mounted his horse and, taking some armed servants with him, set out to seek Black Piet, but not to find him, for the man had gone, nobody knew whither. Indeed this was as well, or so we thought at the time, for though Jan is slow to move, when once he is moved he is a very angry man, and I am sure that if he had met Piet van Vooren that day the grasses would have been richer by the blood of one or both of them. But he did not meet him and so the thing passed over, for afterwards we remembered that Ralph had been the aggressor, since no one would take count of this story of the kissing of a girl, and also that there was no proof at all that it was Piet who had attempted his life, as that shot might have been fired by anyone.

Now from this day forward Suzanne went in terror of Swart Piet, and whenever Ralph rode, he rode armed, for though it was said that he had gone on one of his long journeys trading among the Kaffirs, both of them guessed that they had not seen the last of Van Vooren. Jan and I were afraid also, for we knew the terrible nature of the man and of his father before him, and that they came of a family which never forgot a quarrel or left a desire ungratified.

About fourteen days after Ralph had been shot at and wounded, a Kaffir brought a letter for Jan, which, on being opened, proved to have been written by Swart Piet, or on his behalf, since his name was set at the bottom of it. It read thus:—

To the *Heer* Jan Botmar,
Well-beloved Heer, this is to tell you that your daughter, Suzanne, holds my heart, and that I desire to make her my wife. As it is not convenient for me to come to see you at present, I write to ask you that you will consent to our betrothal. I will make a rich woman of her as I can easily satisfy you, and you will find it better to have me as a dear son-in-law and friend than as a stranger and an enemy, for I am a good friend and a bad enemy. I know there has been some talk of love between Suzanne and the English foundling at your place; but I can overlook that, although you may tell the lad that if he is impertinent to me again as he was the other day, he will not for the second time get off with a whipping only. Be so good as to give your answer to the bearer, who will pass it on to those that can find me, for I am travelling about on business, and do not know where I shall be from day to day. Give also my love to Suzanne, your daughter, and tell her that I think often of the time when she shall be my wife.
I am, well-beloved *Heer*, your friend,
Piet van Vooren."

Now, when Ralph had finished reading this letter aloud, for it had been given to him as the best scholar among us, you might have thought there were four crazy people in the room, so great was our rage. Jan and Ralph said little indeed, although they looked white and strange with anger, and Suzanne not over much, for it was I who talked for all of them.

"What is your answer, girl?" asked her father presently with an angry laugh.

"Tell the *Heer* Piet van Vooren," she replied, smiling faintly, "that if ever his lips should touch my face again it will be only when that face is cold in death. Oh! Ralph," she cried, turning to him suddenly and laying her hand upon his breast, "it may be that this man will bring trouble and separation on us; indeed, my heart warns me of it, but, whatever chances, remember my words, dead I may be, but faithful I shall be—yes, to death and through death."

"Son, take pen and write," said Jan before Ralph could answer. So Ralph wrote down these words as Jan told them to him:

"Piet van Vooren,

"Sooner would I lay my only child out for burial in the grave than lead her to the house of a coloured man, a consorter with witch-doctors and black women and a would-be murderer. That is my answer, and I add this to it. Set no foot within a mile of my house, for here we shoot straighter than you do, and if we find you on this place, by the help of God we will put a bullet through your carcase."

At the foot of this writing, which he would not suffer to be altered, Jan printed his name in big letters; then he went out to seek the messenger, whom he found talking to Sihamba, and having given him the paper bade him begone swiftly to wherever it was he came from. The man, who was a strong red-coloured savage, marked with a white scar across the left cheek, and naked except for his *moocha* and the *kaross* rolled up upon his shoulders, took the letter, hid it in his bundle, and went.

Jan also turned to go, but I who had followed him and was watching him, although he did not know it, saw him hesitate and stop.

"Sihamba," he said, "why were you talking to that man?"

"Because it is my business to know of things, Father of Swallow, and I wished to learn whence he came."

"Did he tell you then?"

"Not altogether, for someone whom he fears has laid a weight upon his tongue, but I learned that he lives at a *kraal* far away in the mountains, and that this *kraal* is owned by a white man who keeps wives and cattle at it, although he is not there himself just now. The rest I hope to hear when Swart Piet sends him back again, for I have given the man a medicine to cure his child, who is sick, and he will be grateful to me."

"How do you know that Swart Piet sent the man?" asked Jan.

She laughed and said: "Surely that was easy to guess; it is my business to twine little threads into a rope."

Again he turned to go and again came back to speak to her.

"Sihamba," he said, "I have seen you talking to that man before. I remember the scar upon his face."

"The scar upon his face you may remember," she answered, "but you have not seen us talking together, for until this hour we never met."

"I can swear it," he said angrily. "I remember the straw hat, the shape of the man's bundle, the line where the shadow fell upon his foot, and the tic-bird that came and sat near you. I remember it all."

"Surely, Father of Swallow," Sihamba replied, eyeing him oddly, "you talk of what you have just seen."

"No, no," he said, "I saw it years ago."

"Where?" she asked, staring at him.

He started and uttered some quick words. "I know now," he said. "I saw it in your eyes the other day."

"Yes," she answered quietly, "I think that, if anywhere, you saw it in my eyes, since the coming of this messenger is the first of all the great things that are to happen to the Swallow and to those who live in her nest. I do not know the things; still, it may happen that another who has Vision may see them in the glass of my eyes."

CHAPTER 12

What the Cow Showed Zinti

Twelve days passed, and one morning when I went out to feed the chickens, I saw the red Kaffir with the scar on his face seated beyond the *stoep* taking snuff.

"What is it?" I asked.

"A letter," he answered, giving me a paper.

I took it into the house, where the others were gathered for breakfast, and as before Ralph read it. It was to this effect:

"Well-beloved *Heer* Botmar,—I have received your honoured letter, and I think that the unchristian spirit which it shows cannot be pleasing to our Lord. Still, as I seek peace and not war, I take no offence, nor shall I come near your place to provoke the shedding of the blood of men. I love your daughter, but if she rejects me for another, I have nothing more to say, except that I hope she may be happy in the life she has chosen. For me, I am leaving this part of the country, and if you, *Heer* Botmar, like to buy my farm, I shall be happy to sell it to you at a fair price; or perhaps the *Heer* Kenzie will buy it to live on after he is married; if so, he can write to me by this messenger. Farewell."

Now, when they heard this letter, the others looked more happy; but for my part I shook my head, seeing guile in it, since the tone of it was too humble for Swart Piet. There was no answer to it, and the messenger went away, but not, as I learned, before he had seen Sihamba. It seems that the medicine which she gave him had cured his child, for which he was so grateful that he drove her down a cow in payment, a fine beast, but very wild, for handling was strange to it; moreover, it had been but just separated from its calf. Still, although she questioned him closely, the man would tell Sihamba but little of the place where he lived, and nothing of the road to it.

Here I will stop to show how great was the cunning of this woman, and yet how simple the means whereby she obtained the

81

most of her knowledge. She desired to learn about this hiding-place, since she was sure that it was one of the secret haunts of Swart-Piet, but when she asked him the messenger grew deaf and blind, and she could find no one else who knew anything of the matter. Still she was certain that the cow which had been brought to her would show the way to its home, if there were anybody to follow it thither and make report of the path.

Now when Sihamba had been robbed and sentenced to death by Swart Piet, the most of her servants and people who lived with her had been taken by him as slaves. Still two or three had escaped, either then or afterwards, and settled about in the neighbourhood of the farm where they knew that their mistress dwelt. From among these people, who still did her service, she chose a young man named Zinti, who, although he was supposed to be stupid, was still very clever about many things, especially the remembering of any path that he had once trodden, and of every *kopje*, stream, or *pan* by which it could traced. This youth she bade to herd the cow which had been given her, telling him to follow it whithersoever it should wander, even if it led him a ten days' journey, and when he saw that it had reached home, to return himself without being seen, and to give to her an exact report of the road which it had travelled.

Now all happened as Sihamba expected, for on the first day that the cow was turned out, watched by the lad, who was provided with food and a blanket, so soon as it had filled itself it started straight over the hills, running at times, and at times stopping to graze, till night came on. Then it lay down for a while and its herd beside it, for he had tied his wrist to its tail with a *rimpi* lest it should escape in the darkness.

At the first breaking of the light the cow rose, filled itself with grass and started forward on its homeward path, followed by Zinti. For three days they travelled thus, the herd milking the cow from time to time when its udder was full. On the evening of the third day, however, the beast would not lie down, but walked forward all night, lowing now and again, by which Zinti, who found it difficult to keep it in sight because of the darkness, guessed that it must be near its home. So it proved indeed, for when the sun rose Zinti saw a *kraal* before him hidden away in a secret valley of the mountains over which they had been travelling. Still following the cow, though at a distance, he moved down towards the *kraal* and hid himself in a patch of bush. Presently the cattle were let out to graze, and the cow rushed to them lowing loudly, till a certain calf came to it, which it made much of and suckled, for it was its own calf.

Now Zinti's errand was done, but still he lay hid in the bush a while, thinking that he might learn some more, and lying thus he fell asleep, for he was weary with travel. When he woke the sun was high, and he heard women talking to each other close by him, as they laboured at their task of cutting wands, such as are used for the making of huts. He rose to run away, then thought better of it and sat down again, remembering that should he be found, it would be easy to tell them that he was a wanderer who had lost his path. Presently one of the women asked:

"For whom does Bull-Head build this fine new hut in the secret *krantz* yonder?"

Now Zinti opened his ears wide, for he knew that this was the name which the natives had given to Swart Piet, taking it from his round head and fierce eye, according to their custom when they note any peculiarity in a man.

"I do not know," answered a second woman, who was young and very pretty, "unless he means to bring another wife here; if so, she must be a chief's daughter, since men do not build such huts for girls of common blood."

"Perhaps," said the other; "but then I think that he has stolen her from her father without payment; else he would not wish to hide her away in the secret *krantz*. Well, let her come, for we women must work hard here where there are so few men, and many hoes clean a field quickly."

"For my part I think there are enough of us already," said the young girl, looking troubled, for she was Swart Piet's last Kaffir wife, and did not desire to be supplanted by a new favourite. "But be silent, I hear Bull-Head coming on his horse," and she began to work very hard at cutting the wands.

A few minutes later Zinti saw Swart Piet himself ride up to the women, who saluted him, calling him "Chief" and "Husband."

"You are idle," he said, eyeing them angrily.

"These wands are tough to cut, husband," murmured the young woman in excuse.

"Still you must cut them quicker, girl," he answered, "if you would not learn how one of them feels upon your back. It will go hard with all of you if the big hut is not finished in seven days from now."

"We will do our best," said the girl, "but who is to dwell in the hut when it is done?"

"Not you, be sure of that," he answered, roughly, "nor any black woman, for I am weary of you, one and all. Listen: I go tomorrow with my servants to fetch a chieftainess, a white lady, to rule over you, but if any of you speak a word of her presence here you will pay for it, for I shall turn you away to starve. Do you understand?"

"We hear you, husband," they replied, somewhat sullenly, for now they understood that this new wife would be a mistress, and not a sister to them.

"Then be careful that you do not forget my words, and—hearken—so soon as you have cut a full load of hut-poles, let two of you carry them up to the *krantz* yonder, where they are wanted, but be careful that no one sees you going in or coming out."

"We hear you, husband," they said again, whereon Swart Piet turned and rode away.

Now, although Zinti was said to be foolish, chiefly, as I think, because he could not, or would not, work, yet in many ways he was cleverer than most Kaffirs, and especially always did he desire to see new places, the more so if they chanced to be secret places. Therefore, when he heard Swart Piet command the women to carry the rods for the hidden *krantz*, he determined that he would follow them, and this he did so skilfully that they neither heard nor saw him. At first he wondered whither they could be going, for they walked straight to the foot of what seemed to be an unclimbable wall of rock more than a hundred feet high. On the face of this rock, however, shrubs grew here and there like the bristles on the back of a hog, and having first glanced round to see that no one was watching them, the women climbed to one of these shrubs, which was rooted in the cliff about the height of a man above the level of the ground, and vanished so quickly that Zinti, who as watching, rubbed his eyes in wonder. After waiting a while, however, he followed in their steps to find that behind the shrub was a narrow cleft or crack such as are often to be seen in cliffs, and that down this cleft ran a pathway which twisted and turned in the rock, growing broader as it went, till at last it ended in the hidden *krantz*. This *krantz* was a very beautiful spot about three *morgen*, or six English acres, in extent, and walled all round with impassable cliffs. Down the face of one of these cliffs fell a waterfall forming a deep pool, out of which a stream ran, and on the banks of this stream the new hut was being built in such a position that the heat of the sun could strike it but little.

While he was taking note of these and other things Zinti saw some of those who were working at the hut leave it and start to walk towards the cleft. So having learnt everything that he could he thought it was time to go, and slipped away back to the bush, and thence homewards by the road which the cow had shown him.

Now, it chanced that as he went Zinti pierced his foot with a large thorn so that he was only able to travel slowly. On the fifth night of his journey he limped into a wood to sleep, which wood grew not much more than two hours on horseback from our farm. When he had been asleep for some hours he woke up, for all his food was done, and he could not rest well because of his hunger, and was astonished to see the light of a fire among the trees at some distance from him. Towards this fire he crept, thinking that there were herds or travellers who would give him food, but when he came to it he did not ask for any, since the first thing he saw was Swart Piet himself walking up and down in front of the fire, while at some distance from it lay a number of his men asleep in their *karosses*. Presently another man appeared slipping through the tree trunks, and coming to Swart Piet saluted him.

"Tell me what you have found out," he said.

"This, Baas," answered the man; "I went down to *Heer* Botmar's place and begged a bowlful of meal there, pretending that I was a stranger on a journey to court a girl at a distant *kraal*. The slaves gave me meal and some flesh with it, and I learned in talk with them that the *Heer* Botmar, his *vrouw*, his daughter Suzanne and the young Englishman, *Heer* Kenzie, all rode away yesterday to the christening party of the first-born of the *Heer* Roozen, who lives about five hours on horseback to the north yonder. I learned also that it is arranged for them to leave the *Heer* Roozen tomorrow at dawn, and to travel homewards by the Tiger's Nek, in which they will off-saddle about two hours before mid-day, for I forgot to say that they have two servants with them to see to their horses."

"That makes six in all," said Swart Piet, "of whom two are women, whereas we are twenty. Yes, it is very good, nothing could be better, for I know the off-saddling place by the stream in Tiger's Nek, and it is a nice place for men to hide behind the rocks and trees. Listen now for the plan, and be sure you understand it. When these people are off-saddled and eating their food, you Kaffirs will fall on them—with the spear and the *kerry* alone, mind—and they will come to their end."

"Does the master mean that we are to kill them?" asked the man doubtfully.

"Yes," answered Swart Piet, with some hesitation. "I do not want to kill them indeed, but I see no other way, except as regards the girl, of course, who must be saved. These people are to be attacked and robbed by Kaffirs, for it must never be known that I had a hand in it, and you brutes of Kaffirs always kill. Therefore, they must die, alas!

especially the Englishman, though so far as I am concerned I should be glad to spare the others if I could, but it cannot be done without throwing suspicion upon me. As for the girl, if she is harmed the lives of all of you pay for it. You will throw a *kaross* over her head, and bring her to the place which I will tell you of tomorrow, where I shall come upon you with some men and seem to rescue her. Do you understand, and do you think the plan good?"

"I understand, and I think the plan good—for you—and yet, Baas, there is one thing that I have not told you which may mar it."

"What is it?"

"This: When I was down there at the *Heer* Botmar's place, I saw the witch-doctoress Sihamba, who has a hut upon the farm. I was some way off, but I think that she recognised me, as she might well do seeing that it was I who set the rope about her neck when you wished to hang her. Now if she did know me all your plans may be in vain, for that woman has the Sight and she will guess them. Even when the cord was round her she laughed at me and told me that I should die soon, but that she would live for years, and therefore I fear her more than anyone living."

"She laughed at you, did she?" said Swart Piet; "well, I laugh at her, for neither she nor anyone who breathes shall stand between me and this girl, who has preferred the suit of another man to mine."

"Ah, master!" said the Kaffir, with admiration, "you are a great one, for when a fruit pleases you, you do not wait for it to drop into your lap, you pluck it."

"Yes," said Swart Piet, striking his breast with pride, "if I desire a fruit I pluck it as my father did before me. But now go you and sleep, for tomorrow you will need all your wit and strength."

****

When the head Zinti had heard this talk he crept away, heading straight for the farm, but his foot was so bad, and he was so weak from want of food, that he could only travel at the pace of a lame ox, now hopping upon one leg and now crawling upon his knees. In this fashion it was that at length, about half-past eight in the morning, he reached the house, or rather the hut of Sihamba, for she had sent him out, and therefore to her, after the Kaffir fashion, he went to make report. Now, when he came to Sihamba, he greeted her and asked for a little food, which she gave him. Then he began to tell his story, beginning as natives do at the first of it, which in his case were all the wanderings of the cow which he had followed, so that although she hurried him much, many minutes went by before he came to that part of the tale which told of what he had heard in the wood some eight hours before.

So soon as he began to speak of this, Sihamba stopped him, and calling to a man who lingered near, she bade him bring to her Jan's famous young horse, the roan *schimmel*, bridled but not saddled. Now this horse was the finest in the whole district, for his sire was the famous stallion which the Government imported from England, where it won all the races, and his dam the swiftest and most enduring mare in the breeding herds at the Paarl. What Jan gave for him as a yearling I never learned, because he was afraid to tell me; but I know that we were short of money for two years after he bought him. Yet in the end that *schimmel* proved the cheapest thing for which ever a man paid gold.

Well, the Kaffir hesitated, for, as might be guessed, Jan was very proud of this horse, and none rode it save himself, but Sihamba sprang up and spoke to him so fiercely that at last he obeyed her, since, although she was small in stature, all feared the magic of Sihamba, and would do her bidding. Nor had he far to go, for the *schimmel* did not run wild upon the *veldt*, but was fed and kept in a stable, where a slave groomed him every morning. Thus it came about that before Zinti had finished his tale, the horse was standing before Sihamba bridled but not saddled, arching his neck and striking the ground with his hoof, for he was proud and full of corn and eager to be away.

"Oh! fool," said Sihamba to Zinti, "why did not you begin with this part of your story? Now, to save five from death and one from dishonour, there is but a short hour left and twenty long miles to cover in it. Ho! man, help me to mount this horse."

The slave put down his hand, and setting her foot in it, the little woman sprang on to the back of the great stallion, which knew and loved her as a dog might do, for she had tended it day and night when it was ill from the sickness we call "thick head," and without doubt had saved its life by her skill. Then, gripping its shoulders with her knees, Sihamba shook the reins and called aloud to the *schimmel*, waving the black rod she always carried in her hand, so that the fiery beast, having plunged once, leapt away like an antelope, and in another minute was nothing but a speck racing towards the mountains.

CHAPTER 13

The Schimmel's First Race

So hard did Sihamba ride, and so swift and untiring proved the horse, to whose strength her light weight was as nothing, that, the *veldt* over which they travelled being flat and free from stones or holes, she reached the mouth of Tiger's Nek, twenty miles away, in very few minutes over the hour of time. But the Nek itself was a mile or more in length, and for aught she knew we might already be taken in Black Piet's trap, and she but riding to share our fate. Still she did not stay, but though it panted like a blacksmith's bellows, and its feet stumbled with weariness among the stones of the Nek, she urged on the *schimmel* at a gallop. Now she turned the corner, and the off-saddling place was before her. Swiftly and fearfully Sihamba glanced around, but seeing no signs of us, she uttered a cry of joy and shook the reins, for she knew that she had not ridden in vain. Then a voice from the rocks called out:

"It is the witch-doctoress, Sihamba, who rides to warn them. Kill her swiftly." With the voice came a sound of guns and of bullets screaming past her, one of which shattered the wand she carried in her hand, numbing her arm. Nor was that all, for men sprang up across the further end of the off-saddling place, where the path was narrow, to bar her way, and they held spears in their hands. But Sihamba never heeded the men or the spears, for she rode straight at them and through them, and so soon was she gone that, although six or seven *assegais* were hurled at her, only one of them struck the horse, wounding it slightly in the shoulder.

A few minutes later, three perhaps, or five, just as the four of us with our Kaffir servants were riding quietly up to the mouth of the Nek, we saw a great horse thundering towards us, black with sweat and flecked with foam, its shoulder bloody, its eyes staring, its red nostrils agape, and perched upon its bare back a little woman who swayed from side to side as though with weariness, holding in her hand a shattered wand.

"*Allemachter!*" cried Jan. "It is Sihamba, and the witch rides my roan *schimmel!*"

By this time Sihamba herself was upon us. "Back," she screamed as she came, "death waits you in the pass;" whereon, compelled to it as it were by the weight of the words and the face of she who spoke them, we turned our horses' heads and galloped after the *schimmel* for the half of a mile or more till we were safe in the open *veldt*.

Then of a sudden the horse stopped, whether of its own accord or because its rider pulled upon the reins I know not. At the least it stood there trembling like a reed and Sihamba lay upon its back clinging to the mane, and as she lay I saw blood running down her legs, for her skin was chafed to the flesh beneath. Ralph sprang to her and lifted her to the ground and Suzanne made her take a draught of peach brandy from Jan's flask, which brought the life to her face again.

"Now," she said, "if you have it to spare, give the *schimmel* yonder a drink of that stuff, for he has saved all your lives and I think he needs it."

"That is a wise word," said Jan, and he bade Ralph and the Kaffirs pour the rest of the spirit down the horse's throat, which they did, thereby, as I believe, saving its life, for until it had swallowed it the beast looked as though its heart were about to burst.

"Now," said Jan, "why do you ride my best horse to death in this fashion?"

"Have I not told you, father of Swallow," she answered, "that it was to save you from death? But a few minutes over an hour ago, fifteen perhaps, a word was spoken to me at your stead yonder and now I am here, seven leagues away, having ridden faster than I wish to ride again, or than any other horse in this country can travel with a man upon its back."

"To save us from death! What death?" asked Jan astounded.

"Death at the hands of Swart Piet and his Kaffir tribesmen for the three of you and the two slaves, and for the fourth, the lady Swallow there, a love which she does not seek, the love of the murderer of her father, her mother, and her chosen."

Now we stared at each other; only Suzanne ran to Sihamba, and putting her arms about her, she kissed her.

"Nay," said the little woman smiling, "nay, Swallow, I do but repay to you one-hundredth part of my debt, and all the rest is owing still."

Then she told her story in few words, and when it was done, having first looked to see that Swart Piet and his men were not coming, at the bidding of Jan we all knelt down upon the *veldt* and thanked the Almighty for our deliverance. Only Sihamba did not kneel, for she was a heathen, and worshipped no one unless it were Suzanne.

"You should pray to the horse, too," she said, "for had it not been for his legs, I could never have reached you in time."

"Peace, Sihamba," I answered, "it is God who made the horse's legs, as God put it into your mind to use them;" but I said no more, though at any other time I should have rated her well for her heathen folly.

Then we consulted together as to what was to be done and decided to make our way to the house by a longer path which ran through the open *veldt*, since we were sure that there, where is no cover, Swart Piet would not attack us. Ralph, it is true, was for going into the Nek and attacking him, but, as Jan showed him, such an act would be madness, for they were many, and we were few; moreover, they could have picked us off from behind the shelter of the rocks. So we settled to leave him alone, and that night came home safely, though not without trouble, for we carried Sihamba the most of the way, and after he grew stiff the *schimmel* could only travel at a walking pace. Very soon that horse recovered, however, for he was a good feeder, and lived to do still greater service, although for a while his legs were somewhat puffed and had to be poulticed with cabbage leaves.

Now Jan and Ralph were mad against Swart Piet, and would have brought him to justice. But this road of justice was full of stones and mud-holes, since the nearest *landdrost*, as we call a magistrate, lived a hundred miles off, and it would not have been easy to persuade Piet to appear and argue the case before him. Moreover, here again we had no evidence against the man except that of a simple black fellow, who would never have been believed, for, in fact, no attack was made upon us, while that upon Sihamba might very well have been the work of some of the low Kaffirs that haunt the *kloofs*, runaway slaves, and other rascals who desired to steal the fine horse upon which she rode. Also we learned that our enemy, acting through some agent, had sold his farm to a stranger for a small sum of money, giving it out that he had no need of the land, as he was leaving this part of the country.

But if we saw Piet's face no more, we could still feel the weight of his hand, since from that time forward we began to suffer from thefts of cattle and other troubles with the natives, which—so Sihamba learned in her underground fashion—were instigated by him, working through his savage tools, while he himself lay hidden far away and in safety. Also he did us another ill turn—for it was proved that his money was at the bottom of it—by causing Ralph to be commandeered to serve on some distant Kaffir expedition, out of which trouble we were obliged to buy him, and at no small cost.

All these matters weighed upon us much, so much, indeed, that

I wished Jan to trek from the Transkei and found a new home; but he would not, for he loved the place which he had built up brick by brick, and planted tree by tree; nor would he consent to be driven out of it through fear of the wicked practices of Swart Piet. To one thing he did consent, however, and it was that Ralph and Suzanne should be married as soon as possible, for he saw that until they were man and wife there would be little peace for any of us. When they were spoken to on the matter, neither of them had anything to say against this plan; indeed, I believe that in their hearts, for the first and last time in their lives, they blessed the name of Black Piet, whose evil-doing, as they thought, was hurrying on their happiness.

Now it was settled that the matter of this marriage should be kept secret for fear it should come to the ears of Van Vooren through his spies, and stir him up to make a last attempt to steal away Suzanne. And, indeed, it did come to his ears, though how to this hour I do not know, unless, in spite of our warning, the *predicant* who was to perform the ceremony, a good and easy man but one who loved gossip, blabbed of it on his journey to the farm, for he had a two days' ride to reach it.

It was the wish of all of us that we should continue to live together after the marriage of Ralph and Suzanne, though not beneath the same roof. Indeed, there would have been no room for another married pair in that house, especially if children came to them, nor did I wish to share the rule of a dwelling with my own daughter after she had taken a husband, for such arrangements often end in bitterness and quarrels. Therefore Jan determined to build them a new house in a convenient spot not far away, and it was agreed that during the two or three months while this house was building Ralph and his wife should pay a visit to a cousin of mine, who owned a very fine farm on the outskirts of the *dorp* which we used to visit from time to time to partake of *Nachtmahl*[2]. This seemed wise to us for several reasons beyond that of the building of the new house. It is always best that young people should begin their married life alone, as by nature they wish to do, and not under the eyes of those who have bred and nurtured them, for thus face to face, with none to turn to, they grow more quickly accustomed to each other's faults and weaknesses, which, perhaps, they have not learned or taken count of before.

Moreover, in the case of Ralph and Suzanne we thought it safer that they should be absent for a while from their own district and the neighbourhood of Swart Piet, living in a peopled place where they

2. That is, Holy Communion.

could not be molested, although, not knowing the wickedness of his heart, we did not believe it possible that he *would* molest them when once they were married. Indeed, there was some talk of their going to the *dorp* for the wedding, and I wish that they had done so, for then much trouble might have been spared to us. But their minds were set against this plan, for they desired to be married where they had met and lived so long, so we did not gainsay them.

At length came the eve of the wedding day and with it the *predicant*, who arrived hungry and thirsty but running over with smiles and blessings. That night we all supped together and were full of joy, nor were Ralph and Suzanne the least joyous of us, though they said little, but sat gazing at each other across the table as though the moon had struck them.

Before I went to bed I had occasion to go out of the house for I remembered that some linen which Suzanne was to take with her had been left drying upon bushes after the wash, and I feared that if it remained there the Kaffir women might steal it. This linen was spread at a little distance from the house, near the huts where Sihamba lived, but I took no lantern with me, for the moon was bright.

As I drew near the spot I thought that I heard a sound of chanting which seemed to come from a little circle of mimosa trees that grew a spear's throw to my left, of chanting very low and sweet. Wondering who it was that sung thus, and why she sang—for the voice was that of a woman—I crept to the nearest of the trees, keeping in its shadow, and peeped through the branches into the grassy space beyond, to perceive Sihamba crouched in the centre of the circle. She was seated upon a low stone in such fashion that her head and face shone strangely in the moonlight, while her body was hidden in the shadow. Before her, placed upon another stone, stood a large wooden bowl, such as the Kaffirs cut out of the trunk of a tree, spending a month of labour, or more, upon the task, and into this bowl, which I could see was filled with water, for it reflected the moonrays, she was gazing earnestly, and, as she gazed, chanting that low, melancholy song whereof I could not understand the meaning.

Presently Sihamba ceased her singing, and turning from the bowl as though she had seen in it something that frightened her, she covered her eyes with her hands and groaned aloud, muttering words in which the name of Suzanne was mixed up, or of Swallow, as she called her. Now I guessed that Sihamba was practising that magic of which she was said to be so great a mistress, although she denied always that she knew anything of the art. At first I made up my mind to call to her to cease from such wickedness, which, as the Holy Book tells us, is a sin in the eyes of the Lord, and a cause of damnation to those who practise it. But I was curious and longed greatly in my heart to know what it was that Sihamba saw in the bowl, and what it had to do with my daughter Suzanne. So I changed my mind, thereby making myself a partaker of the sin, and coming forward said instead:

"What is it that you do here by night, in this solitary place, Sihamba?"

Now although, as I suppose, she had neither seen nor heard me, for I came up from behind her, Sihamba did not start or cry out as any other woman would have done; she did not even turn to look at me as she answered in a clear and steady voice:

"Now while she is still a girl I read the fate of Swallow and of those who love her according to my lore, O mother of Swallow. Look, I read it there."

I looked and saw that the large bowl was filled to the brim with pure water. At the bottom of it lay some white sand, and on the sand were placed five pieces of broken looking-glass, all of which had been filed carefully to a round shape. The largest of these pieces was of the size of a crown of English money. This lay in the exact centre of the bowl. Above it and almost touching its edge, was another piece the size of a half-crown, then to the right and left at a little distance, two more pieces of the size of a shilling, and below, but some way off, where the bowl began to curve, a very small piece not larger than a six-penny bit.

"Swallow," said Sihamba, pointing to the two largest of the fragments, "and husband of Swallow. There to the right and left father and mother of Swallow, and here at her feet, a long way off and very small, Sihamba, servant of Swallow, made all of them from the broken glass that shows back the face, which she gave me, and set, as they must be set, like the stars in the Cross of the Skies."

Now I shivered a little, for in myself I was afraid of this woman's magic, but to her I laughed and said roughly:

"What fool's plaything made of bits of broken glass is this that you have here, Sihamba?"

"It is a plaything that will tell a story to those who can read it," she answered without anger, but like one who knows she speaks the truth.

"Make it tell its story to me, and I will believe you," I said laughing again.

She shook her head and answered, "Lady, I cannot, for you have not the Sight; but bring your husband here, and perhaps he will be able to read the story, or some of it."

Now at this I grew angry, for it is not pleasant to a woman to hear that a man whom all know to be but a child compared to her can see things in water which she is not able to see, even though the things are born only of the false magic of a witch-doctoress. Still, as at that moment I chanced to hear Jan seeking me, for he wondered where I had gone, I called to him and set out the matter, expecting that he would be very angry and dismiss Sihamba, breaking up her magic bowl. But all the while that I talked to him the little woman sat, her chin resting upon her hand, looking into his face, and I think that she had some power over him. At the least, he was not at all angry, although he said that I must not mention the business to the *predicant*, who was well known to be a prejudiced man. Then he asked Sihamba to show him the wonders of the bowl. Replying that she would if she might, and always keeping her eyes fixed upon his face, she bade him kneel down and look into the water in such fashion that he did not shut the moonlight off from it, and to tell us what he saw.

So he knelt and looked, whispering presently that on the midmost piece of glass there appeared the image of Suzanne, and on the others respectively those of Ralph, Jan himself, me his wife, and Sihamba. I asked him what they were doing, but he could give me no clear answer, so I suppose that they were printed there like the heads on postage stamps, if indeed they existed anywhere except in Jan's brain, into which Sihamba had conjured them.

"What do you see more?" asked Sihamba.

"I see a shadow in the water," he answered, "a dark shadow, and— it is like the head of Swart Piet cut out of black paper—it spreads till it almost hides all the faces on the bits of glass. Almost, I say, but not quite, for things are passing beneath the shadow which I cannot distinguish. Now it shrinks quite small, and lies only over your likeness, Sihamba, which shows through it red—yes, and all the water round it is red, and now there is nothing left;" and Jan rose pale with fright, and wiped his brow with a coloured pocket-handkerchief, muttering "*Allemachter*! this is magic indeed."

"Let me look," I said, and I looked for a long while and saw nothing except the five bits of glass. So I told Jan outright that he was a fool whom any conjurer could play with, but he waited until I had done and then asked Sihamba what the vision meant.

"Father of Swallow," she answered, "what I saw in the water mirror you have seen, only I saw more than you did because my sight is keener. You ask me what it means, but I cannot tell you altogether, for such visions are uncertain; they sum up the future but they do not show it all. This, however, is sure, that trouble waits us every one because of Swart Piet, for his shadow lay thick upon the image of each of us; only note this, that while it cleared away from the rest, it remained upon mine, staining it blood-red, which means that while in the end you will escape him, I shall die at his hands, or through him. Well, so be it, but meanwhile this is my counsel—because of other things that I saw in the water which I cannot describe, for in truth I know not rightly what they were—that the marriage of the Swallow and her husband should be put off, and that when they are married it should be at the *dorp* yonder, not here."

Now when I heard this my anger overflowed like water in a boiling pot. "What!" I cried, "when all is settled and the *predicant* has ridden for two days to do the thing, is the marriage to be put off because forsooth this little black idiot declares that she sees things on bits of glass in a bowl, and because you, Jan, who ought to know better, take the lie from her lips and make it your own? I say that I am mistress here and that I will not allow it. If we are to be made fools of in this fashion by the peepings and mutterings of Kaffir witch-doctors we had better give up and die at once to go and live among the dead, whose business it is to peep and mutter. Our business is to dwell in the world and to face its troubles and dangers until such time as it pleases God to call us out of the world, paying no heed to omens and magic and such like sin and folly. Let that come which will come, and let us meet it like men and women, giving glory to the Almighty for the ill as well as for the good, since both ill and good come from His hands and are part of His plan. For my part I trust to Him who made us and who watches us, and I fear not Swart Piet, and therefore chance what may the marriage shall go on."

"Good words," said Jan, "such as my heart approves of;" but he still mopped his head with the coloured pocket-handkerchief and looked troubled as he added, "I pray you, wife, say nothing of this to anybody, and above all to the *predicant*, or he will put me out of the church as a wizard."

"Yes, yes," said Sihamba, "good words, but the Sight is still the Sight for those who have the power to see. Not that I wished you to see, indeed I did not wish it, nor did I think that you would be turned from your purpose by that which you have seen. Father and mother of Swallow, you are right, and now I will tell you the truth. What you beheld in the water was nothing but a trick, a clever trick of the little doctoress, Sihamba, by the help of which and others like it, she earns her living, and imposes on the foolish, though she cannot impose upon you, who are wise, and have the Lord of the skies for a friend. So think no more of it, and do not be angry with the little black monkey whose nature it is to play tricks;" and with a motion of her foot she upset the bowl of water, and collecting the pieces of mirror hid them away in her skin pouch.

Then we went, but as I passed through the thorn trees I turned and looked at Sihamba, and lo! she was standing in the moonlight, her face lifted towards the sky, weeping softly and wringing her hands. Then for the first time I felt a little afraid.

CHAPTER 14

The Wedding

The marriage morning of Ralph and Suzanne broke brightly; never have I seen a fairer. It was spring time, and the *veldt* was clothed with the fresh green grass and starred everywhere with the lily blooms that sprang among it. The wind blew softly, shaking down the dew-drops from the growing corn, while from every bush and tree came the cooing of unnumbered doves. Beneath the eave of the *stoep* the pair of red-breasted swallows which had built there for so many years were finishing their nest, and I watched them idly, for to me they were old friends, and would wheel about my head, touching my cheek with their wings. Just then they paused from their task, or perhaps it was at length completed, and flying to a bough of the peach tree a few yards away, perched there together amidst the bright bloom, and nestling against each other, twittered forth their song of joy and love.

It was at this moment that Sihamba walked up to the *stoep* as though to speak to me.

"The Swallow and the Swallow's mate," she said, following my eyes to where the little creatures swung together on the beautiful bough.

"Yes," I answered, for her fancy seemed to me of good omen, "they have built their nest, and now they are thanking God before they begin to live together and rear their young in love."

As the words left my lips a quick shadow swept across the path of sunlit ground before the house, two strong wings beat, and a brown hawk, small but very fierce, being of a sort that preys upon small birds, swooped downwards upon the swallows. One of them saw it, and slid from the bough, but the other the hawk caught in its talons, and mounted with it high into the air. In vain did its mate circle round it swiftly, uttering shrill notes of distress; up it went steadily as pitiless as death.

"Oh! my swallow," I cried aloud in grief, "the accursed hawk has carried away my swallow."

"Nay, look," said Sihamba, pointing upwards.

I looked, and behold! a black crow that appeared from behind the house, was wheeling about the hawk, striking at it with its beak until, that it might have its talons free to defend itself, it let go the swallow, which, followed by its mate, came fluttering to the earth, while the crow and the falcon passed away fighting, till they were lost in the blue depths of air.

Springing from the *stoep* I ran to where the swallow lay, but Sihamba was there before me and had it in her hands.

"The hawk's beak has wounded it," she said pointing to a blood stain among the red feathers of the breast, "but none of its bones are broken, and I think that it will live. Let us put it in the nest and leave it to its mate and nature."

This we did, and there in the nest it stayed for some days, its mate feeding it with flies as though it were still unfledged. After that they vanished, both of them together, seeking some new home, nor did they ever build again beneath our eaves.

"Would you speak with me, Sihamba?" I asked when this matter of the swallows was done with.

"I would speak with the Baas, or with you, it is the same thing," she answered, "and for this reason. I go upon a journey; for myself I have the good black horse which the Baas gave me after I had ridden to warn you in Tiger Kloof yonder, the one that I cured of sickness. But I need another beast to carry pots and food and my servant Zinti, who accompanies me. There is the brown mule which you use little because he is vicious, but he is very strong and Zinti does not fear him. Will you sell him to me for the two cows I earned from the Kaffir whose wife I saved when the snake bit her? He is worth three, but I have no more to offer."

"Whither do you wish to journey, Sihamba?" I asked.

"I follow my mistress to the *dorp*," she answered.

"Did she bid you follow her, Sihamba?"

"No! is it likely that she would think of me at such a time, or care whether I come or go? Fear not, I shall not trouble her, or put her to cost; I shall follow, but I shall not be seen until I am wanted."

Now I had made up my mind to gainsay Sihamba, not that I could find any fault with her plan, but because if such arrangements are to be made, I like to make them myself, as is the business of the head of the house. I think Sihamba guessed this; at any rate she answered me before I spoke, and that in an odd way, namely, by looking first at the swallow's nest, then at the blooming bough of the peach tree, and lastly into the far distances of air.

"It was the black crow that drove the hawk away," she said, reflectively, as though she were thinking of something else, "though I think, for my eyes are better than yours, that the hawk killed the crow, or perhaps they killed each other; at the least I saw them falling to the earth beyond the crest of the mountain."

At this I was about to break in angrily, for if there was one thing in the world I hated it was Sihamba's nonsense about birds and omens and such things, whereof, indeed, I had had enough on the previous night, when she made that lump Jan believe that he saw visions in a bowl of water. And yet I did not—for the black crow's sake. The cruel hawk had seized the swallow which I loved, and borne it away to devour it in its eyrie, and it was the crow that saved it. Well, the things that happened among birds might happen among men, who also prey upon each other, and—but I could not bear the thought.

"Take the mule, Sihamba," I said; "I will answer for it to the Baas. As for the two cows, they can run with the other cattle till your return."

"I thank you, Mother of Swallow," she answered, and turned to go, when I stopped her and asked:

"Have you heard anything that makes you afraid, Sihamba?"

"I have heard nothing," she replied, "still I am afraid."

"Then you are a fool for your pains, to be afraid of nothing," I answered roughly; "but watch well, Sihamba."

"Fear not, I will watch till my knees are loosened and my eyes grow hollow." Then she went away, and that was the last I saw of her for many a weary month. Ah! Suzanne, child, had it not been for the watching of little Sihamba, the walker-by-moonlight, you had not been sitting there today, looking much as she used to look, the Suzanne of fifty years ago.

****

The marriage was to take place at noon, and though I had much to see to, never have I known a longer morning. Why it was I cannot say, but it seemed to me as though twelve o'clock would never come. Then, wherever I went there was Ralph in my way, wandering about in a senseless fashion with his best clothes on, while after him wandered Jan holding his new hat in his hand.

"In the name of Heaven," I cried at length as I blundered into both of them in the kitchen, "be off out of this. Why are you here?"

"*Allemachter!*" said Jan, "because we have nowhere else to go. They are making the sitting-room ready for the service and the dinner after it; the *predicant* is in Ralph's room writing; Suzanne is in yours trying on her clothes, and the *stoep* and even the stables are full of Kaffirs. Where, then, shall we go?"

"Cannot you see to the wagon?" I asked.

"We have seen to it, mother," said Ralph; "it is packed, and the oxen are already tied to the yokes for fear lest they should stray."

"Then be off and sit in it and smoke till I come to call you," I replied, and away they walked shamefacedly enough, Ralph first, and Jan following him.

At twelve o'clock I went for them, and found them both seated on the wagon-chest smoking like chimneys, and saying nothing.

"Come, Ralph," I said, "it is quite time for you to be married," and he came, looking very pale, and walking unsteadily as though he had been drinking, while after him, as usual, marched Jan, still pulling at the pipe which he had forgotten to take out of his mouth.

Somehow I do not recollect much of the details of that wedding; they seem to have slipped my mind, or perhaps they are buried beneath the memories of all that followed hard upon it. I remember Suzanne standing before the little table, behind which was the *predicant* with his book. She wore a white dress that fitted her very well, but had no veil upon her head after the English fashion, which even Boer girls follow nowadays, only in her hand she carried a bunch of rare white flowers that Sihamba had gathered for her in a hidden *kloof* where they grew. Her face was somewhat pale, or looked so in the dim room, but her lips showed red like coral, and her dark eyes glowed and shone as she turned them upon the lover at her side, the fair-haired, grey-eyed, handsome English lad, whose noble blood told its tale in every feature and movement, yes, and even in his voice, the man whom she had saved from death to be her life-mate.

A few whispered words, the changing of a ring, and one long kiss, and these two, Ralph Kenzie and Suzanne Botmar, were husband and wife in the eyes of God and man. Ah! me, I am glad to think of it, for in the end, of all the many marriages that I have known, this proved the very best and happiest.

Now I thought that it was done with, for they had knelt down and the *predicant* had blessed them; but not so, for the good man must have his word, and a long word it was. On and on he preached about the duties of husbands and wives, and many other matters, till at last, as I expected, he came to the children. Now I could bear it no longer.

"That is enough, reverend Sir," I said, "for surely it is scarcely needful to talk of children to people who have not been married five minutes."

That pricked the bladder of his discourse, which soon came to an end, whereon I called to the Kaffirs to bring in dinner.

The food was good and plentiful, and so was the Hollands, or Squareface as they call it now, to say nothing of the Constantia and peach-brandy which had been sent to me many years before by a cousin who lived at Stellenbosch; and yet that meal was not as cheerful as it might have been. To begin with, the *predicant* was sulky because I had cut him short in his address, and a holy man in the sulks is a bad kind of animal to deal with. Then Jan tried to propose the health of the new married pair and could not do it. The words seemed to stick in his throat, for at the best Jan was never a speaker. In short, he made a fool of himself as usual, and I had to fill up the gaps in his head.

Well, I talked nicely enough till in an evil moment I overdid it a little by speaking of Ralph as one whom Heaven had sent to us, and of whose birth and parents we knew nothing. Then Jan found his tongue and said: "Wife, that's a lie, and you know it," for, doubtless, the Hollands and the peach-brandy had got the better of his reason and his manners. I did not answer him at the time, for I hate wrangling in public, but afterwards I spoke to him on the subject once and for all. Luckily, the *predicant* took no notice of this incident, for he was thinking about himself as he was too prone to do.

Then, to make matters worse, Suzanne must needs throw her arms round her father's neck and begin to cry—thanks be to my bringing up of her, she knew better than to throw them round mine. "Good Lord!" I said, losing my temper, "what is the girl at now? She has got the husband for whom she has been craving, and the first thing she does is to snivel. Well, if I had done that to my husband I should have expected him to box my ears, though Heaven knows that I should have had excuse for it."

Here the *predicant* woke up, seeing his chance.

"*Vrouw* Botmar," he said, blinking at me like an owl, "it is my duty to reprove your irreverent language even at this festive board, for a word must be spoken both in and out of season, and without respect of persons. *Vrouw* Botmar, I fear that you do not remember the Third Commandment, therefore I will repeat it to you," and he did so, speaking very slowly.

What I answered I cannot recollect, but even now I seem to see that *predicant* flying out of the door of the room holding his hands above his head. Well, for once he met his match, and I know that afterwards he always spoke of me with great respect.

After this again I remember little more till the pair started upon their journey. Suzanne asked for Sihamba to say good-bye to her, and when she was told that she was not to be found she seemed vexed, which shows that the little doctoress did her injustice in supposing that just because she was married she thought no more of her. Then she kissed us all in farewell—ah! we little knew for how long that farewell was to be—and went down to the wagon to which the sixteen black oxen, a beautiful team, were inspanned, and standing there ready to start. But Ralph and Suzanne were not going to ride in the wagon, for they had horses to carry them. At the last moment, indeed, Jan, whose head was still buzzing with the peach-brandy, insisted upon giving Ralph the great *schimmel*, that same stallion which Sihamba had ridden when she warned us of the ambush in the pass, galloping twenty miles in the hour. This shows me that Providence can turn even a man's vices to account, for afterwards the *schimmel* was very useful.

So there was much kissing and many good-byes; Ralph and Suzanne saying that they would soon be back, which indeed was the case with one of them, till at last they were off, Jan riding with them a little way towards their first outspan by the sea, fourteen miles distant, where they were to sleep that night.

When they had gone I went into my bedroom, and sitting down, I cried, for I was sorry to lose Suzanne, even for a little and for her own good, and my heart was heavy. Also my quarrel with the *predicant* had put me out of temper. When I had got over this fit I set to work to tidy Suzanne's little sleeping place, and that I found a sad task. Then Jan returned from the wagon, having bid farewell to the young couple, an hour's trek away, and his head being clear by now, we talked over the plans of the new house which was to be built for them to live in, and, going down to the site of it, set it out with sticks and a rule, which gave us occupation till towards sunset, when it was time for him to go to see to the cattle.

That night we went to bed early, for we were tired, and slept a heavy sleep, till at length, about one in the morning, we were awakened by the shoutings of the messengers who came bearing the terrible news.

CHAPTER 15

Ralph Returns Into the Sea

Ralph and Suzanne reached their outspan place in safety a little before sunset. I used to know the spot well; it is where one of the numerous wooden *kloofs* that scar the mountain slopes ends on a grassy plain of turf, short but very sweet. This plain is not much more than five hundred paces wide, for it is bordered by the cliff, that just here is not very high, against which the sea beats at full tide.

When the oxen had been turned loose to graze, and the *voorlooper* set to watch them, the driver of the wagon undid the cooking vessels and built a fire with dry wood collected from the *kloof*. Then Suzanne cooked their simple evening meal, of which they partook thankfully. After it was done the pair left the wagon and followed the banks of the little *kloof* stream, which wandered across the plain till it reached the cliff, whence it fell in a trickling waterfall into the sea. Here they sat down upon the edge of the cliff, and locked in each other's arms, watched the moon rise over the silver ocean, their young hearts filled with a joy that cannot be told.

"The sea is beautiful, is it not, husband?" whispered Suzanne into his ear.

"To-night it is beautiful," he answered, "as our lives seem to be; yet I have seen it otherwise," and he shuddered a little.

She nodded, for she knew of what he was thinking, and did not wish to speak of it. "Neither life nor ocean can be always calm," she said, "but oh! I love that great water, for it brought you to me."

"I pray that it may never separate us," answered Ralph.

"Why do you say that, husband?" she asked. "Nothing can separate us now, for even if you journey far away to seek your own people, as sometimes I think you should, I shall accompany you. Nothing can separate us except death, and death shall bind us more closely each to each for ever and for ever."

"I do not know why I said it, Sweet," he answered uneasily, and just then a little cloud floated over the face of the moon, darkening the world, and a cold wind blew down the *kloof*, causing its trees to rustle and chilling the pair, so that they clung closer to each other for comfort.

The cloud and the wind passed away, leaving the night as beautiful as before, and they sat on for a while to watch it, listening to the music of the waterfall that splashed into the deep sea pool below, and to the soft surge of the waves as they lapped gently against the narrow beach.

At length Ralph spoke in a low voice. "Sweet, it is time to sleep," he said, and kissed her.

"It is time," she whispered back, "but, husband, first let us kneel together here and pray to the Almighty to bless our married life and make us happy."

"That is a good thought," he answered, for in those days young men who had been brought up as Christians were not ashamed to say their prayers even in the presence of others.

So they knelt down side by side upon the edge of the cliff, with their faces set towards the open sea.

"Pray for us both aloud, Ralph," said Suzanne, "for though my heart is full enough I have no words."

So Ralph prayed very simply, saying: "Oh, God, Who madest us, hear us, Thy son and daughter, and bless us. This night our married life begins; be Thou with us ever in it, and if it should please Thee that we should have children, let Thy blessing go with them all their days. Oh! God, I thank Thee that Thou didst save me alive from the sea and lead the feet of the child who is now my wife to the place where I was starving, and Suzanne thanks Thee that through the whisperings of a dream her feet were led thus. Oh! God, as I believe that Thou didst hear my prayer when as a lost child I knelt dying on the rock, so I believe that Thou dost hear this the first prayer of our wedded life. We know that all life is not made up of such joy as Thou hast given us this day, but that it has many dangers and troubles and losses, therefore we pray Thee to comfort us in the troubles, to protect us in the dangers, and to give us consolation in the losses; and most of all we pray Thee that we who love each other, and whom Thou hast joined together, may be allowed to live out our lives together, fearing nothing, however great our peril, since day and night we walk in the shadow of Thy strength, until we pass into its presence."

This was Ralph's prayer, for he told it to me word by word afterwards when he lay sick. At the time the answer to it seemed to be a strange one, an answer to shake the faith out of a man's heart, and yet it was not lost or mocked at, for the true response came in its season. Nay, it came week by week and hour by hour, seeing that every day through those awful years the sword of the Strength they had implored protected those who prayed, holding them harmless in many a desperate peril to reunite them at the last. The devil is very strong in this world of ours, or so it seems to me, who have known much of his ways, so strong that perhaps God must give place to him at times, for if He rules in heaven, I think that Satan shares His rule on earth. But in the end it is God who wins, and never, never, need they fear who acknowledge Him and put their faith in Him, trying the while to live uprightly and conquer the evil of their hearts. Well, this is only an old woman's wisdom, though it should not be laughed at, since it has been taught to her by the experience of a long and eventful life. Such as it is I hope that it may be of service to those who trust in themselves and not in their Maker.

****

As the last words of his prayer left Ralph's lips he heard a man laugh behind him. The two of them sprang to their feet at the sound, and faced about to see Swart Piet standing within five paces of them, and with him eight or ten of his black ruffians, who looked upon him as their chief, and did his needs without question, however wicked they might be.

Now Suzanne uttered a low cry of fear and the blood froze about Ralph's heart, for he was unarmed and their case was hopeless. Black Piet saw their fear and laughed again, since like a cat that has caught a mouse for which it has watched long, he could not resist the joy of torture before he dealt the death blow.

"This is very lucky," he said, "and I am glad that I have to do with such pious people, since it enabled us to creep on you unawares; also I much prefer to have found you engaged in prayer, friend Englishman, rather than in taking the bloom off my peach with kisses, as I feared might be the case. That was a pretty prayer, too; I almost felt as though I were in church while I stood listening to it. How did it end? You prayed that you might be allowed to live together, fearing nothing, however great your peril, since you walked always in the shadow of God's strength. Well, I have come to answer your petition, and to tell you that your life together is ended before it is begun. For the rest, your peril is certainly great, and now let God's strength help you if it can. Come, God, show Your strength. He does not answer, you see, or perhaps He knows that Swart Piet is god here and is afraid."

105

"Cease your blasphemy," said Ralph in a hoarse voice, "and tell me what you want with us."

"What do I want? I want her whose scorn and beauty have driven me mad, her for whom I have been seeking this long time—Suzanne Botmar."

"She is my wife," said Ralph; "would you steal away my wife?"

"No, friend, for that would not be lawful. I will not take your wife, but I shall take your widow, as will be easy, seeing that you are armed with God's strength only."

Now understanding all this man's devilish purpose, Suzanne fell upon her knees before him, imploring him with many piteous words. But knowing that death was at hand Ralph's heart rose to it, as that of a high-couraged man will do, and he bade her to cease her supplications and rise. Then in a loud, clear voice he spoke in the Kaffir tongue, so that those who were with Piet Van Vooren should understand him.

"It seems, Piet Van Vooren," he said, "that you have stolen upon us here to carry off my wife by violence after you have murdered me. These crimes you may do, though I know well that if you do them they will be revenged upon you amply, and upon you men also who take part in them. And now I will not plead to you for mercy, but I ask one thing which you cannot refuse, because those with you, Kaffirs though they be, will not suffer it—five short minutes of time in which to bid farewell to my new-wed wife."

"Not an instant," said Swart Piet, but at the words the black men who were with him, and whose wicked hearts were touched with pity, began to murmur so loudly, that he hesitated.

"At your bidding, Bull-Head," said one of them, "we have come to kill this man and to carry away the white woman, and we will do it, for you are our chief and we must obey you. But, if you will not give him the little space for which he asks, wherein to bid farewell to his wife before she becomes your wife, then we will have nothing more to do with the matter. I say that our hearts are sick at it already, and, Bull-Head, you kill a man, not a dog, and that by murder, not in fair fight."

"As you will, fool," said Swart Piet. "Englishman, I give you five minutes," and he drew a large silver watch from his pocket and held it in his hand.

"Get out of hearing then, murderer," said Ralph, "for I have no breath left to waste on you," and Piet obeying him, fell back a little and stood gnawing his nails and staring at the pair.

"Suzanne, wife Suzanne," whispered Ralph, "we are about to part,

106

since, as you see, I must die, and your fate lies in the Hand of God. Yes, you are made a widow before you are a wife; and, Suzanne, ah! that is the worst of it, another takes you, even my murderer."

Now Suzanne, who till this moment had been as one stupefied, seemed to gather up her strength and answered him calmly, saying:

"Truly, husband, things appear to be as you say, though what we have done that they should be so, I cannot tell. Still comfort yourself, for death comes to all of us soon or late, and whether it comes soon or late makes little difference in the end, seeing that come it must."

"No, not death, it is your fate that makes the difference. How can I bear to die and leave you the prey of that devil? Oh my God! my God! how can I bear to die!"

"Have no fear, husband," went on Suzanne in the same clear, indifferent voice, "for you do not leave me to be his prey. Say, now; if we walk backwards swiftly before they could catch us we might fall together into the pit of the sea beneath."

"Nay, wife, let our deaths lie upon their heads and not upon ours, for self-murder is a crime."

"As you will, Ralph; but I tell you, and through you I tell Him who made me, that it is a crime which I shall dare if need be. Have no fear, Ralph, as I leave your arms, so shall I return to them, whether it be in Heaven or upon earth. That man thinks he has power over me, but I say that he has none, seeing that at the last God will protect me with His hand, or with my own."

"I cannot blame you, Suzanne, for there are some things which are not to be borne. Do therefore as your conscience teaches you, if you have the means."

"I have the means, Ralph. Hidden about me is a little knife which I have carried since I was a child; and if that fails me there are other ways."

"Time is done," said Swart Piet, replacing the watch in his pocket.

"Farewell, sweet," whispered Ralph.

"Farewell, husband," she answered bravely, "until we meet again, whether it be here on earth or above in Heaven; farewell until we meet again," and she flung her arms about his neck and kissed him.

For a moment Ralph clung to her muttering some blessing above her bowed head; then he unloosed her clasping arms, letting her fall gently upon the ground and saying: "Lie thus, shutting your ears and hiding your eyes till all is done. Afterwards you must act as seems best to you. Escape to your father if you can, if not—tell me, do you understand?"

"I understand," she murmured, and hid her face in a tuft of thick grass, placing her hands upon her ears.

Ralph bowed his head for an instant in prayer. Then he lifted it and there was no fear upon his face.

"Come on, murderer," he said, addressing Swart Piet, "and do your butcher's work. Why do you delay? You cannot often find the joy of slaughtering a defenceless man in the presence of his new-made wife. Come on then and win the everlasting curse of God."

Now Swart Piet glanced at him out of the corners of his round eyes; then he ordered one of the Kaffirs to go up to him and shoot him.

The man went up and lifted his gun, but presently he put it down again and walked away, saying that he could not do this deed. Thrice did Van Vooren issue his command, and to three separate men, the vilest of his flock, but with each of them it was the same; they came up lifting their guns, looked into Ralph's grey eyes and slunk away muttering. Then, cursing and swearing in his mad fury, Swart Piet drew the pistol from his belt and rushing towards Ralph fired it into him so that he fell. He stood over him and looked at him, the smoking pistol in his hand, but the wide grey eyes remained open and the strong mouth still smiled.

"The dog lives yet," raved Swart Piet; "cast him into the sea, and let the sea finish him."

But no man stirred; all stood silent as though they had been cut in stone, and there, a little nearer the cliff edge, lay the silent form of Suzanne.

Then Van Vooren seized Ralph and dragged him by the shoulders to the brink of the precipice. His hair brushed the hair of Suzanne as his body was trailed along the ground, and as he passed he whispered one word, "Remember," into her ear, and she raised her head to look at him and answered, "Now, and always." Then she let her head fall again.

Stooping down, Swart Piet lifted Ralph in his great arms, and crying aloud: "Return into the sea out of which you came," he hurled him over the edge of the cliff. Two seconds later the sound of a heavy splash echoed up its sides; then, save for the murmur of the waterfall and the surge of the surf upon the beach, all was still again.

CHAPTER 16

How Ralph Came Back to the Stead

For a few moments Swart Piet and his black ruffians stood staring now at each other and now over the edge of the cliff into the deep sea-hole. There, however, they could see nothing, for the moonbeams did not reach its surface, and the only sound they heard was that of the dripping of the little waterfall, which came to their ears like the tinkle of distant sheep-bells. Then Swart Piet shivered and laughed aloud, a laugh that had more of fear than of merriment in it.

"The Englishman called down the everlasting curse of God on me," he cried. "Well, I have waited for it, and it does not come, so now for man's reward," and going to where Suzanne lay, he set his arms beneath her and turned her over upon her back. "She has swooned," he said; "perhaps it is as well," and he stood looking at her, for thus in her faint she seemed wonderfully fair with the moonbeams playing upon her deathlike face.

"He had good taste, that Englishman," went on Swart Piet. "Well, now our account is squared; he has sown and I shall harvest. Follow me, you black fellows, for we had best be off," and, stooping down he lifted Suzanne in his arms and walked away with her as though she were a child. For a while they followed the windings of the stream, keeping under cover of the reeds and bushes that grew upon its banks. Then they struck out to the right, taking advantage of a cloud which dimmed the face of the moon for a time, for they wished to reach the *kloof* without being seen from the wagon. Nor, indeed, were they seen, for the driver and *voorlooper* were seated by the cooking-fire on its further side, smoking, and dozing as they smoked. Only the great thoroughbred horse winded them and snorted, pulling at the *riem* with which he was tied to the hind wheel of the wagon.

"Something has frightened the *schimmel*," said the driver waking up.

"It is nothing," answered the other boy drowsily; "he is not used to the *veldt*, he who always sleeps in a house like a man; or, perhaps, he smells a hyena in the *kloof*."

"I thought I heard a sound like that of a gun a while ago down yonder by the sea," said the driver again. "Say, brother, shall we go and find out what made it?"

"By no means," answered the *voorlooper*, who did not like walking about at night, fearing lest he should meet spooks. "I have been wide awake and listening all this time, and I heard no gun; nor, indeed, do people go out shooting at night. Also it is our business to watch here by the wagon till our master and mistress return."

"Where can they have gone?" said the driver, who felt frightened, he knew not why. "It is strange that they should be so long away when it is time for them to sleep."

"Who can account for the ways of white people?" answered the other, shrugging his shoulders. "Very often they sit up all night. Doubtless these two will return when they are tired, or perhaps they desire to sleep in the *veldt*. At any rate it is not our duty to interfere with them, seeing that they can come to no harm here where there are neither men nor tigers."

"So be it," said the driver, and they both dozed off again till the messenger of ill came to rouse them.

****

Now Black Piet and his men crept up the *kloof* carrying Suzanne with them, till they came to a little patch of rocky ground at the head of it where they had left their horses.

"That was very well managed," said Piet as they loosed them and tightened their girths, "and none can ever know that we have made this journey. Tomorrow the bride and bridegroom will be missed, but the sea has one and I have the other, and hunt as they may they will never find her, nor guess where she has gone. No, it will be remembered that they walked down to the sea, and folk will think that by chance they fell from the cliff into the deep water and vanished there. Yes, it was well managed and none can guess the truth."

Now the man to whom he spoke, that same man with whom the boy Zinti had heard him plot our murder in the Tiger Kloof, shrugged his shoulders and answered: "I think there is one who will guess."

"Who is that, fool?"

"She about whose neck I once set a rope at your bidding, Bull-Head, and whose life was bought by those lips," and he pointed to Suzanne, "Sihamba Ngenyanga."

"Why should she guess?" asked Piet angrily.

"Has she not done so before? Think of the great *schimmel* and its rider in Tiger Kloof. Moreover, what does her name mean? Does it not mean 'Wanderer-by-moonlight,' and was not this great deed of yours a deed at the telling of which all who hear of it shall grow sick and silent, done in the moonlight, Bull-Head?"

Now as we learned afterwards from a man whom Jan took prisoner, and who told us everything which passed that night, hoping to buy his life, Piet made no answer to this saying, but turned to busy himself with his saddle, for, after his ill dealings with her, he was always afraid of Sihamba, and would never mention her name unless he was obliged. Soon the horses, most of which were small and of the Basuto breed, were ready to start. On one of the best of them there was a soft pad of sheepskins, such as girls used to ride on when I was young, before we knew anything about these new-fangled English saddles with leather hooks to hold the rider in her place. On this pad, which had been prepared for her, they set Suzanne, having first tied her feet together loosely with a *riem* so that she might not slip to the ground and attempt to escape by running. Moreover, as she was still in a swoon, they supported her, Black Piet walking upon one side and a Kaffir upon the other. In this fashion they travelled for the half of an hour or more, until they were deep in among the mountains, indeed, when suddenly with a little sigh Suzanne awoke, and glanced about her with wide, frightened eyes. Then memory came back to her, and she understood, and, opening her lips, she uttered one shriek so piercing and dreadful that the rocks of the hills multiplied and echoed it, and the blood went cold even in the hearts of those savage men.

"Suzanne," said Swart Piet in a low, hoarse voice, "I have dared much to win you, and I wish to treat you kindly, but if you cry out again, for my own safety's sake and that of those with me, we must gag you."

She made no answer to him, nor did she speak at all except one word, and that word "*Murderer.*" Then she closed her eyes as though to shut out the sight of his face, and sat silent, saying nothing and doing nothing, even when Piet and the other man who supported her had mounted and pushed their horses to a gallop, leading that on which she rode by a *riem*.

****

It might be thought after receiving a pistol bullet fired into him at a distance of four paces, and being cast down through fifty feet of space into a pool of the sea, that there was an end of Ralph Kenzie for ever on this earth. But thanks to the mercy of God this was not so, for the ball had but shattered his left shoulder, touching no vital part, and the water into which he fell was deep, so that, striking against no rock, he rose presently to the surface, and the pool being but narrow, was able to swim to one side of it where the beach shelved. Up that beach Ralph could not climb, however, for he was faint with loss of blood and shock. Indeed, his senses left him while he was in the water, but it chanced that he fell forward and not backward, so that his head rested upon the shelving edge of the pool, all the rest of his body being beneath its surface. Lying thus, had the tide been rising, he would speedily have drowned, but it had turned, and so, the water being warm, he took no further harm.

Now Sihamba did not leave the stead till some hours after Ralph and his bride had trekked away. She knew where they would outspan, and as she did not wish that they should see her yet, or until they were too far upon their journey to send her back, it was her plan to reach the spot, or rather a hiding-place in the *kloof* within a stone's throw of it, after they had gone to rest. So it came about that at the time when Ralph and Suzanne were surprised by Swart Piet, Sihamba was riding along quietly upon the horse which Jan had given her, accompanied by the lad Zinti, perched on the strong brown mule in the midst of cooking pots, bags of meal, biltong, and rolls of blankets. Already, half a mile off or more, she could see the cap of the wagon gleaming white in the moonlight, when suddenly away to the left they heard the sound of a pistol shot.

"Now who shoots in this lonely place at night?" said Sihamba to Zinti. "Had the sound come from the wagon yonder I should think that someone had fired to scare a hungry jackal, but all is quiet at the wagon, and the servants of Swallow are there, for, look, the fire burns."

"I know not, lady," answered Zinti, for Sihamba was given the title of Chieftainess among the natives who knew something of her birth, "but I am sure that the sound was made by powder."

"Let us go and see," said Sihamba turning her horse.

For a while they rode on towards the place whence they had heard the shot, till, suddenly, when they were near the cliff and in a little fold of ground beyond the ridge of which ran the stream, Sihamba stopped and whispered, "Be silent, I hear voices." Then she slipped from her horse and crept like a snake up the slope of the rise until she reached its crest, where at this spot stood two tufts of last season's grass, for no fires had swept the *veldt*. From between these tufts, so well hidden herself that unless they had stepped upon her body, none could have discovered her, she saw a strange sight.

There beneath her, within a few paces indeed, for the ground sloped steeply to the stream, men were passing. The first of these was white, and he carried a white woman in his arms; the rest were Kaffirs, some of whom wore *karosses* or cotton blankets, and some tattered soldiers' coats and trousers, while all were well armed with "*roers*" or other guns, and had powder flasks hung about their necks. Sihamba knew at once that the white man was Swart Piet, and the woman in his arms her mistress, Suzanne. She could have told it from her shape alone, but as it happened, her head hung down, and the moonlight shone upon her face so brightly that she could see its every feature. Her blood boiled in her as she looked, for now she understood that her fears were just, and that the Swallow whom she loved above everything in the world, had fallen into the power of the man she hated. At first she was minded to follow, and if might be, to rescue her. Then she remembered the pistol-shot, and remembered also that this new-made wife would have been with her husband and no other. Where, then, was he now? Without doubt, murdered by Bull-Head. If so, it was little use to look for him, and yet something in her heart told her to look.

At that moment she might not help Suzanne, for what could one woman and a Kaffir youth do against so many men? Moreover, she knew whither Van Vooren would take her, and could follow there, but first she must learn for certain what had been the fate of the Baas Ralph her husband. So Sihamba lay still beneath the two tufts of grass until the last of the men had passed in silence, glancing about them sullenly as though they feared vengeance for a crime. Then, having noted that they were heading for the *kloof*, she went back to where Zinti stood in the hollow holding the horse with one hand and the mule with the other, and beckoned him to follow her.

Very soon, tracing the spoor backwards, they reached the edge of the cliff just where the waterfall fell over it into the sea pool. Here she searched about, noting this thing and that, till at last all grew clear to her. Yonder Suzanne had lain, for the impress of her shape could still be seen upon the grass. And there a man had been stretched out, for his blood stained the ground. More, he had been dragged to the edge of the cliff, for this was the track of his body and the spoor of his murderer's feet. Look how his heels had sunk into the turf as he took the weight of the corpse in his arms to hurl it over the edge.

"Tie the horse and the mule together, Zinti," she said, "and let us find a path down this precipice."

The lad obeyed, wondering, though he too guessed much of what had happened, and after a little search they found a place by which they could descend. Now Sihamba ran to the pool and stood upon its brink scanning the surface with her eyes, till at length she glanced downwards, and there, almost at her feet, three parts of his body yet hidden in the water, lay the man she sought.

Swiftly she sprang to him, and, aided by Zinti, dragged him to dry ground.

"Alas! lady," moaned the Kaffir, "it is of no use, the Baas is dead. Look, he has been shot."

Taking no heed of the words, Sihamba opened Ralph's garments, placing first her hand, then her ear, upon his heart. Presently she lifted her head, a light of hope shining in her eyes, and said:

"Nay, he lives, and we have found him in time. Moreover, his wound is not to death. Now help me, for between us we must bear him up the cliff."

So Zinti took him on his back as a man takes a sack of flour, while Sihamba supported his legs, and thus between them, with great toil, for the way was very steep, they carried him by a sloping buck's path to the top of the precipice, and laid him upon the mule.

"Which way now?" gasped Zinti, for being strong he had borne the weight.

"To the wagon if they have not yet stolen it," said Sihamba, and thither they went.

When they were near she crept forward, searching for Swart Piet and his gang, but there were no signs of them, only she saw the driver and his companion nodding by the fire. She walked up to them.

"Do you then sleep, servants of Kenzie," she said, "while the Swallow is borne away to the Hawk's Nest and the husband of Swallow, your master, is cast by Bull-Head back into the sea whence he came?"

Now the men woke up and knew her. "Look, it is Sihamba," stammered one of them to the other, for he was frightened. "What evil thing has happened, Lady Sihamba?"

"I have told you, but your ears are shut. Come then and see with your eyes," and she led them to where Ralph lay in his blood, the water yet dripping from his hair and clothes.

"Alas! he is dead," they groaned and wrung their hands.

"He is not dead, he will live; for while you slept I found him," she answered. "Swift now, bring me the wagon box that is full of clothes, and the blankets off the cartel."

They obeyed her, and very quickly and gently—for of all doctors Sihamba was the best—with their help she drew off his wet garments, and, having dried him and dressed his wounds with strips of linen, she put a flannel shirt upon him and wrapped him in blankets. Then she poured brandy into his mouth, but, although the spirit brought a little colour into his pale face, it did not awaken him, for his swoon was deep.

"Lay him on the cartel in the wagon," she said, and, lifting him, they placed him upon the *rimpi* bed. Then she ordered them to inspan the wagon, and this was done quickly, for the oxen lay tied to the trek-tow. When all was ready she spoke to the two men, telling them what had happened so far as she knew it, and adding these words:

"Trek back to the stead as swiftly as you may, one of you sitting in the wagon to watch the Baas Kenzie and to comfort him should he wake out of his swoon. Say to the father and mother of Swallow that I have taken the horses to follow Swart Piet and to rescue her by cunning if so I can, for as will be plain to them, this is a business that must not wait; also that I have taken with me Zinti, since he alone knows the path to Bull-Head's secret hiding-place in the mountains. Of that road Zinti will tell you all he can and you will tell it to the Baas Botmar, who must gather together such men as he is able, and start tomorrow to follow it and rescue us, remembering what sort of peril it is in which his daughter stands. If by any means I can free the Swallow, we will come to meet him; if not, who knows? Then he must act according to his judgment and to what he learns. But let him be sure of this, and let her husband be sure also, that while I have life in me I will not cease from my efforts to save her, and that if she dies—for I know her spirit and no worse harm than death will overtake her—then if may be, I will die with her or to avenge her, and I have many ways of vengeance. Lastly, let them not believe that we are dead until they have certain knowledge of it, for it may chance that we cannot return to the stead, but must lie hid in the mountains or among the Kaffirs. Now hear what Zinti has to say as to the path of Bull-Head's den and begone, forgetting no one of my words, for if you linger or forget, when I come again I, Sihamba, will blind your eyes and shrivel your livers with a spell."

"We hear you," they answered, "and remember every word of your message. In three hours the Baas shall know it."

Five minutes later they trekked away and so swiftly did they drive and so good were the oxen, that in less than the three hours we were awakened by the barking of the dogs and one knocking on our door, and ran out to learn all the dreadful tidings and to find Ralph bleeding and still senseless, stretched upon that cartel where we thought him sleeping happily with his bride.

Oh! the terror and the agony of that hour, never may I forget them! Never may I forget the look that sprang into Ralph's eyes when at last he awoke and, turning them to seek Suzanne, remembered all.

"Why am I here and not dead?" he asked hoarsely.

"Sihamba saved you and you have been brought back in the wagon," I answered.

"Where then is Suzanne?" he asked again.

"Sihamba has ridden to save her also, and Jan starts presently to follow her, and with him others."

"Sihamba!" he groaned. "What can one woman do against Piet Van Vooren and his murderers, and for the rest they will be too late. Oh! my God, my God, what have we done that such a thing should fall upon us? Think of it, think of her in the hands of Piet Van Vooren. Oh! my God, my God, I shall go mad!"

Indeed I, who watched him, believe that this would have been so, or else his brain must have burst beneath its shock of sorrow, had not nature been kind to him and plunged him back into stupor. In this he lay long, until well on into the morrow indeed, or rather the day, for by now it was three o'clock, when the doctor came to take out the pistol ball and set his shattered bone. For, as it chanced, a doctor, and a clever one, had been sent for from the *dorp* to visit the wife of a neighbour who lay sick not more than twenty miles away, and we were able to summon him. Indeed but for this man's skill, the sleeping medicines he gave him to quiet his mind, and, above all, a certain special mercy which shall be told of in its place, I think that Ralph would have died. As it was, seven long weeks went by before he could sit upon a horse.

CHAPTER 17

The Hidden Krantz

Before the wagon left her, Sihamba took from it Ralph's gun, a very good *roer*, together with powder and bullets. Also she took tinder, a bottle of peach-brandy, a blanket, *mealies* in a small bag, wherewith to bait the horses in case of need, and some other things which she thought might be necessary. These she laded among her own goods upon the mule that with her horse had been fetched by Zinti and hastily fed with corn. Now, at her bidding, Zinti set Suzanne's saddle upon the back of the *schimmel*, and Ralph's on that of Suzanne's grey mare, which he mounted that the mule might travel lighter. Then Sihamba got upon her own horse, a good and quiet beast which she rode with a sheepskin for a saddle, and they started, Sihamba leading the *schimmel* and Zinti the mule that, as it chanced, although bad tempered, would follow well on a *riem*.

Riding up the *kloof* they soon reached the spot where Van Vooren's band had tethered their horses and tracked the spoor of them with ease for so long as the ground was soft. Afterwards when they reached the open country, where the grass had been burnt off and had only just begun to spring again, this became more difficult, and at length, in that light, impossible. Here they wasted a long time, searching for the hoof-marks by the rays of the waning moon, only to lose them again so soon as they were found.

"At this pace we shall take as long to reach Bull-Head's *kraal* as did the cow you followed," said Sihamba presently. "Say, now, can you find the way to it?"

"Without a doubt, lady; Zinti never forgets a road or a landmark."

"Then lead me there as fast as may be."

"Yes, lady, but Bull-Head may have taken the Swallow somewhere else, and if we do not follow his spoor how shall we know where he has hidden her?"

"Fool, I have thought of that," she answered angrily, "else should I have spent all this time looking for hoof-marks in the dark? We must risk it, I say. To his house he has not taken her, for other white folk are living in it, and it is not likely he would have a second, or a better hiding-place than that you saw. I say that we must be bold and risk it since we have no time to lose."

"As you will, mistress," answered Zinti. "Who am I that I should question your wisdom?" and, turning his horse's head, he rode forward across the gloomy *veldt* as certainly as a homing rock-dove wings its flight.

So they travelled till the sun rose behind a range of distant hills. Then Zinti halted and pointed to them.

"Look, lady," he said. "Do you see that peak among the mountains which has a point like a spear, the one that seems as though it were on fire? Well, behind it lies Bull-Head's *kraal*."

"It is far, Zinti, but we must be there by night."

"That may be done, lady, but if so we must spare our horses."

"Good," she answered. "Here is a spring; let us off-saddle a while."

So they off-saddled and ate of the food which they had brought, while the horses filled themselves with the sweet green grass, the *schimmel* being tied to the grey mare, for he would not bear a knee-halter.

All that day they rode, not so very fast but steadily, till towards sunset they off-saddled again beneath the shadow of the spear-pointed peak. There was no water at this spot, but seeing a green place upon the slope of a hill close by, Zinti walked to it, leading the thirsty beasts. Presently he threw up his hand and whistled, whereon Sihamba set out to join him, knowing that he had found a spring. So it proved to be, and now they learned that Sihamba had been wise in heading straight for Swart Piet's hiding-place, since round about this spring was the spoor of many horses and of men. Among these was the print of a foot that she knew well, the little foot of Suzanne.

"How long is it since they left here?" asked Sihamba, not as one who does not know, but rather as though she desired to be certified in her judgment.

"When the sun stood there," answered Zinti, pointing to a certain height in the heavens.

"Yes," she answered, "three hours. Bull-Head has travelled quicker than I thought."

"No," said Zinti, "but I think that he knew a path through the big *vlei*, whereas we rode round it, two hours' ride, fearing lest we should be bogged. Here by this spring they stayed till sunset, for it was needful that the horses should feed and rest, since they would save their strength in them.

"Lady," went on Zinti presently, "beyond the neck of the hill yonder lies the secret *kraal* of Bull-Head. Say, now, what is your plan when you reach it?"

"I do not know," she answered, "but tell me again of the hidden *krantz* where the women built the new hut, and of the way to it."

He told her and she listened, saying nothing.

"Good," she said, when he had done. "Now lead me to this place, and then perhaps I will tell my plan if I have one."

So they started on again, but just as they reached the crest of the Nek a heavy thunderstorm came up, together with clouds and rain, hiding everything from them.

"Now I suppose that we must stay here till the light comes," said Sihamba.

"Not so, lady," answered Zinti, "I have been the path once and I can go it again in storm or shine," and he pressed forward, with the lightning flashes for a candle.

Well was that storm for them indeed, since otherwise they would have been seen, for already Swart Piet had set his scouts about the *kraal*.

At length Sihamba felt that they were riding among trees, for water dripped from them upon her and their branches brushed her face.

"Here is the wood where the women cut poles for the new hut," whispered Zinti in her ear.

"Then let us halt," she answered, and dismounting they tied the three horses and the mule to as many small trees close together, but not near enough for them to kick each other.

Now Sihamba took a piece of biltong from a saddle-bag and began to eat it, for she knew that she would need all her cleverness and strength. "Take the bag of *mealies*," she said, "and divide it among the horses and the mule, giving a double share to the *schimmel*."

Zinti obeyed her, and presently all four of the beasts were eating well, for though they had travelled far their loads were light, nor had the pace been pressed.

Sihamba turned, and, holding out her hands towards the horses, muttered something rapidly.

"What are you doing, mistress?" asked Zinti.

"Perhaps I am throwing a charm upon these animals, that they may neither neigh nor whinny till we come again, for if they do so

119

we are lost. Now let us go, and—stay, bring the gun with you, for you know how to shoot."

So they started, slipping through the wet wood like shadows. For ten minutes or more they crept on thus towards the dark line of cliff, Zinti going first and feeling the way with his fingers, till presently he halted.

"*Hist!*" he whispered. "I smell people."

As he spoke, they heard a sound like to that of someone sliding down rocks. Then a man challenged, saying, "Who passes from the *krantz*?" and a woman's voice answered, "It is I, Asika, the wife of Bull-Head."

"I hear you," answered the man. "Now tell me, Asika, what happens yonder."

"What happens? How do I know what happens?" she answered crossly. "About sunset Bull-Head brought home his new wife, a white chieftainess, for whom we built the hut yonder; but the fashions of marriage among these white people must be strange indeed, for this one came to her husband, her feet bound, and with a face like to the face of a dead woman, the eyes set wide, and the lips parted. Yes, and they blindfolded her in the wood there and carried her through this hole in the rock down to the hut where she is shut in."

"I know something of this matter," answered the man; "the white lady is no willing wife to Bull-Head, for he killed her husband and took her by force. Yes, yes, I know, for my uncle was one of those with him when the deed was done, and he told me something of it just now."

"An evil deed," said Asika, "and one that will bring bad luck upon all of us; but then, Bull-Head, our chief, is an evil man. Oh! I know it who am of the number of his Kaffir wives. Say, friend," she went on, "will you walk a little way with me, as far as the first huts of the *kraal*, for there are ghosts in the wood, and I fear to pass it alone at night."

"I dare not, Asika," he answered, "for I am set here on guard."

"Have no fear, friend, the chief is within, seeing to the comfort of his new wife."

"Well, I will come with you a little way if you wish it, but I must be back immediately," he said, and the listeners heard them walk off together.

"Now, Zinti," whispered Sihamba, "lead me through the hole in the rock."

So he took her by the hand and felt along the face of the cliff till he found the bush which covered the entrance. To this he climbed, dragging her after him, and presently they were in the secret *krantz*.

"We have found our way into the spider's nest," muttered Zinti, who grew afraid; "but say, lady, how shall we find our way out of it?"

"Lead on and leave that to me," she answered. "Where I, a woman, can go, surely you who are a man can go also."

"I trust to your magic to protect us—therefore I come," said Zinti, "though if we are seen our death is sure."

On they crept across the glen, till presently they heard the sound of the small waterfall and saw it glimmering faintly through the gloom and drizzling rain. To their left ran the stream, and on the banks of it stood something large and round.

"There stands the new hut where Swallow is," whispered Zinti.

Now Sihamba thought for a moment and said:

"Zinti, I must find out what passes in that hut. Listen: do you lie hid among the rocks under the bank of the stream, and if you hear me hoot like an owl, then come to me, but not before."

"I obey," answered Zinti, and crept down among the reeds, where he crouched for a long time up to his knees in water, shivering with cold and fear.

CHAPTER 18

What Passed in the Hut

Going on to her hands and knees Sihamba crawled towards the hut. Now she was within ten paces of it and could see that a man stood on guard at its doorway. "I must creep round to the back," she thought, and began to do so, heading for some shrubs which grew to the right. Already she had almost reached them, when of a sudden, and for an instant only, the moon shone out between two thick clouds, revealing her, though indistinctly, to the eyes of the guard. Now Sihamba was wearing a fur cape made of wild dog's hide, and, crouched as she was upon her hands and knees, half-hidden, moreover, by a tuft of dry grass, the man took her to be a wild dog or a jackal, and the hair which stood out round her head for the ruff upon the animal's neck.

"Take that, you four-legged night thief," he said aloud, and hurled the *assegai* in his hand straight at her. The aim was good; indeed, had she been a dog it would have transfixed her. As it was, the spear passed just beneath her body, pinning the hanging edges of the cape and remaining fixed in the tough leather. Now if Sihamba's wit had left her, as would have happened with most, she was lost, but not for nothing had she been a witch-doctoress from her childhood, skilled in every artifice and accustomed to face death. From his words she guessed that the sentry had mistaken her for a wild beast, so instead of springing to her feet she played the part of one, and uttering a howl of pain scrambled away among the bushes. She heard the man start to follow her, then the moonlight went out and he returned to his post grumbling over his lost *assegai* and saying that he would find it in the jackal's body on the morrow. Sihamba, listening not far away, knew his voice; it was that of the fellow who had set the noose about her neck at Swart Piet's bidding and who was to have done the murder in the pass.

"Now, friend, you are unarmed," she thought to herself, "for you have no gun with you, and perhaps we shall settle our accounts before you go to seek that dead jackal by tomorrow's light." Then drawing the *assegai* from the cloak and keeping it in her hand, she crept on till she came to the back of the hut in safety. Still she was not much nearer to her end, for the hut was new and very well built, and she could find no crack to look through, though when she placed her ear against its side she thought that she could hear the sound of a man's voice. In her perplexity Sihamba cast her eyes upwards and saw that a fine line of light shone from the smoke-hole at the very top of the hut, which was hive-shaped, and a thought came into her head.

"If I climb up there," she said to herself, "I can look down through the smoke-hole and see and hear what passes in the hut. Only then if the moon comes out again I may be seen lying on the thatch; well, that I must chance with the rest."

So very slowly and silently, by the help of the *rimpis* which bound the straw, she climbed the dome of the hut, laughing to herself to think that this was the worst of omens for its owner, till at length she reached the smoke-hole at the top and looked down.

This was what she saw: Half seated, half lying upon a rough bedstead spread with blankets, was Suzanne. Her hair had come undone and hung about her, her feet were still loosely bound together, and as the Kaffir, Asika, had said, her face was like that of a dead woman, and her eyes were set in a fixed unnatural stare. Before her was a table cut by natives out of a single block of wood, on which were two candles of sheep's fat set in bottles, and beyond the table stood Swart Piet, who was addressing her.

"Suzanne," he said, "listen to me. I have always loved you, Suzanne, yes, from the time when I was but a boy: we used to meet now and again, you know, when you were out riding with the Englishman who is dead"—here Suzanne's face changed, then resumed its deathlike mask—"and always I worshipped you, and always I hated the Englishman whom you favoured. Well, as you grew older you began to understand and dislike me, and Kenzie began to understand and insult me, and from that seed of slight and insult grew most that is bad in me. Yes, Suzanne, you will say that I am wicked; and I am wicked. I have done things of which I should not like to tell you. I have done such things as you saw last night; I have mixed myself up with Kaffir wizardries and cruelties; I have forgotten God and taken another master, and so far from honouring my own father, why, I struck him down when he was drunk and dared me to do it, and of that blow they say he died. Well, I owed him nothing less for begetting me into such a world as this, and teaching me how to find the devil before my time.

"And now," he went on after a pause, for Suzanne answered nothing, "standing before you as I do here with your husband's blood upon my hands, and seeking your love over his grave, you will look at me and say—'This man is a monster, a madman, one who should be cast from the earth and stamped deep, deep into hell!'Yes, all these things I am, and let the weight of them rest upon your head, for you made me them, Suzanne. I am mad, I know that I am mad, as my father and grandfather were before me, but my madness is mixed with knowledge, for in me runs the blood of the old Pondo witch-doctoress, my grandmother, she who knew many things that are not given to white men. When I saw you and loved you I became half mad—before that I was sane—and when the Englishman, Kenzie, struck me with the whip after our fight at the sheep-*kraal*, ah! then I went wholly mad, and see how wisely, for you are the first-fruits of my madness, you and the body that to-night rolls to and fro in the ocean.

"You do not answer: Well, look you, Suzanne, I have won you by craft and blood, and by craft and blood I will keep you. Here you are in my power, here Heaven itself could not save you from me, in Bull-Head's secret *krantz* which none knew of but some few natives. Choose, therefore; forget the sins that I have committed to win you and become my wife willingly, and no woman shall ever find a better husband, for then the fire and the tempest will leave my brain and it will grow calm as it was before I saw you.

"Have you still no answer? Well, I will not hurry you. See, I must go—do you know what for? To set scouts lest by any chance your father or other fools should have found my hiding-place, though I think that they can never find it except it be through the wisdom of Sihamba, which they will not seek. Still I go, and in an hour I will return for your answer, which you must make then, Suzanne, since whether you desire it, or desire it not, fortune has given you to me. Have you no word for me before I go?"

Now during all this long, half-insane harangue, Suzanne had sat quite silent, making no reply at all, not even seeming to hear the demon, for such he was, whose wicked talk defiled her ears. But when he asked her whether she had nothing to say to him before he went, still looking not at him, but beyond him, she gave him his answer in one word, the same that she had used when she awoke from her swoon:

"*Murderer.*"

Something in the tone in which she spoke, or perhaps in the substance of that short speech, seemed to cow him; at the least he turned and left the hut, and presently Sihamba heard him talking to the sentry without, bidding him to keep close watch till he came back within an hour.

When Piet went out he left the door-board of the hut open, so that Sihamba dared neither act nor speak, fearing lest the guard should hear or see her through it. Therefore she still lay upon the top of the hut, and watched through the smoke-hole. For a while Suzanne sat quiet upon the bed, then of a sudden she rose from it, and shuffling across the hut as well as her bound feet would allow her, she closed the opening with the door-board, and secured it by its wooden bar. Next she returned to the bed and, seating upon it, clasped her hands and began to pray, muttering aloud and mixing with her prayer the name of her husband Ralph. Ceasing presently, she thrust her hand into her bosom and drew from it a knife, not large, but strong and very sharp. Opening this knife she cut the thong that bound her ankles, and made it into a noose. Then she looked earnestly first at the noose, next at the knife, and thirdly at the candles, and Sihamba understood that she meant to do herself to death, and was choosing between steel and rope and fire.

Now all this while, although she dared not so much as whisper, Sihamba had not been idle, for with the blade of the *assegai* she was working gently at the thatch of the smoke-hole, and cutting the *rimpis* that bound it, till at last, and not too soon, she thought that it was wide enough to allow of the passage of her small body. Then watching until the guard leaned against the hut, so that the bulge of it would cut her off from his sight, during the instant that her figure was outlined against the sky, she stood up, and thrusting her feet through the hole, forced her body to follow them, and then dropped lightly as a cat to the floor beneath. But now there was another danger to be faced, and a great one, namely, that Suzanne might cry out in fear, which doubtless she would have done, had not the sudden sight of some living creature in the hut where she thought herself alone, so startled her that for a moment she lost her breath. Before she could find it again Sihamba was whispering in her ear, saying:

"Keep silence for your life's sake, Swallow. It is I, Sihamba, who am come to save you."

Suzanne stared at her, and light came back into the empty eyes, then they grew dark again, as she answered below her breath:

"Of what use is my life? Ralph is dead, and I was about to take it that I may save myself from shame and go to seek him, for surely God will forgive the sin."

Sihamba looked at her and said:

"Swallow, prepare yourself for great joy, and, above all, do not cry out. Your husband is not dead, he was but wounded, and I drew him living from the sea. He lies safe at the stead in your mother's care."

Suzanne heard her, and, notwithstanding the caution, still she would have cried aloud in the madness of her joy, had not Sihamba, seeing her lips opened, thrust her hands upon her mouth and held them there till the danger was past.

"You do not lie to me?" she gasped at length.

"Nay, I speak truth, I swear it. But this is no time to talk. Yonder stand food and milk; eat while I think."

As Sihamba guessed, nothing but a little water had passed Suzanne's lips since that meal which she and her husband took together beside the wagon, nor one minute before she could have swallowed anything had her life been the price of it. But now it was different, for despair had left her, and hope shone in her heart again, and behold! of a sudden she was hungry, and ate and drank with gladness, while Sihamba thought.

Presently the little woman looked up and whispered:

"A plan comes into my head; it is a strange one, but I can find no other, and it may serve our turn, for I think that good luck goes with us. Swallow, give me the noose of hide which you made from the *riem* that bound your feet."

Suzanne obeyed her wondering, whereon Sihamba placed the noose about her own neck, then bade Suzanne stand upon the bed and thrust the end of the *riem* loosely into the thatch of the hut as high up as she could reach, so that it looked as though it were made fast there. Next, Sihamba slipped off her fur cloak, leaving herself naked except for the *moocha* round her middle, and, clasping her hands behind her back with the *assegai* between them, she drew the *riem* taut, and leaned against the wall of the hut after the fashion of one who is about to be pulled from the ground and strangled.

"Now, mistress, listen to me," she said earnestly. "You have seen me like this before, have you not, when I was about to be hanged, and you bought my life at a price? Well, as it chances, that man who guards the hut is he who took me at Bull-Head's bidding and set the rope round my neck, whereon I said some words to him which made him afraid. Now if he sees me again thus in a hut where he knows you to be alone, he will think that I am a ghost and his heart will turn to ice and the strength of his hands to water, and then before he can find his strength again I shall make an end of him with the spear, as I know well how to do although I am so small, and we will fly."

"Is there no other way?" murmured Suzanne aghast.

"None, Swallow. For you the choice lies between witnessing this deed and—Swart Piet or—Death. Nay, you need not witness it even, if you will do as I tell you. Presently, when I give the word, loosen the bar of the door-board, then crouch by the hole and utter a low cry of fear, calling to the man on guard for help. He will enter and see me, whereon you can creep through the door-hole and wait without, leaving me to deal with him. If I succeed I will be with you at once; if I fail, run to the stream and hoot like an owl, when Zinti, who is hidden there, will join you. Then you must get out of the *krantz* as best you can. Only one man watches the entrance, and if needful Zinti can shoot him. The *schimmel* and other horses are hidden in the wood, and he will lead you to them. Mount and ride for home, or anywhere away from this accursed place, and at times when you talk of the matter of your escape with your husband, think kindly of Sihamba Ngenyanga. Nay, do not answer, for there is little time to lose. Quick, now, to the door-hole, and do as I bade you."

So, like one in a dream, Suzanne loosened the bar, and, crouching by the entrance to the hut, uttered a low wail of terror, saying, "Help me, soldier, help me swiftly," in the Kaffir tongue. The man without heard, and, pushing down the board, crept in at once, saying, "Who harms you, lady?" as he rose to his feet. Then suddenly, in this hut, where there was but one woman, a white woman, whom he himself had carried into it, he beheld another woman—Sihamba; and his hair stood up upon his head and his eyes grew round with terror. Yes, it was Sihamba herself, for the light of the candles shone full upon her, or, rather, her ghost, and she was hanging to the roof, the tips of her toes just touching the ground, as once he had seen her hang before.

For some seconds the man stared in his terror, and while he stared Suzanne slipped from the hut. Then muttering, "It is the spirit of the witch, Sihamba, who prophesied my death—her spirit that haunts me," he dropped to his knees, and, trembling like a leaf, turned to creep from the hut. Next second he was *dead*, dead without a sound, for Sihamba was a doctoress, and knew well where to thrust with the spear.

Of all this Suzanne heard nothing and saw nothing, till presently Sihamba stood by her side holding the skin cape in one hand and the spear in the other.

"Now one danger is done with," she said quietly, as she put on the cape, "but many still remain. Follow me, Swallow," and, going to the edge of the stream, she hooted like an owl, whereupon Zinti came out of the reeds, looking very cold and frightened.

"Be swift," whispered Sihamba, and they started along the *krantz* at a run. Before they were half way across it, the storm-clouds, which had been thinning gradually, broke up altogether, and the moon shone out with a bright light, showing them as plainly as though it were day; but as it chanced they met nobody and were seen of none.

At length they reached the cleft in the rock that led to the plain below. "Stay here," said Sihamba, "while I look," and she crept to the entrance. Presently she returned and said:

"A man watches there, and it is not possible to slip past him because of the moonlight. Now, I know of only one thing that we can do; and you, Zinti, must do it. Slip down the rock and cover the man with your gun, saying to him that if he stirs a hand or speaks a word you will shoot him dead. Hold him thus till we are past you on our way to the wood, then follow us as best you can, but do not fire except to save your life or ours."

Now the gifts of Zinti lay rather in tracking and remembering paths and directions than in fighting men, so that when he heard this order he was afraid and hesitated.

But when she saw it, Sihamba turned upon him so fiercely that he feared her more than the watchman, and went at once, so that this man who was half asleep suddenly saw the muzzle of a *roer* within three paces of his head and heard a voice command him to stand still and silent or die. Thus he stood indeed until he perceived that the new wife of his chief was escaping. Then remembering what would be his fate at the hands of Bull-Head he determined to take his chance of being shot, and, turning suddenly, sped towards the *kraal* shouting as he ran, whereon Zinti fired at him, but the ball went wide. A cannon could scarcely have made more noise than did the great *roer* in the silence of the night as the report of it echoed to and fro among the hills.

"Oh! fool to fire, and yet greater fool to miss," said Sihamba. "To the horses! Swift! swift!"

They ran as the wind runs, and now they were in the wood, and now they had found the beasts.

"Praise to the Snake of my house!" said Sihamba, "they are safe, all four of them," and very quickly they untied the *riem*s by which they had fastened the horses to the trees.

"Mount, Swallow," said Sihamba, seizing the head of the great *schimmel*.

Suzanne set her foot upon the shoulder of Zinti, who knelt to receive it, and sprang into the saddle. Then having lifted Sihamba on the grey mare Zinti mounted the other horse himself, holding the mule by a leading *riem*.

"Which way, mistress?" he asked.

"Homewards," she answered, and they cantered forward through the wood.

On the further side of this wood was a little sloping plain not more than three hundred paces wide, and beyond it lay the seaward Nek through which they must pass on their journey to the stead. Already they were out of the wood and upon the plain, when from their right a body of horsemen swooped towards them, seven in all, of whom one, the leader, was Swart Piet himself, cutting them off from the Nek. They halted their horses as though to a word of command, and speaking rapidly, Sihamba asked of Zinti: "Is there any other pass through yonder range, for this one is barred to us?"

"None that I know of," he answered; "but I have seen that the ground behind us is flat and open as far as the great peak which you saw rising on the plain away beyond the sky-line."

"Good," said Sihamba. "Let us head for the peak, since we have nowhere else to go, and if we are separated, let us agree to meet upon its southern slope. Now, Zinti, loose the mule, for we have our lives to save, and ride on, remembering that Death is behind you."

CHAPTER 19

How the Schimmel Crossed the Red Water

When they turned their horses' heads, Swart Piet and his men were not much more than a hundred paces from them, but in the wood they gained much ground, for he did not think that they would dare to leave it, and hunted for them there while they were racing over the open plain more than a mile away. At last he caught sight of them crossing a distant ridge, and the long chase began. For hour after hour they galloped on through the moonlight across the wide and rolling *veldt* until the moon sank, and they must pick their way as best they could in the darkness.

Then came the dawn, and still they rode forward, though now the horses were beginning to grow weary, except the *schimmel*, who pulled upon his bit as though he were fresh from the stable. In front of them, some twenty miles away, rose the lofty peak for which they were heading, and behind lay the great expanse of plain which they had passed. Suzanne looked back over her shoulder, but there was no one in sight.

"Let us halt," she said, "and rest ourselves and the horses." So they pulled up by a stream and suffered the beasts to drink some water, though not much, while they themselves devoured biltong, of which they had a little in the saddle-bags.

"Why do we ride for the peak?" asked Suzanne.

"Because there are places where we may lie hid," Sihamba answered, "and thence we can make our way down to the seashore and so back homewards, whereas here upon the plain we can be seen from miles away."

"Do any people live on the peak?"

"Yes, Swallow; it is the home of the great chief Sigwe, the chief-paramount of the Red Kaffirs, who counts his spears by thousands, but

I have heard that he is away to the north upon a war which he makes against some of the Swazi tribes with whom he has a quarrel."

"Will the people of Sigwe protect us, Sihamba?"

"Perhaps. We shall see. At least, you are safer with them than in the hands of Swart Piet."

At this moment, Zinti, who was watching the plain over which they had travelled, uttered a cry of warning. Looking back, they saw the reason of it, for there, crossing the crest of a wave of ground, not more than a mile away, were five horsemen riding hard upon their spoor.

"Swart Piet and four of his men," said Sihamba, "and by my Spirit, they have fresh horses; they must have taken them from the *kraal* of the half-breed which we passed at daybreak, and that is why we lost sight of them for a while."

Now even as Zinti helped her to mount the *schimmel* Suzanne turned so faint with terror that she almost fell to the ground again.

"Have no fear, Swallow," said Sihamba, "he has not caught us yet, and a voice in me says that we shall escape him."

But though she spoke thus bravely, in her heart Sihamba was much afraid, for except the *schimmel* their horses were almost spent, whereas Van Vooren was fresh mounted, and not a mile behind. Still they galloped forward till they reached a more broken stretch of *veldt*, where trees grew singly, and here and there were *kloofs* with bush in them.

"Mistress," cried Zinti, "my horse can go no more, and Bull-Head is hard upon us. Of your wisdom tell me what I should do or presently I must be killed."

"Ride into that *kloof* and hide yourself," answered Sihamba, "for Bull-Head will never seek you there; he hunts the white Swallow, not the black finch. Afterwards you can follow on our spoor, and if you cannot find us, make your way back to the Baas Botmar and tell him all you know. Quick, into the *kloof*, for here they cannot see you."

"I hear you, lady," said Zinti, and the next minute they saw him leading his weary horse into the shelter of the thick bush, for the poor beast could carry him no more.

For the next three miles the ground trended downwards to the banks of a great river, beyond which were the gentle rising slopes that surrounded the foot of the high peak. On they galloped, the *schimmel* never faltering in his swinging stride, although his flanks grew thin and his eyes large. But with the grey mare it was otherwise, for though she was a gallant nag her strength was gone. Indeed, with any heavier rider upon her back, ere this she would have fallen. But still she answered to Sihamba's voice and plunged on, rolling and stumbling in her gait.

"She will last till the river," she said, seeing Suzanne look at the mare.

"And then——?" gasped Suzanne, glancing behind her to where, not five hundred yards away, Swart Piet and his Kaffirs hunted them sullenly and in silence, as strong dogs hunt down a wounded buck.

"And then—who knows?" answered Sihamba, and they went on without more words, for they had no breath to spare.

Now, not half a mile away, they came in sight of the river, which had been hidden from them before by the lie of the ground, and a groan of despair broke from their lips, for it was in flood. Yes, the storms in the mountains had swollen it, and it rolled towards the sea a red flood of foam-flecked water, well-nigh two hundred yards from bank to bank. Still they rode on, for they dared not stop, and presently behind them they heard a shout of triumph, and knew that their pursuers had also seen the Red Water, and rejoiced because now they had them in a trap.

Within ten yards of the lip of the river, the grey mare stopped suddenly, shivered like a leaf in the wind and sank to the ground.

"Now, Swallow," said Sihamba as she slipped from the saddle, "you must choose between that raging torrent and Swart Piet. If you choose the torrent the great horse is still strong and he may swim through; I can say no more."

"And you?" asked Suzanne.

"I? I bide here, and oh! I would that Zinti had left the gun with me."

"Never," cried Suzanne. "Together we will live or die. Mount, I say—mount. Nay, if you refuse I will throw myself into the water before your eyes."

Then seeing that she would indeed do no less, Sihamba took her outstretched hand, and placing her foot upon the foot of Suzanne, scrambled up upon the pad in front of her, whereat the pursuers, who now were little over two hundred yards away, laughed out loud, and Swart Piet shouted to Suzanne to yield. But they did not laugh long, for Sihamba, having first bent her head and kissed Suzanne on the hand, leaned forward and began to stroke the *schimmel*'s neck and to whisper into his ear, till indeed it seemed as though the great brute that loved her understood. At the least he pricked his ears and tossed his head, then looked, first round at the horses that drew near, and next at the foaming flood in front.

"Sit fast, Swallow," said Sihamba, and then she cried a word aloud to the horse, and struck it lightly with her hand. At the sound of that word the stallion drew himself together, sprang forward with two bounds over the ten paces of level bank and leapt far out into the flood that foamed beneath. Down sank the horse and his riders till the Red Water closed over their heads, then they rose again and heard the shout of wonder of their enemies, who by now had almost reached the bank. With a yell of rage Black Piet rode his horse at the river, for to do him justice he was a brave man, but do what he might it would not face it, so with the others he sat still and watched.

Now the *schimmel* struck out bravely, heading for the other bank, but in the fierce current it was not possible that any horse should reach it swimming in a straight line, for the weight of the stream was too great. Sihamba had noted, however, that from the further shore, but two or three hundred paces lower down the river, a little point of land projected into it, and this the horse had seen also, or perhaps she told him of it, at least for that point he swam steadily. In five minutes they were in the centre of the torrent, and here it ran with a roar and mighty force so that its waves began to break over the *schimmel*'s head, and they feared that he would drown. So much did Sihamba fear it, indeed, that she slipped from his back, and leaving Suzanne to cling to the saddle, caught hold of his mane, floating alongside of him and protected by his neck from the whirl of the water. Lying thus she continued to call to the horse and to urge him forward, and ever he answered to her words, so that although twice he nearly sank, in the end he set his feet upon a sandbank and, having rested there a while, plunged forward, half wading and half swimming, to the projecting point of land, up which he scrambled, still carrying Suzanne and dragging Sihamba with him, until once more they found themselves safe upon the solid earth, where he stood shaking himself and snorting.

Suzanne slipped from the saddle and lay flat upon the ground, looking at the awful water they had passed, and by her lay Sihamba. Presently the little doctoress spoke.

"It is well to have lived," she said, "if only to have dared that deed, for no others have ever made the passage across the Red Water in flood, two of them on one tired horse," and she caught in her arms the muzzle of the *schimmel* that hung above her, pressing it to her breast as though it had been a child, whereon the brute whinnied faintly, knowing well that she was thanking him for his toil and courage.

"I pray God that I may never be called upon to make it again," answered Suzanne, staggering to her feet, the water running from her dripping dress as she turned to look across the river.

Now, when Van Vooren's horse refused to face the stream, he had ridden up and down shouting like a madman; once even he lifted his gun and pointed it, then let it fall again, remembering that he could not make sure of hitting the horse, and that if he did so Suzanne must certainly be drowned. When they were quite beyond his reach in the middle of the stream, he stood still and watched until he saw them come to the further shore in safety. Then he called his men about him and consulted with them, and the end of it was that they rode off in a body up the bank of the river.

"They go to seek a ford," said Suzanne.

"Yes, Swallow, but now we shall have the start of them. Come, let us mount."

So they climbed upon the back of the *schimmel*, and once more he went on with them, not fast, for now he could not even canter, but ambling or walking, according to the nature of the ground, at a rate perhaps of seven miles the hour. Soon they had left the river and were toiling up the slopes of the peak, until presently they struck a well-worn footpath.

"I think that this must lead to the town of Sigwe," said Sihamba.

"I pray that it does," answered Suzanne, "and that it is not far, for I feel as though Death were near to me."

"Keep a great heart," said Sihamba, "for we have met Death face to face and conquered him."

So still they toiled on till at length the path took a turn, and there, in a fold of the hill, they beheld the great *kraal* of Sigwe, a very large Kaffir town. Before the *kraal* was a wide open space, and on that space armed men were assembled, several full regiments of them. In front of this *impi* was gathered a company of chiefs.

"Now we have no choice," said Sihamba, and turned the *schimmel* towards them, while all that army stared at this strange sight of two women, one tall and fair, one black and little, riding towards them mounted together upon a great blood horse which was so weary that he could scarcely set one foot before the other.

When they reached the captains Sihamba slipped to the ground, but Suzanne remained seated upon the *schimmel*.

"Who are you?" asked a broad man in a leopard-skin cloak, of Sihamba; but although she was small and dishevelled, her hair and garments being wet with water, he did not laugh at her, for he saw that this stranger had the air of one who is of the blood of chiefs.

"I am Sihamba Ngenyanga, the doctoress, of whom you may have heard," she answered; and some of the people said, "We have heard of her; she is a great doctoress."

"To what people do you belong, Sihamba?" asked the captain again.

"I belong to the people of Zwide, whom Chaka drove from Zululand, and by birth I am a chieftainess of the Umpondwana, who live in the mountain Umpondwana, and who were the Children of Zwide, but are now the Children of Chaka."

"Why then do you wander so far from home, Sihamba?"

"For this reason. When Zwide and his people, the Endwandwe, were driven back, my people, the Umpondwana, who were subject to Zwide, made peace with Chaka against my will. Therefore, because I would not live as a Zulu dog, I left them."

"Although your body is small you have a large heart," said the captain, and one of his people cried out: "The story of Sihamba is true, for when you sent me as messenger to the Endwandwe, I heard it—it is a tale there."

Then the captain asked, "And who is the beautiful white woman who sits upon the great horse?"

"She is my mother and my sister and my mistress, whom I serve till death, for she saved me from death, and her name is Swallow."

Now at this word *Swallow*, most of those present started, and some uttered exclamations of wonder, especially a little band of people, men and women, who stood to the left, and who from their dress and other tokens it was easy to see were witch-doctors and diviners. Sihamba noted the movements and words of wonder, but pretending to see nothing she went on:

"The lady Swallow and I have fled hither from far, hoping to find the chief Sigwe, for we need his counsel and protection, but he is away, making war to the north, is it not so?"

"Nay," answered the captain. "I am the chief Sigwe, and I have not yet begun my war."

"I am glad," said Sihamba. "Chief, listen to my tale and suffer us to creep into the shadow of your strength——" and in a few words she told them the story of the capture of Suzanne by Swart Piet and of their flight from him. Now when she spoke of Van Vooren, or of Bull-Head rather, for she called him by his native name, she saw that Sigwe and the captains looked at each other, and when she told how they had swum the Red Water in flood, the two of them upon one horse, she was sure that they did not believe her, for such a deed they thought to be impossible. But still Sihamba went on and ended—"Chief, we seek this from you; protection from Bull-Head, who doubtless will be here ere long, and an escort of spears to lead us down the coast to the home of the Swallow, a hundred miles away, where they and you will be well rewarded for the service. Answer us quick, chief, I pray you, for our need is great and we are weary."

CHAPTER 20

The Omen of the White Swallow

Now Sigwe and two of his captains walked to where the diviners stood and took counsel with them, speaking low and earnestly. Then he returned and said:

"Sihamba, Walker-by-Moonlight, and you, Lady Swallow, listen to me. A wonderful thing has come to pass in the *kraal* of Sigwe this day, such a thing as our fathers have not known. You see that my host is gathered yonder: well, tomorrow they start to make war upon these very Endwandwe of whom you have spoken because of a deadly insult which they have put upon me and my house. Therefore, according to custom, this morning the soldiers were assembled at dawn to be doctored and that the diviners might search out the omens of the war. So the diviners searched, and she who was chosen among them ate the medicine and sank into the witch sleep here before us all. Yes, this one," and he pointed to a tall woman with dreamy eyes who was bedizened with bones and snakeskins.

"Now in her sleep she spoke, and we hung upon her words, for we knew that they would be the words of omen. Sihamba, these were the words, as all can testify:

"'Thus say the spirits of your fathers, and thus speaks the Snake of your tribe. Unless a *White Swallow* guide your footsteps in the war with the Men of the Mountains you shall perish and your *impis* shall be scattered, but if a *White Swallow* flies before your spears than but little of your blood shall be shed, and you shall return with honour and with one whom you seek. Only the Swallow shall not return with you, for if she set her face southward, then, Sigwe, woe to you and your armies.'

"Sihamba, these were the words of the dreamer. Scarcely was she awake again, while we wondered at their strangeness, and asked her questions of their meaning, which she could not answer, for here the wisdom of the wisest was at fault, lo! you rode over the hill, and with you a beautiful white woman whose name you say is Swallow. Yes, this is the White Swallow who shall fly in front of my regiments, bringing me honour and good fortune in the war, and therefore, Sihamba, your prayer is granted, though not all of it, for you shall go northward and not southward, and among your own people I will leave you and the Swallow with you, and for her sake I will spare your people, the people of Umpondwana, although they are subject to my foe, the Endwandwe, and of the same blood. Moreover, while you are among us all honour shall be done to you and the Swallow, and of the cattle we capture a tenth part shall be the Swallow's. Still, I tell you this, that had it not been for the omen of the diviner I would have refused your prayer and delivered you and the Swallow over to Bull-Head, for with him I have sworn friendship long ago. But now the face of things is changed, and should he come with a hundred men armed with guns yet I will protect you from him, and the Swallow also; yes, though oaths must be broken to do it."

When they heard this saying, Suzanne and Sihamba looked at each other in dismay.

"Alas!" said Suzanne, "it seems that we do but change one prison for another, for now we must be borne away to the far north to do battle with this Kaffir chief, and there be left among your people, so that none will know what has become of us, and the heart of Ralph will break with doubt and sorrow; yes, and those of my parents also."

"It is bad," answered Sihamba, "but had not yonder diviner dreamed that dream of a swallow, it would have been worse. Better is it to travel in all honour with the *impis* of Sigwe than to be dragged back by Bull-Head to his secret *kraal*—I to be done to death there and you to the choice of which you know. For the rest we must take our chance and escape when the time comes, and meanwhile we will send a message to the stead."

Now Suzanne heard her, and sat upon the horse thinking, for her trouble was sore; still, she could see no way out of the net which had meshed her. As she thought, a man who was herding cattle on the mountains ran up to the chief and saluted him, saying that five men, one of them white, rode towards his *kraal*. When Suzanne heard this she hesitated no more, but cried out to the chief Sigwe, speaking in the Kaffir tongue, which she knew well:

"Chief Sigwe, swear to me that you will not suffer Bull-Head so much as to touch me or my sister Sihamba, and that while we dwell with you you will treat us with all honour, and I, who am named

Swallow, yes, I, the White Swallow of the diviner's dream, will lead your armies to the northern land, bringing you the good fortune which is mine to give to others, though myself I know it not."

"I swear by the spirits of my fathers, lady," answered Sigwe, "and these my counsellors and headmen swear it also."

"Yes," echoed the counsellors, "we swear it, all of it, and while one of us is left alive the oath shall be fulfilled, O White Bird of good omen."

Then Sigwe gave an order, and at his bidding five hundred soldiers, the half of a regiment, ran up and formed a circle about Sihamba and Suzanne, who still sat upon the *schimmel*, white faced and wearied, her hair hanging down her back. Scarcely was the circle made when from round the shoulder of the hill appeared Swart Piet and with him his four after-riders.

Seeing all the great array, he halted for a moment astonished, then catching sight of Suzanne set up above the heads of the ring of soldiers, he rode straight to Sigwe, who, with his counsellors and guards, was standing outside the circle.

"Chief Sigwe," he said, "a wife of mine with her servant has escaped from me, and as I suspected taken refuge in your *kraal*, for I see her sitting yonder surrounded by your soldiers. Now, in the name of our friendship, I pray you hand them over to me that I may lead them back to their duty."

"I give you greeting, Bull-Head," answered Sigwe courteously, "and I thank you for your visit to my town; presently an ox shall be sent for you to eat. As for this matter of the white lady and her companion it is one that we can inquire into at leisure. I hear that she is the daughter of the big Boer whom the natives of the coast name Thick-Arm; also that you murdered the lady's husband and carried her off by force to be your wife instead of his. Now here, as you know, I am chief paramount, for having of our blood in your veins, you understand our customs, and, therefore, I must see justice done, especially as I do not wish to bring a quarrel with the white people upon our heads. So off-saddle a while, and tomorrow before I start upon a certain journey, I will summon my counsellors and we will try the case."

Now by this time Swart Piet, who, as Sigwe had said, understood the customs of the Kaffirs, knew very well that the chief was making excuses, and would not surrender Suzanne to him. For a while he kept himself calm, but when this knowledge came home to his mind his reason left him, and he grew more than commonly mad with rage and disappointment, for after all his crimes and toil Suzanne was now as far from him as ever. Springing from his horse, but still keeping the gun in his hand, he ran up to the triple ring of soldiers, pausing only at the hedge of *assegais* which shone about it.

"Open," he said, "open, you red dogs!" but not a spear moved. Twice he ran round the circle, then he stopped and cried, "Sihamba. Is Sihamba here?"

"Surely, Bull-Head," answered the little woman, walking forward from where she stood behind the *schimmel*. "Where else should I be? I pray you, soldiers, draw a little way but not far apart, that yonder half-breed may satisfy his eyes with the sight of me. So, a little way, but not far, for I who know him like him best at a distance. Now, Bull-Head," she went on, "what is it that you wish to talk about—the English-man, Ralph Kenzie, the husband of Swallow yonder? You thought you killed him. Well, it was not so; I lifted him living from the water, and I, who am a doctoress, tell you that his wound is of no account, and that soon he will be strong again and seeking a word with you, Half-breed. No, not of him? Then perhaps it is of your hidden *krantz* and the new hut you built in it. Bah! I knew its secret long ago and—that hut has too wide a smoke-hole. Go back and ask him who guarded it if this is not true. What! Not of that either? Then would you speak of the ride which we have taken? Ah! man, I thought at least that you were no coward, and yet even when you had us in your hand, you did not dare to face the Red Water which two women swam on one tired horse. Look at him, soldiers, look at the brave cross-bred chief who dared not swim his horse across one little stream."

Now while the soldiers laughed Swart Piet stamped upon the ground, foaming with rage, for Sihamba's bitter words stuck in him like barbed *assegais*.

"Snake's wife, witch!" he screamed, "I will catch you yet, and then you shall learn how slowly a woman may die, yes, and her also, and she shall learn other things, for if that husband of hers is not dead I will kill him before her eyes. I tell you I will follow you both through all Africa and across the sea if needful; yes, whenever you lie down to sleep, you may be sure that Piet van Vooren is not far from you."

"Do you say so?" mocked Sihamba. "Well, now I think of it you have no luck face to face with me, Half-breed, and were I you, I should look the other way when you saw me coming, for I who have the Sight tell you that when you behold the Walker-by-Moonlight for the last time, you will very soon become a walker in the darkness for ever. Bah!" she went on, her clear voice rising to a cry. "Bastard, dog, thief, murderer that you are! I, Sihamba, who have met and beaten you in every pool of the stream, will beat you for the last time where the stream falls into the sea. Be not deceived, yonder Swallow never shall be yours; for many and many a year after you are dead, your rival shall fold her close, and when men name your name they shall spit upon the ground. Nothing, nothing shall be yours, but shame and empty longing and black death, and after it the woe of the wicked. Get you back to your secret *krantz* and your Kaffir wives, Half-breed, and tell them the tale of your ride, and of how you did not dare to face the foam of the Red Water."

Now Van Vooren went mad indeed; so mad that, forgetting he was not on the lonely *veldt*, he lifted his gun and fired straight at Sihamba. But her eye was quick, and seeing the muzzle rise, she threw herself upon the ground, so that the ball passed over her.

"Why, Half-breed, have you even forgotten how to shoot?" she called, springing to her feet again and mocking him. Then the voice of Sigwe broke in, for his anger was deep.

"One thing you have certainly forgotten, Bull-Head," he said, "that these two are my guests and wrapped in my *kaross*, and therefore from this hour we are enemies. Ho! men," he cried to his guard, "I spare Bull-Head's life because once we were friends, therefore do not take his life, but beat him and those with him out of my town with the shafts of your *assegais*, and if ever he sets foot within it again then use their blades upon him."

At their chief's bidding the soldiers of the guard sprang forward, and, falling upon Van Vooren and those with him, they flogged them with sticks and the shafts of their spears until from head to foot they were nothing but blood and bruises, and thus they drove them out of the town of Sigwe back to the ford of the Red River.

When they were gone, Suzanne, who through it all had sat upon the horse watching in silence, now urged him forward to where Sigwe stood, and said:

"Chief, I thank you for that deed, and now, I pray you, give us food and a hut to rest in, for we are wet and hungry and worn out with long travel."

So the guest masters led them into the fence of the town and gave them the guest hut, the largest in the *kraal*, and the best food that they had—milk and meal and beef and eggs, as much as they would of it. The *schimmel* also was fastened to a post in the little courtyard of the hut, and a Kaffir who once had served as groom to a white man, washed him all over with warm water. Afterwards he was given a mash of meal to eat, and, later, when he was a little rested, his fill of good forage, which he ate gladly, for, though he was very tired and his legs were somewhat swollen, otherwise he was none the worse for that great ride.

In the shelter of the hut Suzanne took off her clothes, remembering with a sort of wonder how she had put them on on the morning of her marriage, which now seemed years ago, and bathed herself with water. Then Sihamba having given the garments to a waiting woman to wash, wrapped her in a soft *kaross* of fur, and after drinking some milk and eating a little, Suzanne laid herself down upon a mattress made of the husks of *mealie* cobs, and even as she thanked God Who had brought her safely through so many dangers past, and prayed Him to protect her in those that were to come, and to comfort the heart of her husband in his sickness and affliction, she fell asleep. When she saw her sleeping, but not before, Sihamba crept to her feet, for now that all was over she could scarcely walk, and laying herself down there slept also.

All the rest of the day they slept, and all the night that followed, nor did they wake till sunrise of the next morning, when women of the household of the chief knocked upon the door-board to ask if they needed aught. Then they rose feeling well and strong again except for the stiffness of their limbs, and Suzanne clothed herself in the garments that the woman had washed, combing her dark hair with a Kaffir comb. Afterwards they ate heartily of the good food that was brought to them, and left the hut to visit the *schimmel*, that they found almost recovered and devouring Kaffir sugar-cane, though like themselves he was somewhat stiff.

Presently, while they stroked and fondled him, a messenger came, saying that if it pleased the lady Swallow, the chief Sigwe would take counsel with her in the place of audience. So after a little while they went, and as they passed out of the *kraal* fence, Suzanne was received with a chief's salute by the escort that was waiting for her. Then surrounding her and Sihamba, they led them to the place of audience, a circle of ground enclosed by a high double fence, and as Suzanne entered it once more all present there, including Sigwe himself, gave her the salute of chiefs.

But though it was strange enough that such a thing should happen to a white woman, at the time Suzanne took little notice of the salute or aught else, for there standing before her, looking much bewildered and very weary, was none other than Zinti and with him Sihamba's horse, and also that mule laden with goods, which they had abandoned in the wood nearly a hundred miles away, when they came face to face with Van Vooren and his riders and turned to begin their long flight for life and liberty.

CHAPTER 21

The Vision of Ralph and Suzanne

"Sihamba," said the chief Sigwe, "this man who was found wandering upon the outskirts of the town, declares that he is your servant, and that he comes to seek you. Is it so?"

"It is so, indeed, chief," she answered, "though I scarcely expected to see him again," and she told how they two and Zinti had parted.

Then Zinti was commanded to tell his tale, and from it it seemed that after he had rested some hours in the *kloof* he crept to the mouth of it, and, hidden behind a stone, saw Swart Piet and his servants pass quite close to him on their homeward way. A sorry sight they were, for three of their horses were lame, so that the riders were obliged to walk and lead them, and the men themselves had been so bruised with the spear-shafts that they seemed more dead than alive. Swart Piet rode last of all, and just then he turned, and looking towards the peak shook his fist as though threatening it, and cursed aloud in Dutch and Kaffir. Indeed, Zinti said that his head and face were so swollen with blows that had it not been for his large round eyes he could not have known him, and Sihamba thought that very good tidings.

Well, when they had gone Zinti took heart, for it was plain that they had been roughly handled, and had failed to catch his mistress or the Swallow. So he went back to where he had left his horse eating a little grass, and since it was too weak to carry him he led it, following Van Vooren's spoor backwards till in the evening he came to the ford of the Red River. Here he halted for the night, knee-haltering the horse, and leaving it loose to graze, though he himself had nothing to eat. At the first grey of dawn he awoke, and was astonished to see a second animal feeding with the horse, which proved to be none other than the mule that, as these creatures sometimes will, had followed the spoor of his companion, Sihamba's horse, till it found it again. After this he crossed the drift, riding slowly and leading the mule, till shortly after sunrise he came to the outskirts of the town, where Sigwe's watchmen found him and brought him to the chief.

"This man is a servant worth having," said Sigwe when he had heard the story. "Let food be given to him and to the beasts."

When Zinti had gone Sigwe spoke to Suzanne.

"Lady Swallow," he said, "as you have heard, by the command of the spirits of my ancestors speaking through the mouth of the diviner, while you are with us, you and not I are the captain of my army, and must lead it in this great war which I make against the Endwandwe. Now the regiments are ready to march, and I ask if it be your pleasure that we should set out tomorrow at the dawn, for time presses, and the Endwandwe live very far away?"

"Your will is my will, chief," she answered, for she could see no way of escape from this strange journey, "but I desire to learn the cause of this war which I must lead by the decree of the spirits of your ancestors."

Now Sigwe gave an order to some attendants waiting upon him, who went away to return presently leading with them a woman. This woman was about fifty years of age, very fat in person, sour-faced, yellow-toothed, and with one eye only.

"There is the cause," exclaimed the chief, at the same time turning his back upon the woman and spitting upon the ground as though in disgust.

"I do not understand," said Suzanne.

"Then listen, Lady Swallow. Sikonyana, the chief of the Endwandwe, has a sister named Batwa, whose beauty is famous throughout all the world, and for her by my envoys I made an offer of marriage, intending that she should be my head wife, for I desired to be the husband of the most beautiful woman in the world."

"I saw Batwa when she was still a child," broke in Sihamba; "indeed, she is my cousin, and it is true that she is most beautiful."

"The chief Sikonyana," went on Sigwe, "answered me that he was much honoured by my offer since he knew me to be the greatest man of all this country, but that at the same time his sister was not to be won with a small price; yet if I would send a thousand head of cattle, half of them black and half white, she should be mine. Then with much pain I collected these cattle, two years did it take me to gather them together, for here oxen and cows pure white and pure black are not common, and I sent them with an *impi* to guard them, for nothing less would suffice, to the *kraal* of the chief of the Endwandwe.

"Four moons was that *impi* gone, while I awaited its return, eating out my heart with impatience. At length it did return, bringing with it my bride. At nightfall it marched into the town hungry and tired, for it had suffered much upon the journey, and twice had been forced to give battle to the armies of other chiefs, but although I was eager to see her I did not look upon my new wife that night. No, I sent out messengers and gathered together all my army and all the people young and old, yonder in the plain of assembly. Then when they were mustered from far and near, I commanded that Batwa, the sister of Sikonyana, should be produced in the face of the people that her loveliness might shine upon me and upon them as the sun shines equally upon us all.

"Lady Swallow, the moment came, and this old woman was brought out; yes, she strutted before us proudly, this one-eyed hag, this cat of the mountains. For her I had sent an *impi*, for her I had paid a thousand head of cattle, half of them pure black and half pure white——" and Sigwe ceased, gasping with rage.

Now at this story Suzanne, who had not smiled for days, laughed aloud, while even Sihamba the wise looked down studying the earth. But there was one who did not laugh, and it was the one-eyed woman. No, she sprang up and screamed aloud:

"Dog of a red Kaffir, who are you that dare to talk thus of a princess of the blood of the Endwandwe, a princess whom Chaka, the great king, wished to take to wife? You asked for Batwa in marriage, Batwa, the sister to Sikonyana, and I am Batwa the sister of Sikonyana."

"Then, hag, there must be two Batwas," shouted Sigwe in answer.

"Two Batwas!" she screamed. "Fool and beast, there are *four*! In our race all the women of the royal blood are named Batwa, and I am the eldest and the wisest and the best of them, for I am older than my brother Sikonyana by twenty years, I, who have had three husbands and outlived them all; whereas the chit of whom you talk, a thing with a waist like a reed and an eye like a sick buck, is his junior by ten years, being a child of our father's last wife."

"It may be so," answered Sigwe, "for aught I know, every woman of your accursed tribe is named Batwa, but this I say, that every soon there will be few Batwas left to look upon the sun, for tomorrow I march against them and I will stamp the house of Batwa flat, and you I will hang to the roof-tree of the hut of the chief your brother; yes, I keep you alive that I may hang you there, so until then you have nothing to fear from me."

"Is it is, is it so, indeed?" shrieked the virago; "then I am safe, for, little red Kaffir, I shall live to see you and your cowards beaten out of the country of the Endwandwe with whips of hide."

"Take her away," groaned Sigwe, "before I break my word and hang her at once, which I do not wish to do," and Batwa the eldest was led off still screaming curses.

****

When she had gone, after consulting apart for a while with Sihamba, Suzanne spoke.

"Now, chief," she said, "I understand the cause of this war and in truth it is a strange one. Still, as I must lead your armies, and as I do not love to see men killed for such a quarrel, here and before we start I will lay down the terms of peace if it should please Sikonyana and the people of the Endwandwe to accept them. Subject to your wisdom they shall be these: If Sikonyana will give to you that Batwa whom you desire in the place of the Batwa whom you do not desire, paying back to you the thousand head of cattle, and by way of fine for his deceit, if indeed he meant to deceive you, for you do not seem to have told him which of the many Batwas you sought, two thousand other head of cattle, then no blood shall be shed and you and your *impi* shall return in peace and honour. If he will not do this, then the war must go as it is fated. Say, do you consent as I counsel you to do? for otherwise, although I go with you my goodwill will not go, since I am the Swallow of peace and not the Hawk of war."

Now there followed a great *indaba* or debate between Sigwe and his counsellors and captains, some of them taking one view of the matter, and some of them the other, but the end of it was that the party of peace prevailed, it being agreed between them that if the Endwandwe would grant these terms and in addition an ox for every man who might die or be killed upon the journey, the *impi* should return without putting the matter to the chance of war, and this the chief and his counsellors swore solemnly to Suzanne. Indeed Sigwe was glad to swear it, for he sought that Batwa for whom he longed rather than the dangers of battle and the risk of defeat in a far land, while those who were for fighting at all costs thought that the oath meant little, since they did not believe that the great Sikonyana would make peace upon such terms.

When this matter was settled Suzanne prayed the chief that he would allow her to send Zinti as a messenger to her husband and father to tell them that she lived and was well. But on this matter, and this only, Sigwe would not listen to her, and though he gave many

145

reasons for his refusal, the true one was that he feared lest the white men, on learning her whereabouts, should gather a commando and send it to take her from him, as doubtless we should have done had it been in any way possible.

Indeed, the foolish dream of the diviner as to the leading of his army by a white swallow, followed as it chanced to be by the arrival at his town of a woman who was named Swallow, had taken such a hold of Sigwe—who, like all savages, was very superstitious—that for nothing which could have been offered to him would he have consented to let Suzanne go until the war with the Endwandwe was finished. Rather than do so he would have fought till the last, and he issued an order that if any man, woman, or child spoke of Suzanne's presence in his town to strangers they should be put to death without mercy. Moreover, in his terror lest she should escape, he set a guard over her and Sihamba day and night and other guards over the horses and the lad Zinti, so that they soon learned that all hopes of flight must be abandoned and that it was not possible even to send a messenger or a letter.

As may be guessed this was a sore grief to Suzanne, so great a grief that when they were back in the guest-hut she wept long and bitterly, for her heart ached with her own sorrow, and she knew well how deep would be the torment of mind of Ralph if he still lived, and of us, her father and mother, when we learned that she had vanished quite away, and that none could tell what her fate had been. At first she thought of bidding Zinti slip away under cover of the night, but Sihamba showed her that even if he could do so, which was not likely, the end of it must be that he would be followed and put to death, and that then his blood would be upon their hands and no good done. Afterwards she tried to bribe and to command several men of her guard to take the message, but in this matter alone the people of Sigwe would not obey her, for they knew the doom which awaited them if they listened to her pleading. So, when she spoke, they looked into the air over her head, and did not seem to hear, although afterwards they reported her words to Sigwe, whereupon that chief doubled the guard, setting a second to watch the first.

And now I have to tell you one of the strangest things in the strange story of the love of Ralph Kenzie and my daughter Suzanne. It will be remembered that it was by means of a dream—or so the child declared—that Suzanne was led to where the boy Ralph lay alone and starving in the *kloof*. So now in this second great crisis of their lives, it was by means of a dream that comfort was brought to the hearts of both of them, enabling them, as I believe, to bear the terrors of those long years of tidingless terror and separation, that otherwise would have broken down their minds and perhaps have killed them.

It seems, as Suzanne told me in after days, that before she slept that night, there in the guest-hut of Sigwe, she prayed long and earnestly as those who have faith do pray when they lie under the shadow of an overwhelming grief. She prayed that God would bring about what she was unable to bring about, namely, that her husband should learn that she was unharmed and well, and that she might learn how it went with him, seeing that for aught she knew, by now he might be dead of his wounds. Well, that prayer was heard, for I myself can testify to it, as the prayer of faith is so often heard; yes, that which seemed to be impossible was done, for in the watches of the night these two who lay a hundred miles apart, one of them a prisoner in the town of a savage, and the other helpless upon a bed of pain, had sight and speech of each other.

Still praying, Suzanne fell asleep. Then of a sudden it seemed as though space had no bars for her, for she awoke, or thought that she awoke, in the guest-hut of Sigwe, since she could hear the breathing of Sihamba at her side, and stretching out her hand she touched her face. But in the twinkling of an eye there came a change, for, still wide awake, now she was standing in the stead at home just within the door of her own sleeping-room. There upon the bed lay her husband, fevered and unconscious, but muttering to himself, while bending over him were I, her mother, and a strange man whom she did not know, but who, as she guessed, must have been roused from his sleep, for his hair was dishevelled and he was half-clothed.

To this man she heard me—her mother—talking. "The fever runs so high, doctor," I said, "that I made bold to wake you from your rest, for I fear lest it should burn his life away." Thereupon she saw the man look at Ralph, feeling his pulse, and heard him answer as he examined the bandages of the wound, "His hurt does well, and I do not think that the fever comes from it. It comes from his mind, and it is there that the danger lies, for who can doctor a broken heart?"

"Heaven only," I replied.

"Yes," he said. "Heaven only. And now, *Vrouw* Botmar, go and rest awhile, hoping for the best, for you will hear him if he wakes up, but he will not wake, since the sleep-draught that I gave him holds him fast."

Then she saw us both go—the doctor back to his bed and me to a settle with mattress on it, which was placed just outside his door.

Here I would stop my tale to say that *this thing happened*, and that those words which Suzanne heard while her body lay in Sigwe's guest-hut, passed between the doctor, who was sleeping at the stead, and myself at one o'clock of the morning on the third night after the night of the taking of Suzanne, and moreover, that I never spoke of them to any living creature until Suzanne repeated them to me in later years. Nor could the doctor have told them to her, for he went away to the province of Graff Reinet, where shortly afterwards he was killed by a fall from his horse.

Then it seemed to Suzanne that she moved to the bedside of her husband, and bending down, kissed him upon the forehead, which was hot to her lips, saying, "Awake, dear love." Instantly, in her vision, he awoke with a cry of joy, and said, "Suzanne, how came you here?" to which she answered, "I am not here. I have escaped unharmed from Swart Piet, but I am a prisoner in the hands of red Kaffirs, and tomorrow I lead their army to the north. Yet it has been permitted me to visit you, husband, and to tell you to be of good comfort and to fear no evil tidings, for you will recover and we shall meet again, unharmed in any way, though not till many days are passed."

"Where shall we meet?" he asked. "I do not know," she answered. "Yes, I see now. Look before you."

Then they looked, both of them, and there painted in the air they saw the picture of a great mountain, standing by itself upon a plain, but with other mountains visible to the north and south of it. This mountain was flat-topped, with precipices of red rock, and down its eastern slope ran five ridges shaped like the thumb and fingers of a mighty hand, while between the thumb and the first finger, as it were, a stream gushed out, upon the banks of which grew flat-topped trees with thick green leaves and white bloom.

"You have seen and you will remember, fearing nothing," she said in her vision.

"I have seen and I shall remember, fearing nothing," Ralph answered, and with the sound of his voice still echoing in her ears, Suzanne awoke in the guest-hut of Sigwe, and once more heard Sihamba breathing at her side, and felt the hand which she had outstretched to find her, pressed against her cheek. But now there was a new sense of comfort in her heart, for she believed that without any doubt she had seen her husband, and that although they were separated, still the day would come when they should meet again, not in the spirit but in the flesh.

148

****

Now I, Suzanne Botmar, who tell this tale, had scarcely left Ralph's room upon that very night and laid myself down upon the settle when he called to me. I ran back to the bed to find him sitting up in it wide awake and calm-eyed.

"Mother," he said, for so he still named me, "did you see Suzanne?"

"Hush, Ralph," I answered, "you are talking foolishly; wherever Suzanne may be, alas! she is not here."

"She was here just now," he said, smiling, "for we have been talking together. She has escaped from Swart Piet and is unharmed, but a prisoner among the Kaffirs. And, mother, she and I will meet again upon a great mountain like a fortress, which has ridges on its eastern side resembling the thumb and fingers of a man, and a stream of water gushing out between the thumb and first finger."

"Doubtless, doubtless," I said, for I saw that he was wandering in his mind.

"Ah!" Ralph answered, "you do not believe me, but it is true. I tell you that I saw Suzanne just now wearing a fine *kaross* of tiger skins upon her shoulders, and that she kissed me on the forehead," and even as he spoke he sank into a deep and quiet sleep, and when he awoke in the morning we found that the fever had left him and that he was out of danger of his life.

CHAPTER 22

The War of the Clean Spear

When Sihamba arose next day, Suzanne asked her if the home of her people, the Umpondwana, was a great mountain faced round with slab-sided precipices and having ridges on its eastern face like to the thumb and fingers of a hand, with a stream of water gushing from between the thumb and first finger, upon the banks of which grew flat-topped trees with thick green leaves and white flowers.

Sihamba stared at her, saying:

"Such is the place indeed, and there are no trees like to those you speak of to be found anywhere else. The maidens use the flowers of them to adorn their hair, and from the leaves is made a salve that is very good for wounds. But, say, Swallow, who told you about the mountain Umpondwana that is so far away, since I never described it to you?"

"Nobody told me," she answered, and she repeated the vision to her, or as much of it as she wished.

Sihamba listened, and when the tale was done she nodded her little head, saying:

"So even you white people have something of the power which has been given to us Kaffir witch-doctors from the beginning. Without a doubt your spirit spoke to the spirit of your husband last night and I am glad of it, for now, although you are apart from each other, the hearts of both of you will be rested. Now also I am sure that we must go to my people and live among them for so long as may be appointed, seeing that there and nowhere else you and the Baas Kenzie will come together again."

"I had sooner go back to the stead," sighed Suzanne.

"That cannot be, Swallow, for it is not fated, and for the rest, if you meet, what does it matter where you meet?"

****

That morning Suzanne, mounted upon the great *schimmel*, which by now had almost recovered from his weariness, although he was still somewhat stiff, and followed by Sihamba and Zinti riding the horse and the mule, passed up and down before Sigwe's regiments that saluted her as chieftainess. Then amongst much wailing of women and children, the *impi* started northward, Suzanne, preceded only by scouts and a guard to feel the way, riding in front of it that she might escape the dust raised by so many feet and the hoofs of the great herd of oxen that were driven along to serve as food for the soldiers.

For fourteen days' journey they travelled thus, and during that time nothing of note happened to them, except that twelve men and Sihamba's brown mule were lost in crossing a flooded river, whereof there were many in their path. The country through which they passed was populated by Kaffirs, but these tribes were too small and scattered to attempt to oppose so large an army, nor did the men of Sigwe do them any mischief beyond taking such grain and meal as they required for food.

On the fourteenth day, however, they reached the boundary of the territories of a very powerful tribe of Pondo blood, and here they halted while messengers were sent forward to the Pondo chief, saying that with him Sigwe had no quarrel, and asking for a safe-conduct for the army while passing through his lands. On the third day these messengers returned, accompanied by an embassy from the Pondo chief, that after much talk, though to all appearance unwillingly, gave Sigwe the promise of safe-conduct upon condition that he made a present of ceremony of one ox to their ruler. Now Sihamba noticed that while the envoys were talking, their eyes wandered all about, taking note of every thing, and especially of the number of the soldiers and of Suzanne, who sat beside Sigwe during the *indaba*, or council.

"These are no true men," she thought to herself, and made a plan. In the evening she visited the camp of the envoys who had heard already that she was a famous doctoress, and offered her services to them for payment should any of them chance to need the boon of her magic arts. They laughed, answering that they wanted neither charms nor divinations, but that she should see a certain young man, a servant in their train, who was very sick with love and had bought philtres from every doctor in their country without avail, wherewith to soften the heart of a girl who would have nothing to do with him. When Sihamba, without seeming to speak much of it, had drawn from them all that she wished to know of the story of this man and girl, and with it other information, though they won little enough from her, she took her leave, and so set her trap that at night when all were asleep the young man came to consult her in a place apart.

Now she looked at him and said at once, without suffering him to speak:

"Let me see. Your name is so-and-so, and you are in love with such a girl, who turns away from you;" and she went on to tell him things which he thought were known only to himself.

"Wonderful," he said, "wonderful! But say, lady doctoress, can you help me, for my heart is water because of this girl?"

"It is difficult," she answered. "Do you know that when you come to consult a wise woman you should keep your mind fixed upon the matter about which you would take counsel with her from the first moment that you set out to visit her until you stand in her presence? Now this you have not done, for as you came you were thinking of other things; yes, you were thinking about the ambush which is to be set for these people in the pass yonder, and therefore I cannot see the girl's heart clear, and do not quite know what medicine I should give you to soften it."

"It is true, lady," answered the stupid fellow, "that I was thinking about the ambush of which I have heard some talk, though I do not know who told you of it."

"Who told me? Why to my sight your thoughts are written on your face, yes, they ran before you and reached me as I heard your footsteps. But now, think no more of that matter, which has nothing to do with you or me, think only of the girl, and go on thinking of her, and of her only, until you get back home, and give her the medicine—that is if you wish it to work."

"I am thinking, lady," he muttered, turning his stupid face up to the skies.

"Fool, be quiet. Do I not know that? Ah! now I see her heart, and I tell you that you are lucky, for when you have done as I bid you, she will love you more than if you were the greatest chief in all the land." Then Sihamba gave him a certain harmless powder to sprinkle in the hut where the girl slept, and bade him wait for her on six different days when she came up from bathing, giving her on each day a garland of fresh flowers, a new flower for every day.

The man thanked her and asked what he must pay her for a fee, to which she replied that she took no fee in matters of love, since her reward was to know that she had made two people happy; but she added:

"Remember what I tell you, or instead of earning love you will earn hate. Say nothing of your visit to me, and if you can avoid it, do not speak at all until you have sprinkled the powder in the hut; especially put all things which do not concern you and her out of your mind and think only of her face and how happy you will be when you have married her, which, if you follow my instructions, you will shortly do."

Now the young man went away as though he were walking upon air, and indeed so closely did he obey her that he was dismissed by his masters as a dumb fool before he reached home again. But whether or no Sihamba's medicine softened the heart of the maid I have not heard.

****

So soon as he was gone Sihamba sent Zinti to bring Sigwe and two of his generals to the place where she and Suzanne were encamped in a booth made of branches and long grass. When they were come, she told them of what she had learned from the love-stricken lad, adding that this plan of making sure of what already she had suspected, had been born in the brain of the Swallow, although she had carried it out. For when she deemed that she could serve her mistress or win her honour, Sihamba thought less of the truth than she should have done.

On learning this tidings Sigwe and his captains were full of wrath, and spoke of making war upon the Pondo chief at once, but Sihamba said:

"Listen; the Swallow has whispered a better way into my ear. It is this: the embassy of the Pondos leaves at dawn, and you must bid them farewell, telling them that you will follow and camp tomorrow night at the mouth of the pass, which you will enter at the next daybreak. Meanwhile now at once we will send out my servant, Zinti, dressed like a Pondo lad, to search the country, and find if there is not another path by which the pass can be turned, for if such a way exists he will discover it and report to us tomorrow at nightfall, since he, who is stupid in many things, was born with the gift of seeking out roads and remembering them; also he knows how to be silent if questioned."

The chief and his captains thought this plan good, and thanked the Swallow for it, praising her wisdom, and within an hour, having been instructed what he must do and where he should meet them, Zinti was despatched upon his errand.

Next morning the envoys departed suspecting nothing, and taking with them gifts and the ox of ceremony; and that night the army of Sigwe encamped within a mile of the pass, to the right and left of which stretched tall and difficult cliffs.

About an hour after sunset Zinti crept into the camp and asked for food to eat, for he had travelled far and was hungry; moreover, he had been chased by some Pondo soldiers to whom, feigning the fool he was commonly supposed to be, he would make no answer when they questioned him. When he had eaten he made his report to Sigwe, Suzanne, and Sihamba, and the gist of it was that he had found a good road by which men might safely ascend the cliffs, though not so easily as they could travel through the gorge. Following this road, he added, they could pass round the Pondo town, avoiding its fortifications, and coming out at the cattle kraals at the back of the town, for he had climbed a high tree and mapped out the route with his eye. Then followed a council of war, and the upshot of it was that, under the leadership of Zinti, the army marched off in silence an hour before midnight, leaving its cooking fires burning to deceive the Pondos.

They climbed the cliffs by the path he showed them, and, travelling all night, at dawn found themselves before the cattle kraals, which, as no enemy was expected, were unguarded except by the herds. These they cleared of the cattle, some thousands of them, and marched on at speed, sending a message back to the town by the herds that this was the luck which those must expect who attempted to trap the Swallow in a snare set for a rock-rabbit.

The Pondos were very angry at their loss, and, gathering their strength, followed them for some days, but before they could come up with them Sigwe and his army had reached country so difficult and so far away that the Pondo chief thought it wisest to leave them alone. So they marched on, taking the captured cattle with them, and after this bloodless victory Suzanne and Sihamba were greatly honoured by the soldiers, and even the lad Zinti was treated like a chief.

Now once more they reached wild lands, inhabited only by scattered tribes, and passed through them at their leisure, for they had plenty of food to eat, although from time to time they were obliged to encamp upon the banks of flooded rivers, or to hunt for a road over a mountain. It was on the thirty-first day of their journey that at length they entered the territories of the Endwandwe, against whom they had come to make war, where at once they were met by messengers sent by Sikonyana, the chief of the Endwandwe, desiring to know why they came upon him with so great a force. To these men the case was set out by Sigwe, speaking in his own name and in that of the Swallow. As he had promised Suzanne, for this was a savage who kept his word, he offered to refrain from attack if the young Batwa was exchanged for her one-eyed sister and sent to him, together with the thousand head of cattle which he had paid, and two thousand more by way of fine. At first these terms were refused, but afterwards an embassy came of whom the captain was the brother of the king, who said that he was charged to discuss the matter with the white chieftainess named Swallow, herself, and with none other.

So Suzanne, accompanied only by Sihamba, and mounted upon the great *schimmel* that had come safe and well through all the journey, though the black horse had died of sickness, rode out a hundred paces in front of the army and met the man. There she spoke to him well and wisely, pointing out to him that without doubt a trick had been played upon Sigwe which he was mad to avenge. The captain answered that they were well able to fight. She replied that this might be so, that they might even conquer Sigwe and drive him back, but it could not be done without great loss to themselves, and that if his tribe were at all weakened the Zulus, who hated them, would hear of it, and take the opportunity to stamp them out.

Well, the end of it was that the Endwandwe yielded, and upon the promise of Suzanne—for they would take no other—that no spear should be lifted against them, they sent the true Batwa, a beautiful but sullen girl, to Sigwe, taking back the old Batwa, who departed cursing him and all his race. With her they returned also the thousand head of cattle which he had paid and twelve hundred more by way of fine, for the balance was remitted by agreement.

****

And so came to an end the war of Sigwe with the Endwandwe, which among the Kaffirs is still spoken of as the "War of the White Swallow," or sometimes as "The War of the Clean Spear," because no blood at all was shed in it, and not a man was killed by violence, although when Sigwe passed through that country on his journey home, by means of a clever trick the Pondo chief re-captured most of the cattle that had been taken from him.

CHAPTER 23

How Suzanne Became a Chieftainess

So the cattle were handed over, and the girl Batwa was given to Sigwe, whom by the way she made unhappy for the rest of his days. Indeed, she brought about his ruin, for being ambitious she persuaded him to make war upon the white people in the Transkei, of which the end was that from a great chief he became a very small one. When all was accomplished Sigwe waited upon Suzanne.

"Lady Swallow," he said, "in three days I begin my homeward march, and now I have come to ask whither you wish to go, since you cannot stop here in the *veldt* alone."

"I would return with you to the Transkei," she answered, "and seek out my own home."

"Lady," he said shamefacedly, "alas! that may not be. You remember the dream of the diviner, and you know how that all which she foretold, and more, has come to pass, for you, the White Swallow, appeared and flew in front of my *impi*, and from that hour we have had the best of luck. By your wisdom we outwitted the Pondos and seized their cattle; by your wisdom we have conquered the Endwandwe without lifting a single spear, and that Batwa, whom I desired, is mine; while of the great force which came out with me to war but twenty-one are dead, twelve by drowning, eight by sickness, and one by snakebite. All things have gone well, and she who dreamed the dream of the White Swallow is the greatest of diviners.

"But, lady, this was not all the dream, for it said that if you, the Swallow, should set your face southward with us then the best of luck would turn to the worst, for then utter misfortune should overwhelm me and my regiments. Now, lady, I cannot doubt that as the first part of the prophecy has come true, so the last part would come true also did I tempt the spirits of my ancestors by disregarding it, and, therefore, White Swallow, though all I have is yours, yet you cannot fly home with us."

Now Suzanne pleaded with him long and earnestly, as did Sihamba, but without avail, for he could not be moved. Indeed, had he consented the captains and the army would have disobeyed his order in this matter, for they believed, every man of them, that to take the Swallow with them homewards would be to run to their own deaths. Nor was it safe that she should attempt to follow in the path of the *impi*, since then in their superstitious fear they might send back and kill her to avert the evil fate.

"Now, Swallow," said Sihamba, "there is but one thing for us to do, and it is to seek refuge among my people, the Umpondwana, whose mountain stronghold lies at a distance of four days' journey from this place. But to speak truth, I am not sure how they will receive me, seeing that I parted from them in anger twelve years ago, having quarrelled with them, first about a matter of policy, and secondly about a matter of marriage, and that my half-brother, the son of my father by a slave, was promoted to rule in my place. Still to them we must go, and with them we must stay, if they will suffer it, until we find an opportunity of travelling south in safety."

"If it must be so," answered Suzanne, sighing, "perhaps Sigwe will escort us to the house of the Umpondwana before he turns homewards, for they will think the more of us if they see us at the head of a great army."

To this plan Sigwe and his captains assented with gladness, for they loved and honoured the Swallow, and were sore at heart because their fears forced them to leave her alone in the wilderness. But first they made sure that the mountain Umpondwana lay to the west, and not to the south, for not one step to the southward would they allow Suzanne to travel with them.

On the morrow, then, they marched, and the evening of the third day they set their camp in a mountain pass which led to a wide plain. Before sunrise next morning Sihamba woke Suzanne.

"Dress yourself, Swallow," she said, "and come to see the light break on the house of my people."

So they went out in the grey dawn, and climbing a *koppie* in the mouth of the pass, looked before them. At first they could distinguish nothing, for all the plain beneath was a sea of mist through which in the distance loomed something like a mountain, till presently the rays of the rising sun struck upon it and the veils of vapour parted like curtains that are drawn back, and there before them was the mountain-fortress of Umpondwana separated from the pass by a great space of mist-clad plain. Suzanne looked and knew it.

"Sihamba," she said, "it is the place of my vision and none other. See, the straight sides of red rock, the five ridges upon the eastern slope fashioned like the thumb and fingers of the hand of a man. Yes, and there between the thumb and first finger a river runs."

"I told you that it was so from the beginning, Swallow, for in all the country there is no other such hill as this, and because of the aspect of those ridges when seen from a distance it is named the Mountain of the Great Hand."

Before the words had left her lips another voice spoke, at the sound of which Suzanne nearly fell to the earth.

"Good day to you, Suzanne," it said in Dutch and was silent.

"Sihamba, did you hear, Sihamba?" she gasped. "Do I dream, or did Piet Van Vooren speak to me?"

"You did not dream," answered Sihamba, "for that voice was the voice of Swart Piet and no other, and he is hidden somewhere among the rocks of yonder cliff wall. Quick, Swallow, kneel behind this stone lest he should shoot."

She obeyed, and at that moment the voice spoke again out of the shadows of the cliff that bordered the pass twenty or thirty paces from them.

"What, Suzanne," it said, "is that little witch-doctoress telling you that I shall fire on you? Had I wished I could have shot you three times over while you were standing upon that rock. But why should I desire to kill one who will be my lover? Sihamba I wished to shoot indeed, but her familiar set her so that the bullet must pass through you to reach her heart. Suzanne, you are going to hide yourself among the people of the Umpondwana. Oh! yes, I know your plan. Well, when once you are behind the walls of that mountain it may be difficult to speak to you for a while, so listen to me. You thought that you had left me far away, did you not? but I have followed you step by step and twice I have been very near to you, although I could never find a chance to carry you off safely. Well, I wish to tell you that sooner or later I shall find that chance; sooner or later you will come out of the mountain or I shall get into it, and then it will be my turn; so, love, till that hour fare you well. Stay, I forgot, I have news for you; your husband, the English castaway, is dead."

At this tidings a low moan of pain broke from Suzanne's lips.

"Be silent and take no heed," whispered Sihamba, who was kneeling at her side behind the shelter of the stone, "he does but lie to torment you."

"The bullet and the water together were too much for him," went on Swart Piet, "and he died on the second night after he reached the stead. Your father came to seek me in the place you know, and was carried home badly wounded for his pains, but whether he lived or died I cannot tell you, but I heard that your mother, the good *Vrouw* Botmar, is very sick, for things have so fallen out lately that her mind is troubled, and she flies to drink to comfort it."

Now when she heard this, Sihamba could keep silence no longer, but cried in a mocking voice:

"Get you gone, Bull-Head, and take lessons in lying from your friends of my trade, the Kaffir witch-doctors, for never before did I hear a man bear false witness so clumsily. On the third night of his illness the husband of Swallow was alive and doing well; the *Heer* Jan Botmar was not wounded at all, and as for the *Vrouw* Botmar, never in her life did she drink anything stronger than coffee, for the white man's firewater is poison to her. Get you gone, you silly half-breed, who seek to deceive the ears of Sihamba, and I counsel you, hold fast to your business of theft and murder and give up that of lying, in which you will never succeed. Now be off, you stink-cat of the rocks, lest I send some to hunt you from your hole who this time will use the points and not the shafts of their *assegais*. Come, Swallow, let us be going."

So they went, keeping under cover all the way to the camp, which, indeed, was quite close to them, and if Swart Piet made any answer they did not hear it. So soon as they reached it Sihamba told Sigwe what had passed and he sent men to scour the cliff and the bush behind it, but of Van Vooren they could find no trace, no, not even the spot where he had been hidden, so that Sigwe came to believe that they had been fooled by echoes and had never heard him at all.

But both Suzanne and Sihamba knew that this was not so; indeed, this hearing of the voice of Swart Piet filled Suzanne with fear, since where the voice was, there was the man, her hateful enemy, who had given his life to her ruin and to that of those she loved. Whatever lies he might have spoken—and her heart told her that all his ill tidings were but a cruel falsehood—this at least was true, that he had dogged her step by step through the vast wilderness, and so craftily that none guessed his presence. What might not be feared from such a foe as this, half mad and all wicked, armed with terrible cunning and untiring patience? If the Umpondwana would not receive her she must fall into his hands at once, and if they did receive her she would never dare to leave their *kraal*, for always, always he would be watching and waiting for her. Little wonder then that she felt afraid, though, just as the sun shines ever behind the blackest cloud, still in her heart shone the sure comfort of her hope, and more than hope that in the end God would give her back her husband and her to him unharmed. Yet, which ever way she looked the cloud was very black, and through it she could see no ray of light.

****

When the mists had vanished and the air was warm with the sun, the army of Sigwe marched from the pass heading for the great mountain. As they drew near they saw that the Umpondwana were much terrified at the sight of them, for from all the kraals, of which there were many on the slopes of the mountain, they ran hither and thither like ants about a broken nest, carrying their goods and children upon their shoulders, and driving herds of cattle in towards the central stronghold. Noting this, Sigwe halted and sent heralds forward to say that he came in peace and not in war, and he desired to speak with their chief. In less than two hours the heralds returned, bringing with them some of the headmen of the Umpondwana, who stared round with frightened eyes, for they did not believe that any general would come upon a message of peace with so many regiments. When the *indaba* was set Sigwe told them his name and tribe, of both of which they had heard, and then, before speaking of his business, asked which of them was the chief of the Umpondwana.

"Alas!" answered an old man, "we are in sore trouble here, and wander in the darkness, for our chief, who was named Koraanu, died two days ago of the small-pox which has raged among us for many months, leaving no children behind him, for the sickness killed them also. Moreover, we are suffering from a great drought, for as you may see, the *veldt* is still brown, and there is no green upon the cornfields, and if rain does not fall soon famine will follow the sickness, and then it will only need that the Zulus should follow the famine to make an end of us once and for all."

"It seems that your tribe must have sinned deeply and brought down upon itself the curse of the spirits of its ancestors," said Sigwe, when they had done their melancholy tale, "that so many misfortunes should overtake you. Tell me now, who by right is ruler of the Umpondwana?"

"We do not know, chief," they answered, "or rather, we cannot tell if our ruler is alive or dead, and if she is dead then none are left of the true blood. She was a small woman, but very pretty and full of wisdom as a *mealie*-cob with grains of corn, for in all this country

160

there was no doctoress or diviner like to her. Her name was Sihamba Ngenyanga, the Wanderer-by-Moonlight, which name was given her when she was little, because of her habit of walking in the dark alone, and she was the only child of our late chief's *inkosikaas*, a princess of the Swazis, the father of that lord, Koraanu, who lies dead of the small-pox. But when this chief died and Sihamba was called upon to rule our tribe, quarrels arose between her and the *indunas* of the tribe, for she was a very headstrong woman.

"We, the *indunas*, wished her to marry, but for her own reasons she would not marry; also we wished to swear allegiance to Chaka, but she was against it, saying that as well might a lamb swear allegiance to a wolf as the Umpondwana to the Zulus. The end of it was that in a temper she took a bowl of water, and before us all washed her hands of us, and that same night she vanished away we know not where, though rumours have reached us that she went south. From the day of her departure, however, things have gone ill with us; the Zulus with whom we made peace threaten us continually; her half-brother, Koraanu, the slave-born, was not a good chief, and now he is dead of the sickness. So our heart is heavy and our head is in the dust, and when we saw your *impi* we thought that Dingaan, who now rules over the Zulus, had sent it to eat us up and to take the cattle that still remain to us.

"But you say that you come in peace, so tell us, chief, what it is you desire, and I trust that it may be little, for here we have nothing to give, unless," he added with meaning, "it be the small-pox, although we are ready to fight to the death for what is left to us, our liberty and our cattle; and, chief, even a larger army than yours might fail to take that stronghold which has but one gate."

When the councillor had finished speaking, Sigwe called aloud:

"Lady Sihamba, I pray you come hither, and with you the lady Swallow, your companion."

Then Sihamba, who was prepared for this event, for her hair was freshly dressed and powdered with blue mica, wearing her little cape of fur and the necklace of large blue beads, stepped from the screen of bush behind which she had hidden. With her, and holding her hand, came Suzanne, who covered the raggedness of her clothes beneath a splendid *kaross* of leopards' skins that Sigwe had given her, down which her dark hair flowed almost to her knee. A strange pair they made, the tall Suzanne in the first bloom of her white beauty which had suffered nothing in their journeying, and the small, quick-eyed, delicate-featured Kaffir woman.

"Who are these?" asked Sigwe of the council.

The old man looked at them and answered:

"Of the white lady we can say nothing except that she is very beautiful; but, unless our eyes deceive us, she whom she holds by the hand is Sihamba Ngenyanga, who was our chieftainess, and who left us because she was angry."

"She is Sihamba and no one else," said Sigwe. "Sihamba come back to rule you in the hour of need, and with her own tongue she shall tell you her story and the story of the White Swallow who holds her by the hand."

So Sihamba began, and for an hour or more she spoke to them, for when she chose this little woman had the gift of words, telling them all about herself, and telling them also the story of the Swallow, and of how she had brought good luck to the army of Sigwe, and how she was destined to bring good luck wherever she made her home. At the end of her speech she said:

"Now, my people, although I have wandered from you, yet my eyes, which are far-seeing, have not been blind to your griefs, and in the hour of your need I return to you, bringing with me the White Swallow to sojourn among you for a while. Receive us if you will and be prosperous, or reject us and be destroyed; to us it matters nothing, it is for you to choose. But if we come, we come not as servants but as princes whose word cannot be questioned, and should you accept us and deal ill with us in any way, then your fate is sure. Ask the chief Sigwe here whether or no the flight of the Swallow is fortunate, and whether or no there is wisdom in the mouth of Sihamba, who is not ashamed to serve her."

Then Sigwe told them of all the good fortune that had come to him through Suzanne, and of how wise had been the words of Sihamba, and told them, moreover, that if they dealt ill by either of them he would return from his own country and stamp them flat.

****

Thus it came about that the *indunas* of the Umpondwana took back Sihamba to be their chieftainess with all powers, and with her Suzanne as her equal in rule, and this their act was confirmed that same day by a great council of the tribe. So that evening Suzanne, mounted on the *schimmel*, rode down the ranks of the Red Kaffirs, while they shouted their farewells to her. Then having parted with Sigwe, who almost wept at her going, she passed with Sihamba, the lad Zinti, and a great herd of cattle—her tithe of the spoil—to the mountain Umpondwana, where all the tribe were waiting to receive them. They rode up to the flanks of the mountain, and through the narrow pass and the red wall of rock to the tableland upon its top, where stood the chief's huts and the cattle-*kraal*, and here they found the people gathered.

"Give us a blessing," these cried. "Grant to us that rain may fall."

Sihamba spoke with Suzanne and answered:

"My people, I have entreated of the White Swallow, and for your sake she will pray that rain may fall ere long."

Now Sihamba knew the signs of the water, and as it happened rain began to fall that night in torrents, and fell for three days almost without ceasing, washing the sickness away with it. So the Umpondwana blessed the name of Sihamba and the White Swallow, and these two ruled over them without question, life and death hanging upon their words.

And there, a chieftainess among savages, Suzanne was fated to dwell for more than two long years.

CHAPTER 24

The Madness of Ralph Kenzie

Now my story goes back to that night at the stead when I, Suzanne Botmar and my husband, Jan Botmar, were awakened from our sleep to learn that our daughter had been carried off by that mad villain, Piet Van Vooren, and that her husband Ralph lay senseless and wounded in the wagon at the door. We carried him in, groaning in our bitter grief, and despatched messengers to arouse all the Kaffirs on and about the place whom we could trust and to a party of Boers, six men in all, who chanced to have outspanned that night upon the borders of our farm to shoot vildebeest and blesbok. Also we sent another messenger mounted on a good horse to the house of that neighbour who was being attended by the doctor from the *dorp*, praying that he would come with all speed to visit Ralph, which indeed he did, for he was with us by half-past eight in the morning.

Within an hour of the despatch of the messengers the Boers rode up from their wagons, and to them, as well as to ourselves and to the Kaffirs who had gathered, the driver and *voorlooper* told all they knew of the terrible crime that had been done upon the persons of Ralph Kenzie and his wife by Piet Van Vooren and his band. Also they repeated all that Zinti had taught them of the road to the secret *krantz* whither it was believed that he had carried off Suzanne. Then Jan asked those present if they would help him in this trouble, and being true men, one and all, they answered yes, so by seven in the morning the little commando, numbering twenty-one guns—eight white men and thirteen Kaffirs—started to seek for Swart Piet's hiding-place, and to rescue Suzanne if they might.

"Alas!" I said to Jan as he bade me farewell, "at the best I fear that you will be too late."

"We must trust in God," he answered heavily.

"Never had we more need of trust, husband, but I think that God turns His face from us because of the lies we told to the Englishmen, for now the punishment which you foresaw has fallen."

"Then, wife, it were more just that it should have fallen on us who were guilty, and not on those two who are innocent. But still I say I trust in God—and in Sihamba"—he added by an afterthought, "for she is brave and clever, and can run upon a path which others cannot even see."

Then they went, and were away five days, or it may have been six. They started early on Tuesday, and upon the Thursday morning, after much trouble, by the help of a native whom they captured, they found Swart Piet's *kraal*, but of Swart Piet or Suzanne or the hidden *krantz* they could see nothing. Indeed, it was not until they had gathered together every man they could find in the *kraal* and tied them to trees, saying that they would shoot them, that a woman, the wife of one of the men, led them to a rock wall and showed the secret of the *kloof*. They entered and found the big hut with the body of the man whom Sihamba had killed still lying in it, and also the knife with which Suzanne had intended to destroy herself, and which her father knew again.

Then by degrees they discovered the whole story, for the woman pointed out to them the man who had guarded the entrance to the *kloof*, at whom Zinti had fired, and under fear of death this man confessed all he knew, which was that Suzanne, Sihamba and Zinti had escaped northward upon their horses, followed by Swart Piet and his band.

Accordingly northwards they rode, but they never found any traces of them, for rain had fallen, washing out their spoor, and as might be expected in that vast *veldt* they headed in the wrong direction. So at last worn out, they returned to the stead, hoping that Suzanne and Sihamba would have found their way back there, but hoping in vain.

After that for days and weeks they searched and hunted, but quite without result, for as it chanced the Kaffirs who lived between the territory of Sigwe and the stead rose in arms just then, and began to raid the Boer farms, stealing the cattle, including some of our own, so that it was impossible to travel in their country, and therefore nobody ever reached the town of Sigwe to make inquiries there.

The end of it was that, exhausted by search and sorrow, Jan sat down at home and abandoned hope; nor could the prayers and urgings of Ralph, who all this while was unable even to mount a horse, persuade him to go out again upon so fruitless an errand.

"No, son," he answered, "long before this the girl is either dead or she is safe far away, and in either event it is useless to look for her about here, since Van Vooren's *kraal* is watched, and we know that she is not in it." To which Ralph would answer:

"She is not dead, I know that she is not dead," and we understood that he spoke of the vision which had come to him, for I had told the tale of it to Jan. But in his heart Jan put no faith in the vision, and believed that Suzanne, our beloved child, had been dead for many days, for he was certain that she would die rather than fall again into the hands of Van Vooren, as I was also, and indeed of this we were glad to be sure.

To Ralph, however, that we might comfort him in his sorrow, which was even more terrible than our own, we made pretence that we believed Suzanne to be hiding far away, but unable to communicate with us, as in fact she was.

Oh! our lives were sad during those bitter months. Yes, the light had gone out of our lives, and often we wished, the three of us, that already we were resting in the grave. As he recovered from his wounds and the strength of his body came back to him, a kind of gentle madness took hold of Ralph which it wrung our hearts to see. For hours, sometimes for days indeed, he would sit about the place brooding and saying no word. At other times he would mount his horse and ride away none knew whither, perhaps not to return that night or the next, or the next, till we were terrified by the thought that he too might never come back again. It was useless to be angry with him, for he would only answer with a little smile:

"You forget; I must be seeking my wife, who is waiting for me upon the Mountain of the Hand," and then we learned that he had ridden to a far off hill to examine it, or to see some travellers or natives and ask of them if they knew or had heard of such a mountain, with ridges upon its eastern slopes fashioned like the thumb and fingers of a man's hand. Indeed, in all that countryside, among both Boers and natives, Ralph won the by-name of the "Man of the Mountain" because he rarely spoke of aught else. But still folk, black and white, knew the reason of his madness and bore with him, pitying his grief.

It was, I remember, in the season after Suzanne had vanished that the Kaffirs became so angry and dangerous. For my part I believe that those in our neighbourhood were stirred up by the emissaries of Swart Piet, for though he had gone none knew where, his tools and agents remained behind him. However this may have been, all over the country the black men began to raid the stock, and in our case they ended by attacking the stead also, a great number of them armed with guns. Fortunately we had a little warning, and they were very sad Kaffirs that went away next day; moreover, forty of them never went away at all. Just at dawn, when they had been besieging the house for some hours, shouting, banging off their guns, and trying to fire the roof by means of *assegais* with tufts of blazing grass tied on to them, Jan, Ralph, and about twenty of our people crept down under cover of the orchard wall and sallied out upon them.

Almighty! how those men fought, especially Jan and Ralph. It was a pleasure to see them, for I watched the whole thing from the *stoep*, though I admit that I was anxious, since it was evident that neither of them seemed to care whether he lived or died. However, as it turned out, it was not they who died, but the Kaffirs, who went off with some few cattle and afterwards left us in peace.

And now comes the strange part of the affair, though I scarcely like to tell it, lest after all these years it should not be believed. Someone connected with the London Missionary Society reported us to the Government at the Cape for shooting poor, innocent black men, and it was threatened that Jan and Ralph would be put upon their trial for murder by the British Government. Indeed, I believe that this would have been done had not we and others of our neighbourhood let it be clearly known that before they were dragged to the common gaol there would be killing not only of black but of white men.

Our case was only one of many, since in those times there was no security for us Boers—we were robbed, we were slandered, we were deserted. Our goods were taken and we were not compensated; the Kaffirs stole our herds, and if we resisted them we were tried as murderers; our slaves were freed, and we were cheated of their value, and the word of a black man was accepted before our solemn oath upon the Bible.

No wonder that we grew tired of it and trekked, seeking to shake the dust of British rule from off our feet, and to find a new home for ourselves out of the reach of the hand of the accursed British Government. Oh! I know that there are two sides to the story, and I daresay that the British Government meant well, but at the least it was a fool, and it always will be a fool with its Secretaries of State, who know nothing sitting far away there in London, and its Governors, whose only business is to please the Secretaries of State, that when the country they are sent to rule grows sick of them, they may win another post with larger pay.

Well, this tale is of people and not of politics, so I will say no more of the causes that brought about the great trek of the Boers from the old Colony and sent them forth into the wilderness, there to make war with the savage man and found new countries for themselves. I know those causes, for Jan and Ralph and I were of the number of the *voortrekkers*; still, had it not been for the loss of Suzanne, I do not think that we should have trekked, for we loved the home we had made upon the face of the wild *veldt*.

But now that she was gone it was no home for us; every room of the house, every tree in the garden, every ox and horse and sheep reminded us of her. Yes, even the distant roar of the ocean and the sighing of the winds among the grasses seemed to speak of her. These were the flowers she loved, that was the stone she sat on, yonder was the path which day by day she trod. The very air was thick with memories of her, and the tones of her lost voice seemed to linger in the echoes of the hills at night.

It was upon the anniversary of the marriage of Ralph and Suzanne, yes, on the very day year of her taking by Piet Van Vooren, that we made up our minds to go. We had dined and Ralph sat quite silent, his head bowed a little upon his breast, as was his custom, while Jan spoke loudly of the wrongs of the Boers at the hand of the British Government. I do not think that he was much troubled with those wrongs just then, but he talked because he wished to interest Ralph and turn his mind from sad thoughts.

"What think you of it, son?" said Jan at length, for it is hard work talking all by oneself, even when one has the British Government to abuse, which was the only subject that made Jan a wordy man.

"I, father?" answered Ralph with a start, which showed me that his mind was far away. "I do not quite know what I think. I should like to hear what the English Government say about the matter, for I think that they mean to be fair, only they do not understand the wants and troubles of us Boers who live so far away. Also, without doubt the missionaries mean well, but they believe that a black man has a bigger soul than a white man, whereas we who know the black man see that there is a difference."

"*Allemachter*, son," said Jan, looking at him out of the corner of his eye, "cannot you show some spirit? I hoped that being an Englishman you would have stood up for your own people, and then we might have quarrelled about it, which would have done us both good, but you only sit and talk like a magistrate in his chair, looking at both sides of the case at once, which is an evil habit for men who have to make their way in the world. Well, I tell you that if you had seen the cursed British Government hang your father and uncle at Slagter's Nek, and not satisfied with that, hang them a second time, when the ropes broke, just because they tried to shoot a few Hottentot policemen, you would not think much of its fairness. And as for the missionaries of the London Society, well, I should like to hang *them*, as would be right and proper, seeing that they blacken the names of honest Boers."

Ralph only smiled at this onslaught, for he was not to be stirred from his lethargy by talk about Slagter's Nek and the missionaries. For a while there was silence, which presently was broken by Jan roaring at me in a loud voice as though I were deaf.

"*Vrouw*, let *ons* trek," and, to give weight to his words, he brought his great fist down with a bang upon the table, knocking off a plate and breaking it.

I stooped to pick up the pieces, rating him for his carelessness as I gathered them, for I wished to have time to think, although for a long while I had expected this. When I had found them all I placed them upon the table, saying:

"They cannot be mended, and—hearts or plates—what cannot be mended had best be hidden away. Hearts and plates are brittle things, but the last can be bought in iron, as I wish the first could be also. Yes, husband, we will trek if you desire it."

"What say you, son?" asked Jan.

Ralph answered his question by another. "In which direction will the emigrants trek?"

"North, I believe, to the Vaal River."

"Then, father, I say let us go," he replied with more spirit than he had shown for a long while, "for I have searched and inquired to the south and the east and the west, and in them I can hear of no mountain that has ridges upon its eastern slopes shaped like the thumb and fingers of a man's hand with a stream of water issuing from between the thumb and first finger."

Now once more we were silent, for we saw that his madness had again taken hold of Ralph's mind, and that was a sad silence.

CHAPTER 25

The Great Trek

On the morrow we began to make ready, and a month later we trekked from our much loved home. Jan tried to sell the farm, which was a very good one of over six thousand *morgen*, or twelve thousand English acres, well watered, and having on it a dwelling house built of stone, with large kraals and out-buildings, an orchard of fruit-trees, and twenty *morgen* of crop lands that could be irrigated in the dry season, well fenced in with walls built of loose stones. But no one would make a bid for it, for there were few English about, and most of the farmers were trekking, so at last he parted with it to a cowardly fellow, a Boer by birth, but, as I believe, a spy of the British Government, who gave him fifty pounds and an old wagon in exchange for the place and everything upon it except the stock which we took with us.

Some years ago I heard that this man's grandson sold that same farm for twenty thousand pounds in cash, and that now it is a place where they breed horses, angora goats, and ostriches in great numbers. It makes me mad to think that the descendant of that low spy should have profited so largely out of the land which was ours, but so it often chances that those whose hearts are small and mean reap the reward of the courage and misfortunes of braver men. Nor should we grumble indeed, seeing that the Lord has blessed us greatly in land and goods.

Ah! It was a sad home leaving. The day before we trekked Ralph rode to visit his mother's grave for the last time, and then, following the track which he had taken as a child, he went to the *kloof* where Suzanne had found him, and sat down upon that stone on which as a child he had knelt in prayer, and where in after years he and his lost wife had told their love. Jan accompanied him upon this dismal journey, for to speak truth we did not like to leave him more alone than we could help, since his manner remained strange, and when he set out on his solitary rides we could not be certain that we should ever see him come back again.

Next morning we trekked away, and my eyes were so full of tears as I sat beneath the tent of the first wagon that the familiar landscape and the home where I lived for twenty years and more were blotted from my sight. But I could still hear the long-nosed spy who had bought the farm, and who as waiting to enter into possession, talking to Jan.

"Good-bye, *Heer* Botmar," he said, "and good fortune to you upon your journey. For my part I cannot understand you emigrants. The English Government is an accursed Government, no doubt; still I would not sell a farm and a house like this for fifty pounds and an old wagon in order to wander in the wilderness to escape from it, there to be eaten by lions or murdered by Kaffirs. Still, good-bye, and good luck to you, and I hope that you are as content with your bargain as I am with mine."

"The Lord will be our guide, as He was to the Israelites of old," answered Jan in a somewhat troubled voice.

"Yes, yes; they all say that, *Heer* Botmar, and I trust that they are right, for you will need nothing less than a cloud by day and a pillar of fire in the darkness to protect you from all the dangers in your path. Also I hope that the hosts of Pharaoh, in the shape of English soldiers, will not fetch you back before you cross the border, for then, when you have sold your birthright in Egypt, and are cut off from the Promised Land, your lot will be hard, *Heer* Botmar."

"The Lord will guide and protect us," repeated Jan, and gave the word to trek.

In my heart at the time I was inclined to agree with that cheat's sneering words; and yet Jan was right, and not I, for of the truth the Lord did guide and protect us. Has anything more wonderful happened in the world than this journey of a few farmers, cumbered with women and children, and armed only with old-fashioned muzzle-loading guns, into a vast, unknown land, peopled by savages and wild beasts? Yet, look what they did. They conquered Moselikatse; they broke the strength of Dingaan and all his Zulu *impis*; they peopled the Free State, the Transvaal, and Natal. That was the work of those few farmers, and I say that of their own strength they could never have done it; the strength was given to them from above; the Sword of God was in their hand, and He guided that hand and blessed it.

****

Our first outspan was at the spot where Van Vooren had tried to murder Ralph and carried off Suzanne upon her wedding-day. We did not stop there long, for the place was bad for Ralph, who sat upon the box of the wagon staring moodily at some blackened stones, which, as one of the drivers told me—the same man who accompanied them upon their wedding journey—had been brought from the *kloof* and used by Suzanne to set the kettle on when they took their meal together. Led by this same driver I walked to the edge of the cliff—for I had never visited the place before—and looked at the deep sea-pool, forty feet below me, into which Swart Piet had thrown Ralph after he had shot him. Also I went down to the edge of the pool and climbed up again by the path along which Zinti and Sihamba had staggered with his senseless body. Afterwards I returned to the wagons with a heart full of thankfulness and wonder that he should still be alive among us today, although alas, there was much for which I could not feel thankful, at least not then.

Now it is of little use that I should set down the history of this trek of ours day by day, for if I did my story would have no end. It is enough to tell that in company with other emigrants we crossed the Orange River, heading for Thaba Nchu, which had been the chief town of Maroko before Moselikatse drove him out of the Marico country. Here several bands of emigrants were to meet, and here they did meet, but not until a year or more had passed since we left the colony and wandered out into the *veldt*.

Ah! I tell you, my child, the *veldt* in those days was different indeed from what it is now. The land itself remains the same except where white men have built towns upon it, but all else is changed. Then it was black with game when the grass was green; yes, at times I have seen it so black for miles that we could scarcely see the grass. There were all sorts of them, springbucks in myriads, blesbok and quagga and wildebeeste in thousands, sable antelope, sassaby and hartebeeste in herds, eland, giraffe and koodoo in troops; while the forests were full of elephant and the streams of sea-cow. They are all gone now, the beautiful wild creatures; the guns of the white men have killed them out or driven them away, and I suppose that it is as well that they are gone, for while the game is in such plenty the men will not work. Still I for one am sorry to lose the sight of them, and had it not been for their numbers we Boers should never have lasted through that long trek, for often and often we lived upon buck's flesh and little else for weeks together.

At Thaba Nchu we camped, waiting for other bands of emigrants, but after four or five months some of our number grew so impatient that they started off by themselves. Among these were the companies under the *Heer* Triegaart and the *Heer* Rensenburg, who wished us to accompany him, but Jan would not, I do not know why. It was as well, for the knob-nosed Kaffirs killed him and everybody with him. Triegaart, who had separated from him, trekked to Delagoa Bay, and reached it, where nearly all his people died of fever.

After that we moved northwards in detachments, instead of keeping together as we should have done, with the result that several of our parties were fallen upon and murdered by the warriors of Moselikatse. Our line of march was between where Bloemfontein and Winburg now stand in the Orange Free State, and it was south of the Vaal, not far from the Rhenoster River that Moselikatse attacked us.

I cannot tell the tale of all this way, I can only tell of what I saw myself. We were of the party under the leadership of Carl Celliers, afterwards an elder of the church at Kronnstadt. Celliers went on a commission to Zoutpansberg to spy out the land, and it was while he was away that so many families were cut off by Moselikatse, the remainder of them, with such of their women and children as were left alive, retreating to our *laager*. Then Celliers returned from his commission, and we retired to a place called Vechtkop, near the Rhenoster River; altogether we numbered not more than fifty or sixty souls, including women and children.

Here we heard that Moselikatse was advancing to make an end of us, so we made our *laager* as strong as we could, lashing the *disselboom* of each wagon beneath the framework of that before it and filling the spaces beneath and between with the crowns and boughs of sharp-thorned mimosa trees, which we tied to the trek tows and brake chains so that they could not be torn away. Also in the middle of the *laager* we made an inner defence of seven wagons, in which were placed the women and children, with the spare food and gunpowder, but the cattle we were obliged to leave outside. Early on the morning when we had finished the *laager* we heard that the *impi* of Moselikatse was close to us, and the men to the number of over thirty rode out to look for it, leaving but a few to defend the camp.

About an hour's ride away they found the Kaffirs, thousands of them, and a Hottentot who could speak their tongue was instructed to call to them and ask them why they attacked us. By way of answer they shouted out the name of their chief and began to charge, whereupon our men dismounted from their horses and opened fire upon them, mounting again before they could come near. So the fight went on until the *laager* was reached, and many Kaffirs were killed without any loss to the Boers, for luckily in those days the natives had no firearms.

I remember that we women were moulding bullets when the men rode in, and very thankful we were to find that not one of them was even wounded. While they ate something we washed out their guns, and at intervals near the places where each man must stand behind the wagons we piled little heaps of powder and bullets upon buck-skins and pieces of canvas laid on the ground; also we did all we could to strengthen our defences still further by binding ox-hides over the wagon wheels and thrusting in more thorns between them.

Then, as the enemy was still preparing to attack us, the *Heer* Cel-liers called us together, and there in the *laager*, while all knelt around him, even to the smallest child, he put up a prayer to God asking that we might be forgiven our sins, and that He would look upon us and protect us in our great need.

It was a strange sight. There we all knelt in the quiet sunshine while he prayed in an earnest voice, and we followed his words with our hearts, every one of us, men and women, holding guns or axes in our hands. Never had human beings more need for prayer, for through the cracks between the wagons we could see Moselikatse's Zulus, six or seven thousand of them, forming themselves into three bodies to rush upon us and murder us, and that was a dreadful sight for fifty or sixty people, of whom some were little children.

When we had finished praying, husbands and wives and parents and children kissed each other, and then the little ones and some of the women who were sick or aged were put behind the seven wagons in the centre of the *laager*, round which were tied the horses, while the rest of us went to our stations, men and women together. I stood be-hind Jan and Ralph, who fought side by side, and, assisted by a girl of fourteen years of age, loaded their spare guns. Now there was a great silence in the camp, and suddenly in the silence, Jan, who was looking through his loophole, whispered:

"*Allemachter!* here they come."

And come they did, with a rush and a roar from three sides at once, while men drew in their breath and set their faces for the struggle. Still no one fired, for the order was that we were to save our powder until Celliers let off his gun. Already the savages were within thirty paces of us, a countless mass of men packed like sheep in a *kraal*, their fierce eyes showing white as ivory in the sunlight, their cruel spears quivering in their hands, when the signal was given

174

and every gun, some loaded with slugs and some with bullets, was discharged point-blank into the thick of them.

Over they rolled by dozens, but that did not stop the rest, who, in spite of our pitiless fire, rushed up to the wagons and gripped them with their hands, striving to drag them apart, till the whole line of them rocked and surged and creaked like boats upon the sea, while the air grew thick with smoke rising straight up towards the sky, and through the smoke *assegais* flashed as thick as rain.

But although some of the heavy laden wagons were dragged a foot or more outward they held together, and the storm of spears flying over our heads did little harm. Heavens! what a fight was that, the fight of fifty against six thousand.

Not more than seven feet of space divided us from that shrieking sea of foes into which we poured bullets at hazard, for there was no need to aim, as fast as the guns could be loaded. Suddenly I heard the girl call out:

"*Kek, tante, da is een swartzel!*" (Look, aunt, there is a black man.)

I looked, and just at my side I saw a great savage who had forced his way through the thorns and crawled beneath the wagon into the *laager*. The gun in my hand was empty, but by me lay an axe which I snatched up, and as he rose to his knees I struck him with all my strength upon the neck and killed him at a blow. Yes, my child, that was the kind of work to which we wives of the *voortrekkers* had to put a needle.

Jan had just fired his gun, and seeing the man he sprang to help me, whereon three more Kaffirs following on the dead soldier's path crawled out from under the wagon. Two of them gained their feet and ran at him lifting their *assegais*. I thought that all was lost, for one hole in our defence was like a pin prick to a bladder, but with a shout Jan dropped the empty gun and rushed to meet them. He caught them by the throat, the two of them, one in each of his great hands, and before they could spear him dashed their heads together with such desperate strength that they fell down and never stirred again. This was always thought something of a feat, for as everybody knows the skulls of Kaffirs are thick.

By this time the girl had handed Ralph his second gun loaded, and with it he shot the third Kaffir; then he also did a brave thing, for seeing that more Zulus were beginning to creep through the hole, he snatched the *assegai* from a dead man's hand, and stopped the gap with his own body, lying flat upon his stomach and thrusting at their heads with the spear. Soon we dragged him out with only one slight wound, pushing the bodies of the Kaffirs into his place, and over them spare branches of thorn, so that the breach was made good.

This was the turning point of the fight, for though after it one other Kaffir managed to get into the *laager*, where he was cut down, and two Boers, Nicholas Potgieter and Pieter Botha were killed by *assegais* thrown from without, from that moment the attack began to slacken. In thirty minutes from the time that Celliers had fired the first shot, Moselikatse's general, whose name was Kalipi, had given the order to retire, and his hosts drew off sullenly, for we had beaten them.

****

Thirty minutes! Only thirty minutes—the shadows had shifted but a few inches on the grass, and yet now that it was done with it seemed like half a lifetime. Panting and begrimed with smoke and powder, we stood looking at each other and around us. The tents of the wagons were ripped to pieces, in our own I counted more than sixty spear cuts, and the trampled turf inside the *laager* was like the back of an angry porcupine, for from it we gathered nearly fourteen hundred heavy *assegais*. For the rest, the two men lay dead where they had fallen, their faces turned towards the sky, each of them pierced through by a spear, and out of our little number twelve others were wounded, though none of them died of their wounds. Not a woman or a child was touched.

Outside the *laager* there was a sight to see, for there on the red grass, some lying singly and some in heaps, were over four hundred Zulu soldiers, most of them dead, and how many wounded they carried away with them I cannot tell.

Now we saw that the Kaffirs were collecting our cattle, and about twenty men under Potgieter saddled up and rode out to try and recapture them, since without oxen to draw the wagons we were helpless. Till sunset they followed them, killing many, but being so few they could not recapture the cattle, and in the end were obliged to return empty handed. Ralph went with his party, and, because of an act of mercy which he did then it came about in the end that Suzanne was found and many lives were saved. So plenteously do our good deeds bear fruit, even in this world.

Yes, you may have thought that this tale of the battle of Vetchkop was only put in here because it is one of the great experiences of an old woman's life. But it is not so; it has all to do with the story of Ralph and of my daughter Suzanne.

CHAPTER 26

How Gaasha Brought Good Luck

When Ralph returned from pursuing the Zulus, as he drew near to the *laager* he lingered a little behind the others, for he was very weary of all this work of killing, also the flesh-wound that he had got from the Kaffir's spear having stiffened pained him when his horse cantered. There was no more danger now, for the savages were gone, leaving their path marked by the corpses of those who had been shot down by the Boers, or of men who had limped away wounded either to die upon the road or to be killed by their comrades because their case was hopeless. Following this black trail of death backwards Ralph rode on, and when he was within a hundred yards of the wagons halted his horse to study the scene. He thought that he would never see such another, although, in fact, that at the Blood River when we conquered the Zulu king, Dingaan, was even more strange and terrible.

The last crimson rays of the setting sun were flooding the plain with light. Blood-red they shone upon the spear-torn canvas of the wagons and upon the stained and trampled *veldt*. Even the bodies of the Kaffirs looked red as they lay in every shape and attitude; some as though they slept; some with outstretched arms and spears gripped tight; some with open mouths as they had died shouting their way-cry. Ralph looked at them and was thankful that it was not we white people who lay thus, as it might well have been. Then, just as he was turning towards the *laager*, he thought that he saw something move in a tussock of thick grass, and rode towards it. Behind the tussock lay the body of a young Kaffir, not an uncommon sight just there, but Ralph was so sure that he had seen it move that, stirred by an idle curiosity, he dismounted from his horse to examine it. This he did carefully, but the only hurt that he could see was a flesh wound caused by a slug upon the foot, not serious in any way, but such as might very well prevent a man from running.

"This fellow is shamming dead," he thought to himself, and lifted his gun, for in those times we could not afford to nurse sick Kaffirs.

Then of a sudden the young man who had seemed to be a corpse rose to his knees, and, clasping his hands, began to beg for mercy. Instead of shooting him at once, as most Boers would have done, Ralph, who was tender-hearted, hesitated and listened while the Kaffir, a pleasant-faced lad and young, besought him for his life.

"Why should I spare you," asked Ralph, who understood his talk well, "seeing that, like all the rest of these, you set upon my people to murder them?"

"Nay, chief," answered the young man, "it is not so. I am no Zulu. I belong to another tribe, and was but a slave and a carrier in the army of Kalipi, for I was taken prisoner and forced to carry mats and food and water," and he pointed to a bundle and some gourds that lay beside him.

"It may be so," answered Ralph, "but the dog shares his master's fate."

"Chief," pleaded the man, "spare me. Although it prevented me from running away with the others, my wound is very slight and will be healed in a day or two, and then I will serve you as your slave and be faithful to you all my life. Spare me and I shall bring you good luck."

"I need that enough," said Ralph, "and I am sure that you are no Zulu, for a Zulu would not stoop to beg for his life thus," and he stood thinking.

While he thought, Jan, who had seen him from the *laager*, came up behind.

"What are you doing, son," he asked in an angry voice, "talking to this black devil here alone among the dead? Stand aside and let me settle him if you have not the heart," and he lifted his gun.

"No, father," said Ralph, pushing it aside, "this man is not a Zulu; he is but a slave-carrier and he has prayed me to spare his life, swearing that he will serve me faithfully. Also he says that he brings good luck."

"Certainly he brought good luck to these," answered Jan, pointing to the scattered dead with his hand, and laughing grimly. "*Allemachter!* son, you must be mad to play the fool thus, for doubtless the sneaking villain will murder you the first time your back is turned. Come, stand aside and I will finish it."

Now the young man, whose name was Gaasha, seeing that he was about to be shot, threw himself upon the ground, and clasping Ralph round the knees, implored for mercy.

"Save me, Baas," he prayed, "save me, and you will always be glad of it, for I tell you I bring you good luck, I tell you I bring you good luck."

"Father," said Ralph, setting his mouth, "if you kill this Kaffir it will be a cause of quarrel between us, and we never quarrelled yet."

"Quarrel or no quarrel, he shall die," said Jan in a rage, for he thought it the strangest folly that Ralph should wish to spare a black man.

At that moment, however, something seemed to strike his mind, for his face grew puzzled, and he looked about him almost anxiously.

"Where have I seen it before?" he said, as though he were speaking to himself. "The *veldt* all red with blood and sunset, the *laager* behind and the Kaffir with the wounded foot holding Ralph by the knees. *Allemachter!* I know. It was that day in the *sit-kammer*[3] at the stead yonder, when the little doctoress, Sihamba, made me look into her eyes; yes, yes, I have seen it all in the eyes of Sihamba. Well, let the lad live, for without a doubt Sihamba did not show me this picture that should be for nothing. Moreover, although I am stupid, as your mother says, I have learned that there are many things in the world which we cannot understand but which play a part in our lives nevertheless."

So the lad Gaasha was brought to the *laager*, and upon the prayer of Jan and Ralph, the commandant gave him his life, ordering, however, that he should sleep outside the wagons.

"Well," I said when I heard the tale, "one thing is, that you will never see him again, for he will be off during the night back to his friends the Zulus." But I was wrong, for next morning there was Gaasha, and there he remained even after his foot was quite well, making the best Kaffir servant that ever I had to do with.

After that day we saw no more of the Zulus at Vetchkop, although later with the help of other Boers we attacked them twice, killing more than four thousand of them, and capturing six thousand head of cattle, so that they fled north for good and all, and founded the nation of the Matabele far away.

But oh! our fate was hard there at Vetchkop; never have I known worse days. The Zulus had taken away all our cattle, so that we could not even shift the wagons from the scene of the fight, but must camp there amidst the vultures and the mouldering skeletons, for the dead were so many that it was impossible to bury them all. We sent messengers to other parties of Boers for help, and while they were gone we starved, for there was no food to eat, and game was very scarce. Yes, it was a piteous sight to see the children cry for food and gnaw old bits of leather or strips of hide cut from Kaffir shields to stay the craving of their stomachs. Some of them died of that hunger, and I

---

3. Sitting room.

grew so thin that when I chanced to see myself in a pool of water where I went to wash I started back frightened.

At length, when we were all nearly dead, some oxen came and with them we dragged a few of the wagons to Moroko, where an English clergyman and his wife, taking pity on us, gave us corn, for which reason I have always held that among the British the clergymen must be a great deal better than the rest of that proud and worthless race, for it is true that we judge of people as they deal by us. Yes, and I will go so far as to say that I do not believe that the Reverend Mr. Owen, the English missionary at the *kraal* of the Zulu King Dingaan, did in truth advise him to massacre Retief and his seventy Boers, as was generally reported among my countrymen.

Well, after Moselikatse's Zulus were finally defeated the question arose whether we should proceed to Zoutpansberg and settle there, or follow our brethren who in large numbers had already crossed the Quathlamba Mountains into Natal under the leadership of Retief. In the end we decided for Natal because it was nearer the sea, for in those days we never dreamed that the treacherous British Government would steal that land also; so trekking slowly, we headed for Van Reenen's Pass, our party then numbering thirty wagons and about sixty white people.

It was when we were about four days trek, or sixty miles, from the pass that one evening, as we sat eating our food, Jan, Ralph, and I—I remember it was the fried steaks of an eland that Ralph had shot—the lad Gaasha, who had now served us for some six months, came up to the fire, and having saluted Ralph, squatted down before him Kaffir fashion, saying that he had a favour to ask.

"Speak on," said Ralph. "What is it?"

"Baas," replied Gaasha, "it is this; I want a week or ten days leave of absence to visit my people."

"You mean that you want to desert," I put in.

"No, lady," answered Gaasha; "you know that I love the Baas who saved my life far too well ever to wish to leave him. I desire only to see my parents and to tell them that I am happy, for doubtless they think me dead. The Baas proposes to cross into Natal by Van Reenen's Pass, does he not? Well, not so very far from my home, although none would guess it unless he knew the way, is another pass called Oliver's Hook, and by that pass, after I have spoken with my father and my mother if they still live, I would cross the Quathlamba, finding the Baas again on the further side of the mountains, as I can easily do."

"I think that I will let you go as I can trust you, Gaasha," said Ralph, "but tell me the name of your home, that I may know where to send to seek you if you should not come back as you promise."

"Have I not said that I will come back, Baas, unless the lions or the Zulus should eat me on the way? But the name of the house of my tribe is Umpondwana. It is only a little tribe, for the Zulus killed many of us in the time of Chaka, but their house is a very fine house."

"What does Umpondwana mean?" asked Ralph idly as he lit his pipe.

"It means the Mountain of the Man's Hand, Baas."

Ralph let his pipe fall to the ground, and I saw his face turn white beneath the sunburn, while of a sudden his grey eyes looked as though they were about to leap from their sockets.

"Why is it called the Mountain of the Man's Hand?" he asked in a hollow voice. "Speak quick now, and do not lie to me."

Gaasha looked up at him astonished.

"How should I know, Baas, when the place was named so before I was born, and none have told me? But I think that it may be because upon one of the slopes of the mountain, which has great cliffs of red rock, are five ridges, which, seen from the plain below, look like the four fingers and thumb of a man. Also the place has another name, which means 'where the water springs out of the rock,' because from between two of the ridges, those that are like the thumb and first finger, flows a stream which comes from the heart of the mountain."

"On which side of the mountain are the ridges and the stream?" asked Ralph in the same unnatural voice.

"Baas, when the sun rises it strikes on them."

Now Ralph swung to and fro like a drunken man, and had I not put my arm about him I believe that he would have fallen.

"It is the mountain of my vision," he gasped.

"Be not foolish," I answered, for I feared lest when he found that all this strange resemblance was a chance, the bitterness of his disappointment might overwhelm him. "Be not foolish, son; are there not many hills in this great land with ridges on their flanks, and streams of water running down them?"

Then, as Ralph seemed unable to answer me, I asked of Gaasha:

"Who is the chief of this tribe of yours?"

"He is named Koraanu," he answered, "if he still lives, but a man I met some months ago told me that he has been dead these two years, and that she who used to rule us when I was a little child had come back from the lands whither she had wandered, and is now *Inkoosikaas* of the Umpondwana."

"What is the name of this chieftainess?" I asked in the midst of a great silence.

Gaasha answered at once; that is, after he had taken a pinch of snuff, but to us it seemed a year before the words crossed his lips.

"Her name, lady," and he sneezed, "is"—and he sneezed again, rocking himself to and fro. Then slowly wiping away the tears which the snuff had brought to his eyes with the back of his hand he said, "Ow! this is the best of snuff, and I thank the Baas for giving it to me."

"Answer," roared Jan, speaking for the first time, and in such a fierce voice that Gaasha sprang to his feet and began to run away.

"Come back, Gaasha, come back," I called, and he came doubtfully, for Gaasha was not very brave, and ever since he had wished to shoot him he trembled even at the sight of Jan. "Be silent, you fool," I whispered to the latter as the lad drew near, then said aloud, "Now, Gaasha."

"Lady," he answered, "it is indeed as I have told you; the Baas gave me the snuff a long time ago; he took it out of the ear-boxes of the dead men at Vetchkop. He gave it to me. I did not steal it. He will say so himself."

"Never mind the snuff, Gaasha," I said in a voice half-choked with doubt and anxiety, for the sight of Ralph's piteous face and the strangeness of it all were fast overwhelming me, "but tell us what is the name of this chieftainess whom you have heard is now the ruler of your tribe?"

"Her name, lady," he answered, much relieved, "why it is well known, for though she is small, it is said that she is the best of doctoresses and rain-makers."

Now Jan could no longer be restrained, for stretching out his great hand he gripped Gaasha by the throat, saying:

"Accursed *swartzel*, if you do not tell us the name at once I will kill you."

"Madman," I exclaimed, "how can the lad speak while you are choking him?"

Then Jan shifted his grip and Gaasha began to cry for pity.

"The name, the name," said Jan.

"Why should I hide it? Have I not told it? Baas, it is *Sihamba Ngenyanga.*"

As the words passed his lips Jan let go of him so suddenly that Gaasha fell to the ground and sat there staring at us, for without doubt he thought that we had all gone mad.

Jan looked up to the skies and said, "Almighty, I thank Thee, Who canst make dreams to fly to the heart of a man as a night-bird to its nest through the darkness, and Who, because of what I saw in the eyes of Sihamba, didst turn aside my gun when it was pointed at the breast of this Kaffir."

Then he looked at Ralph, and was quiet, for Ralph had swooned away.

CHAPTER 27

Swart Piet Sets a Snare

It was a strange life that Suzanne led among the Umpondwana during the two years or more that, together with Sihamba, she ruled over them as chieftainess. Upon the top of the mountain was a space of grass land measuring about five hundred *morgen*, or a thousand acres in extent, where were placed the chief's huts and those of the head men and soldiers, surrounding a large cattle *kraal*, which, however, was only used in times of danger. The rest of the people dwelt upon the slopes of the mountain, and even on the rich plains at the foot of it, but if need were they could all retreat to the table-land upon its crest. Here they might have defied attack for ever, for beneath the cattle *kraal* grain was stored in pits, only there was but one spring, which in dry seasons was apt to fail. Therefore it was that the Umpondwana had built stone *schanzes* or fortifications about the mouth of the river which gushed from the mountain between the thumb and finger like ridges on the eastern slope, although it lay below their impregnable walls of rock, seeing that to this river they must look for their main supply of water.

The table-top of the hill, which could only be approached by one path that wound upwards through a ravine cut by water, being swept by every wind of heaven, and so high in the air, was very cold and naked. Indeed, in the winter season, rain fell there twice or thrice a week, and there were many days when it was wrapt in a dense white mist. Still, during the two years and more that she dwelt with the Umpondwana, Suzanne scarcely left this plain, not because she did not desire to do so, but because she did not dare, for word was brought that the foot, and even the slopes, of the mountain were patrolled by men in the employ of Swart Piet. Moreover, soon it became clear that he had knowledge of all her movements, doubtless from spies in his pay who dwelt among the Umpondwana themselves. During the first few months of her sojourn on the mountain, it is true that now and again Suzanne rode out on the *veldt* mounted on the *schimmel*, but this pastime she was forced to abandon because one day Swart Piet and his men saw her and gave chase, so that she was only saved from him by the fleetness of the great horse.

After this, both she and the *schimmel* stayed upon the tableland, where daily they took exercise together, galloping round a prepared path which was laid about the fence of the cattle *kraal*, and thus kept themselves in good health.

Swart Piet had Kaffir blood in his veins, as I have said, and from boyhood it had been his custom to live two lives, one as a white man with white men, and one as a Kaffir with Kaffirs. About three miles distant from the Umpondwana Mountain was a strong *koppie* with fertile valleys to the back of it, and here, being rich and having a great name as a white man, he found it no trouble to establish himself as a native chief, for refugees of all sorts gathered themselves about him, so that within a year he ruled over a little tribe of about a hundred men together with women.

With these men Van Vooren began to harass the Umpondwana, cutting off their cattle if they strayed, and from time to time killing or enslaving small parties of them whom he caught wandering on the plains out of reach of help from the mountain. Whenever he captured such a party he would spare one of them, sending him back with a message to the Umpondwana. They were all to one effect, namely, that if the tribe would deliver over to him the lady Swallow who dwelt among them he would cease from troubling it, but if this were not done, then he would wage war on it day and night until in this way or in that he compassed its destruction.

To these messages Sihamba would reply as occasion offered, that if he wanted anything from the Umpondwana he had better come and take it.

So things went on for a long while. Swart Piet's men did them no great harm indeed, but they harassed them continually, until the people of the Umpondwana began to murmur, for they could scarcely stir beyond the slopes of the mountain without being set upon. Happily for them these slopes were wide, for otherwise they could not have found pasturage for their cattle or land upon which to grow their corn. So close a watch was kept upon them, indeed, that they could neither travel to visit other tribes, nor could these come to them, and thus it came about that Suzanne was as utterly cut off from the rest of the world as though she had been dead. She had but one hope to keep her heart alive, and it was that Ralph and Jan would learn of her fate through native rumours and be able to find her out. Still, as she knew that this could not be counted on, she tried to let us have tidings of her, for when she had been only a week on the mountain Umpondwana she despatched Zinti and two men to bear him company, with orders to travel back over all the hundreds of miles of *veldt* to the far-off stead in the Transkei.

As she had neither pen nor ink, nor anything with which she could write, Suzanne was obliged to trust a long message to Zinti's memory, making him repeat it to her until she was sure that he had it by heart. In this message she told all that had befallen her, and prayed us to take Zinti for a guide and to come to her rescue, since she did not dare to set foot outside the walls of rock, for fear that she should be captured by Van Vooren, who watched for her continually.

Zinti, being brave and faithful, started upon his errand, though it was one from which many would have shrunk. But as ill-luck would have it, one night when they were camped near the *kraal* of a small Basuto tribe, his companions becoming hungry, stole a goat and killed it. Zinti ate of the goat, for they told him that they had bought it for some beads, and while they were still eating the Basutos came upon them and caught them red-handed. Next day they were tried by the councillors of the tribe and condemned to die as thieves, but the chief, who wanted servants, spared their lives and set them to labour in his gardens, where they were watched day and night.

Zinti was a prisoner among these Basutos for nearly a year, but at length he made his escape, leaving his two companions behind, for they were afraid lest if they ran away with him they should be recaptured and killed. As soon as he was free Zinti continued his journey, for he was a man not easily turned from his purpose, nor because it was now over a year old did he cease from his attempt to deliver the message that had been set in his mouth.

Well, after many dangers, footsore and worn-out with travelling, at length he reached the stead, to find that we had all gone, none knew whither, and that the long-nosed cheat to whom we had sold the farm ruled in our place. Zinti sought out some Kaffirs who lived upon the land, and abode with them awhile till he was rested and strong again. Then once more he turned his face northward towards the mountain Umpondwana, for though he greatly feared the journey, he knew that the heart of Suzanne would be sick for news. War raged in the country that he must pass, and food was scarce; still at length he won through, although at the last he was nearly captured by Black Piet's thieves, and one year and nine months after he had left it, a worn and weary figure, he limped up the red rock path of Umpondwana.

Suzanne had been watching for him. It seems strange to say it, but after six months had gone by, which time at the best must be given to his journey, she watched for him every day. On the top of the highest and most precipitous cliff of the mountain fortress of Umpondwana was a little knoll of rock curiously hollowed out to the shape of a chair, difficult to gain and dizzy to sit in, for beneath it was a *sheer* fall of five hundred feet, which chair-rock commanded the plain southward, and the pass where Van Vooren had spoken to Suzanne from his hiding-place among the stones. By this pass and across this plain help must reach her if it came at all, or so she thought; therefore in that eagle's eyrie of a seat Suzanne sat day by day watching ever for those who did not come. A strange sight she must have been, for now long ago such garments as she had were worn to rags, so that she was forced to clothe herself in beautiful skins fashioned to her fancy, and to go sandal-footed, her lovely rippling hair hanging about her.

At length one day from her lonely point of outlook she saw a solitary man limping across the plain, a mere black speck dragging itself forward like a wounded fly upon a wall. Descending from her seat she sought out Sihamba.

"Swallow," said the little woman, "there is tidings in your eyes. What is it?"

"Zinti returns," she answered, "I have seen him from far away."

Now Sihamba smiled, for she thought Zinti lost; also she did not believe it possible that Sihamba could have recognized him from such a distance. Still before two hours were over Zinti came, gaunt and footsore, but healthy and unharmed, and sitting down before Suzanne in her private enclosure, began at the very beginning of his long story, after the native fashion, telling of those things which had befallen him upon the day when he left the mountain nearly two years before.

"Your news? Your news?" said Suzanne.

"Lady, I am telling it," he answered.

"Fool!" exclaimed Sihamba. "Say now, did you find the Baas Kenzie and the Baas Botmar?"

"No, indeed," he replied, "for they were gone."

"Gone where? Were they alive and well?"

"Yes, yes, they were alive and well, but all the Boers in those parts have trekked, and they trekked also, believing the lady Swallow to be dead."

"This is a bitter cup to drink," murmured Suzanne, "yet there is some sweetness in it, for at least my husband lives."

Then Zinti set out all his story, and Suzanne listened to it in silence, praising him much and thanking him when he had done. But after that day her heart failed her, and she seemed to give up hope. Ralph had vanished, and we, her parents, had vanished, and she was left alone a prisoner among a little Kaffir tribe, at the foot of whose stronghold her bitter enemy waited to destroy her. Never was white woman in a more dreadful or more solitary state, and had it not been for Sihamba's tender friendship she felt that she must have died.

Now also Swart Piet grew bolder, appearing even on the slopes of the mountain where his men harried and stole. He did more than this even, for one morning just before dawn he attacked the pass leading to the stronghold so secretly and with such skill that his force was halfway up it before the sentries discovered them. Then they were seen, and the war-horns blew, and there followed a great fight. Indeed, had it not been for a lucky chance, it is doubtful how that fight would have ended, for his onslaught was fierce, and the Umpondwana, who at the best were not the bravest of warriors, were taken by surprise.

It will be remembered that Zinti had brought Ralph's gun with him when first they fled north, and this gun he still had, together with a little powder and ball, for, fearing lest it should be stolen from him, he had not taken it on his great journey to the Transkei and back. Now, hearing the tumult, he ran out with it, and fired point blank at the stormers, who were pushing their way up the narrow path, driving the Umpondwana before them. The *roar* was loaded with slugs, which, scattering, killed three men; moreover, by good fortune, one of the slugs struck Van Vooren himself through the fleshy part of the thigh, causing him to fall, whereon, thinking him mortally wounded, in spite of his curses and commands, his followers lost heart and fled, bearing him with them. Sihamba called upon her people to follow, but they would not, for they feared to meet Swart Piet in the open.

In truth they began to weary of this constant war, which was brought upon them through no fault or quarrel of their own, and to ask where was that good luck which the White Swallow had promised them. Had it not been that they loved Suzanne for her beauty and her gentle ways, and that Sihamba, by her cleverness and good rule, had mastered their minds, there is little doubt indeed but that they would have asked Suzanne to depart from among them.

On the day following the attack Sihamba learned that Swart Piet lay very sick, having lost much blood, and sought to persuade her people to attack him in turn, and make an end of him and his robbers.

But they would not, and so the council broke up, but not before Sihamba had spoken bitter words, telling them that they were cowards, and would meet the end of cowards, whereat they went away sullenly. Afterwards they learned through their spies that Van Vooren had gone to Zululand to visit the King Dingaan, which Sihamba thought evil tidings, for she scented fresh danger in this journey, and not without reason. But to Suzanne she said nothing.

Two more months went by peacefully, when one morning a herd who was tending the cattle that belonged to Suzanne and Sihamba, sought audience of the chieftainess.

"What is it?" asked Sihamba, for she saw by the man's face that something strange had happened.

"This, lady," he answered. "When I went down to the *kloof* at dawn, where your cattle and those of the Lady Swallow are kraaled, I found among them strange oxen to the number of more than a hundred. They are beautiful oxen, such as I have never seen, for every one of them is pure white—white from the muzzle to the tail, and I cannot understand how they came among your cattle, for the mouth of the *kraal* was closed as usual last night; moreover, I found it closed this morning."

When Sihamba heard this she turned cold to the heart, for she knew well that these spotless white cattle must come from the royal herd of Dingaan, king of the Zulus, since none other were known like them in all the land. Also she was sure that Swart Piet had stolen them and placed them among her cattle so as to bring down upon her and her tribe the terrible wrath of Dingaan, for she remembered that this mingling of cattle was a trick which he had played before. But to the herd she said only that doubtless they were cattle which had strayed, and that she would make enquiry as to their owner. Then she dismissed him, bidding him to keep a better watch in future.

Scarcely had he gone when another man appeared saying that he had met a Kaffir from beyond the mountains, who told him that a party of white men with women and children had crossed the Quathlamba range by what is now known as Bezuidenhout's Pass, and were camped near the Tugela River. This was strange news to Sihamba, who had heard nothing of the whereabouts of the Trek Boers, so strange that she would not speak of it to Suzanne, fearing lest it should fill her with false hopes. But she sent for Zinti, and bade him cross the Quathlamba by a little-used pass that was known to her near the place where the Tugela takes its rise, and which today is called Mont aux Sources, and following the river down, to find out whether or no it was true that white men were encamped upon its banks. When he had done this he was to return as swiftly as possible with whatever information he could gather.

This task Zinti undertook gladly, for he loved following a spoor, which was a gift that Nature had given him; also he was weary of being cooped up like a fatting fowl upon the mountain Umpondwana.

When Zinti had gone Sihamba summoned other messengers, and commanded them to travel swiftly to the *kraal* Umgungundlhovo, bearing her homage to Dingaan, king of the Amazulus, and asking whether he had lost any of the cattle from his royal herds, since certain white oxen had been found among her beasts, though how they came there she could not tell. These men went also, though in fear and trembling, since in those days none loved to approach the Lion of the Zulu with tales of cattle of his that had strayed among their herd. Still they went, and with doubt in her heart Sihamba sat awaiting their return.

CHAPTER 28

The Coming of the Impi

Sihamba had not very long to wait, for on the evening of the fifth day from the starting of the messengers they came back at great speed, having run so fast that they could scarcely speak for want of breath, and telling her that a Zulu *impi*, numbering more than three thousand spears, was advancing upon the Umpondwana to destroy them. It seemed that long before the king's oxen had been found mixed with her herd it had been reported to Dingaan that Sihamba had stolen them, which was not altogether strange, seeing that Swart Piet travelled with the *impi*. As she suspected, he had caused the oxen to be stolen, and now he had fixed the deed upon her, knowing well that Dingaan only sought a pretext to destroy her tribe, with which the Zulus had an ancient quarrel.

Now there was but one thing to be done—to make ready their defence, so, without more ado, Sihamba summoned her council and told them that a Zulu *impi* was at hand to eat them up because of the white cattle that had been placed among the herds. Then the councillors wrung their hands, and some of them shed tears even, although they were aged men, for the name of the Zulus struck terror to their hearts, and they expected nothing less than death for themselves, their wives, and their children.

"It is best that we should fly while there is yet time," said the captain of the council.

"There is no time," answered Sihamba; "the *impi* will be here by dawn and will cut you up upon the plain."

"What then shall we do?" they asked; "we who are already dead."

"Do?" she cried. "You shall fight as your fathers fought before you, and beat back these dogs of Dingaan. If you will but be brave, what have you to fear from them? You have water, you have food, you have spears, and even the Zulus have not wings like eagles with which to fly over your walls of cliff. Let them come, and if you will but obey me, I promise you that they shall return again to make report to the 'Elephant' many fewer than they left his *kraal*."

So the Umpondwana made ready to fight, not because they loved it, but because they must, for they knew that no humbleness would help them in face of the spears of Dingaan. The cattle were driven into the centre *kraal*, and great supplies of grass and green corn were cut to feed them. Except for one manhole the pass leading to the top of the mountain was closed, and the *schanzes*, or walls, which protected the mouth of the river that welled from the hillside between the eastern ridges were strengthened and garrisoned. Here, as Sihamba knew, was their weak place, for this river flowed out beneath the impregnable precipices of rock, and to it they must look for their main supply of water, since, although the spring upon the tableland, if husbanded, would suffice for a supply to the tribe, it was not sufficient for the cattle. It was for this reason that Sihamba wished to turn the kine loose and let the Zulus capture them if they would, for she knew that then they could never take the mountain or harm a hair of the head of one of its inhabitants. But the Umpondwana were greedy, and would not consent to the loss of their cattle, forgetting that cattle are of no value to dead men. They said that they could very well defend the *schanzes* which surrounded the source of the river, and that from it sufficient water could be carried to keep the beasts alive, even if the siege were long.

"As you will," answered Sihamba shortly, "but see that you do defend them when the Zulu warriors leap upon the walls, for if you fail then you will lose cattle and life together."

All this time, according to her daily custom, Suzanne had been seated in her chair of rock upon the highest point of the precipice looking for that help which never came. Presently, as she watched with sad eyes, far away upon the plain she saw a cloud of dust in which moved and shone the sheen of spears. Now she climbed down from her seat, and ran to seek Sihamba, whom she found surrounded by her councillors.

"What is it, Swallow?" asked the little chieftainess looking up, though already she had guessed the answer.

Suzanne told her, adding, "Who can it be that travels towards the mountain with so great a force?"

"Lady Swallow," said Sihamba gravely, "it is an army of the Zulus sent by Dingaan to destroy us, and with them marches Bull-Head." And she told her of the trick of the cattle and of what the messengers had seen.

Suzanne heard, and her face grew white as the goatskin cloak she wore.

"Then at last the long story is at an end," she faltered, for she knew the terrible prowess of the Zulus, and how none could stand before their onslaught.

"Yes, of that *impi* there is an end," answered Sihamba proudly, "if these children of mine will but take heart and fight as their fathers fought. Fear not, Lady Swallow, nothing that has not wings can storm the mountain of Umpondwana."

But for all that she could say Suzanne still felt much afraid, which was not strange, for she knew that the heart was out of these soldiers of Sihamba, and knew, moreover, that a Zulu army did not dare to be defeated, for which reason it must either take the mountain or fight till it was destroyed.

Now all was confusion; the horns blew and women wailed, while the captains of the Umpondwana issued their commands, and the men piled up stones upon the brink of the precipice to roll down upon the foe, and drove the herds of cattle into the great *kraal* upon the tableland.

Marching quickly, the *impi* drew near and the defenders could see that it numbered about four thousand spears and was composed of two separate regiments. At a distance of a mile it halted and throwing out horns or wings surrounded the mountain, up the slopes of which it advanced in a thin circle, much as beaters do who are driving game to a certain point. As the circle drew nearer to the cliffs, it thickened, having less ground to cover, though still there was a gap here and there.

Presently those who were watching saw a man dart through one of these gaps and run up hill at great speed, followed by Zulu soldiers, who tried to kill him. But he was the swifter of foot, moreover he knew the path, so that before they could come up with him he reached the great stone walls which were built about the source of the river, and was dragged over them by the defenders.

A while later this man appeared upon the top of the mountain and proved to be none other than Zinti, who had returned from his errand, and, having news to tell, risked his life to pass through the *impi* before the stronghold was altogether surrounded. Sihamba received him at once, Suzanne standing at her side, and bade him be brief for she had little time to listen to long stories.

"I will be brief," Zinti answered. "Lady, as you bade me I crossed the mountains by the road of which you told me. It is a good road for men on foot or horseback, but wagons could not travel it. Having reached the plain on the further side I followed the bank of the river, till suddenly I came in sight of thirty wagons drawn up in a *laager* upon a knoll of ground, and among the wagons I saw Boers with their wives and children. I tried to go up to speak to them, but a young Boer, seeing me, shot at me with his gun, so I thought it safer to lie hid. At nightfall, however, I met the driver of one of the wagons, a Kaffir man, at some distance from the *laager*, where he was watching by a pit made to catch bucks, and fell into talk with him. He told me that this was a party of the Boers who had trekked from Cape Colony, and were taking possession of Natal, and that there were other such parties scattered about the country. He said that in this party there were five-and-twenty men with women and children, but he did not know the names of any of them. Also he told me that he meant to run away, as he heard that Dingaan was going to attack the white people, and was sure that if he did so they would be eaten up, for these Boers, thinking themselves quite safe, had grown very careless, and neither made their *laager* as strong as it should be nor set any watch at night. Having learned this I returned at once to make report to you, nor did I come too quickly, for the Zulus nearly caught me as I passed their ranks. I saw Bull-Head as I ran; he is riding a brown horse, and seems quite recovered from his wound."

"How far is the Boer *laager* from this place?" asked Sihamba before Suzanne could speak.

"Lady, a man on a good horse could reach it in seven hours, nor is it possible to mistake the way. After crossing the plain you enter the gorge by the saw-edged rock yonder, and follow its windings across the mountains till you come out the other side, where the river runs down to the flat country. Then you can keep along the bank of the river as I did when I went, or if you wish to go more quickly you must head for a large white-topped hill, or *koppie*, which can be seen from the mountains, and when you come to it you will find the Boer *laager* upon the knoll at its foot, but near to the banks of the river, which winds round it."

"Oh! let us go; let us go quickly," said Suzanne springing to her feet, for the thought even of seeing a white man again made her drunk with hope.

"Alas! sister," answered Sihamba sadly, "an hour ago we might have gone, or rather you might have gone, mounted on the great *schimmel*, but now—look," and she pointed to where the Zulus clustered like bees along the banks of the river by which the path ran. "See," she added, "there is but one road out of this stronghold, for nowhere else can the surest-footed climber in the world descend its cliffs, no, not with a rope to help him, and that road is thick with Zulu spears; moreover, a certain man whom you do not wish to see waits for you upon it."

Suzanne looked. "Too late," she moaned. "Oh! surely my God has forsaken me! Within six hours of safety and doomed to perish here; oh! surely my God has forsaken me!" and she burst out weeping in the bitterness of her disappointed hope.

"Say not so," answered Sihamba gently, "for I think that the Great one whom you worship will save you yet."

As she spoke a messenger arrived saying that the Zulus had sent forward heralds who desired to speak with her, and that these heralds waited within earshot of the first wall.

"I will come," said Sihamba, and she passed down the cleft and through the man hole into the fortifications which were built about the source of the river. But she would not allow Suzanne to accompany her.

When she reached the outer wall she climbed it and stood upon it, for Sihamba was a woman who knew no fear, and there, about forty paces away, she saw three great Zulus standing, and with them him whom she dreaded more than all the Zulus on the earth—Piet Van Vooren himself. When the Zulu captains caught sight of her upon the wall, they jeered aloud and asked whether this was indeed Sihamba Ngenyanga, or if a she-monkey had been sent to talk with them.

"I am Sihamba," she answered quietly, "or I am a monkey, as it may please you, though the white man with you can tell you what I am."

"I can," said Piet with a laugh. "You are a witch and a thief, and the fate that I promised you long ago is with you at last."

"Murderer," mocked Sihamba in answer, "I see Death standing behind you, and with him shadows of the Fear to come. But I would speak with these chiefs and not with an outcast half-breed. Tell me, chiefs, why do you come up against my stronghold with so great a force?"

"Because that 'Elephant whose tread shakes the earth,' our master, Dingaan the king, has sent us," answered the spokesman of the captains.

"Say, now, on what errand, chief?"

"On this errand; to take your stronghold and cattle, to burn your *kraal*, and to kill your people, all of them save the marriageable girls and such children as are old enough to travel, who must be brought with the cattle to Dingaan. But you yourself and the white woman who is called Swallow who rules with you are to be handed over to Bull-Head here to do with as he will, for that is the bargain between him and the king."

"And why are these things to come upon us who have done no wrong?" asked Sihamba.

"Why, little woman!" answered the chief, "because you have dared to steal cattle from the king's herd, even the royal white cattle; yes, and they have been traced to your mountain and seen among your oxen."

"It is true that the cattle are here," said Sihamba, "but it is not true that we have stolen them, seeing that they were lifted by the white man, Bull-Head, and mixed up with our herds to bring us into trouble with the king."

"A fit tale for the king's ears," replied the captain, laughing. "Why it was Bull-Head who told the king of the theft; but let that pass. Dingaan the king is merciful, and he makes you this offer through my mouth: If you will return the cattle together with all your own by way of fine, and hand over your councillors and head men to be killed, then he will grant the rest their lives. But all the young men and the girls must come with me to pass into the service of the king, the married women and the children going where they will. Perhaps Bull-Head here will take them with yourself and White Swallow. What is your word, little chieftainess?"

"My word is that we will have none of such mercy. It is better that we should die together, but I tell you, men of Dingaan, that these rocks will be white with your bones before ever you drive our cattle and maidens back to Dingaan."

"As you will, little chieftainess. We captains of the Zulus have heard many such proud words in our time, but ah! where are those who spoke them? Ask the jackals and the vultures, little chieftainess."

CHAPTER 29

Thirst

When Sihamba finished her talk with the captains of Dingaan the sun was already sinking. Still the Umpondwana thought that the Zulus would attack at once, but these shouted to the defenders that they might rest easily till the dawn, since they wished to have day-light by which to divide the spoil. And at daylight the attack came. Driving the men of Bull-Head in front of them much against their will, for they knew these to be cowards, and wished to make mock of them, company by company the Zulus rushed at the stone wall, though many of them were killed and often they were driven back. But always they came on laughing and shouting their war-cry till the arms of the Umpondwana grew weary with stabbing at them as their plumed heads appeared above the level of the wall. Still, fight-ing under the eye of Sihamba, whose bitter tongue they feared, her people held their own, for indeed the place was almost impregnable to the attacks of men armed only with spears however brave they might be, and had it been defended by warriors of true Zulu blood it could never have been taken.

When the fight had raged for an hour or more the Zulu captains withdrew their men, and went apart to consult with Van Vooren, for their loss was heavy, and they saw that if they were to capture the head waters of the river they must seek some other plan. Very soon they found it. The river issued from the side of the mountain not as a little stream but as a broad fierce water. So deep and rapid was it that the triple line of defence works of the Umpondwana were built only to its edge, for the water ran through a rocky gorge, although thorn trees fastened by their trunks were thrust out for ten or twelve feet over the banks of the gorge from either side of the stream. Now, in the centre of this river, which may have been thirty paces wide, was a long ridge or saddle of rock over which the water boiled furiously, although here it was not more than three feet deep. This ridge began at a point within the last line of walls and ran down to some five-and-twenty paces below the first wall. Swart Piet had noted the ridge.

"There is a saddle on which you may ride to victory," he said.

"How so, Bull-Head?" asked the captain.

"Thus. Yonder stand trees with tall stems and green tops; cut them down and make a bridge from the bank to the saddle; then wade up the saddle where the water is not more than waist deep, till you are past the third wall and reach the bank inside it as best you can."

Now although he was a brave man, as were all the Zulus in those days, the captain looked long and doubtfully at the white water which foamed upon the ridge.

"There is death in that water," he said.

"Death for some and victory for others," answered Van Vooren, "but if you fear it, go back to Dingaan and tell him so, for in no other way can this mountain be taken, seeing that it is impregnable, and that thirst alone can conquer it."

"I fear nothing, white man," answered the Zulu, "but if you are so brave, why, show us black people the way along yonder ridge!"

Piet shrugged his shoulders. "I wish to keep alive for reasons of my own; besides, I am not a soldier of Dingaan," he answered.

Then the captain turned and commanded such men as had battle axes to cut down three of the longest trees, which they did, although the task was difficult, for the wood was hard and their axes were light. When at length the trees were down they rolled them uphill to a spot where the ridge of rock ended, which was not more than thirty paces from the face of the outer wall. Now it was that Sihamba guessed their purpose for the first time, for until then she had believed that they were cutting the trees to use them as battering rams against the walls.

"They are coming on us by the path of the river," she said, and called for men to sally out and prevent them making the bridge from the bank to the saddle. But none answered her, for they dared not face the Zulus in the open.

"The water will sweep them away," they said; "moreover, when they try to land we can spear them."

"Cowards," she moaned, "on your own heads be your doom."

So the Umpondwana contented themselves with standing behind the first wall and casting volleys of spears at those who thrust out the trees within thirty paces of them, while Zinti shot at them with his gun, killing several. But coming between, the Zulus made a shield hedge to protect their comrades, so that the light throwing *assegais* did little hurt, and of the few that the gun killed they thought nothing.

Presently the ends of the trees lay beneath the water on the ridge of rock, and the captain commanded a certain *induna* to lead his men across. Now all natives fear a wet death, and though he was a brave man who would gladly have rushed the fortifications alone had he been so commanded, this soldier to whom the captain spoke looked askance at the furious torrent and hesitated. But that captain had served under Chaka, and knew how to deal with those who showed doubt or fear. Lifting his heavy *assegai*, he drove it through the man, so that he fell dead, and as he smote cried, "Coward, take this gift from the king!"

Then, calling to the soldiers, he himself ran out upon the bridge of tree-trunks and leaped into the water that rose to his middle. In an instant he would have been swept away, for the current was very fierce, had not those who followed sprang down at his side and behind him. For a moment they managed to keep their feet till others came, giving them support and being themselves protected by a breakwater built of the men who had gone first. Then, forming in a double line, each man linked his arms round the middle of his comrade in front, as Kaffir girls link themselves in a dance, and very slowly this human chain began to struggle forward along the back of the ridge. At times, indeed, the weight of the stream was almost too much for them, and swept some of them off into the deep water which ran on either side, but the strong rope of human muscles held, and they were dragged back again. Now they were between the lip of the first walls, and the Umpondwana soldiers hurled spears at them from the banks, killing many. But if a man was slain, or even badly wounded, his companions who held him let go, and, if needful, thrust him into the water, who could no longer serve the king. Then he gripped the soldier who stood in front of the lost one, and the chain dragged on.

"Oh! men of the Umpondwana," cried Sihamba, "had you but half the heart of these, who are brave, we need fear nothing from Dingaan," and the Zulus in the stream who heard her called in answer:—

"You are right, little chieftainess, we are brave."

Slowly the black snake-like line pressed forward through the white foam, never heeding the storm of spears that slew continually, till the point of it was well within the third line of walls. Then the captain, who by some chance had escaped, called an order to those behind him, and the head of the double line leapt off the ridge of rock into deep water, and swimming with their feet, but still gripping with their hands, suffered themselves to be swung round by the current towards the bank, twenty yards away. Here some rocks jutted out, and these, after a great struggle, they were able to grasp and hold.

Then followed what Suzanne, who was watching from above, afterwards declared to be the strangest sight she had ever seen, for these men, who swung to and fro in the current, anchored, as it were, to the ridge and the bank, made of their living bodies a bridge for their fellows. Yes, their companions ran and crawled over them, springing from shoulder to shoulder, and driving their heads beneath the water with the push of their clinging feet. Half-drowned and almost torn in two as they were, still they held on till enough men were safe on shore to finish the fray. For when the Umpondwana saw that the Zulus had won the bank they did not stay to kill them while they landed, as might easily have been done; no, dragging Sihamba with them, they ran into the gorge leading to the flat top of the mountain, and blocked it with great stones that were ready. And so it came about that the Zulus won this fight, though with great loss to themselves, and cut off the Umpondwana from their main supply of water.

But though they had won the fight they had not won the mountain. After resting a while they began the work of storming the narrow gorge that led upwards to the tableland, for this gorge was its only gate, and at first were suffered to pull down or climb over the walls which were built across it with but little resistance. Soon, however, they found out the reason of this, for when a number of them were in the gorge stones began to roll upon them from the edges of the cliffs above, crushing the life out of many, so that presently they were driven back to the head of the river. Afterwards they searched long and earnestly but could find no other path by which to attack, for there was none.

"Well," said the Zulu captain, "it seems that we must fight the fight of 'sit-down,' and since these rock-rabbits will not let us come to them we must wait till they come to us to ask for water."

So they waited for seven whole days, setting guards about the mountain in case there should be secret ways of egress of which they knew nothing.

****

When they reached the tableland Sihamba spoke words so bitter to her councillors and captains that some of them stopped their ears that they might hear no more, while others answered that they could do nothing against men who walked upon the boiling waters.

"Now, indeed, you can do nothing against them," Sihamba cried, "for Thirst will fight for them, and he is the best of friends. Because of your cowardice we must perish, everyone of us, and for my part I should be glad of it were it not that you have given the Lady Swallow to death also."

Then she buried her face in the ground and would say no more, even when they told her that the Zulus had been beaten back by the rocks that were rolled down upon them.

For some days the little spring gave enough water for the thousands of people who were crowded upon the mountain top, though there was none to spare for the cattle. But on the third night the poor beasts being maddened by thirst, broke out of the *kraal* and rushing to the spring, so trampled it with their hoofs that its waters were sealed up, and only very little could be obtained even by digging, for here the rock came near to the surface of the soil, and it would seem as though the course of the spring was turned or choked beneath it.

Then all those upon that mountain began to suffer the horrors of thirst. Soon the cattle were altogether mad and rushing to and fro in herds, bellowing furiously and goring everyone they met, or trampling them to the earth. Now the Umpondwana strove to be rid of them by driving them down the gorge, but the Zulus, guessing the trouble that the presence of these beasts was bringing upon the besieged would not suffer them to pass. Next they attempted to force them over the edge of the precipice, but when they were driven to it the oxen turned and charged through them, killing several men. After this they contented themselves with stabbing the most dangerous of the animals, and leaving the rest to rush to and fro as they would, for they did not care to kill them all lest their carcasses should breed a pestilence.

The sixth day came, and, oh! the great *kraal* of the Umpondwana was but as a hell wherein lost souls wandered in torment, for the sun beat down upon it fiercely and everywhere roamed or lay men, women and children overcome with the torture of thirst; indeed, of the last, some were already dead, especially those who were at the breast, for their mothers' milk was dry. Here three men had dragged an old wife from her hut, and were beating her to make her reveal the store of water which she was believed to have hidden; there others were cutting the throat of an ox that they might drink its blood, and yonder a little girl was turning stones to lick the damp side of them with her poor parched tongue.

In the midst of these scenes which passed outside her hut, sat

Sihamba brooding. As chieftainess she still had about a pint of water stored in a jar, but though she had made Suzanne drink, herself she drank but little, for she would not consent to suffer less than those about her.

Now Sihamba's eyes fell upon the child who was licking stones, and her heart was wrung with pity. Going into the hut she fetched most of the water in a gourd, and calling to the child, who staggered towards her, for she could scarcely walk, she gave it to her, bidding her drink slowly.

In a moment it was gone, every drop of it, and, behold! the dim eyes brightened, and the shrunken limbs seemed to grow round again, while the young voice, no longer high and cracked, praised and blessed her name. Sihamba motioned the child away, then she went into the hut to weep, only weep she could not, since her eyes were too dry for tears.

"Three more days," she thought to herself, "and they will all be dead unless rain should fall. Yes, the cowards, and those whom their cowardice has betrayed will all be dead together."

As she thought thus, Suzanne entered the hut, and there was tidings in her eyes.

"What is it, sister," asked Sihamba, "and whence do you come?"

"I come from the high seat upon the edge of the cliff," she answered, "where I have sat all day, for I can no longer bear these sights, and I have this to tell, that the Zulus are marching across the plain, but not towards Zululand, since they head for the Quathlamba Mountains."

CHAPTER 30

Sihamba Prevails

Now a fire of hope shot up in Sihamba's eyes, but soon it died out again.

"It is a trick, it must be a trick," she said, "for who ever heard of a Zulu loosing the prey that was in his hand? Never dare he do it save by the command of the king," and she left the hut to be met by others running with the same tidings. Of these she sent some down the gorge to bring her report of what had happened, and with them Zinti, for she could not altogether trust the word of her own people.

Within an hour the messengers returned, and on their faces was a strange look which, clever as she was, Sihamba did not understand.

"Is the path clear?" she asked.

"No, chieftainess," they replied, "it is still blocked, for though the Zulus have gone we know not where by order received from Dingaan, Bull-Head holds it with such of his own men as are left alive."

"Had you speech with the white man?" she asked.

"Yes, lady."

"Say on."

Now they looked about them like people who are ashamed, but at last the oldest of them spoke.

"Chieftainess," he said, "Bull-Head made us this offer and in these words: 'You people of the Umpondwana, you are dying of thirst and I know it; yes, though the Zulus have gone and but few of us are left here, yet you cannot force the narrow way against us, so that I have only to sit here for a few days longer and you will be dead of thirst, everyone of you, you and your cattle together. But I do not wish that you should die, for with you I have no quarrel; also if you die one will perish among you whom I desire to keep alive. Therefore I make you this offer. Hand over to me your ruler, Sihamba Ngenyanga, and with her the white woman named Swallow, and you yourselves shall go free, everyone of you; more, although I will take this stronghold of yours to live in myself, I will give back to you the half of the cattle. Now, answer.'

"Lady, when he had finished speaking we consulted together and answered Bull-Head thus: 'We cannot give over to you our chieftainess and her white sister, for it is better to die than that such dishonour should lie upon our names. But if you will let us go, you can take them from among our number as we pass before you, for that will be no fault of ours, or if they do not choose to accompany us, after we have gone by you can ascend the mountain and take them.'

"To this Bull-Head assented, saying, 'Set the Lady Swallow in her chair upon the cliff edge and Sihamba at her side so that my eyes seeing them may know that they are safe, and you shall go.' So it was agreed between us that tomorrow at the dawn he will open the wall and let us down to the river to drink, after which we may pass whither we will."

Now when Sihamba heard these shameful words her rage was so great that for a while she could not even speak. At length she found her tongue and gasped out:

"Oh! father of cowards, do you dare to sing such a song in my ears? Why do not you, who are many, storm the pass and take the water?"

"Lady," answered the old man coldly, "we dare because we must, for honour cannot live before the *assegai* of thirst. You talk to us of storming the pass; we cannot storm it, for ten men can hold that place against a hundred; also our arms are weak and we are weary of war. Listen; on the one hand are the lives of thousands, with them your own and that of the White Swallow, and on the other this dishonour. We choose the dishonour, since if you and the Swallow do not desire to fall into the hands of Bull-Head, you can still do what you must have done had we chosen honour. Lady, you can die, knowing that by your death you have saved the lives of the multitude over whom you rule.

"Listen again, lady, we did not seek you, it was you who came back to us after the death of the chief, your brother. We accepted you and you have ruled us justly for these two years, but you wish to make of us a fighting people who are and who desire to remain a people of peace. Moreover, you promised that the white chieftainess, your companion, would bring us prosperity and good, whereas to us she has been a bird of ill-omen, for since she came here on her account there has been war and nothing but war. Yes, because of her we have been cooped up on this mountain and killed whenever we ventured on to the plains beyond; therefore we will have no more of her, she must find her own fortune, for we have our lives and those of our wives and children to save.

"Further, I say this: the news of the offer of Bull-Head has gone abroad among the people, and had we refused they would have torn us limb from limb, yes, and you and the White Swallow also. Our hearts are sad, but lady, who can fight against fate?"

"I can," answered Sihamba, "but have no fear; tomorrow at the dawn you shall see us sit out upon the cliff point; and now, father of cowards, begone, and let me see your face no more. Betray us if you will, you who were not men enough to hold the water, you who are not men enough to cut a path to it as you might, and therefore must complete your cowardice with treachery. Betray us if you will, but I tell you that you shall not go free from this disgrace. The curse of Chaka shall fall upon you and the blade of the spear shall be the inheritance of you who are afraid to grasp its shaft. Begone!" and withered by her words and the fire of her eyes, the spokesmen of the Umpondwana crept like beaten hounds from the presence of their deserted chieftainess.

****

Here I will stop the tale to say that this prophecy of Sihamba's came true, as did all the prophecies of that strange woman, who, with other gifts, without doubt had that of foresight. A few years later, when Panda was king, and their wars with us Boers were ended, the Zulus, who never forgot a quarrel, swooped down upon the Umpondwana unawares, and storming the mountain by night, put all the men on it to the spear, and carried away the women and children to Zululand, so that of this tribe there remains nothing but some crumbling walls and a name of shame.

****

Now the sun had set upon that home of thirst, and all was silent in it save for the sound of the hoofs of the galloping cattle as they rushed hither and thither, and the groaning of the women and children, who wandered about seeking grass to chew, for the sake of the night damps that gathered on it. Sihamba went into the great hut where she always slept with Suzanne, whom she found seated upon a stool, wan-faced, and her eyes set wide with misery of mind and body.

"What passes now?" asked Suzanne.

The little woman came to her, and throwing her arms about her neck she kissed her, answering:

"Alas! sister, all things pass, and with them our lives," and she told her of the surrender of the Umpondwana and its terms.

Suzanne listened in silence, for grief and despair had done their worst with her, and her heart could hold no more pain.

"So it is finished at last," she said, when Sihamba had spoken, "and this is the end of all our toil and strivings and of our long fight against fate. Yes, this is the end: that we must die, or at the least I must die, for I will choose death rather than that Van Vooren should lay a finger upon me. Well, I should care little were it not that now I believe my husband to be still alive, and it is hard to go before him into yonder darkness, though I believe also that the darkness which we fear will prove such a happy light as does not shine upon this earth," and she laid her head upon Sihamba's breast and they wept together.

Presently Sihamba said, "My mind, that was wont to be so clear, is darkened. Pray to your God, you who are of His people that He may send light upon it, so that I can think once more while there is yet time. Now we wander in the forest of despair, but never yet was there a forest so thick that it cannot be passed. Pray then that I may be given light, for your life hangs upon it."

So Suzanne prayed, and presently, as she prayed, her weariness overcame her and she slept, and Sihamba slept also. When Sihamba awoke it was within an hour of midnight. A little lamp of oil burnt in the hut, and by the light of it she could see the white face of Suzanne lying at her side, and groaned in her bitterness to think that before the sun set again that face must be whiter still, for she knew that the Swallow was not of the mind of the Umpondwana, who preferred dishonour to death. "Oh! that my wisdom might come back to me," she murmured. "Oh! Great-Great, God of my sister, give me back my wisdom and I will pay my life for it. Oh! Lighter of the stars, for myself I ask nothing, who am not of Thy children. Let eternal death be my portion, but give me back my wisdom that I may save my sister who serves Thee."

Thus prayed Sihamba out of the depth of her untutored heart, not for herself but for another, and it would seem that her prayer was heard; though many among our people think that God does not listen to the black creatures. At the least, as her eyes wandered around the hut, they fell upon certain jars of earthenware. Now during the years that she dwelt among the Umpondwana Suzanne had but two pastimes. One of them was to carve wood with a knife, and the other to paint pictures upon jars, for which art she always had a taste, these jars being afterwards burnt in the fire. For pigments she used certain clays or ochres, red and black and white and yellow, which were found in abundance on the slopes of the mountain, and also a kind of ink that she made by boiling down the kernels of the fruit of the green-leaved tree which grew by the banks of the river.

Now it was as she gazed at these jars of pigments and the brushes of goat's hair that the wisdom which she sought came to Sihamba; yes, in a moment it came to her, in a moment her plan was made, and she knew that it would not fail. Tomorrow at the dawn the Umpondwana, to the number of several thousands, would pour through the pass on to the plain beyond. Well, Suzanne should go with them, she should go *as a black woman!* Already her hair and eyes were dark, and with those pigments her snow-white flesh could be darkened also, and then in the crowd who would know her from a Kaffir girl, she who could talk the language as though she had been born a Kaffir. Stay! Bull-Head was artful and clever, and perhaps he might be ready for such a trick. How could she deceive him?

Again she looked at the jars, and again wisdom came to her. It was the habit of Suzanne to sit in her dizzy chair of rock and watch the sunrise, hoping ever that in the light of it she might see white men riding to rescue her, and this Van Vooren knew, for she could be seen from the mouth of the pass below, where from hour to hour he would stand gazing at her five hundred feet above his head.

Well, tomorrow at the dawn another white woman should be seated yonder to satisfy his eyes, or at least a woman who seemed to be white. On the cliff edge, not far from this very rock lay the body of a poor girl who that day had died of thirst. If its face and arms and feet were painted white, and Suzanne's cloak of white goat's hair were set upon its shoulders, and the corpse itself placed upright in the chair, who, looking at it from hundreds of feet beneath, could guess that it was not Suzanne, and who, seeing it set aloft, would seek for Suzanne among the crowd of escaping Kaffirs? The plan was good; it could scarcely fail, only time pressed.

"Sister, awake," whispered Sihamba. Suzanne sat up at once, for the sleep of the doomed is light. "Listen, sister," went on Sihamba, "that wisdom for which you prayed has come to me," and she told her all the plan.

"It is very clever, and it may serve," answered Suzanne, "for I understand these paints and can stain myself so that if my hair is cut none would know me from a Kaffir. But, Sihamba, there is one thing which I do not understand. What will you do? For if you attempt to escape your stature will betray you."

"I?" hesitated the little woman, "nay, I do not know, I have never thought of it. Doubtless I shall win through in this way or in that."

"You are deceiving me, Sihamba. Well, there is an end, I will not go without you."

"Can you think of death and say that you will not go without me?"

"I can Sihamba."

"Can you think of your father and your mother and say that you will not go without me?"

"I can, Sihamba."

"Can you think of your husband and say that you will not go without me?"

"I can," faltered Suzanne.

"Truly you are brave," laughed the little woman. "There is more courage in that white heart of yours than in those of all the Umpondwana. Well, sister, I also am brave, or at the least for these many moons I have set myself a task, nor will I shrink from it at the end, and that is to save you from Piet Van Vooren as once at a dearer price you saved me. Now, hearken, for myself I have no fear; as I have said, doubtless in this way or in that I shall win through, but it cannot be at your side. I must rejoin you afterwards. What, you refuse to go? Then, Lady Swallow, you send me down to death and your hands are red with my blood. I am weary, I will not live to see more trouble; life is hard and death is easy. Finish your own battle, Swallow, and fly out your flight alone," and drawing a knife from her girdle Sihamba laid it upon her knee.

"Do you mean that you will kill yourself if I refuse your prayer?"

"Nothing less, sister, and at once, for I thirst, and would seek some land where there is water, or where we need none. It comes to this, then: if you consent I may live, if you refuse I must die."

"I cannot do it," moaned Suzanne. "Let us die together."

Now Sihamba crept to her and whispered in her ear:

"Think of Ralph Kenzie and of what his life must be if you should die. Think of those children who will come, and of that first kiss of love found again which you must miss in death, whatever else it may have to give. Think of the knife's point that you would change for it, or the last sick rush down a mountain height of space. Think of your husband. Hark! I hear him calling you."

Then Suzanne yielded.

"O woman with a noble heart," she murmured, "I listen to your tempting; may God forgive me and God reward you, O woman with the noble heart."

CHAPTER 31

Sihamba's Farewell

Then they began the work, for much must be done before the daylight came. First Sihamba took a sharp knife, and with it cut off Suzanne's beautiful hair close to the head, over which what was left of it curled naturally. To disguise it further, for though it was dark it was too fine for the hair of a native, she put grease upon it and powdered it with the blue dust that Kaffir women use. This done, the poor girl stripped herself, and with the help of Sihamba smeared all her body, every inch of it down to the soles of her feet, with the ink-like juice mixed with the black earth and grease, which when it was dry made her the colour of a Kaffir. Next Sihamba dressed her in a native woman's *moocha* made of skin and beads, and gave her an old skin blanket to wear upon her shoulders and hide sandals for her feet, together with anklets of beads and copper wire. Then having examined her all over to see that no sign of her white skin could be seen through the pigments, and burned the long tresses of her hair, Sihamba went to the door of the hut.

"Where are you going?" asked Suzanne.

"To find Zinti," she answered, "for now we must have his help."

"No, no," cried Suzanne, "I am ashamed to be seen thus by any man."

"Wherefore, Swallow, seeing that for some days you are but a Kaffir woman, and this is their dress, of which none think harm? Nay, you must, for remember that if you show doubt or shame, you will betray yourself."

Then with a groan Suzanne yielded, and crouching upon the floor like a native, awaited the return of Sihamba. Presently she came, followed by Zinti, who was in good case, though somewhat thin, for Zinti was clever and provident, and, foreseeing what would come, he had hidden water for himself among the rocks.

"Zinti," said Sihamba, "I would speak with you of secret matters."

"Speak on, lady," he answered—here his eyes fell upon Suzanne crouched on the ground in the full light of the lamp—"but there is a stranger present."

"This is no stranger, Zinti," said Sihamba, "but one whom you know well."

"Indeed, lady, I know her not. Should I forget one so beautiful? And yet—and yet—" and he rubbed his eyes and stared, gasping, "it cannot be."

"Yes, it is, Zinti. There sits the lady Swallow and none other."

Now although there was little mirth left in him, Zinti burst out laughing till the tears ran from his eyes, and Sihamba struck him with her hands, calling him "Fool," and commanding him to be silent.

"Wow!" he said, "this is wonderful. This is magic indeed. She who was white as snow has become black as coal, and yes, she looks best black. Oh! this is magic indeed."

At his words Suzanne sprang up looking as though she were about to weep, and Sihamba stopped his lips with fierce words and blows, though he took small heed of either, but stood staring.

"Zinti," Sihamba said, "you have done me many services, but today you must do me the greatest of all. This morning at the daylight the lady Swallow will pass with the multitude down the cleft yonder and none will know her in that disguise. You must go with her, but not too near her, and cross the plain, meeting her by the saw-edged rock which stands yonder at the mouth of the gorge in the Quathlamba mountains. Then you must lead her as fast as you can travel to that camp of the Boers which is near the Tugela River, where she will be safe. Do you understand?"

"I understand, lady. But what of yourself?"

"It is my plan to hide on the mountain," Sihamba answered quickly, "in a secret place I know of, seeing that it is impossible that I should escape because my stature would betray me. I will join you at the Boer camp later; or, failing that, you can return in a while—say on the first night of the new moon—to search for me. But talk no more, for we have still much to do. Yes, we who have made a white woman black, must make a black woman white. Follow me, both of you," and giving Zinti a jar of pigment and the long goat-skin cloak, which Suzanne wore for an outer garment, she left the hut, carrying in her hand strips of ox-hide tanned white.

Avoiding the groups of thirst-tormented people who sat or wandered about in the coolness of the night, they passed through the gates of the *kraal* unheeded, and walking quickly across the wide stretch of tableland reached the eastern edge of the cliff. Now upon the very verge of this cliff rose a sharp pinnacle of rock fifty feet or more into the air, and upon the top of this pinnacle was that stone shaped like a great chair, in which Suzanne sat day by day, poised like an eagle over the dizzy gulf of space, for the slopes of the mountain swelled five hundred feet beneath, watching for the help that never came. Not far from the base of this point Sihamba began to search in the starlight till she found what she wanted, the body of a young woman who had crept here to die of thirst, and whose death and the place of it had been reported to her.

Now she took the jar of white clay, and, aided by Zinti, set about her ghastly task, daubing the stuff thickly upon the cold features and the neck and arms and feet. Soon it was done, for such work needed little care, but then began their true toil since the corpse must be carried up the sharp point of rock, and that by no easy path. Had not Zinti been so strong it could never have been done; still, with the aid of Suzanne and Sihamba herself, at last it was finished.

Up that steep place they toiled, the three of them, dragging the dead body from knob to knob of rock, well knowing that one false step in the gloom would send them to be broken to pieces hundreds of feet beneath. At length they reached the little platform where there was scarcely room for all of them to stand with their burden, and climbing on to the stone which was called the Chair, Zinti drew the dead woman into the seat of it.

Then as Sihamba bade him he wrapped her in Suzanne's long white cape of goat-skin, putting the hood of it upon her head, after which he made the corpse fast in a sitting posture, lashing it round the neck and middle to the back of the stone with the white tanned *rimpis* in such fashion that it could not fall or even slip.

"So," said Sihamba grimly, "there sits the bridge upon whom Swart Piet can feast his eyes while you seek safety across the mountains. Now back to the town, for from this height I can already see light glimmering in the east."

Accordingly they returned to the hut and entered it, leaving Zinti without, none noting them since by now the multitudes were thronging the narrow way. Here Sihamba lit the lamp, and by its light once more examined Suzanne carefully, retouching the dye in this place and in that, till she was sure that no gleam of white showed through it.

"It is good," she said at length; "unless you betray yourself, your skin will not betray you. And now, lady Swallow, the hour has come for us to part, and I rejoice to think that some of the debt I owe you I have repaid. Long ago I told you that very far away I should live to save you as you saved me, and I am sure that I have saved you; there is no doubt of it in my heart. Yes, yes, Swallow, I see you most happy in the love of husband and of children, thinking of all these things as a far-off evil dream, as of a dream that never will return. What more do I desire? What more have I to ask?

"I say that I have repaid to you part of the debt I owe, but all of it I can never repay, for, Swallow, you have given me love which elsewhere has been denied to me. Others have parents and brothers and sisters and husbands to love them; I have none of these. I have only you who are to me father and mother and sister and lover.

"How then can I repay you who have taught this cold heart of mine to love, and have deigned to love me in return? Oh! and the love will not die; no, no, it will live on when all else is dead, for although I am but a Kaffir doctoress, at times light shines upon my heart, and in that light I see many new things. Yes, yes, I see that this life of ours is but a road, a weary road across the winter *veldt*, and this death but the black gate of a garden of flowers——"

"Oh! why do you speak thus?" broke in Suzanne. "Is this then our last farewell, and does your wisdom tell you that we part to meet no more?"

"I know not, Swallow," answered Sihamba hastily, "but if it should be so I care nothing, for I am sure that through all your days you will not forget me, and that when your days are done I shall meet you at the foot of the death-bed. Nay, you must not weep. Now go swiftly, for it is time, and even in your husband's love be mindful always that a woman can love also; yes, though she be but a dwarfed Kaffir doctoress. Swallow—Sister Swallow, fare you well," and, throwing herself upon her breast, Sihamba kissed her again and again. Then, with a strange strength, she thrust her from the hut, calling to Zinti to take charge of her and do as she had bidden him, adding that if he failed in this task she would blast his body and haunt his spirit.

****

Thus parted Sihamba, the Kaffir witch-doctoress, and my daughter Suzanne, whom she kept safe for nearly three years, and saved at last at the cost of her own life. Yes, thus they parted, and for always in the flesh, since it was not fated that they should meet again in this world, and whether it has been permitted to Sihamba—being a Kaffir, and no Christian—to enter a better one is more than I can say. In her case, however, I hope that she has found some hole to creep through, for although she was a black witch-doctoress, according to her knowledge she was a good woman and a brave one, as the reader will say also before he comes to the end of this story.

****

Outside the hut Zinti took Suzanne by the arm and led her through the mazes of the town to the open ground that lay between it and the mouth of the steep cleft which ran down to the slopes of the mountain.

All this space was crowded with people, for as yet they could not enter the cleft, which nowhere was more than ten feet wide, because it was filled with cattle, some alive and some dead, that, drawn by the smell of water beneath, had gathered as near to it as the stone walls which blocked the pass would allow.

Suzanne and Zinti mingled with this crowd of fugitives, taking a position almost in the midst of it, for they did not wish to pass out either among the first or the last. There they waited a while, none noting them, for in their great agony of thirst all thought of themselves and not of their neighbours. Indeed, husbands deserted their sick wives and mothers their children, which were too heavy to carry; yes, they deserted them to be trampled by the feet of men and the hoofs of cattle.

Now, the eastern sky grew grey, and though the sun had not yet risen the light was such that a man could see the veins upon the back of his hand and the white moons on his finger-nails. Presently, as though moved by one impulse, thousands of voices uttered a hoarse cry of "It is dawn! Open, open!"

But it would seem that the wall still stood, for the cattle remained packed in so dense a mass that a man could have walked upon their backs, as, indeed, some tried to do.

At last the sun rose, or rather its rays shot upwards across the eastern skies like a fan of fire. Suzanne turned her head and watched till presently the arrows of light struck upon the tall chair rock which was the highest point of all the mountain. Yes, there in the chair sat the white figure and by its side stood what seemed to be a black child. It was Sihamba. Far below other eyes were watching also, the eyes of Swart Piet, for he would not let the people go until he knew that Suzanne and Sihamba stayed behind. But now he saw them, Suzanne in her accustomed place, and at her side Sihamba.

"Pull down the walls," he shouted to his men, for he was eager to clear the pass of cattle and Kaffirs that he might go up it, and they obeyed him. Before they were more than half down the oxen, pushing and leaping forward madly, cleared what was left of them and, open-mouthed, their lolling tongues hanging from their dry jaws, rushed downward to the water, goring or trampling to death some of those who worked at the wall.

"The *schanzes* are down," screamed the people, seeing the long line of cattle move, and immediately they began to press forward also.

At Suzanne's side was a young woman so weak with thirst that she could scarcely walk, and on her back a year-old boy, insensible but living, for a red froth bubbled from his lips. A man thrust this woman to one side and she fell; it was that aged councillor who on the yesterday had brought news of the surrender to Sihamba. She tried to struggle to her feet but others trampled upon her.

"Sister, sister!" she cried, catching Suzanne by the hide blanket which she wore, "I am dead, but oh! save my child."

"Let it be," whispered Zinti, but Suzanne could not deny those piteous eyes, and as she passed she snatched up the boy and the sling in which he was carried by the dying woman, setting the band of it beneath her own breast. So she went forward, bearing him upon her hip, nor did that act of mercy lack its reward, for as shall be seen it was her salvation. Also the child lived, and to this day is a faithful servant in our house, though now his beard is white.

Down the narrow way surged the crowd, scrambling over rocks and dead cattle and crushed women and children, till at the last Suzanne drew near its opening, where stood Swart Piet and some twenty of his followers, watching the multitude pass out.

"Lady," whispered Zinti into her ear, "now I fall behind, for Bull-Head may know me. If I win through I will rejoin you on the plain, or by the saw-edged rock; if I do not, throw away that child, and follow the road of which I have told you, you can scarcely mistake it. Go on, showing no fear, and—stay, let that blanket hang open in front, it is not the custom of these women to wear their garments wrapped so closely."

Suzanne groaned, but she obeyed.

CHAPTER 32

The Pass of the Quathlamba

Like wild beasts escaping from a pen, that red-eyed, gasping mob rushed and staggered to the edge of the water, and, plunging their heads into it with hoarse grunts and cries, drank and drank and drank. Indeed, several lost their lives there, for some filled themselves so full that their vitals were ruptured, and some were thrust into the river by the cattle or those pressing behind them, to be carried away by the swift stream.

Just at the mouth of the pass Suzanne, laden with the child, was pushed down by those who followed, and doubtless would have been trampled to death, had not one of Swart Piet's men, desiring to clear the way, or, perhaps, moved to pity at her plight, dragged her to her feet again. But when he had done this he did not let her go, but held her, staring at her beauty with greedy eyes.

"Here is a rock-rabbit whom I shall keep for a wife," he cried. "I would rather take her than twenty fat oxen."

Now Suzanne's heart nearly stood still with terror.

"Water, water," she moaned; "let me drink, I pray you."

"Do not fear, I will take you to drink, my pretty," went on the man, still staring at her.

Then, losing command of herself, Suzanne screamed and struggled, and the sound of her cries reached the ears of Swart Piet, who was standing close at hand.

"What is this?" he asked of the man.

"Nothing, Bull-Head, except that I have taken a woman whom I wish for a wife because she is so fair."

Van Vooren let his eyes rest upon her, but dreamily, for all his thoughts were given to her who sat aloft five hundred feet above his head, and, feeling their glance, Suzanne's blood froze in her veins.

"Yes, she is fair," he answered, "but she is a married woman, and I will have no Umpondwana brats among my people. Let her go, and take a girl if you will." For Van Vooren did not wish that the few men who remained with him should cumber themselves just then with women and children, since they were needed to look after the cattle.

"Maid or wife, I choose this one and no other," said the man sulkily.

Then Black Piet, whose sullen temper could not brook to be crossed, broke into a blaze of rage.

"Do you dare to disobey me?" he shouted with an awful Kaffir oath. "Let her go, dog, or I will kill you."

At this the man, who knew his master, loosed hold of Suzanne, who ran away, though it was not until she reached the water that she noticed a white ring round her arm, where his grip had rubbed the paint off the skin beneath. Strangely enough Van Vooren saw the ring, and at that distance mistook it for an ivory ornament such as Kaffir women often wear above the elbow. Still more strangely its white colour made him think again of the white woman who sat aloft yonder, and he turned his face upwards, forgetting all about the black girl with the child.

Thrusting herself through the crowd, Suzanne ran on for a while till she was clear of the worst of it, then terrified though she was, she could resist the temptation of the water no longer, for her mouth and throat felt dry and rough. Climbing down to the edge of the river she drank greedily under the shelter of a rock, and when she had satisfied some of her thirst, she poured water into the mouth of the child, dipping its shrunken little body into the stream, whereon it seemed to increase before her eyes like a dry sponge that is left out in the rain.

While she tended the child thus, and just as it began to find its senses and to wail feebly, she chanced to look up, and to her terror saw that man from whom she had escaped walking along the bank looking for her. Happy was it for Suzanne that the rock under which she was crouched hid her, for the man stood for thirty seconds or more within two paces, so that she was obliged to plunge the body of the boy under water to stifle its crying.

Then, as it happened, the Kaffir caught sight of another woman and infant, more than a hundred yards away, and ran off towards them. Thereon Suzanne, replacing the half-choked child upon her back, climbed the bank, hiding the white mark upon her arm beneath the blanket, and taking such shelter as she could behind stones or cattle, or knots of people who, their thirst appeased, were hastening to escape, she slipped across the shoulder of the slope.

Now she was out of sight of Swart Piet and his men, and for the first time for many a day began to breathe freely. For a while she crept on round the flank of the mountain, then at the best of her speed she struck across the plain straight for the saw-edged rock ten miles away, which marked the entrance to the pass over the Quathlamba range.

From time to time Suzanne looked behind her, but none followed her, nor, search as she would, could she discover any trace of Zinti, who, she began to fear, must have come to some harm. One thing she could see, however—the whitened corpse set on high in the chair of rock, and by the side of it a black dot that she knew to be Sihamba. Twice she turned round and gazed at it, but the second time the dot had become almost imperceptible, although it still was there. Long and earnestly she looked, sending her farewell through space to that true friend and deliverer whose eyes, as she knew well, watched her flight and whose heart went with her.

Then she travelled on sadly, wondering what was that plan of escape of which Sihamba had spoken, and why it was that she stood there by the corpse and did not put it into practice, wondering also when they should meet again and where. A third time she turned, and now the dead woman on the rock was but as a tiny point of white, and now it had altogether vanished away.

After this Suzanne halted no more, but pressed on steadily towards the saw-edged spur, which she reached about twelve o'clock, for the grass was so tall, the untrodden *veldt* so rough, and the sun so hot that, weak as she felt with grief and the effects of thirst, and laden with a heavy child, her progress was very slow. At length, however, she stood gasping in its shadow, gazing dismayed at the huge range of mountains before her and the steep rough cliffs up which she must climb.

"Never shall I cross them without foot and weighted with this child, so the end of it will be that I must die after all," thought Suzanne as she sank down by the banks of a little rivulet, resting her swollen feet in its cool stream, for then, and indeed for weeks after, it seemed to her that she could never have enough of the taste and smell and feel of water.

As she sat thus, striving to still the wailing of the hungry boy, suddenly the shadow of a man fell upon her. With a cry she sprang to her feet to find herself face to face with Zinti.

"Oh! I thought that they had taken you," she exclaimed.

"No, lady, I escaped, but I crossed the plain far to your left, for it seemed better that we should not be seen travelling together from the mountain. Now let us eat who have eaten little for so many days, lacking water to wash down the food," and from the large skin wallet which he bore Zinti drew out dried flesh and roasted corn.

Suzanne looked at the food with longing, but before she touched any she took some corn, and having pounded it into a pulp with a stone, she mixed it with water and fed the child, who devoured the stuff greedily and presently fell asleep. Then they ate as much as they wanted, since Zinti carried enough for three such meals, and never did Suzanne take meat with a greater relish. Afterwards, though she yearned to sleep, they pressed on again, for Zinti said it was not safe to stay, since long before this Van Vooren would be seeking her far and wide, and if he chanced to discover the secret of her flight he would travel further in one hour on horseback than they could in four on foot. So they went forward up the pass much refreshed, Zinti carrying the child.

All day long they walked thus, resting at intervals, till by sunset they reached the crest of the pass, and saw the wide plains of Natal stretched out like a map beneath them, and on them, not so very far away and near to the banks of the river that wound at their feet, a white-topped *koppie*, beneath which, said Zinti, was the Boer camp.

Suzanne sat down and looked, and there, yes, there the caps of the wagons gleamed in the fading light; and oh! her heart leapt at the sight of them, for in those wagons were white men and women such as she had not seen for years, and with whom at length she would be safe. But even as her breast heaved at the thought of it, an icy, unnatural wind seemed to stir her hair, and of a sudden she felt, or seemed to feel, the presence of Sihamba. For a moment, and one only, it was with her, then it was gone, nor during all her life did it ever come back again.

"Oh! Sihamba is dead!" she cried.

Zinti looked at her in question.

"It may well be so," he said sadly, "but I pray that it is not so, for she is the best of chieftainesses. At least we have our own lives to save, so let us go on," and again they pressed forward through the gathering gloom.

Soon it grew dark, and had her guide been any other man than Zinti Suzanne must have stopped where she was till the moon rose at midnight. But Zinti could find any path that his feet had trod even in the dark; yes, although it ran through piled-up rocks on the mountain side, and was cut with the course of streams which must be forded.

In wading through one of these rivulets, Suzanne struck her bare ankle against a stone and lamed herself, so that from this time forward, shivering and wet with water, for her hurt was so sharp and sudden that she had fallen in the stream, she was forced to walk leaning on Zinti's shoulder, and indeed over some rough places he was obliged to carry her. Now again Zinti wished to abandon that heavy child, for strong though he was the weight of the two of them proved almost more than he could bear, but Suzanne would not listen to him.

"Nay," she said, "this child that was sent to me by Heaven has saved me from shame and death, and shame and death be my portion if I will leave it while I live. Go on alone if you will, Zinti, and I will stay here with the child."

"Truly white people are strange," answered Zinti, "that they should wish to burden themselves with the child of another when their own lives are at stake, but be it as you will, lady," and he struggled forward as best he could, carrying the one and supporting the other.

Thus for hour after hour, slowly they crept onward with only the stars to light and guide them, till at length about midnight the moon rose and they saw that they were near the foot of the mountain. Now they rested awhile, but not long enough to grow stiff, then hastening down the slope they reached the plain, and headed for the white-topped *koppie* which shone in the moonlight some six miles away. On they crept, Suzanne now limping painfully, for her ankle had begun to swell, and now crawling upon her hands and knees, for Zinti had no longer the strength to carry her and the child. Thus they covered three miles in perhaps as many hours. At last, with something like a sob, Suzanne sank to the earth.

"Zinti, I can walk no more," she said. "Either I must rest or die."

He looked at her and saw that she spoke truth, for she was quite outworn.

"Is it so?" he said, "then we must stay here till the morning, nor do I think that you will take hurt, for Bull-Head will scarcely care to cross that pass by night."

Suzanne shook her head and answered:

"He will have begun to climb it at the rising of the moon. Hear me, Zinti. The Boer camp is close and you still have some strength left; take the child and go to it, and having gained an entrance in this way or in that tell them my plight and they will ride out and save me."

"That is a good thought," he said; "but, lady, I do not like to leave you alone, since here there is no place for you to hide."

"You could not help me if you stayed, Zinti, therefore go, for the sooner you are gone, the sooner I shall be rescued."

"I hear your command, lady," he answered, and having given her most of the food that was left, he fastened the sleeping child upon his shoulder and walked forward up the rise.

In something less than an hour Zinti came to the camp, which was formed of un*laagered* wagons and tents pitched at the foot of a *koppie*, along one base of which ran the river. About fifty yards in front of the camp stood a single buck-wagon, and near to it sill glowed the embers of a cooking-fire.

"Now if I try to pass that wagon those who watch by it will shoot at me," thought Zinti, though, indeed, he need have had no fear, for they were but camp-Kaffirs who slept soundly.

Not knowing this, however, he stood at a distance and called aloud, till at last a Hottentot crept out with a gun, and, throwing back the blanket from his head, asked who he was and what he wanted.

"I want to see the Baas of the camp," he answered, "for my mistress, a white woman, lies exhausted upon the *veldt* not far away and seeks his help."

"If you want to see the Baas," yawned the man, "you must wait till daylight when he wakes up."

"I cannot wait," answered Zinti, and he made as though to pass towards the camp, whereupon the man raised his gun and covered him, saying:

"If you go on I will shoot you, for stray Kaffir dogs are not allowed to prowl about the camp at night."

"What then must I do?" asked Zinti.

"You can go away, or if you will you may sit by the wagon here till it is light, and then when the Boers, my masters, wake up you can tell your story, of which I believe nothing."

So, having no choice, Zinti sat down by the wagon and waited, while the man with the gun watched him, pretending to be asleep all the while.

****

Now Suzanne was left alone upon the great *veldt*, and fear took hold of her, for she was broken in body and mind, and the place was very desolate; also she dreaded lest lions should take her, for she could hear them roaring in the distance, or Swart Piet, who was worse than any lion. Still she was so weary that after washing her face and hands in a spring close by, presently she fell asleep. When she awoke the east was tinged with the first grey light of the coming dawn, and it seemed to her as though some cold hand of fear had gripped her heart of a sudden and aroused her from heavy sleep. A sound caused her to look up, and there on the crest of the rise before her, some three hundred yards away, she saw dark forms moving, and caught sight of spears that glimmered in the moonlight.

"Now there is an end," thought Suzanne to herself, "for without doubt yonder stands a Zulu *impi*; the same that attacked the Umpond-wana, for I can see the crane's feathers in their head-dresses," and she crouched upon the ground in an extremity of dread.

CHAPTER 33

Ralph Finds the Dream Mountain

Now I must go back to that evening when we learned the great tidings from the lips of the lad Gaasha, whose life Ralph had saved after the attack by the Kaffirs upon the *laager*. There sat Gaasha on the ground staring, and there, not far away, Ralph was lying in his swoon, while Jan and I looked at each other like people who have suddenly beheld a sign from heaven.

"What evil magic is there in my words," said Gaasha presently, "that they should strike the Baas yonder dead like a spear?"

"He is not dead," I answered, "but for long he has sought that mountain Umpondwana of which you speak. Tell us now, did you hear of any white woman dwelling with the chieftainess Sihamba?"

"No, lady, I heard of none."

This answer of Gaasha's saddened me, for I made sure that if so strange a thing had happened as that a white woman had come to live among his tribe, the man who told him of the return of Sihamba would have told him of this also. Therefore, so I argued, either Suzanne was dead or she was in the power of Piet Van Vooren, or Sihamba had deserted her, though this last I did not believe. As it turned out afterwards, had not Gaasha been the stupidest of Kaffirs, we should have been saved those long days of doubt and trouble, for though he had not heard that Sihamba was accompanied by a white woman, he had heard that she brought with her a white *bird* to the mountain Umpondwana. Of course if he had told us this we should have guessed that the white bird could be none other than Suzanne, whose native name was Swallow.

Well, we set about reviving Ralph, which was done by throwing water on to his face. When he had found his senses again I prayed him not to suffer himself to be carried away with hope, since although Gaasha had heard of Sihamba, he had heard nothing of Suzanne.

To this he answered that now when God had pointed out to him the mountain of his vision and in so strange a manner, he had no fear but that he would find his wife upon it, since God was merciful and did not desire to mock or torment His servants.

I replied that I trusted it might be so, but the ways of the Almighty were beyond our understanding, nor did it become us to pass judgment upon them. Ralph scarcely heeded my words, but, springing to his feet, said:

"Come, let us be going to the mountain Umpondwana."

"First we must consult with the commandant and get aid from him," said Jan, "for it would not be safe that we should wander into these wild places alone, where there are many Kaffirs who doubtless would murder us."

In his eagerness Ralph would not listen to this, for he desired to start at once. But I pointed out to him that we had no horses, all ours being dead of the sickness; moreover, that the night was dark, and we could not trek till the moon rose, so at length he consented. Then we went into the *laager*, and Jan called the older men together in a quiet place.

"What is it, *Heer* Botmar?" asked the commandant when they were assembled.

"It is this, cousin," said Jan. "I desire to ask you to go a three days' trek out of your march to a mountain called Umpondwana, whither this servant of mine, Gaasha, can guide you."

"For what reason?" asked the commandant astonished.

"Friend," said Jan, "you have all of you heard the story of how that outcast devil Piet Van Vooren, stole away my only child, Suzanne, the wife of Ralph Kenzie the Englishman here."

"That is an old tale," said the commandant, "and, doubtless, the poor girl is dead long ago; why then do you speak of it now, and what has it to do with your request that we should trek to the mountain Umpondwana?"

"Only this, cousin; we think that my daughter Suzanne is living there among the Kaffirs, and we seek to rescue her. At least this is certain, for only now we have learnt it from the lips of Gaasha that Sihamba, her friend and servant whom we believe was with her, rules over this tribe as chieftainess."

"That may be so," said the commandant, "but did Gaasha tell you that your daughter was there also?"

"No," answered Jan.

"Then how do you know it?"

Now Jan hesitated and turned red as he replied:

"We know it because Ralph Kenzie here saw this very mountain in a vision more than two years ago, and in that vision was told that there he would find the wife who was taken from him on his marriage day."

Now, on hearing this most of the Boers broke out laughing, for, though very religious, we are not a people who place faith in visions. Thereupon I grew angry, and spoke to them more strongly, perhaps, than I should have done, reducing them to silence, for they were all of them a little afraid of my tongue. Also I told them the story of that dream of Ralph's and of what had just passed with Gaasha, showing them that there was more in it than they imagined. After I had done Ralph spoke also, saying:

"Friends, doubtless this tale sounds foolish in your ears; but I ask what has been my nickname among you? Has it not been 'Man of the Mountain,' because I have always spoken and inquired for a certain mountain which had ridges on it shaped like the fingers of a man's hand, and have you not thought me mad for this reason? Now I have heard of such a mountain and I have heard also that Sihamba, who was with my wife, rules there as chieftainess. Is it strange, therefore, that I, believing now as ever in that vision, should wish to visit this mountain where, as I am sure, I shall find the wife that is lost to me?"

After this the Boers laughed no more but consulted apart till at last the elder, *Heer* Celliers, spoke.

"*Heer*en Botmar and Kenzie," he said, "of all this story of a vision we can say little. For aught we know it may be true, but if true then it is the work of magic and we will have nothing to do with it. Should you wish to go to seek this mountain Umpondwana you must go alone, for we cannot alter our plans to trek there with you. But we counsel you not to go, since no good can come of visions and magic."

When I heard this I answered him back, but Jan and Ralph went away, and presently I found them talking together outside the *laager*.

"Let me go alone," Ralph was saying.

"Nay," Jan answered, "I will accompany you, for two are better than one; also I shall not sleep till I find out the truth and know whether Suzanne lives or is dead."

"Indeed! and what is to become of me?" I asked.

"You, *vrouw*, can stop with the neighbours here, and we will join you in Natal."

"You will do no such thing, Jan Botmar," I answered, "for where you two go there I can go. What! Am I not sick also with love for my daughter and anxious to learn her fate?"

"As you will, wife," answered Jan; "perhaps it is well that we three should not separate who have been together always," and he went to see about the wagon.

As soon as the moon rose, which was about eleven o'clock, the oxen were inspanned. Before we started, however, several of our friends came praying us not to venture on so perilous a journey; indeed, they threatened even to use force to prevent us, and I think would have done so had not Jan told them outright that we were our own masters and free to go where we wished. So they departed, grieving over our obstinacy, and little guessing that their danger was far greater than our own, since as it chanced just as they had trekked through the Van Reenen's Pass a few days later a Zulu *impi*, returning from the Weenen massacres, fell upon them unawares and killed more than half their number before they were beaten off.

So we trekked with the moon, Gaasha guiding us, and did not out-span till dawn. As I have said, we had no horses, but never until I made that journey did it come home to me how slow are oxen, for never before then was I in a hurry, nor, indeed, have I been since that time. It is the Englishmen who are always in a hurry, and that is one of the reasons why we Boers are so superior to them, and when we choose can master them in everything, except shopkeeping, and especially in fighting. Well, at the best the cattle could not drag the wagon over the roadless *veldt* at a greater rate than two miles an hour, or cover more than twenty miles a day in all. It was pitiful to see Ralph's impatience; again and again he walked on and returned; indeed, had we allowed it, I think that he would have pressed forward on foot, leaving us to follow in the wagon.

At daylight on the third day we inspanned as usual, and trekked through the morning mists until the sun sucked them up. Then Gaasha, who was sitting on the wagon-box beside Ralph, touched his shoulder, and pointed before him. Ralph looked, and far away upon the plain saw what seemed to be a white cloud, above which towered the flat cliffs of a mountain of red rock.

"See, Baas," he said, "yonder is Umpondwana, my home, and now by nightfall I shall know whether my parents are still alive, or, if they are dead, whether they have left any cattle that I can claim by law," and he began to whistle cheerfully.

"And I," said Ralph aloud, "shall know whether my life is to be a heaven or a hell," and all day long, neither eating nor drinking, he sat upon the wagon-box and stared at the mountain, not lifting his eyes from it.

****

It was about one o'clock in the afternoon when we seemed to be quite close to the green flanks of Umpondwana, that of a sudden we cut a wide spoor trampled by thousands of naked feet. Jan and Gaasha got off the wagon to examine it, but Ralph did not move.

"An *impi* has passed here," said Jan presently.

"Yes, and a Zulu *impi* as I think, Baas, but more than one whole day ago," and Gaasha began to hunt about amongst some low bushes which grew near the trail. Presently he held up his hand and shouted, and Jan ran to him.

"Look, Baas," he said, pointing to a bush.

Jan looked, and there beneath the bush lay a man, a Zulu soldier, for his tall grey plume was still fixed upon his head, and near him was his broad *assegai*. At that moment the man, who was still alive, although he was very near his death from dysentery, seemed to hear, for he sat up and opened his eyes, saying, *"Manzie, umlungho, manzie."* (Water, white man, water.)

"Bring a pannikin of water, here lies a sick Kaffir," shouted Jan to Ralph, who was still seated on the wagon-box staring at the mountain.

Ralph brought the water, and the soldier drank it greedily.

"Who are you, and how come you here?" asked Jan.

"I am a soldier of Dingaan," answered the man, "but when we were attacking the little people on that mountain I fell sick. Still I came away with the *impi*, but here my strength failed me, and here I have lain for a round of the sun and a round of the moon. I begged them to kill me, but my brothers would not, for they said that I might recover and join them."

"Where have they gone?" asked Jan.

"They have gone to eat up the Boers in Natal," the Zulu answered in a hollow voice, his empty eyes wandering towards the mountains of the Quathlamba range. "Yes, they have gone to do the King's bidding on the white men, for his word came to us while we besieged yonder stronghold. Tomorrow at the dawn they attack the little *laager* beneath the white *koppie* by the banks of the Tugela, and I must reach them by then—yes, yes, now I am strong again, and I shall attack with them tomorrow at the dawn. Farewell, white men, I will not kill you because you gave me the water which has made me strong again," and, rising from the ground, he grasped his spear and started forward at a run.

"Stay," cried Ralph. "I would question you as to what has hap-

226

pened on that mountain;" but the man did not seem to hear him. For thirty paces or so he ran on, then suddenly he halted and saluted with his spear, crying in a loud voice:

"Chief, I report myself, I am present."

Next he stretched his arms wide and fell forward upon his face. When they reached him he was quite dead.

"This is a strange story that we have heard about the Zulus and the folk in Natal," said Jan, rubbing his forehead.

"I think that the man was wandering in his mind," answered Ralph, "still there may be truth in it; but, father," he added, with a gasp of fear, and, catching Jan by the arm, "what has happened on the mountain Umpondwana? The Zulus have been there, and—what has happened on the mountain?"

Jan shook his head, but did not answer, for he knew too well what happens where the Zulu *impis* pass.

Notwithstanding that Ralph was mad with impatience we halted the wagon for a few minutes to take counsel, and in the end decided to send the *voorlooper* back to the camp which we had left to warn our friends of what we had learned as to the onslaught on our brethren in Natal, though we had small faith in the story. But either the lad ran away, or some accident befell him, or he failed to find the Boers who had already trekked, at the least our message never reached them, nor did we see him again. Then we went on, Gaasha leading the oxen as quickly as they could walk. All that afternoon we travelled almost in silence, following the spoor of the *impi* backwards, for our hearts were full of fear. We met no man, but once or twice we saw groups of cattle wandering unherded, and this astonished us, giving us hope, for it was not the custom of a victorious *impi* to leave the cattle of its enemy behind it, though if the people of the Umpondwana had conquered, it was strange that we should see no herds with the beasts.

At length, within two hours of sunset, we passed round the shoulder of the mountain and beheld its eastern slope.

"It is the very place of my vision," cried Ralph, and certainly there before us were the stone ridges shaped like the thumb and fingers of a man, while between the thumb and first finger gushed the river, upon the banks of which grew flat-topped green-leaved trees.

"Onward, onward!" he cried again, and, taking the long wagon whip, he thrashed the oxen till they bellowed in the yokes. But I, who was seated beneath the tent of the wagon, turned to look behind me, and in the far distance saw that men were driving herds of cattle towards the mountains.

"We are too late," I thought in my heart, "for, without doubt, whether it be the Zulus or others, the place has been taken, since yonder go the victors with the cattle. Now they will fall upon us and kill us. Well, should God will it, so let it be, for if Suzanne is dead indeed I care little if we die also; and to Ralph at least death will be welcome, for I think that then death alone can save him from madness."

Now we had reached the banks of the river, and were trekking up them towards the spot where it issued from the side of the mountain. Everywhere was spoor, but we saw no people, although here and there the vultures were hissing and quarrelling over the bones of a man or a beast.

"There has been war in this place," whispered Jan, "and now the peace of death has fallen upon it," but Ralph only flogged the weary oxen, saying nothing.

At length they could drag the wagon no further, for the path grew too steep for them, whereupon Ralph, seizing the first weapon that came to hand, which, as it chanced, was the broad *assegai* that Gaasha had taken that day from the side of the dead Zulu, ran forward up the trail followed by Jan and myself. Another two hundred yards and the path took a turn which led to the entrance of the first *scherm*, the same that the Zulus had captured by forcing the passage of the river. The gateway was open now, and Ralph entered.

At first he could see no one, but presently he heard a voice saying:

"Will you not tell, for death is very near you? Drink, witch, tell and drink."

"Fool," answered another voice, a grating, broken voice, "I say that death is near to both of us, and since she is saved I die gladly, taking my secret with me."

"Then witch, I will try steel," said the first voice.

Now Ralph looked over the rock from behind which the sound of voices came and saw the body of a little woman tied to a stone by the edge of the water, while over her leant a man, a white man, holding a knife in one hand and in the other a gourd of water, which he now placed close to her lips, and now withdrew from them. He knew that woman, it was Sihamba. Just at this moment the man looked up and their eyes met, and Ralph knew him also.

It was Piet Van Vooren.

228

Chapter 34

The Avenger of Blood

For a moment the two men stood looking at each other, yes, the shedder of blood and the avenger of blood stood quite still and silent, and looked each other in the eyes, as though a spell had fallen upon them striking them into stone. It was the voice of Sihamba that broke the spell, and it issued from her parched throat with a sound like the sound of a death-rattle.

"Ah! devil and torturer," it said, "did I not tell you that doom was at hand? Welcome, Ralph Kenzie, husband of Swallow."

Then with a roar like that of a wounded beast, Ralph sprang forward, in his hand the uplifted spear. For one instant Swart Piet hesitated, but at the words of Sihamba a sudden terror had taken hold of him and he dared not wait. Like a startled buck he turned and fled up the mountain, but as he passed her he struck downwards with the knife he held, stabbing Sihamba in the body.

Once also he looked round for help, but there was none, for during the long torment of Sihamba all the black villains who served him had slipped away, fearing lest others should secure their share of the stolen cattle. Then he sped on up the pass and never did a man run more swiftly. But after him came one who was swifter than he, the light-footed, long-limbed Englishman with rage in his heart, and an awful fire of vengeance blazing in his eyes.

Up the pass they ran, leaping over stones and dead cattle till at length they reached the tableland at the top. Here once again Van Vooren paused for an instant, for he bethought him that, perhaps, he might hold the mouth of the cleft against his pursuer. But his wicked heart was too full of fear to let him stay, so at full speed he set forward across the plain, heading for that chair rock where still sat the whitened corpse, for there he thought he could defend himself. Ralph followed him somewhat more slowly, for of a sudden he had grown cold and cunning, and, knowing that his foe could not escape him, he desired to save his breath for the last struggle.

For six hundred yards or more they ran thus, and when Van Vooren began to climb the pedestal of rock Ralph was fifty paces behind him. Presently he also reached the pedestal and paused to look. Already Swart Piet was standing by the stone chair, but it was not at him that he looked, but rather at the figure which was tied in the chair that he now saw for the first time. That figure no longer sat upright, draped in its white fur cloak, for it had been disturbed, as I shall tell presently, and the cloak was half torn from it. Now it hung over the arm of the chair, the ghastly white face looking down towards Ralph and beneath it the bare black breast.

Ralph stared, wondering what this might mean. Then the answer to the riddle flashed into his mind, and he laughed aloud, for here he saw the handiwork of Sihamba. Yes, that grisly shape told him that his love still lived and that it was to win the secret of her whereabouts that the devil above him had practised torment upon the little doctoress.

Ralph laughed aloud and began to climb the pinnacle. He might have waited till Jan, who was struggling up the pass after them, arrived with his gun, but he would not wait. He had no fear of the man above and he was certain of the issue of the fray, for he knew that God is just. As for that man above, he grinned and gibbered in his disappointed rage and the agony of his dread; yes, he stood there by the painted corpse and gibbered like an ape.

"Your evil doing has not prospered over much, Piet Van Vooren," called Ralph, "and presently when you are dead you will taste the fruits of it. Suzanne shall be mine till the end as she was mine from the beginning, but look upon the Death-wife that your wickedness has won," and he pointed at the body with his spear.

Black Piet made no answer, nor did Ralph speak any more, for he must set himself to finish his task. The Boer took a heavy stone and threw it at him, but it missed him and he could find no more. Then gripping the wrist of the corpse in his left hand to steady himself upon that giddy place, he leant forward and prepared to stab Ralph with the knife as he set foot upon the platform. Ralph saw his plan, and stopping in his climb, he took off his coat and wound it round his left arm as a shield. Then he came on slowly, holding the broad spear in front of him. At the last he made a rush and reached the flat space of rock. Piet stabbed at him, but the strength of the thrust lost itself in the folds of the coat.

Now who can say what happened. Round and round the rock

chair they swung, Van Vooren still holding fast to the arm of the dead woman who was lashed in it. Yes, even from where I stood five hundred feet below I could see the flash of spear and knife as they struck and struck again.

At length a blow went home; the Zulu *assegai* sank deep into Van Vooren's chest and he hung backwards over the edge of the abyss, supported only by his grip of the dead arm—from below it looked as though he were drawing the corpse to him against its will. Yes, he hung back and groaned aloud. Ralph looked at him and laughed again, since though he was gentle-hearted, for this man he had no pity. He laughed, and crying "That curse of God you mocked at falls at last," with a sudden stroke he drew the sharp edge of the spear across the lashing that held the body to the seat.

The *rimpi* parted, and with a swift and awful rush, like that of a swooping bird, the dead woman and the living man plunged headlong into space. One dreadful yell echoed down the pitiless precipices, followed presently by a soft thudding sound, and there, lodged upon a flat rock hundreds of feet beneath, lay what had been Piet Van Vooren, though, indeed, none could have told that it was he.

Thus ended the life of this man, this servant of the devil upon earth, and even now, after all these years, I can find but one excuse for him, that the excess of his own wickedness had made him drunk and mad. Yes, I believe that he who was always near to it, went quite mad when Ralph struck him with the whip after the fight by the sheep *kraal*, mad with hate of Ralph and love of Suzanne. Also his father was wicked before him, and he had Kaffir blood in his veins. Ah! for how much must our blood be called upon to answer, and how good is that man who can conquer the natural promptings of his blood!

****

Jan and I were following Ralph when he entered the river *scherm*, and reached it just in time to see pursued and pursuer vanishing up the narrow cleft. I caught sight of Van Vooren's back only, but although I had not seen him for years, I knew it at once.

"We have found the tiger at home," I said, "yonder goes Swart Piet."

"*Allemachter!* it is so," answered Jan. "Look, there lies the tiger's prey," and pointing to Sihamba he followed them up the mountain side as fast as his weight would allow, for in those days Jan was a very heavy man.

Meanwhile I made my way to the little figure that was stretched upon the rock at the edge of the river. She had fainted, but even before I reached her I saw from her small size and the strange hoop of stiff hair that she wore about her head, that it was none other than Sihamba, Sihamba whom I had last seen upon the eve of that unlucky marriage day.

But oh! she was sadly changed. One of her legs, I forget which, had been broken by a gunshot; the blood trickled from the wound where Van Vooren had stabbed her in the back; her little body was wasted by the want of water, and her face had shrunk to the size of that of a small child, although strangely enough it still was pretty. I knelt down by her, and placing my hand upon her heart felt that it still beat, though very slowly. Then I took water and sprinkled it upon her, and at the touch of it she opened her eyes at once.

"Give me to drink," she moaned, and I did so, pouring the water down her throat, which was ridged and black like a dog's palate. Her eyes opened and she knew me.

"Greeting, mother of Swallow," she said, "you come in a good hour, for now I shall be able to tell you all before I die, and I am glad that I was strong enough to endure the torment of thirst for so many hours."

"Tell me one thing, Sihamba," I said. "Does Suzanne live, and is she safe?"

"Yes, she lives, and I hope that this night she will be safe with your own people, the Boers, for she has crossed the mountains to seek shelter in that *laager* which is by the white-topped *koppie* near the banks of the Tugela in Natal."

"The *laager* by the white-topped *koppie*——" I gasped. "Oh, my God! that must be the camp which the Zulus attack tomorrow at the dawn."

"What do you say?" Sihamba asked.

In a few words I told her the tale that we had heard from the dying soldier, and she listened eagerly.

"I fear it must be true," she said, when I had finished, "for while he was tormenting me Bull-Head let it fall that Dingaan's regiments had gone hence by order of the King to make war upon the Boers in Natal, but I took little heed, thinking that he lied.

"Well," she went on after resting a while, "they may be beaten off, or—stay, in the glade yonder is the great *schimmel* horse; Bull-Head's people brought him down for him and I know that hours ago he has been well fed and watered. If her husband mounts him at sunset, he can be with the Swallow in the *laager* well before the dawn, in time to warn them all. Presently, when he returns from killing Bull-Head, I will show him the road, for I shall live till sunset. Give me more water, I pray you."

Now I saw that nothing could be done till Ralph and Jan returned, if they ever should return, so I prayed of Sihamba to tell me what had passed, for I saw that she could not live long, and desired to know the truth before she died. And she told me, with many rests and at no great length indeed, but very clearly, and as I listened I marvelled more and more at this Kaffir woman's love, faithfulness, and courage. At last she came to the tale of how she had disguised Suzanne, and set up the corpse in her place in the chair of rock.

"Step but a few paces there to the right," she said, "and you will see it."

I did as she bade me, and then it was that on looking upwards I saw Ralph and Swart Piet struggling together. They were so high above me that their shapes seemed small, but I could see the light flashing from the stabbing steel and I called out to Sihamba what I saw.

"Have no fear, lady," she answered, "it will only end one way." So indeed it did as has been told, for presently Van Vooren and the corpse rushed downwards to vanish in the abyss, while Ralph remained standing by the empty chair of stone.

"It is finished," I said, returning to Sihamba.

"I know it, lady," she answered. "Bull-Head's last cry reached my ears, and do you give thanks to the Spirit you worship that he is dead. You wished to know what happened after the Swallow and I parted. Well, I went and stood by the body on the pinnacle of rock, and there, as I expected, came Bull-Head to seek his captive. He commanded us to come down, but I refused, telling him that if he attempted to take the Swallow—for he thought that the body wrapped in the white cloak was she—she would certainly escape him by hurling herself from the cliff. Thus I gained much time, for now from my height I could see her whom I knew to be the lady Swallow travelling across the plain towards the saw-edge rock, although I was puzzled because she seemed to carry a child upon her back; but perhaps it was a bundle.

"At last he grew impatient, and without warning lifted his gun and fired at me, aiming low, for he feared lest the ball should pierce my mistress. The shot struck my leg where you see, and being unable to stop myself, although I broke my fall by clutching with my hands, I rolled down the rock to the ground beneath, but not over the edge of the precipice as I could have wished to do, for at the last I had intended to escape him by throwing myself from it.

"Leaving me unable to move he began to ascend the pinnacle, calling your daughter Swallow by sweet names as a man calls a shy horse which he fears will escape him. I watched from below, and even in my pain I laughed, for now I knew what must come. Since the Swallow did not answer, Bull-Head, wishing to be cunning, crept behind her in silence, and of a sudden seized the cloak and the arm beneath it, for he feared lest she should choose death and cheat him.

"Then it was that the body rolled over toward him; then it was that he saw the whitened face and the black breast beneath. Ah! lady, you should have heard his oaths and his yell of rage as he scrambled down the rocks towards me.

"'What think you of your bride?' I asked him as he came, for I knew that I must die and did not care how soon.

"'This is your trick, witch,' he gasped, 'and now I will kill you.'

"'Kill on, butcher,' I answered, 'at least I shall die happy, having beaten you at last.'

"'No, not yet,' he said presently, 'for if you grow silent, how shall I learn where you have hidden Suzanne Botmar?'

"'Suzanne Kenzie, wife of the Englishman, butcher,' I answered again.

"'Also,' he went on, grinding his teeth, 'I desire that you should die slowly.' Then he called some of his men, and they carried me in a *kaross* to this place. Here by the river he lashed me to the stone, and, knowing that already, from loss of blood and lack of drink, I was in the agonies of thirst, he tormented me by holding water to my lips and snatching it away.

"All day long, lying in the burning sun, have I suffered thus, waiting for death to heal my pain. But in vain did he torture and question, for not one word could he wring from my lips as to where he should seek for the lady Swallow. He thought that she was hidden somewhere on the mountain, and sent men to search for her till they grew tired and ran away to steal the cattle; he never guessed that disguised as a black woman she had passed beneath his very eyes.

"Yet this was so, for I, Sihamba, know it from the talk I overheard between Bull-Head and one of his servants, who had held her awhile wishing to take her for a wife.[4] Yes, she passed beneath his eyes and escaped him, and I—I have won the game."

---

4. In after days, when there was talk far and wide of the wonderful escape of my daughter Suzanne, disguised as a Kaffir woman, the man who had sought to take her captive told the story of the white mark which his grip left upon her arm. He said, indeed, that both he and Bull-Head saw the mark when she was at a little distance from them, but believing it to be an ivory ring they took no heed.

Now the effects of the water, which for a little while had given new life to Sihamba, began to pass off, and she grew weak and silent. Presently I saw Ralph returning down the steep cleft, and with him Jan, and went to meet them.

"It is finished," Ralph said, looking at me with quiet eyes.

"I know it," I answered, "but, son, there is still work to do if you want to save your wife——" and I told him what I had learned.

"The *schimmel*," he exclaimed, growing pale to the lips, "where is the *schimmel*?" and he turned to seek him.

"No, no," I said, "let Jan fetch the horse. Come you to Sihamba, that she may show you the path before she dies."

Now Jan went to the glade that I pointed out to find the *schimmel*, while I led Ralph to Sihamba. She heard him coming and opened her eyes.

"Welcome, husband of Swallow," she said, "you have done well and bravely, yet it was the hand of fate and not yours that smote yonder on the rock point. Now hearken——" and she told the road which he must follow across the Quathlamba, if he would hope to reach the white *koppie* camp by dawn.

Before she had done, for the dying Sihamba spoke slowly and with pain, Jan came leading the *schimmel* saddled and bridled, for Swart Piet's saddle had been put upon it, the mare he was riding having been taken by one of his men whom he had sent to drive in the captured cattle.

The great roan horse, which I rejoiced to see once more, was somewhat thin, for he had lacked water like the rest, but throughout the siege he had been well tended by Sihamba and Zinti, and fed with green corn, and since that morning he had drunk all he would, so that now he was strong again and fit to run.

"Bring me the *schimmel*," said Sihamba, but there was no need, for the brute which loved her now as always, had winded her, and coming to where she lay, put down his head and fondled her with his black lips. Catching him by the forelock, she drew herself up, and as once before she had done when he swam the Red Water, she whispered into his ear, and as I live the beast seemed to listen and understand.

"Not I, not I," she said aloud when she had finished whispering, "not I but the Englishman, yet, Horse, I think that I shall ride you again, but it will be beyond the darkness. Stay not, stumble not, for you go on your last and greatest gallop. Speed like the swallow to save the Swallow, for so shall you live on when your swift bones are dust. Now, Englishman, away."

Ralph stooped down and kissed the woman, the angel whom God had sent to save him and his, and with her dying lips she blessed him and Suzanne, prophesying to them life and joy. Then he leapt into the saddle, and with a snort and a quick shake of its head the *schimmel* plunged forward in the red glow of the sunset.

****

Sihamba leaned against the rock and watched the light pass. As its last ray fell upon her quivering face, she lifted her arms and cried, "Swallow, I have kept my oath. Swallow, I have served you well and saved you. Sister, forget me not."

With these words upon her lips Sihamba Ngenyanga died; yes, she and the daylight died together, while Jan and I stood over her and wept.

CHAPTER 35

The Schimmel's Last Race

Ralph cleared the mountain slope, but before he had covered a mile of way the darkness began to fall, till presently the night was black. Now he must ride slowly, steering his path by the stars, and searching the dim outline of the mountains with his eyes.

But search as he would Ralph could not see the saw-edged rock. He reached the range indeed, and for hour after hour roamed up and down it, his heart torn with helpless haste and fears, but it was of no use, so at last he dismounted, and holding the *schimmel* by the bridle allowed him to eat a little grass while he waited for the moon to rise. Oh! never was the moon so long in coming, but at length it came, and with it clear, soft light. He looked, and there, not half a mile away, just showing in the shadows, was the saw-edged rock he sought.

"There is little time to lose," Ralph muttered to himself as the stallion swept across the plain towards the rock. "In three hours it will be dawn, and these mountains are *sheer* and wide."

Now he was in the pass and galloping up its rocky steeps as fast as the horse dare travel and not fall. Up he went through the moonlit silence that was broken only by the distant roaring of lions; up for one hour and for two. Now he was at the crest of the mountains, and beneath him, miles away, lay the dim *veldt*, and there—yes, there in the far distance—the moonbeams sparkled upon a white-topped *koppie* and the waters of a river that washed its base. Miles and miles away, and but one hour left to cover them. One short hour, and if it was not enough then death by the Zulu *assegai* would be the portion of Suzanne and of those among whom she sheltered. For a moment Ralph breathed the horse, then he shook the reins, and with a snort of pride the *schimmel* started upon his last gallop.

Ah! what a ride was that. Had ever man the like of it? Rushing down an untrodden mountain way swifter than others dare travel on a plain, bounding from rock to rock like a buck, dashing through streams, and leaping dim gullies at a stride. On, on went the *schimmel*, with never a slip and never a stumble. On, swifter than a sassaby and surer-footed than a fox; now the worst of the road was passed, and a long, smooth slope, almost free from stones, led them to the grassy plain beneath. The *schimmel* swept down it at a fearful pace and reached the level land in safety, but the strain of that mad gallop told its tale upon him, for he was drenched with sweat, his eye was red with blood, and the breath whistled in his throat.

Ralph raised himself in his stirrups and scanned the sky, which began to brighten with the coming dawn.

"There is time," he muttered, "for the *koppie* is near, and the Zulus will not attack till they can see the white moons upon their finger nails."

Now he was speeding up a long rise, for here the land lies in waves like a frozen sea. He topped it, and in an instant—almost before he saw them—he had swept through a Zulu *impi* marching stealthily in a triple line with companies thrown forward to the right and left. They shouted in astonishment, but before they could harm him or the horse he was out of reach of their spears and galloping forward with a glad heart, for now he thought the danger done with.

Down the slope he thundered, and the sound of his horse's hoofs came to the ears of Suzanne, who, frozen with terror, crouched in the grass near the spring at the foot of it. Turning her eyes from the ridge where she had seen the Zulus, she looked behind her. At first she could see nothing except a great horse with a man upon its back, but as she stared, presently she recognised the horse—it was the *schimmel*, and none other.

And the man. Whose shape was that? No, this one had a golden beard. Ah! He lifted his head, from which the hat had fallen, and—did she dream? Nay, by Heaven, it was her husband, grown older and bearded, but still her husband. In the piercing agony of that happiness she sank back half-fainting, nor was it till he was almost upon her that she could gain her feet. He saw her, and in the dim light, mistaking her for a Zulu soldier who way-laid him, lifted the gun in his hand to fire. Already he was pressing the trigger when—when she found her voice and cried out:

"Ralph, Ralph, I am Suzanne, your wife."

As the words left her lips it seemed to her as though some giant had thrown the big horse back upon its haunches, for he slipped past her, his flanks almost touching the ground, which he ploughed with outstretched hoofs. Then he stopped dead.

"Have I found you at last, wife?" cried Ralph, in a voice of joy so strange that it sounded scarcely human. "Mount swiftly, for the Zulus are behind."

Thus, then, these two met again, not on the Mountain of the Man's Hand indeed, as the vision had foretold, but very near to it.

"Nay," Suzanne answered, as she sprang on to the saddle before him, "they are in front, for I saw them."

Ralph looked. Yes, there they were in front and to the side and behind. All round them the Zulu *impi* gathered and thickened, crying, *"Bulala umlungu"* (Kill the white man) as they closed in upon them at a run.

"Oh! Ralph, what can we do?" murmured Suzanne.

"Charge them and trust to God," he answered.

"So be it, husband," and, turning herself upon the pommel of the saddle, she threw her arms round his neck and kissed him on the lips, whispering, "At least we have met again, and if we die it shall be together."

"Hold fast," said Ralph, and calling aloud to the horse he set his teeth and charged.

By now the Zulus in front were running down the opposing slope in clusters not much more than a hundred yards away; indeed, the space between them was so narrow that the *schimmel*, galloping up hill under his double load, could scarcely gather speed before they were among them. When they were within ten yards Ralph held out the gun in one hand and fired it, killing a man. Then he cast it away as useless, and placing his right arm about the waist of Suzanne, he bent his body over her to protect her if he might, urging on the horse with feet and voice.

Now they were in them and ploughing through their ever-thickening ranks, throwing their black bodies to this side and to that as a ship throws the water from its bows. Here, there, everywhere spears flashed and stabbed, but as yet they were unhurt, for the very press saved them, although an *assegai* was quivering in the flank of the *schimmel*. Ah! a pang as of the touch of red-hot iron and a spear had pierced Ralph's left shoulder, remaining fast in the wound. Still lower he bent his body till his head was almost hidden in the flowing mane of the *schimmel*, but now black clutching hands caught feet and bridle rein, and slowly the great horse lost way and stopped. A tall Zulu stabbed it in the chest, and Ralph gasped, "It is over!"

But it was not over, for, feeling the pain of this new wound, of a sudden the stallion went mad. He shrieked aloud as only a horse can shriek, and laying back his ears till his face was like the face of a wolf, he reared up on his hind legs and struck out with his hoofs, crushing the skulls and bodies of his tormentors. Down he came again, and with another scream rushed open-mouthed at the man who had stabbed him; his long white teeth gripped him across the body where the ribs end, and then the awful sight was seen of a horse holding in his mouth a man who yelled in agony, and plunging forward with great bounds while he shook him to and fro, as a dog will shake a rat.[5]

Yes, he shook and shook till the flesh gave, and the man fell dying on the *veldt*. Again the furious beast opened his jaws from which gore dripped and rushed upon another, but this one did not wait for him—none waited. To the Zulus in those days a horse was a terrible wild beast, and this was a beast indeed, that brave as they were they dared not face.

"It is a devil! and wizards ride it!" they cried, as they opened a path before its rush.

They were through, and behind them like the voice of hounds that hunt swelled the cry of the war-dogs of Dingaan. They were through and living yet, though one broad *bangwan* was fast in Ralph's shoulder, and another stood in the *schimmel's* chest.

Not two miles away rose the *koppie*. "The horse will die," thought Ralph as he drew Suzanne closer to him, and gripped the saddle with his knees. Indeed, he was dying; yet never since he was a colt did the *schimmel* cover two miles of plain so fast as those that lay between the *impi* and the camp. Slowly and surely the spear worked its way into his vitals, but stretching out his head, and heedless of his burden, he rushed on with the speed of a racer.

****

The Boers in the *laager* were awake at last, the sound of the gun and the war-cry of the Zulus had reached them faintly. Half-clad, men and women together, they stood upon their wagon-boxes looking towards the west. Behind them the pencils of daylight were creeping across the sky, and presently in their low rays they saw such a sight as they would never see again. Fast, fast towards them thundered a great roan horse, blood dripping from his chest, and jaws, and flank, and on its back a yellow-bearded man, in whose shoulder stood a spear, and who held in front of him a fainting woman.

"Soon he will fall suddenly, and we shall be crushed," thought Ralph, and had the horse died while travelling at that speed it must

---

5. The reader may think this incident scarcely credible, but for an authenticated instance of such behaviour on the part of a horse he may be referred to the *Memoirs of General Marbot*.

have been so. But he did not. When within fifty yards of the *laager* suddenly he began to lurch and roll in his stride; then with three bounds he stopped, and standing still, looked round with piteous blood-shot eyes, and whinnied faintly as though he heard some voice that he knew and loved.

Ralph slipped from his back, dragging Suzanne after him, and watched.

For a moment the *schimmel* stood, his head touching the ground, till presently a bloody foam came upon his mouth, and blood poured from his eyes and ears. Now for the last time he arched his neck and shook his mane, then roaring straight up on his hind legs as he had done when he beat down the Zulus, he pawed the air with his fore feet and fell over upon his back to move no more.

Suzanne had fainted, and Ralph carried her to the camp. There they drew out the spear from his shoulder and tended them both, though beyond gasping the words "Prepare, for the Zulus are upon you," it was long before either of them could speak.

****

Yes, yes, they beat off the *impi* with the loss of only one man, but Ralph took no part in that fight. Indeed, when we joined them four days later, for after burying Sihamba Jan and I trekked round through the wagon pass, by the mercy of Heaven escaping the Zulus, they still lay prostrate on a cartel, clasping each other's hands and smiling, but speaking little. The Boers, being warned and awake, beat off the Zulus with great loss to Dingaan, for they had the wagons in front, the *koppie* behind, and the river to one side.

But there were many on that dreadful night whom no *schimmel* galloped to warn. Ah! God, six hundred of them, men and women, maids and children, and little babies at the breast, went down beneath the Zulu *assegai* in that red dawn. Six hundred of them slaughtered!

Is not the name of the land Weenen—"The Land of Weeping"— to this day?

We avenged them at the battle of the Blood River indeed; but could vengeance give us back their lives which it had pleased the Lord to take thus fearfully?

So, so, that is the end of my story of the forgotten bygone years. As I, old Suzanne Botmar, tell it the shadow of that white-topped *koppie* falls upon this house and beneath my feet is the very spot where the brave *schimmel* died. Ralph and Jan would not leave it—no, not even when the British hoisted their flag in Natal, making us English again after all that we had undergone to escape their usurping rule. We suffered much at that event, Jan and I, but though he said nothing, for indeed he did not dare to in my presence, I believe that Ralph did not suffer at all. Well, he was of English blood and it was natural that he should like his own flag best, though to this day I am very angry with my daughter Suzanne, who, for some reason or other, would never say a hard word of the accursed British Government—or listen to one if she could help it.

Yet, to be just, that same Government has ruled us well and fairly, though I never could agree with their manner of dealing with the natives, and our family has grown rich under its shadow. Yes, we were rich from the beginning, for Ralph and some Boers fetched back the cattle of Suzanne and Sihamba which Swart Piet's thieves had stolen, and they were a very great herd.

For many long and happy years after all these events that I have told of did Ralph and Suzanne live together, till at last God took my child Suzanne as she began to grow old. From that day life had no joys for Ralph, or indeed for any of us, and he fought with the English against Cetywayo at Isandlhwana, and fell there bravely, he and his son together, for his son's wife, an English-woman of good blood was dead also in childbirth.

Then all the world grew dark for Jan and me, but now in my extreme age once more it lightens like the dawn.

O God, who am I that I should complain? Nay, nay, to Thee, Almighty God, be praise and thanks and glory. Quite soon I must fall asleep, and how rich and plentiful is that store which awaits me beyond my sleep; that store of friends and kindred who have passed me in the race and won the immortal crown of peace, which even now their dear hands prepare for me. Therefore to Thee, Maker of the world, be praise and thanks and glory. Yes, let all things praise Thee as do my aged lips.

****

NOTE BY THE BARONESS GLENTHIRSK,
FORMERLY KNOWN AS SUZANNE KENZIE

It is something over three years since my great-grandmother, the *Vrouw* Suzanne Botmar, finished dictating to me this history of her early days and of my grandparents, Ralph Kenzie, the English castaway, and Suzanne Botmar, her daughter. Now, if it be only as an instance of the wonderful workings of fate, or, as I prefer to call it, of Providence,

I add this note to her narrative. As I write there stretches before me, not the bushy *veldt* of Weenen in Natal cut by the silver line of the Tugela, but a vast prospect of heather-clad mountains, about whose feet brawls a salmon river. For this is Scotland, and I sit in the castle of Glenthirsk, while on the terrace beneath my window passes my little son, who, if he lives, will one day be lord of it. But I will tell the story, which is indeed a strange one.

As I think my great-grandmother has said, I was educated at a school in Durban, for, although she was in many ways so prejudiced and narrow, she wished that I should be able to hold my own with other girls in learning as in all things. Also she knew well that this would have been the desire of my dear father, who was killed in the Zulu war with *his* father, the Ralph Kenzie of the story, whom, by the way, I can remember as a handsome grey-headed man. For my father was a thorough Englishman, with nothing of the Boer about him, moreover he married an English lady, the daughter of a Natal colonist, and for these reasons he and his grandmother did not get on very well.

After I had finished my schooling I used to stay with friends in Durban, the parents of one of my schoolfellows, and it was at their house that I met my husband, Mr. Ralph Mackenzie, who then was called Lord Glenthirsk, his father having died about six months previous to our acquaintance.

Ralph, my husband, was then quite young, only three-and-twenty indeed, and a subaltern in a Scotch regiment which was quartered at Durban, whither it had come from India. As the term of this regiment's foreign service was shortly to expire, and as at the time there was a prospect of further troubles in South Africa, my husband did not resign his commission on succeeding to the peerage, as his mother wished him to do, for he said that this was a step which he could consider when the regiment returned home, as it would do shortly.

Well, we met, and since we are now quite old married people I may as well admit at once that we fell in love with each other, though to me it seemed a marvellous thing that this handsome and brilliant young lord, with his great wealth and all the world before him, should come to care for a simple Dutch girl who had little to recommend her except her looks (of which my great-grandmother thought, or pretended to think, so little) and some small inheritance of South African farms and cattle. Indeed, when at last he proposed to me, begging me to be his wife, as though I were the most precious thing on the whole earth, I told him so plainly, having inherited some sense with my strain of Huguenot and Dutch blood, and though I trembled at the risk I ran, when everything lay in my own hand, I refused to become engaged to him until he had obtained the consent of his mother and relations, or, at the least, until he had taken a year to think the matter over.

The truth is that, although I was still so young I had seen and heard enough of the misfortunes of unsuitable marriages, nor could I bear that it should ever be said of me that I had taken advantage of some passing fancy to entangle a man so far above me in wealth and station. Therefore I would permit him to say nothing of our engagement, nor did I speak a single word of it to my great-grandmother or my friends. Still Ralph and I saw a great deal of each other during the month which I remained in Durban, for it is a gay town, and almost every day there were parties, and when there were none we rode out together.

It was during one of these rides on the Berea that I told him what I knew of the strange history of my grandfather and grandmother, not all of it indeed, for it was not until the book was dictated to me that I learned the exact facts, the matter being one of which our family spoke little. Ralph listened very attentively, and when I had done asked if I had the ring and locket of which I spoke.

"Here they are," I answered, for since my father's death I had always made a practice of wearing both of them.

He examined the ring with its worn device and proud motto of "Honour first," and as he deciphered it I saw him start, but when he came to look at the miniatures in the locket he turned quite pale.

"Do you know, Suzanne," he said presently, "I believe that we must be distant cousins; at the least I am sure that I have seen the picture from which one of these miniatures was originally copied, and the crest and motto are those of my family."

Now I became very curious, and plied him with questions, but he would say no more, only he led me on to talk of my grandfather, Ralph Kenzie, the castaway, and from time to time made a note in his pocket-book. Also afterwards I showed him the writing in the testament which was found on the body of the shipwrecked lady, my great-grandmother, and he asked me for an impression of the ring, and to allow the ivory miniatures and the writing to be photographed, which I did.

Within three days of that ride we separated for a while, not without heartache on both our parts and some tears on mine, for I feared that once he had lost sight of me he would put me from his mind, and as I loved him truly that thought was sore. But he, speaking very quietly, said that outside death only one thing should divide us from each other, namely, my own decree.

"Then, Ralph, we shall be one for ever," I answered, for at the moment I was too sad for any artifice of maiden coyness.

"You think so now, dear," he said, "but time will show. Supposing that I were not——" and he stopped, nor would he complete the sentence. Indeed those words of his tormented me day and night for weeks, for I finished them in a hundred ways, each more fatal than the last.

Well, I returned to the farm, and immediately afterwards my great-grandmother took the fancy of dictating her history, the ending of which seemed to affect her much, for when it was done she told me sharply to put the typed sheets away and let her hear or see no more of them. Then she rose with difficulty, for the dropsy in her limbs made her inactive, and walked with the help of a stick to the *stoep*, where she sat down, looking across the plain at the solemn range of the Drakensberg and thinking without doubt, of that night of fear when my grandfather had rushed down its steeps upon the great *schimmel* to save her daughter and his wife from an awful death.

The stead where we lived in Natal was built under the lea of a projecting spur of the white-topped *koppie*, and over that spur runs a footpath leading to the township. Suddenly the old lady looked up and, not twenty yards away from her, saw standing on the ridge of it, as though in doubt which way to turn, a gentleman dressed in the kilted uniform of an officer of a Highland regiment the like of which she had never seen before.

"Dear Lord!" I heard her exclaim, "here is a white man wearing the *moocha* of a Kaffir. Suzanne! Suzanne! come and send away this half-clad fellow."

Putting down my papers I ran from the room and at a single glance saw that "the half-clad fellow" was none other than Ralph himself. In my delight I lost my head, and forgetting everything except that my betrothed was there before me, I sprang from the *stoep* and, flying up the little slope, I fell into his open arms. For a few seconds there was silence, then from behind me rose a dreadful shriek followed by cries for help. Freeing myself from Ralph's embrace, I looked round to see my great-grandmother hobbling towards us with uplifted stick. Ralph put his eye-glass in his eye and looked at her.

"Who is this old lady, Suzanne?" he asked.

Before I could answer there came from her lips such a torrent of indignation as I had never heard before.

"What is she saying?" asked Ralph again, who could not understand one word of Dutch. "She seems put out."

"It is my great-grandmother, the *Vrouw* Botmar," I faltered, "and she does not understand—I have never told her."

"Ah! I see. Well, perhaps it would be as well to explain," he answered, which I accordingly began to do as best I could, feeling more foolish than ever I did before. As I stammered out my excuses I saw her face change, and guessed that she was no longer listening to me.

"Who does the man remind me of?" she said, speaking aloud, but to herself. "*Allemachter*! his face is the face of that English lord who visited us with the lawyer more than fifty years ago. Yes, his face is the face of Ralph's cousin. Girl," she added, turning on me fiercely, "tell me that man's name."

"His name is Lord Glenthirsk"

"Lord Glenthirsk! The same face and the same name and *you* in his arms. Is God then making a sequel to the story which I finished this day? Come," and she hobbled back to the *stoep*. "Be seated," she said when we had reached it. "Now, speak; no, Suzanne, give me that *kaross*."

I handed her the rug, wondering what she meant to do with it, and disturbed as I was, nearly burst into hysterics when I saw her solemnly place it upon Ralph's knees saying, "The man has lost his garments and will catch a chill."

"Would you kindly explain," said Ralph blandly, "what the old lady is at now? Really I do not feel cold."

"Your kilt surprises her," I stammered; whereat he began to laugh.

"Silence," she exclaimed in so vigorous a voice that he stopped at once. "Now tell your story; no, I forgot, the man is not educated, do you interpret for him, Suzanne."

"First I have something to say for myself, grandmother," I answered, and in a few words I told that Ralph and I were affianced, though I had said nothing of it, because I wished to give him opportunity to change his mind if he should desire to do so.

"Change his mind!" said the old lady, with a glare of indignation, "I should like to see him dare to change his mind, this Englishman whom you seem to have honoured thus, *opsitting* with him without my leave. A lord indeed? What do I care for lords? The question is whether I should not order the English creature off the place; yes, and I would do it were not his face the face of Ralph's cousin, and his name the name Glenthirsk."

When I had interpreted as much of this speech as I thought necessary, there was a little silence, after which Ralph began to speak very solemnly.

"Listen, Suzanne," he said, "and repeat my words to your great-grandmother. She says that my name is Lord Glenthirsk, but within the last few days I have come to believe that it is nothing of the sort, but only plain Ralph Mackenzie."

"What do you mean?" I asked, astonished.

"I mean, Suzanne, that if your legitimate descent from that Ralph Mackenzie who was cast away about sixty years ago on the coast of the Transkei can be proved—as I believe it can, for I have made inquiries, and find that his marriage to your grandmother to which her mother who still lives can bear witness, was duly registered—then *you* are the Baroness Glenthirsk of Glenthirsk, and I, the descendant of a younger son, am only Lieutenant Ralph Mackenzie of Her Majesty's—Highlanders."

"Oh! Ralph, how can this be?" I gasped. "I thought that in England men took rank, not the women."

"So they do generally," he answered; "but as it happens in our family the title descends in the female line, and with it the entailed estates, so that you would succeed to your father's rights although he never enjoyed them. Suzanne, I am not speaking lightly; all this while that I have kept away from you I have been inquiring in Scotland and the Cape, for I sent home photographs of those miniatures and a statement of the facts, and upon my word I believe it to be true that you and no other are the heiress of our house."

Almost mechanically, for I was lost in amazement, I translated his words. My great-grandmother thought a while and said:

"Wonderful are the ways of the Lord who thus in my old age answers my prayers and rolls from my back the load of my sin. Suzanne, ask that Scotchman if he still means to marry you," and seeing me hesitate, as well I might, she struck her stick upon the floor and added, "Obey, girl, and ask."

So with great shame I asked, explaining that I was forced to it.

"Do I still mean to marry you, Suzanne?" he said, astonished. "Why surely you must understand that the question is, do you still intend to marry me? When I begged you to take me some months ago I had much to offer; today if things be as I am sure they are, I am but a penniless Scottish gentleman, while you are one of the richest and most noble ladies in Great Britain."

By way of answer I looked at him in a fashion which I trust he understood, but before I could speak, *Vrouw* Botmar broke in, for, as usual, I had translated.

"Tell the man to stop talking about money and rank after his godless English manner. I wish to inquire of his character and religion." And so she did clearly and at length, but I do not think that I need set down her questions or his answers.

At last, when we were both overwhelmed and gasping for breath, I refused flatly to ask anything more, whereon she ceased her examinations, saying:

"Well, if he speaks the truth, which is doubtful, he does not seem to be any worse than other men, though that is saying little enough. Is he sound in wind and limb, and what illnesses has he had?"

"You must ask him yourself," I replied, losing patience, whereon she called me a "mealy-mouthed little fool" and laughed. Then of a sudden she said, "Kneel, both of you," and, strange as it may seem, we obeyed her, for we, and especially Ralph, were afraid of the old lady. Yes, there we knelt on the *stoep* before her, while a Kaffir girl stood outside and stared with her mouth open.

"Ralph Kenzie," she said, "whatever else you may be, at least you are an honest man like your grandfather before you, for were it not so you would never have come to tell this child that your fortune is her fortune, and your title her title, though whether this be the case or not, I neither know nor care, since at least you are of the blood of my long-dead adopted son, and that is more to me than any wealth or rank.

"As for you, Suzanne, you are pert and deceitful, for you have kept secret from me that which I had a right to learn; also you have too good an opinion of your own looks, which as I tell you now for the last time, are nothing compared to mine at your age, or even to those of my daughter Suzanne, your grandmother. But this I will say, you have a good heart and some of the spirit of your forbears, therefore"—and she laid one of her heavy hands on the head of each of us—"I, old Suzanne Botmar, bless you both. You shall be married next week, and may you be happy in your marriage, and have children that would be a credit to me and your great-grandfather, could we have lived to see them.

"There, there, Ralph and Suzanne—the first ones, my own lost Ralph and Suzanne—will be glad to hear of this when I come to tell them of it, as I shall do shortly. Yes, they will be glad to hear of it—" and she rose and hobbled back to the *sit-kammer*, turning at the open door to call out:

"Girl, where are your manners? Make that Scotchman some of your coffee."

****

248

So we were married, and within the week, for, all my protestations notwithstanding, the *Vrouw* Botmar would suffer no delay. Moreover, by means of some other interpreter, Ralph, playing traitor, secretly brought my arguments to nothing, and indeed there was a cause for hurry, for just then his regiment was ordered to return to England.

It was a strange sight, that marriage, for my great-grandmother attended it seated on the *voorkisse* of her best wagon drawn by eighteen white oxen, the descendants of Dingaan's royal cattle that Swart Piet stole to bring destruction upon the Umpondwana. By her side was her husband, old Jan Botmar, whom she caused to be carried to the wagon and tied in it in his chair. He, poor old man, knew nothing of what was passing, but from some words he let fall we gathered that he believed that he was once more starting on the great trek from the Transkei. My Ralph, he thought, was his adopted child, perhaps because of some inherited similarity of voice, for he called him "son," but my own presence puzzled him, for he said once or twice, "So Suzanne has escaped from that hell-hound, Swart Piet. Have you killed the dog, Ralph? Ralph, have you killed the dog?"

Thus we went to the little church where the chaplain of the regiment was to wed us, the pipers going first, playing a wild marriage march on their bagpipes. Next came Ralph and I walking side by side, and after us the wagon with my great-grandparents, while the rear was brought up by a guard of honour formed of every available soldier in the company. Outside the open door of the church the wagon was halted, and from it the *Vrouw* Botmar witnessed the ceremony, causing the register to be brought to her to sign. This she did, resting the book upon the head of the Kaffir driver, down whose back she managed to upset the ink.

"Never mind," she said, not the least disturbed, "it cannot make the poor creature any blacker than he is."

"Oh! how can I leave you, grandmother?" I said to her afterwards.

"Child," she answered, with a stern face, "in my youth, to keep one I loved near me, I committed a great sin. Now by way of penance I part from one I love; yes, being yet alive I say farewell for ever to the last of my race. Thus in our age do we pay for the sins of youth. Go, and God with you."

So I placed my hand in that of my husband and went. When we reached this country it was proved that the rank and estates were mine by law, for the evidence of my descent was too strong to be disputed. I did not wish to take either, but Ralph insisted on it and I was overruled. Indeed, had I not done so, it seems that confusion and endless law-suits might have resulted in the future, perhaps after I am dead.

****

Six months afterwards, in this castle of Glenthirsk, I received a letter, at the foot of which was faintly scrawled the signature of Suzanne Botmar. It was short and ran thus:

"Grand-daughter Suzanne,

"Last night your great-grandfather died. Today I buried him, and tomorrow I shall die also, for after being together for so many years I miss his company and mean to seek it again. Till we meet in Heaven, if your pomp and riches will allow you to come there through the eye of whatever needle it has pleased God to choose for you, farewell to you and your husband, whom I love because Ralph Kenzie's blood is in his veins."

As I learnt by other letters on that morrow of which she spoke my great-grandmother, the *Vrouw* Botmar, did die, for even in this she would not be thwarted, and was buried on the evening of the same day by the side of her husband, Jan Botmar.

Benita

Notes

It may interest readers of this story to know that its author believes it to have a certain foundation in fact. It was said about five-and-twenty or thirty years ago that an adventurous trader, hearing from some natives in the territory that lies at the back of Quilimane, the legend of a great treasure buried in or about the sixteenth century by a party of Portuguese who were afterwards massacred, as a last resource attempted its discovery by the help of a mesmerist. According to this history the child who was used as a subject in the experiment, when in a state of trance, detailed the adventures and death of the unhappy Portuguese men and women, two of whom leapt from the point of a high rock into the Zambesi. Although he knew no tongue but English, this clairvoyant child is declared to have repeated in Portuguese the prayers these unfortunates offered up, and even to have sung the very hymns they sang. Moreover, with much other detail, he described the burial of the great treasure and its exact situation so accurately that the white man and the mesmerist were able to dig for and find the place where *it had been*—for the bags were gone, swept out by the floods of the river.

Some gold coins remained, however, one of them a ducat of Aloysius Mocenigo, Doge of Venice. Afterwards the boy was again thrown into a trance (in all he was mesmerized eight times), and revealed where the sacks still lay; but before the white trader could renew his search for them, the party was hunted out of the country by natives whose superstitious fears were aroused, barely escaping with their lives.

It should be added that, as in the following tale, the chief who was ruling there when the tragedy happened, declared the place to be sacred, and that if it were entered evil would befall his tribe. Thus it came about that for generations it was never violated, until at length his descendants were driven farther from the river by war, and from one of them the white man heard the legend.

CHAPTER 1

Confidences

Beautiful, beautiful was that night! No air that stirred; the black smoke from the funnels of the mail steamer *Zanzibar* lay low over the surface of the sea like vast, floating ostrich plumes that vanished one by one in the starlight. Benita Beatrix Clifford, for that was her full name, who had been christened Benita after her mother and Beatrix after her father's only sister, leaning idly over the bulwark rail, thought to herself that a child might have sailed that sea in a boat of bark and come safely into port.

Then a tall man of about thirty years of age, who was smoking a cigar, strolled up to her. At his coming she moved a little as though to make room for him beside her, and there was something in the motion which, had anyone been there to observe it, might have suggested that these two were upon terms of friendship, or still greater intimacy. For a moment he hesitated, and while he did so an expression of doubt, of distress even, gathered on his face. It was as though he understood that a great deal depended on whether he accepted or declined that gentle invitation, and knew not which to do.

Indeed, much did depend upon it, no less than the destinies of both of them. If Robert Seymour had gone by to finish his cigar in solitude, why then this story would have had a very different ending; or, rather, who can say how it might have ended? The dread, foredoomed event with which that night was big would have come to its awful birth leaving certain words unspoken. Violent separation must have ensued, and even if both of them had survived the terror, what prospect was there that their lives would again have crossed each other in that wide Africa?

But it was not so fated, for just as he put his foot forward to continue his march Benita spoke in her low and pleasant voice.

"Are you going to the smoking-room or to the saloon to dance,

255

Mr. Seymour? One of the officers just told me that there is to be a dance," she added, in explanation, "because it is so calm that we might fancy ourselves ashore."

"Neither," he answered. "The smoking-room is stuffy, and my dancing days are over. No; I proposed to take exercise after that big dinner, and then to sit in a chair and fall asleep. But," he added, and his voice grew interested, "how did you know that it was I? You never turned your head."

"I have ears in my head as well as eyes," she answered with a little laugh, "and after we have been nearly a month together on this ship I ought to know your step."

"I never remember that anyone ever recognized it before," he said, more to himself than to her, then came and leaned over the rail at her side. His doubts were gone. Fate had spoken.

For a while there was silence between them, then he asked her if she were not going to the dance.

Benita shook her head.

"Why not? You are fond of dancing, and you dance very well. Also there are plenty of officers for partners, especially Captain——" and he checked himself.

"I know," she said; "it would be pleasant, but—Mr. Seymour, will you think me foolish if I tell you something?"

"I have never thought you foolish yet, Miss Clifford, so I don't know why I should begin now. What is it?"

"I am not going to the dance because I am afraid, yes, horribly afraid."

"Afraid! Afraid of what?"

"I don't quite know, but, Mr. Seymour, I feel as though we were all of us upon the edge of some dreadful catastrophe—as though there were about to be a mighty change, and beyond it another life, something new and unfamiliar. It came over me at dinner—that was why I left the table. Quite suddenly I looked, and all the people were different, yes, all except a few."

"Was I different?" he asked curiously.

"No, you were not," and he thought he heard her add "Thank God!" beneath her breath.

"And were you different?"

"I don't know. I never looked at myself; I was the seer, not the seen. I have always been like that."

"Indigestion," he said reflectively. "We eat too much on board ship, and the dinner was very long and heavy. I told you so, that's why I'm taking—I mean why I wanted to take exercise."

"And to go to sleep afterwards."

"Yes, first the exercise, then the sleep. Miss Clifford, that is the rule of life—and death. With sleep thought ends, therefore for some of us your catastrophe is much to be desired, for it would mean long sleep and no thought."

"I said that they were changed, not that they had ceased to think. Perhaps they thought the more."

"Then let us pray that your catastrophe may be averted. I prescribe for you bismuth and carbonate of soda. Also in this weather it seems difficult to imagine such a thing. Look now, Miss Clifford," he added, with a note of enthusiasm in his voice, pointing towards the east, "look."

Her eyes followed his outstretched hand, and there, above the level ocean, rose the great orb of the African moon. Lo! of a sudden all that ocean turned to silver, a wide path of rippling silver stretched from it to them. It might have been the road of angels. The sweet soft light beat upon their ship, showing its tapering masts and every detail of the rigging. It passed on beyond them, and revealed the low, foam-fringed coast-line rising here and there, dotted with *kloofs* and their clinging bush. Even the round huts of Kaffir kraals became faintly visible in that radiance. Other things became visible also—for instance, the features of this pair.

The man was light in his colouring, fair-skinned, with fair hair which already showed a tendency towards greyness, especially in the moustache, for he wore no beard. His face was clean cut, not particularly handsome, since, their fineness notwithstanding, his features lacked regularity; the cheekbones were too high and the chin was too small, small faults redeemed to some extent by the steady and cheerful grey eyes. For the rest, he was broad-shouldered and well-set-up, sealed with the indescribable stamp of the English gentleman. Such was the appearance of Robert Seymour.

In that light the girl at his side looked lovely, though, in fact, she had no real claims to loveliness, except perhaps as regards her figure, which was agile, rounded, and peculiarly graceful. Her foreign-looking face was unusual, dark-eyed, a somewhat large and very mobile mouth, fair and waving hair, a broad forehead, a sweet and at times wistful face, thoughtful for the most part, but apt to be irradiated by sudden smiles. Not a beautiful woman at all, but exceedingly attractive, one possessing magnetism.

She gazed, first at the moon and the silver road beneath it, then, turning, at the land beyond.

"We are very near to Africa, at last," she said.

"Too near, I think," he answered. "If I were the captain I should stand out a point or two. It is a strange country, full of surprises. Miss Clifford, will you think me rude if I ask you why you are going there? You have never told me—quite."

"No, because the story is rather a sad one; but you shall hear it if you wish. Do you?"

He nodded, and drew up two deck chairs, in which they settled themselves in a corner made by one of the inboard boats, their faces still towards the sea.

"You know I was born in Africa," she said, "and lived there till I was thirteen years old—why, I find I can still speak Zulu; I did so this afternoon. My father was one of the early settlers in Natal. His father was a clergyman, a younger son of the Lincolnshire Cliffords. They are great people there still, though I don't suppose that they are aware of my existence."

"I know them," answered Robert Seymour. "Indeed, I was shooting at their place last November—when the smash came," and he sighed; "but go on."

"Well, my father quarrelled with his father, I don't know what about, and emigrated. In Natal he married my mother, a Miss Ferreira, whose name—like mine and her mother's—was Benita. She was one of two sisters, and her father, Andreas Ferreira, who married an English lady, was half Dutch and half Portuguese. I remember him well, a fine old man with dark eyes and an iron-grey beard. He was wealthy as things went in those days—that is to say, he had lots of land in Natal and the Transvaal, and great herds of stock. So you see I am half English, some Dutch, and more than a quarter Portuguese— quite a mixture of races. My father and mother did not get on well together. Mr. Seymour, I may as well tell you all the truth: he drank, and although he was passionately fond of her, she was jealous of him. Also he gambled away most of her patrimony, and after old Andreas Ferreira's death they grew poor. One night there was a dreadful scene between them, and in his madness he struck her.

"Well, she was a very proud woman, determined, too, and she turned on him and said—for I heard her—'I will never forgive you; we have done with each other.' Next morning, when my father was sober, he begged her pardon, but she made no answer, although he was starting somewhere on a fortnight's trek. When he had gone my mother ordered the Cape cart, packed up her clothes, took some money that she had put away, drove to Durban, and after making arrangements at the bank about a small private income of her own, sailed with me for England, leaving a letter for my father in which she said that she would never see him again, and if he tried to interfere with me she would put me under the protection of the English court, which would not allow me to be taken to the home of a drunkard.

"In England we went to live in London with my aunt, who had married a Major King, but was a widow with five children. My father often wrote to persuade my mother to go back to him, but she never would, which I think was wrong of her. So things went on for twelve years or more, till one day my mother suddenly died, and I came into her little fortune of between £200 and £300 a year, which she had tied up so that nobody can touch it. That was about a year ago. I wrote to tell my father of her death, and received a pitiful letter; indeed, I have had several of them. He implored me to come out to him and not to leave him to die in his loneliness, as he soon would do of a broken heart, if I did not. He said that he had long ago given up drinking, which was the cause of the ruin of his life, and sent a certificate signed by a magistrate and a doctor to that effect. Well, in the end, although all my cousins and their mother advised me against it, I consented, and here I am. He is to meet me at Durban, but how we shall get on together is more than I can say, though I long to see him, for after all he is my father."

"It was good of you to come, under all the circumstances. You must have a brave heart," said Robert reflectively.

"It is my duty," she answered. "And for the rest, I am not afraid who was born to Africa. Indeed, often and often have I wished to be back there again, out on the *veld*, far away from the London streets and fog. I am young and strong, and I want to see things, natural things—not those made by man, you know—the things I remember as a child. One can always go back to London."

"Yes, or at least some people can. It is a curious thing, Miss Clifford, but as it happens I have met your father. You always reminded me of the man, but I had forgotten his name. Now it comes back to me; it *was* Clifford."

"Where on earth?" she asked, astonished.

"In a queer place. As I told you, I have visited South Africa before, under different circumstances. Four years ago I was out here big-game shooting. Going in from the East coast my brother and I—he is dead now, poor fellow—got up somewhere in the Matabele country, on the banks of the Zambesi. As we didn't find much game there we were going to strike south, when some natives told us of a wonderful ruin that stood on a hill overhanging the river a few miles farther on. So, leaving the wagon on the hither side of the steep *nek*, over which it would have been difficult to drag it, my brother and I took our rifles and a bag of food and started. The place was farther off than we thought, although from the top of the *nek* we could see it clearly enough, and before we reached it dark had fallen.

"Now we had observed a wagon and a tent outside the wall which we thought must belong to white men, and headed for them. There was a light in the tent, and the flap was open, the night being very hot. Inside two men were seated, one old, with a grey beard, and the other, a good-looking fellow—under forty, I should say—with a Jewish face, dark, piercing eyes, and a black, pointed beard. They were engaged in examining a heap of gold beads and bangles, which lay on the table between them. As I was about to speak, the black-bearded man heard or caught sight of us, and seizing a rifle that leaned against the table, swung round and covered me.

"'For God's sake don't shoot, Jacob,' said the old man; 'they are English.'

"'Best dead, any way,' answered the other, in a soft voice, with a slight foreign accent, 'we don't want spies or thieves here.'

"'We are neither, but I can shoot as well as you, friend,' I remarked, for by this time my rifle was on him.

"Then he thought better of it, and dropped his gun, and we explained that we were merely on an archaeological expedition. The end of it was that we became capital friends, though neither of us could cotton much to Mr. Jacob—I forget his other name. He struck me as too handy with his rifle, and was, I gathered, an individual with a mysterious and rather lurid past. To cut a long story short, when he found out that we had no intention of poaching, your father, for it was he, told us frankly that they were treasure-hunting, having got hold of some story about a vast store of gold which had been hidden away there by Portuguese two or three centuries before. Their trouble was, however, that the Makalanga, who lived in the fortress, which was called Bambatse, would not allow them to dig, because they said the place was haunted, and if they did so it would bring bad luck to their tribe."

"And did they ever get in?" asked Benita.

"I am sure I don't know, for we went next day, though before we left we called on the Makalanga, who admitted us all readily enough so long as we brought no spades with us. By the way, the gold we saw your father and his friend examining was found in some ancient graves outside the walls, but had nothing to do with the big and mythical treasure."

"What was the place like? I love old ruins," broke in Benita again.

"Oh! wonderful. A gigantic, circular wall built by heaven knows who, then half-way up the hill another wall, and near the top a third wall which, I understood, surrounded a sort of holy of holies, and above everything, on the brink of the precipice, a great cone of granite."

"Artificial or natural?"

"I don't know. They would not let us up there, but we were introduced to their chief and high priest, Church and State in one, and a wonderful old man he was, very wise and very gentle. I remember he told me he believed we should meet again, which seemed an odd thing for him to say. I asked him about the treasure and why he would not let the other white men look for it. He answered that it would never be found by any man, white or black, that only a woman would find it at the appointed time, when it pleased the Spirit of Bambatse, under whose guardianship it was."

"Who was the Spirit of Bambatse, Mr. Seymour?"

"I can't tell you, couldn't make out anything definite about her, except that she was said to be white, and to appear sometimes at sunrise, or in the moonlight, standing upon the tall point of rock of which I told you. I remember that I got up before the dawn to look for her—like an idiot, for of course I saw nothing—and that's all I know about the matter."

"Did you have any talk with my father, Mr. Seymour—alone, I mean?"

"Yes, a little. The next day he walked back to our wagon with us, being glad, I fancy, of a change from the perpetual society of his partner Jacob. That wasn't wonderful in a man who had been brought up at Eton and Oxford, as I found out he had, like myself, and whatever his failings may have been—although we saw no sign of them, for he would not touch a drop of spirits—was a gentleman, which Jacob wasn't. Still, he—Jacob—had read a lot, especially on out-of-the-way subjects, and could talk every language under the sun—a clever and agreeable scoundrel in short."

"Did my father say anything about himself?"

"Yes; he told me that he had been an unsuccessful man all his life, and had much to reproach himself with, for we got quite confidential at last. He added that he had a family in England—what family he didn't say—whom he was anxious to make wealthy by way of reparation for past misdeeds, and that was why he was treasure-hunting. However, from what you tell me, I fear he never found anything."

"No, Mr. Seymour, he never found it and never will, but all the same I am glad to hear that he was thinking of us. Also I should like to explore that place, Bambatse."

"So should I, Miss Clifford, in your company, and your father's, but not in that of Jacob. If ever you should go there with him, I say:— 'Beware of Jacob.'"

"Oh! I am not afraid of Jacob," she answered with a laugh, "although I believe that my father still has something to do with him—at least in one of his letters he mentioned his partner, who was a German."

"A German! I think that he must have meant a German Jew."

After this there was silence between them for a time, then he said suddenly, "You have told me your story, would you like to hear mine?"

"Yes," she answered.

"Well, it won't take you long to listen to it, for, Miss Clifford, like Canning's needy knife-grinder, I have really none to tell. You see before you one of the most useless persons in the world, an undistinguished member of what is called in England the 'leisured class,' who can do absolutely nothing that is worth doing, except shoot straight."

"Indeed," said Benita.

"You do not seem impressed with that accomplishment," he went on, "yet it is an honest fact that for the last fifteen years—I was thirty-two this month—practically my whole time has been given up to it, with a little fishing thrown in in the spring. As I want to make the most of myself, I will add that I am supposed to be among the six best shots in England, and that my ambition—yes, great Heavens! my ambition—was to become better than the other five. By that sin fell the poor man who speaks to you. I was supposed to have abilities, but I neglected them all to pursue this form of idleness. I entered no profession, I did no work, with the result that at thirty-two I am ruined and almost hopeless."

"Why ruined and hopeless?" she asked anxiously, for the way in which they were spoken grieved her more than the words themselves.

"Ruined because my old uncle, the Honourable John Seymour Seymour, whose heir I was, committed the indiscretion of marrying a young lady who has presented him with thriving twins. With the appearance of those twins my prospects disappeared, as did the allowance of £1,500 a year that he was good enough to make me on which to keep up a position as his next-of-kin. I had something of my own, but also I had debts, and at the present moment a draft in my pocket for £2,163-14-5d, and a little loose cash, represents the total of my worldly goods, just about the sum I have been accustomed to spend per annum."

"I don't call that ruin, I call that riches," said Benita, relieved. "With £2,000 to begin on you may make a fortune in Africa. But how about the hopelessness?"

"I am hopeless because I have absolutely nothing to which to look forward. Really, when that £2,000 is gone I do not know how to earn a sixpence. In this dilemma it occurred to me that the only thing I could do was to turn my shooting to practical account, and become a hunter of big game. Therefore I propose to kill elephants until an elephant kills me. At least," he added in a changed voice, "I did so propose until half an hour ago."

CHAPTER 2

The End of the Zanzibar

"Until half an hour ago? Then why——" and Benita stopped.

"Have I changed my very modest scheme of life? Miss Clifford, as you are so good as to be sufficiently interested, I will tell you. It is because a temptation which hitherto I have been able to resist, has during the last thirty minutes become too strong for me. You know everything has its breaking strain." He puffed nervously at his cigar, threw it into the sea, paused, then went on: "Miss Clifford, I have dared to fall in love with you. No; hear me out. When I have done it will be quite time enough to give me the answer that I expect. Meanwhile, for the first time in my life, allow me the luxury of being in earnest. To me it is a new sensation, and therefore very priceless. May I go on?"

Benita made no answer. He rose with a certain deliberateness which characterized all his movements—for Robert Seymour never seemed to be in a hurry—and stood in front of her so that the moonlight shone upon her face, while his own remained in shadow.

"Beyond that £2,000 of which I have spoken, and incidentally its owner, I have nothing whatsoever to offer to you. I am an indigent and worthless person. Even in my prosperous days, when I could look forward to a large estate, although it was often suggested to me, I never considered myself justified in asking any lady to share—the prospective estate. I think now that the real reason was that I never cared sufficiently for any lady, since otherwise my selfishness would probably have overcome my scruples, as it does tonight. Benita, for I will call you so, if for the first and last time, I—I—love you.

"Listen now," he went on, dropping his measured manner, and speaking hurriedly, like a man with an earnest message and little time in which to deliver it, "it is an odd thing, an incomprehensible thing, but true, true—I fell in love with you the first time I saw your face. You remember, you stood there leaning over the bulwark when I came on board at Southampton, and as I walked up the gangway, I looked and my eyes met yours. Then I stopped, and that stout old lady who got off at Madeira bumped into me, and asked me to be good enough to make up my mind if I were going backward or forward. Do you remember?"

"Yes," she answered in a low voice.

"Which things are an allegory," he continued. "I felt it so at the time. Yes, I had half a mind to answer 'Backward' and give up my berth in this ship. Then I looked at you again, and something inside of me said 'Forward.' So I came up the rest of the gangway and took off my hat to you, a salutation I had no right to make, but which, I recall, you acknowledged."

He paused, then continued: "As it began, so it has gone on. It is always like that, is it not? The beginning is everything, the end must follow. And now it has come out, as I was fully determined that it should not do half an hour ago, when suddenly you developed eyes in the back of your head, and—oh! dearest, I love you. No, please be quiet; I have not done. I have told you what I am, and really there isn't much more to say about me, for I have no particular vices except the worst of them all, idleness, and not the slightest trace of any virtue that I can discover. But I have a certain knowledge of the world acquired in a long course of shooting parties, and as a man of the world I will venture to give you a bit of advice. It is possible that to you my life and death affair is a mere matter of board-ship amusement. Yet it is possible also that you might take another view of the matter. In that case, as a friend and a man of the world, I entreat you—don't. Have nothing to do with me. Send me about my business; you will never regret it."

"Are you making fun, or is all this meant, Mr. Seymour?" asked Benita, still speaking beneath her breath, and looking straight before her.

"Meant? Of course it is meant. How can you ask?"

"Because I have always understood that on such occasions people wish to make the best of themselves."

"Quite so, but I never do what I ought, a fact for which I am grateful now come to think of it, since otherwise I should not be here tonight. I wish to make the worst of myself, the very worst, for whatever I am not, at least I am honest. Now having told you that I am, or was half an hour ago, an idler, a good-for-nothing, prospectless failure, I ask you—if you care to hear any more?"

She half rose, and, glancing at him for the first time, saw his face contract itself and turn pale in the moonlight. It may be that the sight of it affected her, even to the extent of removing some adverse impression left by the bitter mocking of his self-blame. At any rate, Benita seemed to change her mind, and sat down again, saying:

"Go on, if you wish."

He bowed slightly, and said:

"I thank you. I have told you what I *was* half an hour ago; now, hoping that you will believe me, I will tell you what I *am*. I am a truly repentant man, one upon whom a new light has risen. I am not very old, and I think that underneath it all I have some ability. Opportunity may still come my way; if it does not, for your sake I will make the opportunity. I do not believe that you can ever find anyone who would love you better or care for you more tenderly. I desire to live for you in the future, more completely even than in the past I have lived for myself. I do not wish to influence you by personal appeals, but in fact I stand at the parting of the ways. If you will give yourself to me I feel as though I might still become a husband of whom you could be proud—if not, I write 'Finis' upon the tombstone of the possibilities of Robert Seymour. I adore you. You are the one woman with whom I desire to pass my days; it is you who have always been lacking to my life. I ask you to be brave, to take the risk of marrying me, although I can see nothing but poverty ahead of us, for I am an adventurer."

"Don't speak like that," she said quickly. "We are all of us adventurers in this world, and I more than you. We have just to consider ourselves, not what we have or have not."

"So be it, Miss Clifford. Then I have nothing more to say; now it is for you to answer."

Just then the sound of the piano and the fiddle in the saloon ceased. One of the waltzes was over, and some of the dancers came upon deck to flirt or to cool themselves. One pair, engaged very obviously in the former occupation, stationed themselves so near to Robert and Benita that further conversation between them was impossible, and there proceeded to interchange the remarks common to such occasions.

For a good ten minutes did they stand thus, carrying on a mock quarrel as to a dance of which one of them was supposed to have been defrauded, until Robert Seymour, generally a very philosophical person, could have slain those innocent lovers. He felt, he knew not why, that his chances were slipping away from him; that sensation of something bad about to happen, of which Benita had spoken, spread from her to him. The suspense grew exasperating, terrible even, nor could it be ended. To ask her to come elsewhere was under the circumstances not feasible, especially as he would also have been obliged to request the other pair to make way for them, and all this time, with a sinking of the heart, he felt that probably Benita was beating down any tenderness which she might feel towards him; that when her long-delayed answer did come the chances were it would be "No."

The piano began to play again in the saloon, and the young people, still squabbling archly, at length prepared to depart. Suddenly there was a stir upon the bridge, and against the tender sky Robert saw a man dash forward. Next instant the engine-room bell rang fiercely. He knew the signal—it was "Stop," followed at once by other ringings that meant "Full speed astern."

"I wonder what is up?" said the young man to the young woman.

Before the words had left his lips they knew. There was a sensation as though all the hull of the great ship had come to a complete standstill, while the top part of her continued to travel forward; followed by another sensation still more terrible and sickening in its nature—that of slipping over something, helplessly, heavily, as a man slips upon ice or a polished floor. Spars cracked, ropes flew in two with a noise as of pistol shots. Heavy objects rushed about the deck, travelling forwards all of them. Benita was hurled from her chair against Robert so that the two of them rolled into the scuppers. He was unhurt and picked himself up, but she lay still, and he saw that something had struck her upon the head, for blood was running down her cheek. He lifted her, and, filled with black horror and despair—for he thought her gone—pressed his hand upon her heart. Thank God! it began to beat again—she still lived.

The music in the saloon had stopped, and for a little while there was silence. Then of an instant there arose the horrible clamour of shipwreck; wild-eyed people rushed to and fro aimlessly; here and there women and children shrieked; a clergyman fell upon his knees and began to pray.

This went on for a space, till presently the second officer appeared and, affecting an unconcerned air, called out that it was all right, the captain said no one was to be afraid. He added that they were not more than six miles from the shore, and that the ship would be beached in half an hour. Indeed, as he spoke the engines, which had been stopped, commenced to work again, and her head swung round in a wide circle, pointing to the land. Evidently they had passed over the rock and were once more in deep water, through which they travelled at a good speed but with a heavy list to starboard. The pumps got to work also with a monotonous, clanging beat, throwing out great columns of foaming water on to the oily sea. Men began to cut the covers off the boats, and to swing some of them outboard. Such were the things that went on about them.

With the senseless Benita clasped to his breast, the blood from her cut head running down his shoulder, Robert stood still awhile, thinking. Then he made up his mind. As it chanced, she had a deck cabin, and thither he forced his way, carrying her tenderly and with patience through the distracted throng of passengers, for there were five hundred souls on board that ship. He reached the place to find that it was quite empty, her cabinmate having fled. Laying Benita upon the lower bunk, he lit the swinging candle. As soon as it burned up he searched for the lifebelts and by good fortune found two of them, one of which, not without great difficulty, he succeeded in fastening round her. Then he took a sponge and bathed her head with water. There was a great bruise upon her temple where the block or whatever it was had struck her, and the blood still flowed; but the wound was not very deep or extensive, nor, so far as he could discover, did the bone appear to be broken or driven in. He had good hope that she was only stunned, and would revive presently. Unable to do more for her, a thought struck him. On the floor of the cabin, thrown by the shock from the rack, lay her writing case. He opened it, and taking a piece of paper wrote these words hurriedly in pencil:

You gave me no answer, and it is more than probable that I shall receive none in this world which one or both of us may be upon the verge of leaving. In the latter case we can settle the matter elsewhere—perhaps. In the former, should it be my lot to go and yours to stay, I hope that you will think kindly of me at times as of one who loved you truly. Should it be yours to go, then you will never read these words. Yet if to the dead is given knowledge, be assured that as you left me so you shall find me, yours and yours alone. Or perhaps we both may live; I pray so.—S. R. S.

Folding up the paper, he undid a button of Benita's blouse and thrust it away there, knowing that thus she would certainly find it should she survive. Then he stepped out on to the deck to see what was happening. The vessel still steamed, but made slow progress; moreover, the list to starboard was now so pronounced that it was difficult to stand upright. On account of it nearly all the passengers were huddled together upon the port side, having instinctively taken refuge as far as possible above the water. A man with a white, distraught face staggered towards him, supporting himself by the bulwarks. It was the captain. For a moment he paused as though to think, holding to a stanchion. Robert Seymour saw his opportunity and addressed him.

"Forgive me," he said; "I do not like interfering with other people's business, but for reasons unconnected with myself I suggest to you that it would be wise to stop this ship and get out the boats. The sea is calm; if it is not left till too late there should be no difficulty in launching them."

The man stared at him absently, then said:

"They won't hold everybody, Mr. Seymour. I hope to beach her."

"At least they will hold some," he answered, "whereas——" And he pointed to the water, which by now was almost level with the deck.

"Perhaps you are right, Mr. Seymour. It doesn't matter to me, anyway. I am a ruined man; but the poor passengers—the poor passengers!" And he scrambled away fiercely towards the bridge like a wounded cat along the bough of a tree, whence in a few seconds Robert heard him shouting orders.

A minute or so afterwards the steamer stopped. Too late the captain had decided to sacrifice his ship and save those she carried. They were beginning to get out the boats. Now Robert returned to the cabin where Benita was lying senseless, and wrapped her up in a cloak and some blankets. Then, seeing the second lifebelt on the floor, by an afterthought he put it on, knowing that there was time to spare. Next he lifted Benita, and feeling sure that the rush would be for the starboard side, on which the boats were quite near the water, carried her, with difficulty, for the slope was steep, to the port-cutter, which he knew would be in the charge of a good man, the second officer, whom he had seen in command there at Sunday boat-drills.

Here, as he had anticipated, the crowd was small, since most people thought that it would not be possible to get this boat down safely to the water; or if their powers of reflection were gone, instinct told them so. That skilful seaman, the second officer, and his appointed crew, were already at work lowering the cutter from the davits.

"Now," he said, "women and children first."

A number rushed in, and Robert saw that the boat would soon be full.

269

"I am afraid," he said, "that I must count myself a woman as I carry one," and by a great effort, holding Benita with one arm, with the other he let himself down the falls and, assisted by a quartermaster, gained the boat in safety.

One or two other men scrambled after him.

"Push her off," said the officer; "she can hold no more," and the ropes were let go.

When they were about twelve feet from the ship's side, from which they thrust themselves clear with oars, there came a rush of people, disappointed of places in the starboard boats. A few of the boldest of these swarmed down the falls, others jumped and fell among them, or missed and dropped into the sea, or struck upon the sides of the boat and were killed. Still she reached the water upon an even keel, though now much overladen. The oars were got out, and they rowed round the bow of the great ship wallowing in her death-throes, their first idea being to make for the shore, which was not three miles away.

This brought them to the starboard side, where they saw a hideous scene. Hundreds of people seemed to be fighting for room, with the result that some of the boats were overturned, precipitating their occupants into the water. Others hung by the prow or the stern, the ropes having jammed in the davits in the frantic haste and confusion, while from them human beings dropped one by one. Round others not yet launched a hellish struggle was in progress, the struggle of men, women, and children battling for their lives, in which the strong, mad with terror, showed no mercy to the weak.

From that mass of humanity, most of them about to perish, went up a babble of sounds which in its sum shaped itself to one prolonged scream, such as might proceed from a Titan in his agony. All this beneath a brooding, moonlit sky, and on a sea as smooth as glass. Upon the ship, which now lay upon her side, the siren still sent up its yells for succour, and some brave man continued to fire rockets, which rushed heavenwards and burst in showers of stars.

Robert remembered that the last rocket he had seen was fired at an evening fete for the amusement of the audience. The contrast struck him as dreadful. He wondered whether there were any power or infernal population that could be amused by a tragedy such as enacted itself before his eyes; how it came about also that such a tragedy was permitted by the merciful Strength in which mankind put their faith.

The vessel was turning over, compressed air or steam burst up the decks with loud reports; fragments of wreckage flew into the air. There the poor captain still clung to the rail of the bridge. Seymour could see his white face—the moonlight seemed to paint it with a ghastly smile. The officer in command of their boat shouted to the crew to give way lest they should be sucked down with the steamer.

Look! Now she wallowed like a dying whale, the moonrays shone white upon her bottom, showing the jagged rent made in it by the rock on which she had struck, and now she was gone. Only a little cloud of smoke and steam remained to mark where the *Zanzibar* had been.

CHAPTER 3

How Robert Came Ashore

In place of the *Zanzibar* a great pit on the face of the ocean, in which the waters boiled and black objects appeared and disappeared.

"Sit still, for your lives' sake," said the officer in a quiet voice; "the suck is coming."

In another minute it came, dragging them downward till the water trickled over the sides of the boat, and backward towards the pit. But before ever they reached it the deep had digested its prey, and, save for the great air-bubbles which burst about them and a mixed, unnatural swell, was calm again. For the moment they were safe.

"Passengers," said the officer, "I am going to put out to sea—at any rate, till daylight. We may meet a vessel there, and if we try to row ashore we shall certainly be swamped in the breakers."

No one objected; they seemed too stunned to speak, but Robert thought to himself that the man was wise. They began to move, but before they had gone a dozen yards something dark rose beside them. It was a piece of wreckage, and clinging to it a woman, who clasped a bundle to her breast. More, she was alive, for she began to cry to them to take her in.

"Save me and my child!" she cried. "For God's sake save me!"

Robert recognized the choking voice; it was that of a young married lady with whom he had been very friendly, who was going out with her baby to join her husband in Natal. He stretched out his hand and caught hold of her, whereon the officer said, heavily: "The boat is already over-laden. I must warn you that to take more aboard is not safe."

Thereon the passengers awoke from their stupor.

"Push her off," cried a voice; "she must take her chance." And there was a murmur of approval at the dreadful words.

"For Christ's sake—for Christ's sake!" wailed the drowning wom-an, who clung desperately to Robert's hand.

"If you try to pull her in, we will throw you overboard," said the voice again, and a knife was lifted as though to hack at his arm. Then the officer spoke once more.

"This lady cannot come into the boat unless someone goes out of it. I would myself, but it is my duty to stay. Is there any man here who will make place for her?"

But all the men there—seven of them, besides the crew—hung their heads and were silent.

"Give way," said the officer in the same heavy voice; "she will drop off presently."

While the words passed his lips Robert seemed to live a year. Here was an opportunity of atonement for his idle and luxurious life. An hour ago he would have taken it gladly, but now—now, with Benita senseless on his breast, and that answer still locked in her sleeping heart? Yet Benita would approve of such a death as this, and even if she loved him not in life, would learn to love his memory. In an instant his mind was made up, and he was speaking rapidly.

"Thompson," he said to the officer, "if I go, will you swear to take her in and her child?"

"Certainly, Mr. Seymour."

"Then lay to; I am going. If any of you live, tell this lady how I died," and he pointed to Benita, "and say I thought that she would wish it."

"She shall be told," said the officer again, "and saved, too, if I can do it."

"Hold Mrs. Jeffreys, then, till I am out of this. I'll leave my coat to cover her."

A sailor obeyed, and with difficulty Robert wrenched free his hand.

Very deliberately he pressed Benita to his breast and kissed her on the forehead, then let her gently slide on to the bottom of the boat. Next he slipped off his overcoat and slowly rolled himself over the gunwale into the sea.

"Now," he said, "pull Mrs. Jeffreys in."

"God bless you; you are a brave man," said Thompson. "I shall remember you if I live a hundred years."

But no one else said anything; perhaps they were all too much ashamed, even then.

"I have only done my duty," Seymour answered from the water. "How far is it to the shore?"

"About three miles," shouted Thompson. "But keep on that plank, or you will never live through the rollers. Goodbye."

"Goodbye," answered Robert.

Then the boat passed away from him and soon vanished in the misty face of the deep.

Resting on the plank which had saved the life of Mrs. Jeffreys, Robert Seymour looked about him and listened. Now and again he heard a faint, choking scream uttered by some drowning wretch, and a few hundred yards away caught sight of a black object which he thought might be a boat. If so, he reflected that it must be full. Moreover, he could not overtake it. No; his only chance was to make for the shore. He was a strong swimmer, and happily the water was almost as warm as milk. There seemed to be no reason why he should not reach it, supported as he was by a lifebelt, if the sharks would leave him alone, which they might, as there was plenty for them to feed on. The direction he knew well enough, for now in the great silence of the sea he could hear the boom of the mighty rollers breaking on the beach.

Ah, those rollers! He remembered how that very afternoon Benita and he had watched them through his field glass sprouting up against the cruel walls of rock, and wondered that when the ocean was so calm they had still such power. Now, should he live to reach them, he was doomed to match himself against that power. Well, the sooner he did so the sooner it would be over, one way or the other. This was in his favour: the tide had turned, and was flowing shorewards. Indeed, he had little to do but to rest upon his plank, which he placed crosswise beneath his breast, and steered himself with his feet. Even thus he made good progress, nearly a mile an hour perhaps. He could have gone faster had he swum, but he was saving his strength.

It was a strange journey upon that silent sea beneath those silent stars, and strange thoughts came into Robert's soul. He wondered whether Benita would live and what she would say. Perhaps, however, she was already dead, and he would meet her presently. He wondered if he were doomed to die, and whether this sacrifice of his would be allowed to atone for his past errors. He hoped so, and put up a petition to that effect, for himself and for Benita, and for all the poor people who had gone before, hurled from their pleasure into the halls of Death.

So he floated on while the boom of the breakers grew ever nearer, companioned by his wild, fretful thoughts, till at length what he took to be a shark appeared quite close to him, and in the urgency of the moment he gave up wondering. It proved to be only a piece of wood, but later on a real shark did come, for he saw its back fin. However, this cruel creature was either gorged or timid, for when he splashed upon the water and shouted, it went away, to return no more.

Now, at length, Robert entered upon the deep hill and valley swell which preceded the field of the rollers. Suddenly he shot down a smooth slope, and without effort of his own found himself borne up an opposing steep, from the crest of which he had a view of white lines of foam, and beyond them of a dim and rocky shore. At one spot, a little to his right, the foam seemed thinner and the line of cliff to be broken, as though here there was a cleft. For this cleft, then, he steered his plank, taking the swell obliquely, which by good fortune the set of the tide enabled him to do without any great exertion.

The valleys grew deeper, and the tops of the opposing ridges were crested with foam. He had entered the rollers, and the struggle for life began. Before him they rushed solemn and mighty. Viewed from some safe place even the sight of these combers is terrible, as any who have watched them from this coast, or from that of the Island of Ascension, can bear witness. What their aspect was to this shipwrecked man, supported by a single plank, may therefore be imagined, seen, as he saw them, in the mysterious moonlight and in utter loneliness. Yet his spirit rose to meet the dread emergency; if he were to die, he would die fighting. He had grown cold and tired, but now the chill and weariness left him; he felt warm and strong. From the crest of one of the high rollers he thought he saw that about half a mile away from him a little river ran down the centre of the gorge, and for the mouth of this river he laid his course.

At first all went well. He was borne up the seas; he slid down the seas in a lather of white foam. Presently the rise and fall grew steeper, and the foam began to break over his head. Robert could no longer guide himself; he must go as he was carried. Then in an instant he was carried into a hell of waters where, had it not been for his lifebelt and the plank, he must have been beaten down and have perished. As it was, now he was driven into the depths, and now he emerged upon their surface to hear their seething hiss around him, and above it all a continuous boom as of great guns—the boom of the breaking seas.

The plank was almost twisted from his grasp, but he clung to it desperately, although its edges tore his arms. When the rollers broke over him he held his breath, and when he was tossed skywards on their curves, drew it again in quick, sweet gasps. Now he sat upon the very brow of one of them as a merman might; now he dived like a dolphin, and now, just as his senses were leaving him, his feet touched bottom. Another moment and Robert was being rolled along that bottom with a weight on him like the weight of mountains. The plank was rent from him, but his cork jacket brought him up. The backwash drew him with it into deeper water, where he lay helpless and despairing, for he no longer had any strength to struggle against his doom.

Then it was that there came a mighty roller, bigger than any that he had seen—such a one as on that coast the Kaffirs call "a father of waves." It caught him in the embrace of its vast green curve. It bore him forward as though he were but a straw, far forward over the stretch of cruel rocks. It broke in thunder, dashing him again upon the stones and sand of the little river bar, rolling him along with its resistless might, till even that might was exhausted, and its foam began to return seawards, sucking him with it.

Robert's mind was almost gone, but enough of it remained to tell him that if once more he was dragged into the deep water he must be lost. As the current haled him along he gripped at the bottom with his hands, and by the mercy of Heaven they closed on something. It may have been a tree-stump embedded there, or a rock—he never knew. At least, it was firm, and to it he hung despairingly. Would that rush never cease? His lungs were bursting; he must let go! Oh! the foam was thinning; his head was above it now; now it had departed, leaving him like a stranded fish upon the shingle. For half a minute or more he lay there gasping, then looked behind him to see another comber approaching through the gloom. He struggled to his feet, fell, rose again, and ran, or rather, staggered forward with that tigerish water hissing at his heels. Forward, still forward, till he was beyond its reach—yes, on dry sand. Then his vital forces failed him; one of his legs gave way, and, bleeding from a hundred hurts, he fell heavily onto his face, and there was still.

The boat in which Benita lay, being so deep in the water, proved very hard to row against the tide, for the number of its passengers encumbered the oarsmen. After a while a light off land breeze sprang up, as here it often does towards morning; and the officer, Thompson, determined to risk hoisting the sail. Accordingly this was done—with some difficulty, for the mast had to be drawn out and shipped—although the women screamed as the weight of the air bent their frail craft over till the gunwale was almost level with the water.

"Anyone who moves shall be thrown overboard!" said the officer, who steered, after which they were quiet.

Now they made good progress seawards, but the anxieties of those who knew were very great, since the wind showed signs of rising, and if any swell should spring up that crowded cutter could scarcely hope to live. In fact, two hours later they were forced to lower the sail again and drift, waiting for the dawn. Mr. Thompson strove to cheer them, saying that now they were in the track of vessels, and if they could see none when the light came, he would run along the shore in the hope of finding a place free of breakers where they might land. If they did not inspire hope, at least his words calmed them, and they sat in heavy silence, watching the sky.

At length it grew grey, and then, with a sudden glory peculiar to South Africa, the great red sun arose and began to dispel the mist from the surface of the sea. Half an hour more and this was gone, and now the bright rays brought life back into their chilled frames as they stared at each other to see which of their company were still left alive. They even asked for food, and biscuit was given to them with water.

All this while Benita remained unconscious. Indeed, one callous fellow, who had been using her body as a footstool, said that she must be dead, and had better be thrown overboard, as it would lighten the boat.

"If you throw that lady into the sea, living or dead," said Mr. Thompson, with an ominous lift of his eye, "you go with her, Mr. Batten. Remember who brought her here and how he died."

Then Mr. Batten held his peace, while Thompson stood up and scanned the wide expanse of sea. Presently he whispered to a sailor near him, who also stood up, looked, and nodded.

"That will be the other Line's intermediate boat," he said, and the passengers, craning their heads round, saw far away to the right a streak of smoke upon the horizon. Orders were given, a little corner of sail was hoisted, with a white cloth of some sort tied above it, and the oars were got out. Once more the cutter moved forward, bearing to the left in the hope of intercepting the steamer.

She came on with terrible swiftness, and they who had miles of water to cover, dared hoist no more sail in that breeze. In half an hour she was nearly opposite to them, and they were still far away. A little more sail was let out, driving them through the water at as quick a rate as they could venture to go. The steamer was passing three miles or so away, and black despair took hold of them. Now the resourceful Thompson, without apologies, undressed, and removing the white shirt that he had worn at the dance, bade a sailor to tie it to an oar and wave it to and fro.

Still the steamer went on, until presently they heard her siren going, and saw that she was putting about.

"She has seen us," said Thompson. "Thank God, all of you, for there is wind coming up. Pull down that sail; we shan't need it any more."

Half an hour later, with many precautions, for the wind he proph-esied was already troubling the sea and sending little splashes of wa-ter over the stern of their deeply laden boat, they were fast to a line thrown from the deck of the three thousand ton steamer *Castle*, bound for Natal. Then, with a rattle, down came the accommodation ladder, and strong-armed men, standing on its grating, dragged them one by one from the death to which they had been so near. The last to be lifted up, except Thompson, was Benita, round whom it was necessary to reeve a rope.

"Any use?" asked the officer on the grating as he glanced at her quiet form.

"Can't say; I hope so," answered Thompson. "Call your doctor." And gently enough she was borne up the ship's side.

They wanted to cast off the boat, but Thompson remonstrated, and in the end that also was dragged to deck. Meanwhile the news had spread, and the awakened passengers of the *Castle*, clad in pyjamas, dressing-gowns, and even blankets, were crowding round the poor castaways or helping them to their cabins.

"I am a teetotaller," said second officer Thompson when he had made a brief report to the captain of the *Castle*, "but if anyone will stand me a whiskey and soda I shall be obliged to him."

CHAPTER 4

Mr Clifford

Although the shock of the blow she had received upon her head was sufficient to make her insensible for so many hours, Benita's injuries were not of a really serious nature, for as it happened the falling block, or whatever it may have been, had hit her forehead slantwise, and not full, to which accident she owed it that, although the skin was torn and the scalp bruised, her skull had escaped fracture. Under proper medical care her senses soon came back to her, but as she was quite dazed and thought herself still on board the *Zanzibar*, the doctor considered it wise to preserve her in that illusion for a while. So after she had swallowed some broth he gave her a sleeping draught, the effects of which she did not shake off till the following morning.

Then she came to herself completely, and was astonished to feel the pain in her head, which had been bandaged, and to see a strange stewardess sitting by her with a cup of beef-tea in her hand.

"Where am I? Is it a dream?" she asked.

"Drink this and I will tell you," answered the stewardess.

Benita obeyed, for she felt hungry, then repeated her question.

"Your steamer was shipwrecked," said the stewardess, "and a great many poor people were drowned, but you were saved in a boat. Look, there are your clothes; they were never in the water."

"Who carried me into the boat?" asked Benita in a low voice.

"A gentleman, they say, Miss, who had wrapped you in a blanket and put a lifebelt on you."

Now Benita remembered everything that happened before the darkness fell—the question to which she had given no answer, the young couple who stood flirting by her—all came back to her.

"Was Mr. Seymour saved?" she whispered, her face grey with dread.

"I dare say, Miss," answered the stewardess evasively. "But there is no gentleman of that name aboard this ship."

At that moment the doctor came in, and him, too, she plied with questions. But having learned the story of Robert's self-sacrifice from Mr. Thompson and the others, he would give her no answer, for he guessed how matters had stood between them, and feared the effects of the shock. All he could say was that he hoped Mr. Seymour had escaped in some other boat.

It was not until the third morning that Benita was allowed to learn the truth, which indeed it was impossible to conceal any longer. Mr. Thompson came to her cabin and told her everything, while she listened silently, horrified, amazed.

"Miss Clifford," he said, "I think it was one of the bravest things that a man ever did. On the ship I always thought him rather a head-in-air kind of swell, but he was a splendid fellow, and I pray God that he has lived, as the lady and child for whom he offered himself up have done, for they are both well again."

"Yes," she repeated after him mechanically, "splendid fellow indeed, and," she added, with a strange flash of conviction, "I believe that he *is* still alive. If he were dead I should know it."

"I am glad to hear you say so," said Mr. Thompson, who believed the exact contrary.

"Listen," she went on. "I will tell you something. When that dreadful accident occurred Mr. Seymour had just asked me to marry him, and I was going to answer that I would—because I love him. I believe that I shall still give him that answer."

Mr. Thompson replied again that he hoped so, which, being as honest and tender-hearted as he was brave and capable, he did most earnestly; but in his heart he reflected that her answer would not be given this side of the grave. Then, as he had been deputed to do, he handed her the note which had been found in the bosom of her dress, and, able to bear no more of this painful scene, hurried from the cabin. She read it greedily twice, and pressed it to her lips, murmuring:

"Yes, I will think kindly of you, Robert Seymour, kindly as woman can of man, and now or afterwards you shall have your answer, if you still wish for it. Whenever you come or wherever I go, it shall be ready for you."

That afternoon, when she was more composed, Mrs. Jeffreys came to see Benita, bringing her baby with her. The poor woman was still pale and shaken, but the child had taken no hurt at all from its immersion in that warm water.

"What can you think of me?" she said, falling on her knees by Benita. "But oh! I did not know what I was doing. It was terror and my child," and she kissed the sleeping infant passionately. "Also I did not understand at the time—I was too dazed. And—that hero—he gave his life for me when the others wished to beat me off with oars. Yes, his blood is upon my hands—he who died that I and my child might live."

Benita looked at her and answered, very gently:

"Perhaps he did not die after all. Do not grieve, for if he did it was a very glorious death, and I am prouder of him than I could have been had he lived on like the others—who wished to beat you off with oars. Whatever is, is by God's Will, and doubtless for the best. At the least, you and your child will be restored to your husband, though it cost me one who would have been—my husband."

That evening Benita came upon the deck and spoke with the other ladies who were saved, learning every detail that she could gather. But to none of the men, except to Mr. Thompson, would she say a single word, and soon, seeing how the matter stood, they hid themselves away from her as they had already done from Mrs. Jeffreys.

The *Castle* had hung about the scene of the shipwreck for thirty hours, and rescued one other boatload of survivors, also a stoker clinging to a piece of wreckage. But with the shore she had been unable to communicate, for the dreaded wind had risen, and the breakers were quite impassable to any boat. To a passing steamer bound for Port Elizabeth, however, she had reported the terrible disaster, which by now was known all over the world, together with the names of those whom she had picked up in the boats.

On the night of the day of Benita's interview with Mrs. Jeffreys, the *Castle* arrived off Durban and anchored, since she was too big a vessel to cross the bar as it was in those days. At dawn the stewardess awoke Benita from the uneasy sleep in which she lay, to tell her that an old gentleman had come off in the tug and wished to see her; for fear of exciting false hopes she was very careful to add that word "old." With her help Benita dressed herself, and as the sun rose, flooding the Berea, the Point, the white town and fair Natal beyond with light, she went on to the deck, and there, leaning over the bulwark, saw a thin, grey-bearded man of whom after all these years the aspect was still familiar.

A curious thrill went through her as she looked at him leaning there lost in thought. After all, he was her father, the man to whom she owed her presence upon this bitter earth, this place of terrors and delights, of devastation and hope supernal. Perhaps, too, he had been as much sinned against as sinning. She stepped up to him and touched him on the shoulder.

"Father," she said.

He turned round with all the quickness of a young man, for about him there was a peculiar agility which his daughter had inherited. Like his mind, his body was still nimble.

"My darling," he said, "I should have known your voice anywhere. It has haunted my sleep for years. My darling, thank you for coming back to me, and thank God for preserving you when so many were lost." Then he threw his arms about her and kissed her.

She shrank from him a little, for by inadvertence he had pressed upon the wound in her forehead.

"Forgive me," she said; "it is my head. It was injured, you know."

Then he saw the bandage about her brow, and was very penitent.

"They did not tell me that you had been hurt, Benita," he exclaimed in his light, refined voice, one of the stamps of that gentility of blood and breeding whereof all his rough years and errors had been unable to deprive him. "They only told me that you were saved. It is part of my ill-fortune that at our first moment of greeting I should give you pain, who have caused you so much already."

Benita felt that the words were an apology for the past, and her heart was touched.

"It is nothing," she answered. "You did not know or mean it."

"No, dear, I never knew or meant it. Believe me, I was not a willing sinner, only a weak one. You are beautiful, Benita—far more so than I expected."

"What," she answered smiling, "with this bandage round my head? Well, in your eyes, perhaps." But inwardly she thought to herself that the description would be more applicable to her father, who in truth, notwithstanding his years, was wonderfully handsome, with his quick blue eyes, mobile face, gentle mouth with the wistful droop at the corners so like her own, and grey beard. How, she wondered, could this be the man who had struck her mother. Then she remembered him as he had been years before when he was a slave to liquor, and knew that the answer was simple.

"Tell me about your escape, love," he said, patting her hand with his thin fingers. "You don't know what I've suffered. I was waiting at the Royal Hotel here, when the cable came announcing the loss of the *Zanzibar* and all on board. For the first time for many a year I drank spirits to drown my grief—don't be afraid, dear—for the first time and the last. Then afterwards came another cable giving the names of those who were known to be saved, and—thank God, oh! thank God—yours among them," and he gasped at the recollection of that relief.

"Yes," she said; "I suppose I should thank—Him—and another. Have you heard the story about—how Mr. Seymour saved me, I mean?"

"Some of it. While you were dressing yourself, I have been talking to the officer who was in command of your boat. He was a brave man, Benita, and I am sorry to tell you he is gone."

She grasped a stanchion and clung there, staring at him with a wild, white face.

"How do you know that, Father?"

Mr. Clifford drew a copy of the *Natal Mercury* of the previous day from the pocket of his Ulster, and while she waited in an agony he hunted through the long columns descriptive of the loss of the *Zanzibar*. Presently he came to the paragraph he sought, and read it aloud to her. It ran:

"The searchers on the coast opposite the scene of the shipwreck report that they met a Kaffir who was travelling along the seashore, who produced a gold watch which he said he had taken from the body of a white man that he found lying on the sand at the mouth of the Umvoli River. Inside the watch is engraved, 'To Seymour Robert Seymour, from his uncle, on his twenty-first birthday.' The name of Mr. Seymour appears as a first-class passenger to Durban by the *Zanzibar*. He was a member of an old English family in Lincolnshire. This was his second journey to South Africa, which he visited some years ago with his brother on a big-game shooting expedition. All who knew him then will join with us in deploring his loss. Mr. Seymour was a noted shot and an English gentleman of the best stamp. He was last seen by one of the survivors of the catastrophe, carrying Miss Clifford, the daughter of the well-known Natal pioneer of that name, into a boat, but as this young lady is reported to have been saved, and as he entered the boat with her, no explanation is yet forthcoming as to how he came to his sad end."

"I fear that is clear enough," said Mr. Clifford, as he folded up his paper.

"Yes, clear enough," she repeated in a strained voice. "And yet—yet—oh! Father, he had just asked me to marry him, and I can't believe that he is dead before I had time to answer."

"Good Heavens!" said the old man, "they never told me that. It is dreadfully sad. God help you, my poor child! There is nothing more to say except that he was only one among three hundred who have gone with him. Be brave now, before all these people. Look—here comes the tug."

The following week was very much of a blank to Benita. When

they reached shore some old friends of her father's took her and him to their house, a quiet place upon the Berea. Here, now that the first excitement of rescue and grief was over, the inevitable reaction set in, bringing with it weakness so distressing that the doctor insisted upon her going to bed, where she remained for the next five days. With the healing up of the wound in her head her strength came back to her at last, but it was a very sad Benita who crept from her room one afternoon on to the veranda and looked out at the cruel sea, peaceful now as the sky above.

Her father, who had nursed her tenderly during these dark days, came and sat by her, taking her hand in his.

"This is capital," he said, glancing at her anxiously. "You are getting quite yourself again."

"I shall never be myself again," she answered. "My old self is dead, although the outside of me has recovered. Father, I suppose that it is wrong, but I wish that I were dead too. I wish that he had taken me with him when he jumped into the sea to lighten the boat."

"Don't speak like that," he broke in hastily. "Of course I know that I am not much to you—how can I be after all that is past? But I love you, dear, and if I were left quite alone again——" And he broke off.

"You shall not be left alone if I can help it," she replied, looking at the old man with her dark and tender eyes. "We have only each other in the world now, have we? The rest have gone, never to return."

He threw his arms about her, and, drawing her to him, kissed her passionately.

"If only you could learn to love me!" he said.

"I do love you," she answered, "who now shall never love any other man upon the earth."

This was the beginning of a deep affection which sprang up between Mr. Clifford and his daughter, and continued to the end.

"Is there any news?" she asked a little later.

"None—none about him. The tide took his body away, no doubt, after the Kaffir had gone. I remember him well now. He was a fine young man, and it comes into my mind that when I said goodbye to him above those old ruins, I wished that I had a son like that. And to think that he went so near to becoming a son to me! Well, the grass must bend when the wind blows, as the natives say."

"I am glad that you knew him," she answered simply.

Then they began talking about other matters. He told her that all the story had become known, and that people spoke of Robert Seymour as "the hero"; also that there was a great deal of curiosity about her.

"Then let us get away as soon as we can," she said nervously. "But, Father, where are we going?"

"That will be for you to decide, love. Listen, now; this is my position. I have been quite steady for years, and worked hard, with the result that I and my partner have a fine farm in the Transvaal, on the high land near Lake Chrissie, out Wakkerstroom way. We breed horses there, and have done very well with them. I have £1,500 saved, and the farm brings us in quite £600 a year beyond the expenses. But it is a lonely place, with only a few Boers about, although they are good fellows enough. You might not care to live there with no company."

"I don't think that I should mind," she answered, smiling.

"Not now, but by-and-by you would when you know what it is like. Now I might sell my share in the farm to my partner, who, I think, would buy it, or I might trust to him to send me a part of the profits, which perhaps he would not. Then, if you wish it, we could live in or near one of the towns, or even, as you have an income of your own, go home to England, if that is your will."

"Is it your will?" she asked.

He shook his head. "No; all my life is here. Also, I have something to find before I die—for your sake, dear."

"Do you mean up among those ruins?" she asked, looking at him curiously.

"Yes. So you know about it?" he answered, with a flash of his blue eyes. "Oh! of course, Seymour told you. Yes, I mean among the ruins—but I will tell you that story another time—not here, not here. What do you wish to do, Benita? Remember, I am in your hands; I will obey you in all things."

"Not to stop in a town and not to go to England," she replied, while he hung eagerly upon her words, "for this has become my holy land. Father, I will go with you to your farm; there I can be quiet, you and I together."

"Yes," he answered rather uneasily; "but, you see, Benita, we shall not be quite alone there. My partner, Jacob Meyer, lives with me."

"Jacob Meyer? Ah! I remember," and she winced. "He is a German, is he not—and odd?"

"German Jew, I imagine, and very odd. Should have made his fortune a dozen times over, and yet has never done anything. Too unpractical, too visionary, with all his brains and scheming. Not a good man, Benita, although he suits me, and, for the matter of that, under our agreement I cannot get rid of him."

"How did he become your partner?" she asked.

285

"Oh! a good many years ago he turned up at the place with a doleful story. Said that he had been trading among the Zulus; he was what we call a *'smouse'* out here, and got into a row with them, I don't know how. The end of it was that they burned his wagon, looted his trade-goods and oxen, and killed his servants. They would have killed him too, only, according to his own account, he escaped in a very queer fashion."

"How?"

"Well, he says by mesmerising the chief and making the man lead him through his followers. An odd story enough, but I can quite be-lieve it of Jacob. He worked for me for six months, and showed him-self very clever. Then one night, I remember it was a few days after I had told him of the story of the Portuguese treasure in Matabeleland, he produced £500 in Bank of England notes out of the lining of his waistcoat, and offered to buy a half interest in the farm. Yes, £500! Although for all those months I had believed him to be a beggar. Well, as he was so *slim*, and better than no company in that lonely place, in the end I accepted. We have done well since, except for the expedition after the treasure which we did not get, although we more than paid our expenses out of the ivory we bought. But next time we shall suc-ceed, I am sure," he added with enthusiasm, "that is, if we can persuade those Makalanga to let us search on the mountain."

Benita smiled.

"I think you had better stick to the horse breeding," she said.

"You shall judge when you hear the story. But you have been brought up in England; will you not be afraid to go to Lake Chrissie?"

"Afraid of what?" she asked.

"Oh! of the loneliness, and of Jacob Meyer."

"I was born on the *veld*, Father, and I have always hated London. As for your odd friend, Mr. Meyer, I am not afraid of any man on earth. I have done with men. At the least I will try the place and see how I get on."

"Very well," answered her father with a sigh of relief. "You can always come back, can't you?"

"Yes," she said indifferently. "I suppose that I can always come back."

CHAPTER 5

Jacob Meyer

More than three weeks had gone by when one morning Benita, who slept upon the cartel or hide-strung bed in the wagon, having dressed herself as best she could in that confined place, thrust aside the curtain and seated herself upon the *voorkisse*, or driving-box. The sun was not yet up, and the air was cold with frost, for they were on the Transvaal high-*veld* at the end of winter. Even through her thick cloak Benita shivered and called to the driver of the wagon, who also acted as cook, and whose blanket-draped form she could see bending over a fire into which he was blowing life, to make haste with the coffee.

"By and by, Missie—by and by," he answered, coughing the rank smoke from his lungs. "Kettle no sing yet, and fire black as hell."

Benita reflected that popular report painted this locality red, but without entering into argument sat still upon the chest waiting till the water boiled and her father appeared.

Presently he emerged from under the side flap of the wagon where he slept, and remarking that it was really too cold to think of washing, climbed to her side by help of the *disselboom*, and kissed her.

"How far are we now from Rooi Krantz, Father?" she asked, for that was the name of Mr. Clifford's farm.

"About forty miles, dear. The wagon cannot make it tonight with these two sick oxen, but after the midday outspan we will ride on, and be there by sundown. I am afraid you are tired of this trekking."

"No," she answered. "I like it very much; it is so restful, and I sleep sound upon that cartel. I feel as though I should like to trek on for the rest of my life."

"So you shall if you wish, dear, for whole months. South Africa is big, and when the grass grows, if you still wish it, we will take a long journey."

She smiled, but made no answer, knowing that he was thinking of the place so far away where he believed that once the Portuguese had buried gold.

The kettle was singing now merrily enough, and Hans, the cook, lifting it from the fire in triumph—for his blowing exertions had been severe—poured into it a quantity of ground coffee from an old mustard tin. Then, having stirred the mixture with a stick, he took a red ember from the fire and dropped it into the kettle, a process which, as travellers in the *veld* know well, has a clearing effect upon the coffee. Next he produced pannikins, and handed them up with a pickle jar full of sugar to Mr. Clifford, upon the wagon chest. Milk they had none, yet that coffee tasted a great deal better than it looked; indeed, Benita drank two cups of it to warm herself and wash down the hard biscuit. Before the day was over glad enough was she that she had done so.

The sun was rising; huge and red it looked seen through the clinging mist, and, their breakfast finished, Mr. Clifford gave orders that the oxen, which were filling themselves with the dry grass near at hand, should be got up and inspanned. The *voorlooper*, a Zulu boy, who had left them for a little while to share the rest of the coffee with Hans, rose from his haunches with a grunt, and departed to fetch them. A minute or two later Hans ceased from his occupation of packing up the things, and said in a low voice:

"*Kek!* Baas"—that is "Look!"

Following the line of his outstretched hand, Benita and her father perceived, not more than a hundred yards away from them, a great troop of wildebeest, or gnu, travelling along a ridge, and pausing now and again to indulge in those extraordinary gambols which cause the Boers to declare that these brutes have a worm in their brains.

"Give me my rifle, Hans," said Mr. Clifford. "We want meat."

By the time that the Westley-Richards was drawn from its case and loaded, only one buck remained, for, having caught sight of the wagon, it turned to stare at it suspiciously. Mr. Clifford aimed and fired. Down went the buck, then springing to its feet again, vanished behind the ridge. Mr. Clifford shook his head sadly.

"I don't often do that sort of thing, my dear, but the light is still very bad. Still, he's hit. What do you say? Shall we get on the horses and catch him? A canter would warm you."

Benita, who was tender-hearted, reflected that it would be kinder to put the poor creature out of its pain, and nodded her head. Five minutes later they were cantering together up the rise, Mr. Clifford having first ordered the wagon to trek on till they rejoined it, and slipped a packet of cartridges into his pocket. Beyond the rise lay a wide stretch of marshy ground, bordered by another rise half a mile or more away, from the crest of which—for now the air was clear enough—they saw the wounded bull standing. On they went after him, but before they could come within shot, he had moved forward once more, for he was only lightly hurt in the flank, and guessed whence his trouble came.

Again and again did he retreat as they drew near, until at length, just as Mr. Clifford was about to dismount to risk a long shot, the beast took to its heels in earnest.

"Come on," he said; "don't let's be beat," for by this time the hunter was alive in him.

So off they went at a gallop, up slopes and down slopes that reminded Benita of the Bay of Biscay in a storm, across half-dried *vleis* that in the wet season were ponds, through stony ground and patches of ant-bear holes in which they nearly came to grief. For five miles at least the chase went on, since at the end of winter the wildebeest was thin and could gallop well, notwithstanding its injury, faster even than their good horses. At last, rising a ridge, they found whither it was going, for suddenly they were in the midst of vast herds of game, thousands and tens of thousands of them stretching as far as the eye could reach.

It was a wondrous sight that now, alas! will be seen no more—at any rate upon the Transvaal *veld*; wildebeest, blesbok, springbok, in countless multitudes, and amongst them a few quagga and hartebeest. With a sound like that of thunder, their flashing myriad hoofs casting up clouds of dust from the fire-blackened *veld*, the great herds separated at the appearance of their enemy, man. This way and that they went in groups and long brown lines, leaving the wounded and exhausted wildebeest behind them, so that presently he was the sole tenant of that great cup of land.

At him they rode till Mr. Clifford, who was a little ahead of his daughter, drew almost alongside. Then the poor maddened brute tried its last shift. Stopping suddenly, it wheeled round and charged head down. Mr. Clifford, as it came, held out his rifle in his right hand and fired at a hazard. The bullet passed through the bull, but could not stop its charge. Its horns, held low, struck the forelegs of the horse, and next instant horse, man, and wildebeest rolled on the *veld* together.

Benita, who was fifty yards behind, uttered a little cry of fear, but before ever she reached him, her father had risen laughing, for he was quite unhurt. The horse, too, was getting up, but the bull could rise no more. It struggled to its forefeet, uttered a kind of sobbing groan, stared round wildly, and rolled over, dead.

"I never knew a wildebeest charge like that before," said Mr. Clifford. "Confound it! I believe my horse is lamed."

Lamed it was, indeed, where the bull had struck the foreleg, though, as it chanced, not badly. Having tied a handkerchief to the horn of the buck in order to scare away the vultures, and thrown some tufts of dry grass upon its body, which he proposed, if possible, to fetch or send for, Mr. Clifford mounted his lame horse and headed for the wagon. But they had galloped farther than they thought, and it was midday before they came to what they took to be the road. As there was no spoor upon it, they followed this track backwards, expecting to find the wagon outspanned, but although they rode for mile upon mile, no wagon could they see. Then, realizing their mistake, they retraced their steps, and leaving this path at the spot where they had found it, struck off again to the right.

Meanwhile, the sky was darkening, and at about three o'clock in the afternoon a thunderstorm broke over them accompanied by torrents of icy rain, the first fall of the spring, and a bitter wind which chilled them through. More, after the heavy rain came drizzle and a thick mist that deepened as evening approached.

Now their plight was very wretched. Lost, starved, soaked to the skin, with tired horses one of which was lame, they wandered about on the lonely *veld*. Only one stroke of fortune came to them. As the sun set, for a few moments its rays pierced the mist, telling them in what direction they should go. Turning their horses, they headed for it, and so rode on until the darkness fell. Then they halted a while, but feeling that if they stood still in that horrible cold they would certainly perish before morning, once more pushed on again. By now Mr. Clifford's horse was almost too lame to ride, so he led it, walking at his daughter's side, and reproaching himself bitterly for his foolishness in having brought her into this trouble.

"It doesn't matter, Father," she answered wearily, for she was very tired. "Nothing matters; one may as well die upon the *veld* as in the sea or anywhere else."

On they plodded, they knew not whither. Benita fell asleep upon her saddle, and was awakened once by a hyena howling quite close to them, and once by her horse falling to its knees.

"What is the time?" she said at last.

Her father struck a match and looked at his watch. It was ten o'clock; they had been fifteen hours away from the wagon and without food. At intervals Mr. Clifford, who had remounted, fired his rifle. Now there was but one cartridge left, and having caught sight of his daughter's exhausted face by the light of the match, he fired this also, though in that desperate wilderness there was little hope of its bringing succour.

"Shall we stop or go on?" he asked.

"I do not care," she answered. "Only if I stop I think it will be for ever. Let us go on."

Now the rain had ceased, but the mist was as dense as before. Also they seemed to have got among bush, for wet leaves brushed their faces. Utterly exhausted they stumbled forward, till suddenly Benita felt her horse stop as though a hand had seized its bridle, and heard a man's voice, speaking with a foreign accent, say:

"*Mein Gott!* Where are you going?"

"I wish I knew," she answered, like one in a dream.

At this instant the moon rose above the mists, and Benita saw Jacob Meyer for the first time.

In that light his appearance was not unpleasing. A man of about forty years of age, not over tall, slight and active in build, with a pointed black beard, regular, Semitic features, a complexion of an ivory pallor which even the African sun did not seem to tan, and dark, lustrous eyes that appeared, now to sleep, and now to catch the fire of the thoughts within. Yet, weary though she was, there was something in the man's personality which repelled and alarmed Benita, something wild and cruel. She felt that he was filled with unsatisfied ambitions and desires, and that to attain to them he would shrink at nothing. In a moment he was speaking again in tones that compelled her attention.

"It was a good thought that brought me here to look for you. No; not a thought—what do you call it?—an instinct. I think your mind must have spoken to my mind, and called me to save you. See now, Clifford, my friend, where you have led your daughter. See, see!" And he pointed downwards.

They leaned forward and stared. There, immediately beneath them, was a mighty gulf whereof the moonlight did not reveal the bottom.

"You are no good *veld* traveller, Clifford, my friend; one more step of those silly beasts, and down below there would have been two red heaps with bits of bones sticking out of them—yes, there on the rocks five hundred feet beneath. Ah! you would have slept soundly tonight, both of you."

"Where is the place?" asked Mr. Clifford in a dazed fashion. "Leopard's Kloof?"

"Yes; Leopard's Kloof, no other. You have travelled along the top of the hill, not at the bottom. Certainly that was a good thought which came to me from the lady your daughter, for she is one of the thought senders, I am sure. Ah! it came to me suddenly; it hit me like a stick whilst I was searching for you, having found that you had lost the wagon. It said to me, 'Ride to the top of Leopard's Kloof. Ride hard.' I rode hard through the rocks and the darkness, through the mist and the rain, and not one minute had I been here when you came and I caught the lady's bridle."

"I am sure we are very grateful to you," murmured Benita.

"Then I am paid back ten thousand times. No; it is I who am grateful—I who have saved your life through the thought you sent me."

"Thought or no thought, all's well that ends well," broke in Mr. Clifford impatiently. "And thank Heaven we are not more than three miles away from home. Will you lead the way, Jacob? You always could see in the dark?"

"Yes, yes," and he took hold of Benita's bridle with his firm, white hand. "Oh! my horse will follow, or put your arm through his rein—so. Now come on, Miss Clifford, and be afraid no more. With Jacob Meyer you are safe."

So they began their descent of the hill. Meyer did not speak again; all his attention seemed to be concentrated upon finding a safe path on which the horses would not stumble. Nor did Benita speak; she was too utterly exhausted—so exhausted, indeed, that she could no longer control her mind and imagination. These seemed to loose themselves from her and to acquire new powers, notably that of entering into the secret thoughts of the man at her side. She saw them pass before her like living things, and yet she could not read them. Still, something she did understand—that she had suddenly grown important to this man, not in the way in which women are generally important to men, but otherwise. She felt as though she had become interwoven with the objects of his life, and was henceforth necessary to their fulfilment, as though she were someone whom he had been seeking for years on years, the one person who could give him light in his darkness.

These imaginings troubled her, so that she was very thankful when they passed away as swiftly as they had arisen, and she knew only that she was half dead with weariness and cold; that her limbs ached and that the steep path seemed endless.

At length they reached level ground, and after travelling along it for a while and crossing the bed of a stream, passed through a gate, and stopped suddenly at the door of a house with lighted windows.

"Here is your home at last, Miss Clifford," said the musical voice of Jacob Meyer, "and I thank the Fate which rules us that it has taught me to bring you to it safely."

Making no answer she slid from the saddle, only to find that she could not stand, for she sank into a heap upon the ground. With a gentle exclamation he lifted her, and calling to two Kaffirs who had appeared to take the horses, led her into the house.

"You must go to bed at once," he said, conducting her to a door which opened out of the sitting-room. "I have had a fire lit in your chamber in case you should come, and old *Tante* Sally will bring you soup with brandy in it, and hot water for your feet. Ah! there you are, old *vrouw*. Come now; help the lady, your mistress. Is all ready?"

"All, Baas," answered the woman, a stout half-breed with a kindly face. "Come now, my little one, and I will undress you."

Half an hour later Benita, having drunk more brandy than ever she had done in her life before, was wrapped up and fast asleep.

When she awoke the sun was streaming through the curtained window of her room, and by the light of it she saw that the clock which stood upon the mantelpiece pointed to half-past eleven. She had slept for nearly twelve hours, and felt that, notwithstanding the cold and exposure, save for stiffness and a certain numb feeling in her head—the result, perhaps, of the unaccustomed brandy—she was well and, what was more, quite hungry.

Outside on the veranda she heard the voice of Jacob Meyer, with which she seemed already to have become familiar, telling some natives to stop singing, as they would wake the chieftainess inside. He used the Zulu word *Inkosikaas*, which, she remembered, meant head-lady or chieftainess. He was very thoughtful for her, she reflected, and was grateful, till suddenly she remembered the dislike she had taken to the man.

Then she looked round her room and saw that it was very pretty, well furnished and papered, with water-colour pictures on the walls of no mean merit, things that she had not expected in this far-off place. Also on a table stood a great bowl of arum lilies. She wondered who had put them there; whether it were the old half-breed, Sally, or Jacob Meyer. Also she wondered who had painted the pictures, which were all of African scenery, and something told her that both the flowers and the pictures came from Jacob Meyer.

On the little table by her bed was a handbell, which presently she rang. Instantly she heard the voice of Sally calling for the coffee "quick," and next minute the woman entered, bringing a tray with it, and bread and butter—yes, and toast and eggs, which had evidently been made ready for her. Speaking in English mixed with Dutch words, she told Benita that her father was still in bed, but sent her his love, and wished to know how she did. Then, while she ate her breakfast with appetite, Sally set her a bath, and subsequently appeared carrying the contents of the box she had used upon the wagon, which had now arrived safely at the farm. Benita asked who had ordered the box to be unpacked, and Sally answered that the *Heer* Meyer had ordered it so that she might not be disturbed in her sleep, and that her things should be ready for her when she woke.

"The *Heer* Meyer thinks a great deal about other people," said Benita.

"*Ja, ja!*" answered the old half-breed. "He tink much about people when he want to tink about them, but he tink most about himself. Baas Meyer, he a very clever man—oh! a very clever man, who want to be a great man too. And one day, Missee, he be a great man, great and rich—if the *Heer* God Almighty let him."

CHAPTER 6

The Gold Coin

Six weeks had gone by since the eventful evening of Benita's arrival at Rooi Krantz. Now the spring had fully come, the *veld* was emerald with grass and bright with flowers. In the *kloof* behind the house trees had put out their leaves, and the mimosas were in bloom, making the air heavy with their scent. Amongst them the ringdoves nested in hundreds, and on the steep rocks of the precipice the red-necked vultures fed their young. Along the banks of the stream and round the borders of the lake the pig-lilies bloomed, a sheet of white. All the place was beautiful and full of life and hope. Nothing seemed dead and hopeless except Benita's heart.

Her health had quite come back to her; indeed, never before had she felt so strong and well. But the very soul had withered in her breast. All day she thought, and all night she dreamed of the man who, in cold blood, had offered up his life to save a helpless woman and her child. She wondered whether he would have done this if he had heard the answer that was upon her lips. Perhaps that was why she had not been given time to speak that answer, which might have made a coward of him. For nothing more had been heard of Robert Seymour; indeed, already the tragedy of the ship *Zanzibar* was forgotten. The dead had buried their dead, and since then worse disasters had happened in the world.

But Benita could not bury her dead. She rode about the *veld*, she sat by the lake and watched the wild fowl, or at night heard them flighting over her in flocks. She listened to the cooing of the doves, the booming of the bitterns in the reeds, and the drumming of the snipe high in air. She counted the game trekking along the ridge till her mind grew weary. She sought consolation from the breast of Nature and found none; she sought it in the starlit skies, and oh! they were very far away. Death reigned within her who outwardly was so fair to see.

In the society of her father, indeed, she took pleasure, for he loved her, and love comforted her wounded heart. In that of Jacob Meyer also she found interest, for now her first fear of the man had died away, and undoubtedly he was very interesting; well-bred also after a fashion, although a Jew who had lost his own faith and rejected that of the Christians.

He told her that he was a German by birth, that he had been sent to England as a boy, to avoid the conscription, which Jews dislike, since in soldiering there is little profit. Here he had become a clerk in a house of South African merchants, and, as a consequence—having shown all the ability of his race—was despatched to take charge of a branch business in Cape Colony. What happened to him there Benita never discovered, but probably he had shown too much ability of an oblique nature. At any rate, his connection with the firm terminated, and for years he became a wandering "*smouse*," or trader, until at length he drifted into partnership with her father.

Whatever might have been his past, however, soon she found that he was an extremely able and agreeable man. It was he and no other who had painted the water-colours that adorned her room, and he could play and sing as well as he painted. Also, as Robert had told her, Mr. Meyer was very well-read in subjects that are not usually studied on the *veld* of South Africa; indeed, he had quite a library of books, most of them histories or philosophical and scientific works, of which he would lend her volumes. Fiction, however, he never read, for the reason, he told her, that he found life itself and the mysteries and problems which surround it so much more interesting.

One evening, when they were walking together by the lake, watching the long lights of sunset break and quiver upon its surface, Benita's curiosity overcame her, and she asked him boldly how it happened that such a man as he was content to live the life he did.

"In order that I may reach a better," he answered. "Oh! no, not in the skies, Miss Clifford, for of them I know nothing, nor, as I believe, is there anything to know. But here—here."

"What do you mean by a better life, Mr. Meyer?"

"I mean," he answered, with a flash of his dark eyes, "great wealth, and the power that wealth brings. Ah! I see you think me very sordid and materialistic, but money is God in this world, Miss Clifford—money is God."

She smiled and answered: "I fear, then, that he is likely to prove an invisible god on the high *veld*, Mr. Meyer. You will scarcely make a great fortune out of horse-breeding, and here there is no one to rule."

"Do you suppose, then, that is why I stop at Rooi Krantz, just to breed horses? Has not your father told you about the great treasure hidden away up there among the Makalanga?"

"I have heard something of it," she answered with a sigh. "Also that both of you went to look for it and were disappointed."

"Ah! The Englishman who was drowned—Mr. Seymour—he spoke of it, did he not? He found us there."

"Yes; and you wished to shoot him—do you remember?"

"God in Heaven! Yes, because I thought he had come to rob us. Well, I did not shoot, and afterwards we were hunted out of the place, which does not much matter, as those fools of natives refused to let us dig in the fortress."

"Then why do you still think about this treasure which probably does not exist?"

"Why, Miss Clifford, do you think about various things that probably do not exist? Perhaps because you feel that here or elsewhere they *do* exist. Well, that is what I feel about the treasure, and what I have always felt. It exists, and I shall find it—now. I shall live to see more gold than you can even imagine, and that is why I still continue to breed horses on the Transvaal *veld*. Ah! you laugh; you think it is a nightmare that I breed——"

Then suddenly he became aware of Sally, who had appeared over the fold of the rise behind them, and asked irritably:

"What is it now, old *vrouw*?"

"The Baas Clifford wants to speak with you, Baas Jacob. Messengers have come to you from far away."

"What messengers?" he asked.

"I know not," answered Sally, fanning her fat face with a yellow pocket-handkerchief. "They are strange people to me, and thin with travelling, but they talk a kind of Zulu. The Baas wishes you to come."

"Will you come also, Miss Clifford? No? Then forgive me if I leave you," and lifting his hat he went.

"A strange man, Missee," said old Sally, when he had vanished, walking very fast.

"Yes," answered Benita, in an indifferent voice.

"A very strange man," went on the old woman. "Too much in his kop," and she tapped her forehead. "I tink it will burst one day; but if it does not burst, then he will be great. I tell you that before, now I tell it you again, for I tink his time come. Now I go cook dinner."

Benita sat by the lake till the twilight fell, and the wild geese began to flight over her. Then she walked back to the house thinking no more of *Heer* Meyer, thinking only that she was weary of this place in which there was nothing to occupy her mind and distract it from its ever present sorrow.

At dinner, or rather supper, that night she noticed that both her father and his partner seemed to be suffering from suppressed excitement, of which she thought she could guess the cause.

"Did you find your messengers, Mr. Meyer?" she asked, when the men had lit their pipes, and the square-face—as Hollands was called in those days, from the shape of the bottle—was set upon the rough table of speckled *buchenhout* wood.

"Yes, I found them," he answered; "they are in the kitchen now." And he looked at Mr. Clifford.

"Benita, my dear," said her father, "rather a curious thing has happened." Her face lit up, but he shook his head. "No, nothing to do with the shipwreck—that is all finished. Still, something that may interest you, if you care to hear a story."

Benita nodded; she was in a mood to hear anything that would occupy her thoughts.

"You know something about this treasure business," went on her father. "Well, this is the tale of it. Years ago, after you and your mother had gone to England, I went on a big game shooting expedition into the interior. My companion was an old fellow called Tom Jackson, a rolling stone, and one of the best elephant hunters in Africa. We did pretty well, but the end of it was that we separated north of the Transvaal, I bringing down the ivory that we had shot, and traded, and Tom stopping to put in another season, the arrangement being that he was to join me afterwards, and take his share of the money. I came here and bought this farm from a Boer who was tired of it—cheap enough, too, for I only gave him £100 for the 6,000 acres. The kitchens behind were his old house, for I built a new one.

"A year had gone by before I saw any more of Tom Jackson, and then he turned up more dead than alive. He had been injured by an elephant, and lay for some months among the Makalanga to the north of Matabeleland, where he got fever badly at a place called Bambatse, on the Zambesi. These Makalanga are a strange folk. I believe their name means the People of the Sun; at any rate, they are the last of some ancient race. Well, while he was there he cured the old Molimo, or hereditary high-priest of this tribe, of a bad fever by giving him quinine, and naturally they grew friendly. The Molimo lived among ruins of which there are many over all that part of South Africa. No one knows who built them now; probably it was people who lived thousands of years ago. However, this Molimo told Tom Jackson a more recent legend connected with the place.

"He said that six generations before, when his great-great-great grandfather was chief (Mambo, he called it), the natives of all that part of South Africa rose against the white men—Portuguese, I suppose—who still worked the gold there. They massacred them and their slaves by thousands, driving them up from the southward, where Lobengula rules now, to the Zambesi by which the Portuguese hoped to escape to the coast. At length a remnant of them, not more than about two hundred men and women, arrived at the stronghold called Bambatse, where the Molimo now lives in a great ruin built by the ancients upon an impregnable mountain which overhangs the river. With them they brought an enormous quantity of gold, all the stored-up treasure of the land which they were trying to carry off. But although they reached the river they could not escape by it, since the natives, who pursued them in thousands, watched day and night in canoes, and the poor fugitives had no boats. Therefore it came about that they were shut up in this fortress which it was impossible to storm, and there slowly perished of starvation.

"When it was known that they were all dead, the natives who had followed them from the south, and who wanted blood and revenge, not gold, which was of no use to them, went away; but the old priest's forefather who knew the secret entrance to the place, and who had been friendly to the Portuguese, forced his way in and there, amidst the dead, found one woman living, but mad with grief—a young and beautiful girl, the daughter of the Portuguese lord or captain. He gave her food, but in the night, when some strength had returned to her, she left him, and at daybreak he found her standing on the peak that overhangs the river, dressed all in white.

"He called some of his councillors, and they tried to persuade her to come down from the rock, but she answered, 'No, her betrothed and all her family and friends were dead, and it was her will to follow them.' Then they asked where was the gold, for having watched day and night they knew it had not been thrown into the river. She answered that it was where it was, and that, seek as he might, no black man would ever find it. She added that she gave it into his keeping, and that of his descendants, to safeguard until she came again. Also she said that if they were faithless to that trust, then it had been revealed to her from heaven above that those same savages who had killed her father and her people, would kill his people also. When she had spoken thus she stood a while praying on the peak, then suddenly hurled herself into the river, and was seen no more.

"From that day to this the ruin has been held to be haunted, and save the Molimo himself, who retires there to meditate and receive revelations from the spirits, no one is allowed to set a foot in its upper part; indeed, the natives would rather die than do so. Consequently the gold still remains where it was hidden. This place itself Tom Jackson did not see, since, notwithstanding his friendship for him, the Molimo refused to allow him to enter there.

"Well, Tom never recovered; he died here, and is buried in the little graveyard behind the house which the Boers made for some of their people. It was shortly before his death that Mr. Meyer became my partner, for I forgot to say that I had told him the story, and we determined to have a try for that great wealth. You know the rest. We trekked to Bambatse, pretending to be traders, and found the old Molimo who knew of me as having been Tom Jackson's friend. We asked him if the story he had told to Jackson were true, and he answered that, surely as the sun shone in the heavens, it was true—every word of it—for it, and much more than he had spoken of, had been handed down from father to son, and that they even knew the name of the white lady who had killed herself. It was Ferreira—your mother's name, Benita, though a common one enough in South Africa.

"We asked him to allow us to enter the topmost stronghold, which stands upon the hill, but he refused, saying that the curse still lay upon him and his, and that no man should enter until the lady Ferreira came again. For the rest the place was free to us; we might dig as we would. So we did dig, and found some gold buried with the ancients, beads and bangles and wire—about £100 worth. Also—that was on the day when the young Seymours came upon us, and accounts for Meyer's excitement, for he thought that we were on the track of the treasure—we found a single gold coin, no doubt one that had been dropped by the Portuguese. Here it is." And he threw a thin piece of gold on the table before her. "I have shown it to a man learned in those matters, and he says that it is a ducat struck by one of the doges of Venice.

"Well, we never found any more. The end of it was that the Makalanga caught us trying to get in to the secret stronghold by stealth, and gave us the choice of clearing out or being killed. So we cleared out, for treasure is not of much use to dead men."

Mr. Clifford ceased speaking, and filled his pipe, while Meyer helped himself to squareface in an absent manner. As for Benita, she stared at the quaint old coin, which had a hole in it, wondering with what scenes of terror and of bloodshed it had been connected.

"Keep it," said her father. "It will go on that bracelet of yours."

"Thank you, dear," she answered. "Though I don't know why I should take all the Portuguese treasure since we shall never see any more of it."

"Why not, Miss Clifford?" asked Meyer quickly.

"The story tells you why—because the natives won't even let you look for it; also, looking and finding are different things."

"Natives change their minds sometimes, Miss Clifford. That story is not done, it is only begun, and now you shall hear its second chapter. Clifford, may I call in the messengers?" And without waiting for an answer he rose and left the room.

Neither Mr. Clifford nor his daughter said anything after he had gone. Benita appeared to occupy herself in fixing the broad gold coin to a little swivel on her bracelet, but while she did so once more that sixth sense of hers awoke within her. As she had been afraid at the dinner on the doomed steamer, so again she was afraid. Again death and great fear cast their advancing shadows on to her soul. That piece of gold seemed to speak to her, yet, alas! she could not understand its story. Only she knew that her father and Jacob Meyer and—yes, yes, yes—Robert Seymour, had all a part in that tragedy. Oh! how could that be when he was dead? How could this gold link him to her? She knew not—she cared not. All she knew was that she would follow this treasure to the edge of the world, and if need be, over it, if only it brought her back to him again.

CHAPTER 7

The Messengers

The door opened, and through it came Jacob Meyer, followed by three natives. Benita did not see or hear them; her soul was far away. There at the head of the room, clad all in white, for she wore no mourning save in her heart, illuminated by the rays of the lamp that hung above her, she stood still and upright, for she had risen; on the face and in her wide, dark eyes a look that was very strange to see. Jacob Meyer perceived it and stopped; the three natives perceived it also and stopped. There they stood, all four of them, at the end of the long sitting-room, staring at the white Benita and at her haunted eyes.

One of the natives pointed with his thin finger to her face, and whispered to the others. Meyer, who understood their tongue, caught the whisper. It was:

"Behold the Spirit of the Rock!"

"What spirit, and what rock?" he asked in a low voice.

"She who haunts Bambatse; she whom our eyes have seen," answered the man, still staring at Benita.

Benita heard the whispering, and knew it was about herself, though not one word of it did she catch. With a sigh she shook herself free from her visions and sat down in a chair close by. Then one by one the messengers drew near to her, and each, as he came, made a profound obeisance, touching the floor with his finger-tips, and staring at her face. But her father they only saluted with an uplifted hand. She looked at them with interest, and indeed they were interesting in their way; tall, spare men, light coloured, with refined, mobile faces. Here was no negro-blood, but rather that of some ancient people such as Egyptians or Phoenicians: men whose forefathers had been wise and civilized thousands of years ago, and perchance had stood in the courts of Pharaoh or of Solomon.

Their salutations finished, the three men squatted in a line upon the floor, drawing their fur *karosses*, or robes, about them, and waited in silence. Jacob Meyer thought a while, then said:

"Clifford, will you translate to your daughter, so that she may be sure she is told exactly what passes?"

Next he turned and addressed the natives.

"Your names are Tamas, Tamala, and Hoba, and you, Tamas, are the son of the Molimo of Bambatse, who is called Mambo, and you, Tamala and Hoba, are his initiated councillors. Is it so?"

They bowed their heads.

"Good. You, Tamas, tell the story and give again your message that this lady, the lady Benita, may hear it, for she has a part in the matter."

"We understand that she has a part," answered Tamas. "We read in her face that she has the greatest part. Doubtless it is of her that the Spirit told my father. These, spoken by my mouth, are the words of the Molimo, my father, which have travelled so far to deliver.

"'When you two white men visited Bambatse four years ago, you asked of me, Mambo, to be admitted to the holy place, that you might look for the treasure there which the Portuguese hid in the time of my ancestor in the sixth generation. I refused to allow you to look, or even to enter the holy place, because I am by birth the guardian of that treasure, although I know not where it lies. But now I am in a great strait. I have news that Lobengula the usurper, who is king of the Matabele, has taken offence against me for certain reasons, among them that I did not send him a sufficient tribute. It is reported to me that he purposes next summer to despatch an *impi* to wipe me and my people out, and to make my kraal black as the burnt *veld*. I have little strength to resist him who is mighty, and my people are not warlike. From generation to generation they have been traders, cultivators of the land, workers in metal, and men of peace, who desire not to kill or be killed. Also they are few. Therefore I have no power to stand against Lobengula.

"'I remember the guns that you and your companion brought with you, which can kill things from far away. If I had a supply of those guns from behind my walls I might defy the *impi* of Lobengula, whose warriors use the *assegai*. If you will bring me a hundred good guns and plenty of powder and bullets for them, it is revealed to me that it will be lawful for me to admit you to the secret, holy place, where you may look for the buried gold for as long as you wish, and if you can find it, take it all away without hindrance from me or my people. But I will be honest with you. That gold will never be found save by the one appointed. The white lady said so in the time of my forefather; he heard it with his ears, and I have heard it from his descendants with my ears, and so it shall be. Still, if you bring the guns you can come and see if either of you is that one appointed. But I do not think that any man is so appointed, for the secret is hid in woman. But of this you can learn for yourselves. I do but speak as I am bidden.

"'This is my message spoken by my mouth, Tamas, son of my body, and my councillors who go with him will bear witness that he speaks the truth. I, Mambo, the Molimo of Bambatse, send you greeting, and will give you good welcome and fulfil my promise, if you come with the far-shooting guns, ten times ten of them, and the powder, and the bullets wherewith I may drive off the Matabele, but not otherwise. My son, Tamas, and my councillors will drive your wagon into my country but you must bring no strange servants. The Spirit of the white woman who killed herself before the eyes of my forefather has been seen of late standing upon the point of rock; also she has visited me at night in my secret place where her companions died. I do not know all that this portends, but I think that amongst other things she wished to tell me that the Matabele are about to attack us. I await the decree of the Heavens. I send you two *karosses* as a gift, and a little ancient gold, since ivory is too heavy for my messengers to carry, and I have no wagon. Farewell.'"

"We have heard you," said Meyer, when Mr. Clifford had finished translating, "and we wish to ask you a question. What do you mean when you say that the Spirit of the white woman has been seen?"

"I mean what I say, white man," answered Tamas. "She was seen by all three of us, standing upon the pinnacle at the dawn; also my father saw and spoke with her alone in his sleep at night. This is the third time in my father's day that she has appeared thus, and always before some great event."

"What was she like?" asked Meyer.

"Like? Oh! like the lady who sits yonder. Yes, quite the same, or so it seemed to us. But who knows? We have seen no other white women, and we were not very near. Let the lady come and stand side by side with the Spirit, so that we can examine them both, and we shall be able to answer better. Do you accept the offer of the Molimo?"

"We will tell you tomorrow morning," replied Meyer. "A hundred rifles are many to find, and will cost much money. Meanwhile, for you there is food and a sleeping-place."

The three men seemed disappointed at his answer, which they evidently believed to be preliminary to a refusal. For a moment or two they consulted together, then Tamas put his hand into a pouch and drew from it something wrapped in dry leaves, which he undid, revealing a quaint and beautiful necklace, fashioned of twisted gold links, wherein were set white stones, that they had no difficulty in recognising as uncut diamonds of considerable value. From this necklace also hung a crucifix moulded in gold.

"We offer this gift," he said, "on behalf of Mambo, my father, to the lady yonder, to whom the *karosses* and the rough gold are of no use. The chain has a story. When the Portuguese lady hurled herself into the river she wore it about her neck. As she fell into the river she struck against a little point of rock which tore the chain away from her—see where it is broken and mended with gold wire. It remained upon the point of rock, and my forefather took it thence. It is a gift to the lady if she will promise to wear it."

"Accept it," muttered Mr. Clifford, when he had finished translating this, "or you will give offence."

So Benita said: "I thank the Molimo, and accept his gift."

Then Tamas rose, and, advancing, cast the ancient, tragic thing over her head. As it fell upon her shoulders, Benita knew that it was a chain of destiny drawing her she knew not where, this ornament that had last been worn by that woman, bereaved and unhappy as herself, who could find no refuge from her sorrow except in death. Had she felt it torn from her breast, she wondered, as she, the living Benita of today, felt it fall upon her own?

The three envoys rose, bowed, and went, leaving them alone. Jacob Meyer lifted his head as though to address her, then changed his mind and was silent. Both the men waited for her to speak, but she would not, and in the end it was her father who spoke first.

"What do you say, Benita?" he asked anxiously.

"I? I have nothing to say, except that I have heard a very curious story. This priest's message is to you and Mr. Meyer, father, and must be answered by you. What have I to do with it?"

"A great deal, I think, my dear, or so those men seemed to believe. At any rate, I cannot go up there without you, and I will not take you there against your wish, for it is a long way off, and a queer business. The question is, will you go?"

She thought a space, while the two men watched her anxiously.

"Yes," she answered at length, in a quiet voice. "I will go if you wish to go, not because I want to find treasure, but because the story and the country where it happened interest me. Indeed, I don't believe much in the treasure. Even if they are superstitious and afraid to look for it themselves, I doubt whether they would allow you to look if they thought it could be found. To me the journey does not seem a good business speculation, also there are risks."

"We think it good enough," broke in Meyer decidedly. "And one does not expect to get millions without trouble."

"Yes, yes," said her father; "but she is right—there are risks, great risks—fever, wild beasts, savages, and others that one cannot foresee. Have I a right to expose her to them? Ought we not to go alone?"

"It would be useless," answered Meyer. "Those messengers have seen your daughter, and mixed her up with their superstitious story of a ghost, of which I, who know that there are no such things, believe nothing. Without her now we shall certainly fail."

"As for the risks, father," said Benita, "personally I take no account of them, for I am sure that what is to happen will happen, and if I knew that I was to die upon the Zambesi, it would make no difference to me who do not care. But as it chances, I think—I cannot tell you why—that you and Mr. Meyer are in more danger than I am. It is for you to consider whether you will take the risks."

Mr. Clifford smiled. "I am old," he said; "that is my answer."

"And I am accustomed to such things," said Meyer, with a shrug of his shoulders. "Who would not run a little danger for the sake of such a glorious chance? Wealth, wealth, more wealth than we can dream of, and with it, power—power to avenge, to reward, to buy position, and pleasure, and all beautiful things which are the heritage of the very rich alone," and he spread out his hands and looked upwards, as though in adoration of this golden god.

"Except such trifles as health and happiness," commented Benita, not without sarcasm, for this man and his material desires disgusted her somewhat, especially when she contrasted him with another man who was lost to her, though it was true that *his* past had been idle and unproductive enough. Yet they interested her also, for Benita had never met anyone like Mr. Meyer, so talented, so eager, and so soulless.

"Then I understand it is settled?" she said.

Mr. Clifford hesitated, but Meyer answered at once:

"Yes, settled as far as anything can be."

She waited a moment for her father to speak, but he said nothing; his chance had gone by.

"Very well. Now we shall not need to trouble ourselves with further doubts or argument. We are going to Bambatse on the Zambesi, a distant place, to look for buried gold, and I hope, Mr. Meyer, that if you find it, the results will come up to your expectations, and bring you all sorts of good luck. Good-night, father dear, good-night."

"My daughter thinks it will bring us ill-luck," said Mr. Clifford, when the door had closed behind her. "That is her way of saying so."

"Yes," answered Meyer gloomily; "she thinks that, and she is one of those who have vision. Well, she may be wrong. Also, the question is, shall we seize our opportunity and its dangers, or remain here and breed bad horses all our lives, while she who is not afraid laughs at us? I am going to Bambatse."

Again Mr. Clifford made no direct answer, only asked a question:

"How long will it take to get the guns and ammunition, and what will they cost?"

"About a week from Wakkerstroom," replied Meyer. "Old Potgieter, the trader there, has just imported a hundred Martinis and a hundred Westley-Richards falling-blocks. Fifty of each, with ten thousand rounds of cartridges, will cost about £600, and we have as much as that in the bank; also we have the new wagon, and plenty of good oxen and horses. We can take a dozen of the horses with us, and sell them in the north of the Transvaal for a fine price, before we get into the tsetse fly belt. The oxen will probably carry us through, as they are most of them salted."

"You have thought it all out, Jacob, I see; but it means a lot of money one way and another, to say nothing of other things."

"Yes, a lot of money, and those rifles are too good for Kaffirs. Birmingham gas-pipes would have done for them, but there are none to be had. But what is the money, and what are the guns, compared to all they will bring us?"

"I think you had better ask my daughter, Jacob. She seems to have her own ideas upon the subject."

"Miss Clifford has made up her mind, and it will not change. I shall ask her no more," replied Meyer.

Then he, too, left the room, to give orders about the journey to Wakkerstroom that he must take upon the morrow. But Mr. Clifford sat there till past midnight, wondering whether he had done right, and if they would find the treasure of which he had dreamed for years, and what the future had in store for them.

If only he could have seen!

When Benita came to breakfast the next morning, she asked where Mr. Meyer was, and learned that he had already departed for Wakkerstroom.

"Certainly he is in earnest," she said with a laugh.

"Yes," answered her father; "Jacob is always in earnest, though, somehow, his earnestness has not brought him much good so far. If we fail, it will not be want of thought and preparation on his part."

Nearly a week went by before Meyer returned again, and meanwhile Benita made ready for her journey. In the intervals of her simple preparations also she talked a good deal, with the help of her father, to the three sturdy-looking Makalanga, who were resting thankfully after their long journey. Their conversation was general, since by tacit consent no further mention was made of the treasure or of anything to do with it, but it enabled her to form a fair opinion of them and their people. She gathered that although they spoke a dialect of Zulu, they had none of the bravery of the Zulus, and indeed lived in deadly terror of the Matabele, who are bastard Zulus—such terror, in fact, that she greatly doubted whether the hundred rifles would be of much use to them, should they ever be attacked by that tribe.

They were what their fathers had been before them, agriculturists and workers in metals—not fighting men. Also she set herself to learn what she could of their tongue, which she did not find difficult, for Benita had a natural aptitude for languages, and had never forgotten the Dutch and Zulu she used to prattle as a child, which now came back to her very fast. Indeed, she could already talk fairly in either of those languages, especially as she spent her spare hours in studying their grammar, and reading them.

So the days went on, till one evening Jacob Meyer appeared with two Scotch carts laden with ten long boxes that looked like coffins, and other smaller boxes which were very heavy, to say nothing of a multitude of stores. As Mr. Clifford prophesied, he had forgotten nothing, for he even brought Benita various articles of clothing, and a revolver for which she had not asked.

Three days later they trekked away from Rooi Krantz upon a peculiarly beautiful Sunday morning in the early spring, giving it out that they were going upon a trading and shooting expedition in the north of the Transvaal. Benita looked back at the pretty little stead and the wooded *kloof* behind it over which she had nearly fallen, and the placid lake in front of it where the nesting wildfowl wheeled, and sighed. For to her, now that she was leaving it, the place seemed like home, and it came into her mind that she would never see it any more.

CHAPTER 8

Bambatse

Nearly four months had gone by when at length the wagon with which were Mr. Clifford, Benita, and Jacob Meyer camped one night within the country of the Molimo of Bambatse, whose name was Mambo. Or perhaps that was his title, since (according to Tamas his son) every chief in succession was called Mambo, though not all of them were Molimos, or representatives and prophets of God, or the Great Spirit whom they knew as Munwali. Thus sometimes the Molimo, or priest of Munwali, and the Mambo or chief were different persons. For instance, he said that he, Tamas, would be Mambo on his father's death, but no visions were given to him; therefore as yet, at any rate, he was not called to be Molimo.

In the course of this long journey they had met with many adventures, such as were common to African travellers before the days of railroads; adventures with wild beasts and native tribes, adventures with swollen rivers also, and one that was worst, with thirst, since for three days (owing to the failure of a pit or pan, where they expected to find water) they were obliged to go without drink. Still, none of these were very serious, nor had any of the three of them ever been in better health than they were at this moment, for by good luck they had escaped all fever. Indeed, their rough, wild life had agreed with Benita extraordinarily well, so well that any who had known her in the streets of London would scarcely have recognized her as the sunburnt, active and well-formed young woman who sat that night by the camp fire.

All the horses they had brought with them had been sold, except some which had died, and three that were "salted," or proof against the deadly horse sickness, which they took on with them. Their own servants also had been sent back to Rooi Krantz in charge of a Scotch cart laden with ivory, purchased from Boer hunters who had brought it down from the north of the Transvaal. Therefore, for this was part of the bargain, the three Makalanga were now their only attendants who drove and herded the cattle, while Benita cooked the food which the two white men shot, or sometimes bought from natives.

For days they had been passing through a country that was practically deserted, and now, having crossed a high *nek*, the same on which Robert Seymour had left his wagon, they were camped in low land which, as they could see by the remains of walls that appeared everywhere, had once been extensively enclosed and cultivated. To their right was a rising mountainous ground, beyond which, said the Makalanga, ran the Zambesi, and in front of them, not more than ten miles away, a great isolated hill, none other than that place that they had journeyed so far to reach, Bambatse, round which flowed the great river. Indeed, thither one of the three Makalanga, he who was named Hoba, had gone on to announce their approach.

They had outspanned amongst ruins, most of them circular in shape, and Benita, studying them in the bright moonlight, guessed that once these had been houses. That place now so solitary, hundreds or thousands of years ago was undoubtedly the home of a great population. Thousands, rather than hundreds, she thought, since close at hand in the middle of one of these round houses, grew a mighty baobab tree, that could not have seen less than ten or fifteen centuries since the seed whence it sprang pierced the cement floor which was still visible about its giant bole.

Tamas, the Molimo's son, saw her studying these evidences of antiquity, and, approaching, saluted her.

"Lady," he said in his own language, which by now she spoke very well, "lady"—and he waved his hand with a fine gesture—"behold the city of my people."

"How do you know that it was their city?" she asked.

"I do not know, lady. Stones cannot speak, the spirits are silent, and we have forgotten. Still, I think so, and our fathers have told us that but six or eight generations ago many folk lived here, though it was not they who built these walls. Even fifty years ago there were many, but now the Matabele have killed them, and we are few; tomorrow you will see how few. Come here and look," and he led her through the entrance of a square cattle kraal which stood close by. Within were tufts of rank grass, and a few bushes, and among these scores of skulls and other bones.

"The Matabele killed these in the time of Moselikatse," he said. "Now do you wonder that we who remain fear the Matabele, and desire guns to defend ourselves from them, even if we must sell our secrets, in order to buy those guns, who have no money to pay for them?"

"No," she answered, looking at the tall, dignified man, into whose soul the irons of fear and slavery had burnt so deep. "No, I do not wonder."

Next morning at daybreak they trekked on, always through these evidences of dead, forgotten people. They had not more than ten miles to cover to reach their long journey's end, but the road, if so it could be called, ran up-hill, and the oxen, whereof only fourteen were now left to drag the heavy-laden wagon, were thin and footsore, so that their progress was very slow. Indeed, it was past midday when at length they began to enter what by apology might be called the town of Bambatse.

"When we go away from this, it will have to be by water, I think, unless we can buy trek-cattle," said Meyer, looking at the labouring oxen with a doubtful eye.

"Why?" asked Mr. Clifford anxiously.

"Because several of those beasts have been bitten by tsetse fly, like my horse, and the poison is beginning to work. I thought so last night, but now I am sure. Look at their eyes. It was down in that bit of bush *veld* eight days ago. I said that we ought not to camp there."

At this moment they came to the crest of the ridge, and on its further side saw the wonderful ruins of Bambatse close at hand. In front of them stood a hill jutting out, as it were into the broad waters of the Zambesi river, which, to a great extent, protected it upon three sides. The fourth, that opposite to them, except at one place where a kind of natural causeway led into the town, was also defended by Nature, since here for more than fifty feet in height the granite rock of the base of the hill rose sheer and unclimbable. On the mount itself, that in all may have covered eight or ten acres of ground, and surrounded by a deep donga or ditch, were three rings of fortifications, set one above the other, mighty walls which, it was evident, had been built by no modern hand. Looking at them Benita could well understand how it came about that the poor fugitive Portuguese had chosen this as their last place of refuge, and were overcome at length, not by the thousands of savages who followed and surrounded them, but by hunger. Indeed, the place seemed impregnable to any force that was not armed with siege guns.

On the hither side of this natural fosse, which, doubtless, in ancient times had been filled with water led from the Zambesi, stood the village of the Bambatse Makalanga, a collection of seventy or eighty wretched huts, round, like those of their forefathers, but built of mud and thatch. About them lay the gardens, or square fields, that were well cultivated, and at this season rich with ripening corn. Benita, however, could see no cattle, and concluded, therefore, that these must be kept on the hill for safety, and within its walls.

Down the rough road they lumbered, and through the village, where the few women and children stared at them in a frightened way. Then they came to the causeway, which, on its further side, was blocked with thorns and rough stones taken from the ruins. While they waited for these to be removed by some men who now appeared, Benita looked at the massive, circular wall still thirty or forty feet in height, by perhaps twenty through its base, built of granite blocks without mortar, and ornamented with quaint patterns of other coloured stones. In its thickness she could see grooves, where evidently had once been portcullises, but these had disappeared long ago.

"It is a wonderful place," she said to her father. "I am glad that I came. Have you been all over it?"

"No; only between the first and second walls, and once between the second and third. The old temple, or whatever it is, is on the top, and into that they would never admit us. It is there that the treasure lies."

"That the treasure is supposed to lie," she answered with a smile. "But, Father, what guarantee have you that they will do so now? Perhaps they will take the guns and show us the door—or rather the gate."

"Your daughter is right, there is none; and before a box is taken off the wagon we must get one," said Meyer. "Oh! I know it is risky, and it would have been better to make sure first, but it is too late to talk of that now. Look, the stones are cleared. Trek on—trek!"

The long wagon-whip cracked, the poor, tired-out oxen strained at the yokes, and on they went through the entrance of that fateful fortress that was but just wide enough to admit them. Inside lay a great open space, which, as they could see from the numerous ruins, had once been filled with buildings that now were half hidden by grass, trees, and creepers. This was the outer ring of the temple where, in ancient days, the priests and captains had their home. Travelling across it for perhaps a hundred and fifty yards, they came near the second wall, which was like the first, only not quite so solid, and saw that on a stretch of beaten ground, and seated in the shadow, for the day was hot, the people of Bambatse were gathered to greet them.

When within fifty yards they dismounted from the horses, which were left with the wagon in the charge of the Makalanga, Tamala. Then Benita taking her position between her father and Jacob Meyer, they advanced towards the ring of natives, of whom there may have been two hundred—all of them adult men.

As they came, except one figure who remained seated with his back against the wall, the human circle stood up as a token of respect, and Benita saw that they were of the same stamp as the messengers—tall and good-looking, with melancholy eyes and a cowed expression, wearing the appearance of people who from day to day live in dread of slavery and death. Opposite to them was a break in the circle, through which Tamas led them, and as they crossed it Benita felt that all those people were staring at her with their sad eyes. A few paces from where the man crouched against the wall, his head hidden by a beautifully worked blanket that was thrown over it, were placed three well-carved stools. Upon these, at a motion from Tamas, they sat themselves down, and, as it was not dignified for them to speak first, remained silent.

"Be patient and forgive," said Tamas at length. "My father, Mambo, prays to the Munwali and the spirits of his fathers that this coming of yours may be fortunate, and that a vision of those things that are to be may descend upon him."

Benita, feeling nearly two hundred pairs of eyes concentrated upon her, wished that the vision might come quickly, but after a minute or two fell into tune with the thing, and almost enjoyed this strange experience. Those mighty ancient walls built by hands unknown, which had seen so much history and so much death; the silent, triple ring of patient, solemn men, the last descendants of a cultured race, the crouching figure hidden beneath the blanket, who imagined himself to be communicating with his god—it was all very strange, very well worth the seeing to one who had wearied of the monotony of civilization.

Look, the man stirred, and threw back his blanket, revealing a head white with age, a spiritual, ascetic face, so thin that every bone showed in it, and dark eyes which stared upwards unseeingly, like those of a person in a trance. Thrice he sighed, while his tribesmen watched him. Then he let his eyes fall upon the three white people seated in front of him. First he looked at Mr. Clifford, and his face grew troubled; then at Jacob Meyer, and it was anxious and alarmed. Lastly, he stared at Benita, and while he did so the dark eyes became calm and happy.

"White maiden," he said in a soft, low voice, "for you, at least, I have good tidings. Though Death come near to you, though you see him on your right hand and your left, and in front of you and behind you, I say, fear not. Here you, who have known deep sorrow, shall find happiness and rest, O maiden, with whom goes the spirit of one pure and fair as you, who died so long ago."

313

Then, while Benita wondered at his words, spoken with such sweet earnestness that although she believed nothing of them, they brought a kind of comfort to her, he looked once more at her father and Jacob Meyer, and, as it were with an effort, was silent.

"Have you no pleasant prophecy for me, old friend," said Jacob, "who have come so far to hear it?"

At once the aged face grew inscrutable, all expression vanished behind a hundred wrinkles, and he answered:

"None, white man—none that I am charged to deliver. Search the skies for yourself, you who are so wise, and read them if you can. Lords," he went on in another voice, "I greet you in the name and presence of my children. Son Tamas, I greet you also; you have done your mission well. Listen, now—you are weary and would rest and eat; still, bear with me, for I have a word to say. Look around you. You see all my tribe, not twenty times ten above the age of boys, we who once were countless as the leaves on yonder trees in spring. Why are we dead? Because of the Amandabele, those fierce dogs whom, two generations ago, Moselikatse, the general of Chaka, brought up to the south of us, who ravish us and kill us year by year.

"We are not warlike, we who have outlived war and the lust of slaying. We are men of peace, who desire to cultivate the land, and to follow our arts which have descended to us from our ancestors, and to worship the Heavens above us, whither we depart to join the spirits of our forefathers. But they are fierce and strong and savage, and they come up and murder our children and old people, and take away the young women and the maidens to be slaves, and with them all our cattle. Where are our cattle? Lobengula, chief of the Amandabele, has them; scarce a cow is left to give milk to the sick or to the motherless babe. And yet he sends for cattle. Tribute, say his messengers, deliver tribute, or my *impi* will come and take it with your lives. But we have no cattle—all are gone. We have nothing left to us but this ancient mountain and the works built thereon, and a little corn on which we live. Yes, I say it—I, the Molimo—I whose ancestors were great kings—I who have still more wisdom in me than all the hosts of the Amandabele," and as he spoke the old man's grey head sank upon his breast and the tears ran down his withered cheeks, while his people answered:

"Mambo, it is true."

"Now listen again," he went on. "Lobengula threatens us, therefore I sent to these white men who were here before, saying that if they would bring me a hundred guns, and powder and ball, to enable us

314

to beat off the Amandabele from behind these strong walls of ours, I would take them into the secret holy place where for six generations no white man has set a foot, and there suffer them to search for the treasure which is hid therein, no man knows where, that treasure which they asked leave to find four winters gone. We refused it then and drove them hence, because of the curse laid upon us by the white maid who died, the last of the Portuguese, who foretold her people's fate for us if we gave up the buried gold save to one appointed. My children, the Spirit of Bambatse has visited me; I have seen her and others have seen her, and in my sleep she said to me: 'Suffer the men to come and search, for with them is one of the blood to whom my people's wealth is given; and great is your danger, for many spears draw nigh.' My children, I sent my son and other messengers on a far journey to where I knew the men dwelt, and they have returned after many months bringing those men with them, bringing with them also another of whom I knew nothing—yes, her who is appointed, her of whom the Spirit spoke."

Then he lifted his withered hand and held it towards Benita, saying: "I tell you that yonder she sits for whom the generations have waited."

"It is so," answered the Makalanga. "It is the White Lady come again to take her own."

"Friends," asked the Molimo, while they wondered at his strange speech, "tell me, have you brought the guns?"

"Surely," answered Mr. Clifford, "they are there in the wagon, every one of them, the best that can be made, and with them ten thousand cartridges, bought at a great cost. We have fulfilled our share of the bargain; now will you fulfil yours, or shall we go away again with the guns and leave you to meet the Matabele with your *assegais*?"

"Say you the agreement while we listen," answered the Molimo.

"Good," said Mr. Clifford. "It is this: That you shall find us food and shelter while we are with you. That you shall lead us into the secret place at the head of the hill, where the Portuguese died, and the gold is hidden. That you shall allow us to search for that gold when and where we will. That if we discover the gold, or anything else of value to us, you shall suffer us to take it away, and assist us upon our journey, either by giving us boats and manning them to travel down the Zambesi, or in whatever fashion may be most easy. That you shall permit none to hurt, molest, or annoy us during our sojourn among you. Is that our contract?"

"Not quite all of it," said the Molimo. "There is this to add: first that you shall teach us how to use the guns; secondly, that you shall search for and find the treasure, if so it is appointed, without our help, since in this matter it is not lawful for us to meddle; thirdly, that if the Amandabele should chance to attack us while you are here, you shall do your best to assist us against their power."

"Do you, then, expect attack?" asked Meyer suspiciously.

"White man, we always expect attack. Is it a bargain?"

"Yes," answered Mr. Clifford and Jacob Meyer in one voice, the latter adding: "the guns and the cartridges are yours. Lead us now to the hidden place. We have fulfilled our part; we trust to the honour of you and all your people to fulfil yours."

"White Maiden," asked the Molimo, addressing Benita, "do you also say that it is a bargain?"

"What my father says, I say."

"Good," said the Molimo. "Then, in the presence of my people, and in the name of the Munwali, I, Mambo, who am his prophet, declare that it is so agreed between us, and may the vengeance of the heavens fall upon those who break our pact! Let the oxen of the white men be outspanned, their horses fed, their wagon unloaded, that we may count the guns. Let food be brought into the guest-house also, and after they have eaten, I, who alone of all of you have ever entered it, will lead them to the holy place, that there they may begin to search for that which the white men desire from age to age—to find it if they can; if not, to depart satisfied and at peace."

CHAPTER 9

The Oath of Maduna

Mr. Clifford and Meyer rose to return to the wagon in order to superintend the unyoking of the oxen and to give directions as to their herding, and the off-saddling of the horses. Benita rose also, wondering when the food that had been promised would be ready, for she was hungry. Meanwhile, the Molimo was greeting his son Tamas, patting his hand affectionately and talking to him, when suddenly Benita, who watched this domestic scene with interest, heard a commotion behind her. Turning to discover its cause, she perceived three great man clad in full war panoply, shields on their left arms, spears in their right hands, black ostrich plumes rising from the polished rings woven in their hair, black *moochas* about their middles, and black oxtails tied beneath their knees, who marched through the throng of Makalanga as though they saw them not.

"The Matabele! The Matabele are on us!" cried a voice; while other voices shouted, "Fly to your walls!" and yet others, "Kill them! They are few."

But the three men marched on unheeding till they stood before Mambo.

"Who are you, and what do you seek?" the old man asked boldly, though the fear that had taken hold of him at the sight of these strangers was evident enough, for his whole body shook.

"Surely you should know, chief of Bambatse," answered their spokesman with a laugh, "for you have seen the like of us before. We are the children of Lobengula, the Great Elephant, the King, the Black Bull, the Father of the Amandabele, and we have a message for your ear, little Old Man, which, finding that you leave your gate open, we have walked in to deliver."

"Speak your message then, envoys of Lobengula, in my ear and in those of my people," said the Molimo.

"Your people! Are these all your people?" the spokesman replied contemptuously. "Why then, what need was there for the *indunas* of the King to send so large an *impi* under a great general against you, when a company of lads armed with sticks would have served the turn? We thought that these were but the sons of your house, the men of your own family, whom you had called together to eat with the white strangers."

"Close the entrance in the wall," cried the Molimo, stung to fury by the insult; and a voice answered:

"Father, it is already done."

But the Matabele, who should have been frightened, only laughed again, and their spokesman said:

"See, my brothers, he thinks to trap us who are but three. Well, kill on, Old Wizard, if you will, but know that if a hand is lifted, this spear of mine goes through your heart, and that the children of Lobengula die hard. Know also that then the *impi* which waits not far away will destroy you every one, man and woman, youth and maiden, little ones who hold the hand and infants at the breast; none shall be left—none at all, to say, 'Here once lived the cowardly Makalanga of Bambatse.' Nay, be not foolish, but talk softly with us, so that perhaps we may spare your lives."

Then the three men placed themselves back to back, in such fashion that they faced every way, and could not be smitten down from behind, and waited.

"I do not kill envoys," said the Molimo, "but if they are foulmouthed, I throw them out of my walls. Your message, men of the Amandabele."

"I hear you. Hearken now to the word of Lobengula."

Then the envoy began to speak, using the pronoun I as though it were the Matabele king himself who spoke to his vassal, the Makalanga chief: "I sent to you last year, you slave, who dare to call yourself Mambo of the Makalanga, demanding a tribute of cattle and women, and warning you that if they did not come, I would take them. They did not come, but that time I spared you. Now I send again. Hand over to my messengers fifty cows and fifty oxen, with herds to drive them, and twelve maidens to be approved by them, or I wipe you out, who have troubled the earth too long, and that before another moon has waned.

"Those are the words of Lobengula," he concluded, and taking the horn snuff-box from the slit in his ear, helped himself, then insolently passed it to the Molimo.

So great was the old chief's rage that, forgetting his self-control, he struck the box from the hand of his tormentor to the ground, where the snuff lay spilled.

"Just so shall the blood of your people be spilled through your rash foolishness," said the messenger calmly, as he picked up the box, and as much of the snuff as he could save.

"Hearken," said the Molimo, in a thin, trembling voice. "Your king demands cattle, knowing that all the cattle are gone, that scarce a cow is left to give drink to a motherless babe. He asks for maidens also, but if he took those he seeks we should have none left for our young men to marry. And why is this so? It is because the vulture, Lobengula, has picked us to the bone; yes, while we are yet alive he has torn the flesh from us. Year by year his soldiers have stolen and killed, till at last nothing is left of us. And now he seeks what we have not got to give, in order that he may force a quarrel upon us and murder us. There is nought left for us to give Lobengula. You have your answer."

"Indeed!" replied the envoy with a sneer. "How comes it, then, that yonder I see a wagon laden with goods, and oxen in the yokes? Yes," he repeated with meaning, "with goods whereof we have known the like at Buluwayo; for Lobengula also sometimes buys guns from white men, O! little Makalanga. Come now, give us the wagon with its load and the oxen and the horses, and though it be but a small gift, we will take it away and ask nothing more this year."

"How can I give you the property of my guests, the white men?" asked the Molimo. "Get you gone, and do your worst, or you shall be thrown from the walls of the fortress."

"Good, but know that very soon we shall return and make an end of you, who are tired of these long and troublesome journeys to gather so little. Go, tend your corn, dwellers in Bambatse, for this I swear in the name of Lobengula, never shall you see it ripen more."

Now the crowd of listening Makalanga trembled at his words, but in the old Molimo they seemed only to rouse a storm of prophetic fury. For a moment he stood staring up at the blue sky, his arms outstretched as though in prayer. Then he spoke in a new voice—a clear, quiet voice, that did not seem to be his own.

"Who am I?" he said. "I am the Molimo of the Bambatse Makalanga; I am the ladder between them and Heaven; I sit on the topmost bough of the tree under which they shelter, and there in the crest of the tree Munwali speaks with me. What to you are winds, to me are voices whispering in my spirit's ears. Once my forefathers were great kings, they were Mambos of all the land, and that is still my

319

name and dignity. We lived in peace; we laboured, we did wrong to no man. Then you Zulu savages came upon us from the south-east and your path was red with blood. Year after year you robbed and you destroyed; you raided our cattle, you murdered our men, you took our maidens and our children to be your women and your slaves, until at length, of all this pit filled with the corn of life, there is left but a little handful. And this you say you will eat up also, lest it should fall into good ground and grow again. I tell you that I think it will not be so; but whether or no that happens, I have words for the ear of your king—a message for a message. Say to him that thus speaks the wise old Molimo of Bambatse.

"I see him hunted like a wounded hyena through the rivers, in the deep bush, and over the mountain. I see him die in pain and misery; but his grave I see not, for no man shall know it. I see the white man take his land and all his wealth; yea, to them and to no son of his shall his people give the *Bayéte*, the royal salute. Of his greatness and his power, this alone shall remain to him—a name accursed from generation to generation. And last of all I see peace upon the land and upon my children's children." He paused, then added: "For you, cruel dog that you are, this message also from the Munwali, by the lips of his Molimo. I lift no hand against you, but you shall not live to look again upon your king's face. Begone now, and do your worst."

For a moment the three Matabele seemed to be frightened, and Benita heard one of them say to his companions:

"The Wizard has bewitched us! He has bewitched the Great Elephant and all his people! Shall we kill him?"

But quickly shaking off his fears their spokesman laughed, and answered:

"So that is what you have brought the white people here for, old traitor—to plot against the throne of Lobengula."

He wheeled round and stared at Mr. Clifford and Jacob Meyer; then added:

"Good, Grey-beard and Black-Beard: I myself will put you both to such a death as you have never heard of, and as for the girl, since she is well favoured, she shall brew the king's beer, and be numbered amongst the king's wives—unless, indeed, he is pleased to give her to me."

In an instant the thing was done! At the man's words about Benita, Meyer, who had been listening to his threats and bombast unconcerned, suddenly seemed to awake. His dark eyes flashed, his pale face turned cruel. Snatching the revolver from his belt he seemed to point and fire it with one movement, and down—dead or dying—went the Matabele.

Men did not stir, they only stared. Accustomed as they were to death in that wild land, the suddenness of this deed surprised them. The contrast between the splendid, brutal savage who had stood before them a moment ago, and the limp, black thing going to sleep upon the ground, was strange enough to move their imaginations. There he lay, and there, over him, the smoking pistol in his hand, Meyer stood and laughed.

Benita felt that the act was just, and the awful punishment deserved. Yet that laugh of Jacob's jarred upon her, for in it she thought she heard the man's heart speaking; and oh, its voice was merciless! Surely Justice should not laugh when her sword falls!

"Behold, now," said the Molimo in his still voice, pointing at the dead Matabele with his finger; "do I speak lies, or is it true that this man shall not look more upon his king's face? Well, as it was with the servant, so it shall be with the lord, only more slowly. It is the decree of the Munwali, spoken by the voice of his Mouth, the Molimo of Bambatse. Go, children of Lobengula, and bear with you as an offering this first-fruit of the harvest that the white men shall reap among the warriors of his people."

The thin voice died away, and there was silence so intense that Benita thought she heard the scraping of the feet of a green lizard which crept across a stone a yard or two away.

Then of a sudden it ended. Of a sudden the two remaining Matabele turned and fled for their lives, and as, when dogs run, a flock of sheep will wheel about and pursue them, so did the Makalanga. They grabbed at the messengers with their hands, tearing their finery from them; they struck them with sticks, they pounded them with stones, till at length two bruised and bleeding men, finding all escape cut off, and led perhaps by some instinct, staggered back to where Benita stood horrified at this dreadful scene, and throwing themselves upon the ground, clutched at her dress and prayed for mercy.

"Move a little, Miss Clifford," said Meyer. "Three of those brutes will not weigh heavier than one upon my conscience."

"No, no, you shall not," she answered. "Mambo, these men are messengers; spare them."

"Hearken to the voice of pity," said the old prophet, "spoken in a place where pity never was, and not in vain. Let them go. Give mercy to the merciless, for she buys their lives with a prayer."

"They will bring the others on us," muttered Tamas, and even old Mr. Clifford shook his head sadly. But the Molimo only said:

"I have spoken. Let them go. That which will befall must befall, and from this deed no ill shall come that would not have come otherwise."

"You hear? Depart swiftly," said Benita, in Zulu.

With difficulty the two men dragged themselves to their feet, and supporting each other, stood before her. One of them, a clever, powerful-faced man, whose black hair was tinged with grey, addressing himself to Benita, gasped:

"Hear me. That fool there," and he pointed to his dead companion, "whose boasting brought his death upon him, was but a low fellow. I, who kept silence and let him talk, am Maduna, a prince of the royal house who justly deserve to die because I turned my back upon these dogs. Yet I and my brother here take life at your hands, Lady, who, now that I have had time to think, would refuse it at theirs. For, whether I stay or go does not matter. The *impi* waits; the slayers are beneath the walls. Those things which are decreed will happen; there, yonder old Wizard speaks true. Listen, Lady: should it chance that you have cause to demand two lives at the hands of Maduna, in his own name and the name of his king he promises them to you. In safety shall they pass, they and all that is theirs, without toll taken. Remember the oath of Maduna, Lady, in the hour of your need, and do you, my brother, bear witness to it among our people."

Then, straightening themselves as well as they were able, these two sorely hurt men lifted their right arms and gave Benita the salute due to a chieftainess. This done, taking no note of any other creature there, they limped away to the gate that had been opened for them, and vanished beyond the wall.

All this while Meyer had stood silent; now he spoke with a bitter smile.

"Charity, Miss Clifford, said a certain Paul, as reported in your New Testament, covers a multitude of sins. I hope very much that it will serve to cover our remains from the *aasvogels*, after we have met our deaths in some such fashion as that brute promised us," and he pointed to the dead man.

Benita looked at her father in question.

"Mr. Meyer means, my dear, that you have done a foolish thing in begging the lives of those Matabele. It would have been safer for us if they were dead, who, as it is, have gone off burning for revenge. Of course, I understand it was natural enough, but——" and he hesitated and stopped.

"The chief did not say so," broke in Benita with agitation; "besides, if he had, I should not have cared. It was bad enough to see one man killed like that," and she shivered; "I could not bear any more."

"You should not be angry at the fellow's death, seeing that it was what he said of you which brought it upon him," Meyer replied with meaning. "Otherwise he might have gone unharmed as far as I was concerned. For the rest, I did not interfere because I saw it was useless; also I am a fatalist like our friend, the Molimo, and believe in what is decreed. The truth is," he added sharply, "among savages ladies are not in place."

"Why did you not say that down at Rooi Krantz, Jacob?" asked Mr. Clifford. "You know I thought so all the while, but somehow I was over-ruled. Now what I suggest is, that we had better get out of this place as fast as we can—instantly, as soon as we have eaten, before our retreat is cut off."

Meyer looked at the oxen which had been outspanned: nine were wandering about picking up what food they could, but the five which were supposed to have been bitten by tsetse fly had lain down.

"Nine worn-out and footsore oxen will not draw the wagon," he said; "also in all probability the place is already surrounded by Matabele, who merely let us in to be sure of the guns which their spies must have told them we were carrying. Lastly, having spent so much and come so far, I do not mean to go without what we seek. Still, if you think that your daughter's danger is greater within these walls than outside of them, you might try, if we can hire servants, which I doubt. Or possibly, if any rowers are to be had, you could go down the Zambesi in a canoe, risking the fever. You and she must settle it, Clifford."

"Difficulties and dangers every way one looks. Benita, what do you say?" asked her father distractedly.

Benita thought a moment. She wished to escape from Mr. Meyer, of whom she was weary and afraid, and would have endured much to do so. On the other hand, her father was tired out, and needed rest; also to turn his back upon this venture now would have been a bitter blow to him. Moreover, lacking cattle and men, how was it to be done? Lastly, something within her, that same voice which had bidden her to come, seemed to bid her to stay. Very soon she had made up her mind.

"Father, dear," she said, "thank you for thinking of me, but as far as I can see, we should run more risks trying to get away than we do in stopping here. I wanted to come, though you warned me against it, and now I must take my chance and trust to God to bring us safe through all dangers. Surely with all those rifles the Makalanga ought to be able to hold such a place as this against the Matabele."

"I hope so," answered her father; "but they are a timid folk. Still, though it would have been far better never to have come, I think with you that it is best to stay where we are, and trust to God."

CHAPTER 10

The Mountain Top

If our adventurers, or any of them, hoped that they were going to be led to the secret places of the fortress that day, they were destined to disappointment. Indeed, the remainder of it was employed arduously enough in unpacking rifles, and a supply of ammunition; also in giving to a few of the leading Makalanga preliminary lessons in the method of their use, a matter as to which their ideas were of the vaguest. The rest of the tribe, having brought their women and children into the outer enclosure of the ancient stronghold, and with them their sheep and goats and the few cattle which remained to them, were employed in building up the entrance permanently with stones, a zigzag secret path upon the river side, that could be stopped in a few minutes, being now their only method of ingress and egress through the thickness of the walls. A certain number of men were also sent out as spies to discover, if possible, the whereabouts of the Matabele *impi*.

That there was some *impi* they were almost sure, for a woman who had followed them reported that the injured captain, Maduna, and his companion had been met at a distance of about three miles from Bambatse by a small party of Matabele, who were hiding in some bushes, and that these men had made litters for them, and carried them away; whither she did not know, for she had not dared to pursue them further.

That night Benita passed in the guesthouse, which was only a hut rather larger than the others, while the two men slept in the wagon just outside. She was so tired that for a long while she could not rest. Her mind kept flying back to all the events of the day: the strange words of that mystic old Molimo, concerning herself; the arrival of the brutal messengers and the indaba that followed; then the sudden and awful destruction of their spokesman at the hand of Jacob Meyer. The scene would not leave her eyes, she saw it again and yet again:

the quick transformation of Meyer's indifferent face when the soldier began to insult and threaten her, the lightning-like movement of his hand, the flash, the report, the change from life to death, and the slayer's cruel laugh. He could be very terrible, Jacob Meyer, when his passions were roused!

And what had roused them then? She could not doubt that it was herself—not mere chivalry towards a woman. Even if he were capable of chivalry, merely for that he would never have taken such risk of future trouble and revenge. No; it was something deeper. He had never said anything or done anything, yet long ago instinct or insight had caused Benita to suspect the workings of his mind, and now she was sure of them. The thought was terrible—worse than all her other dangers put together. True, she had her father to rely on, but he had been somewhat ailing of late; age and these arduous journeys and anxieties had told upon him. Supposing that anything were to happen to him— if he died, for instance, how dreadful her position might become, left alone far from the reach of help, with savages—and Jacob Meyer.

Oh! if it had not been for that dreadful shipwreck, how different might be her lot today! Well, it was the thought of the shipwreck and of him whom she had lost therein, which had driven her on to this adventure, that in it perhaps her suffering mind might be numbed to rest; and now she must face its issues. God still remained above her, and she would put her trust in Him. After all, if she died, what did it matter?

But that old Molimo had promised her that she was safe from death, that she should find here happiness and rest, though not that of the grave. He promised this, speaking as one who knew of all her grief, and a very little while afterwards, in the case of the Matabele soldier, he had proved himself a prophet of awful power. Also—she knew not how, she knew not why—now, as before, her inmost heart seemed to bear witness that this old dreamer's words were true, and that for her, in some strange manner unforeseen, there still remained a rest.

Comforted a little by this intuition, at length Benita fell asleep.

Next morning, when she came out of the hut, Benita was met by her father, who with a cheerful countenance informed her that at any rate as yet there was no sign of the Matabele. A few hours later, too, some spies came in who said that for miles round nothing could be seen or heard of them. Still the preparations for defence went on, and the hundred best men having been furnished with the rifles, were being drilled in the use of them by Tamas and his two companions, Tamala and Hoba, who had learned how to handle a gun very well in the course of their long journey. The shooting of these raw recruits, however, proved to be execrable; indeed, so dangerous were they that when one of them fired at a mark set upon the wall, it was found necessary to order all the rest to lie down. As it was, a poor trek ox— luckily it was sick—and two sheep were killed.

Foreseeing a scarcity of provisions in the event of a siege, Meyer, provident as ever, had already decreed the death of the tsetse-bitten cattle. These were accordingly despatched, and having been skinned and cut up, their flesh was severed into long strips to be dried in the burning sun as biltong, which secretly Benita hoped she might never be called upon to eat. Yet the time was to come when she would swallow that hard, tsetse-poisoned flesh with thankfulness.

At midday, after they had eaten, Mr. Clifford and Meyer went to the Molimo, where he sat against the second wall, and, pointing to the men with the guns, said:

"We have fulfilled our bargain. Now fulfil yours. Lead us to the holy place that we may begin our search."

"So be it," he answered. "Follow me, white people."

Then, quite unattended, he guided them round the inner wall till they came to a path of rock not more than a yard wide, beneath which was a precipice fifty feet or so in depth that almost overhung the river. This giddy path they followed for about twenty paces, to find that it ended in a cleft in the wall so narrow that only one person could walk through it at a time. That it must have been the approach to the second stronghold was evident, however, since it was faced on either side with dressed stones, and even the foundation granite had been worn by the human feet which had passed here for ages upon ages. This path zigzagged to and fro in the thickness of the wall till it brought them finally within its circle, a broad belt of steeply-rising ground, covered like that below with the tumbled ruins of buildings amidst which grew bush and trees.

"Heaven send that the gold is not buried here," said Mr. Clifford, surveying the scene; "for if it is, we shall never find it."

The Molimo seemed to guess the meaning of his words from his face, for he answered:

"I think not here. The besiegers won this place and camped in it for many weeks. I could show you were they built their fires and tried to undermine the last wall within which the Portuguese sat about until hunger killed them, for they could not eat their gold. Follow me again."

So on they went up the slope till they came to the base of the third wall, and as before, passed round it, and reached a point above the river. But now there was no passage, only some shallow and almost precipitous steps cut from single stones leading from the foot of the wall to its summit, more than thirty feet above.

"Really," said Benita, contemplating this perilous ascent with dismay, "the ways of treasure seekers are hard. I don't think I can," while her father also looked at them and shook his head.

"We must get a rope," said Meyer to the Molimo angrily. "How can we climb that place without one, with such a gulf below?"

"I am old, but I climb it," said the aged man in mild surprise, since to him, who had trodden it all his life, it seemed not difficult. "Still," he added, "I have a rope above which I use upon dark nights. I will ascend and let it down."

Ascend he did accordingly; indeed, it was a wondrous sight to see his withered legs scrambling from step to step as unconcernedly as though he were going upstairs. No monkey could have been more agile, or more absolutely impervious to the effects of height. Soon he vanished in—or, rather, through—the crest of the wall, and presently appeared again on the top step, whence he let down a stout hide rope, remarking that it was securely tied. So anxious was Meyer to enter the hidden place of which he had dreamed so long that he scarcely waited for it to reach his hand before he began the climb, which he accomplished safely. Then, sitting on the top of the wall, he directed Mr. Clifford to fasten the end of the rope round Benita's waist, and her turn came.

It was not so bad as she expected, for she was agile, and the knowledge that the rope would prevent disaster gave her confidence. In a very little while she had grasped Meyer's outstretched hand, and been drawn into safety through a kind of aperture above the top step. Then the rope was let down again for her father, who tied it about his middle. Well was it that he did so, since when he was about half-way up, awkwardness, or perhaps loss of nerve—neither of them wonderful in an old man—caused his foot to slip, and had it not been for the rope which Meyer and the Molimo held, he would certainly have fallen into the river some hundreds of feet below. As it was, he recovered himself, and presently arrived panting and very pale. In her relief Benita kissed him, and even as she did so thought again that she had been very near to being left alone with Jacob Meyer.

"All's well that ends well, my dear," he said. "But upon my word I am beginning to wish that I had been content with the humble profits of horse-breeding."

Benita made no answer; it seemed too late for any useful consideration of the point.

"Clever men, those ancients," said Meyer. "See," and he pointed out to her how, by drawing a heavy stone which still lay close by over the aperture through which they had crept, the ascent of the wall could be made absolutely impossible to any enemy, since at its crest it was battened outwards, not inwards, as is usual in these ancient ruins.

"Yes," she answered, "we ought to feel safe enough inside here, and that's as well since I do not feel inclined to go out again at present."

Then they paused to look about them, and this was what they saw:

The wall, built like those below, of unmortared blocks of stone, remained in a wonderfully good state of preservation, for its only enemies had been time, the tropical rains, and the growth of shrubs and trees which here and there had cracked and displaced the stones. It enclosed all the top of the hill, perhaps three acres of ground, and on it at intervals were planted soap-stone pillars, each of them about twelve feet in height, and fashioned at the top to a rude resemblance of a vulture. Many of these columns, however had been blown down, or perhaps struck by lightning, and lay broken upon the wall, or if they had fallen inward, at its foot; but some, six or eight perhaps, were still standing.

Benita learned afterwards that they must have been placed there by the ancient Phoenicians, or whatever people constructed this gigantic fortification, and had something to do with the exact recordings of the different seasons of the year, and their sub-divisions, by means of the shadows which they cast. As yet, however, she did not pay much attention to them, for she was engaged in considering a more remarkable relic of antiquity which stood upon the very verge of the precipice, the wall, indeed, being built up to its base on either side.

It was the great cone of which Richard Seymour had told her, fifty feet high or more, such as once was found in the Phoenician temples. But in this case it was not built of masonry, but shaped by the hand of man out of a single gigantic granite monolith of the sort that are sometimes to be met with in Africa, that thousands or millions of years ago had been left standing thus when the softer rock around it was worn away by time and weather. On the inner side of this cone were easy steps whereby it could be ascended, and its top, which might have been six feet in diameter, was fashioned in the shape of a cup, probably for the purposes of acts of worship and of sacrifice. This extraordinary monument, which, except on the river side, could not be seen from below on account of the slope of the hill, leaned slightly outwards, so that a stone dropped from its crest would fall into the waters of the stream.

"Thence it was," said the Molimo, "that my forefathers saw the last of the Portuguese, the fair daughter of the great Captain Ferreira, hurl herself to death after she had given the gold into our keeping, and laid the curse upon it, until she came again. So in my dreams have I seen and heard her also, ay, and others have seen her, but these only from by the river far below."

He paused awhile, looking at Benita with his queer, dreamy eyes; then said suddenly:

"Say, Lady, do you remember nothing of that matter?"

Now Benita grew vexed, for the whole thing was uncanny and jarred upon her.

"How can I remember," she asked, "who was born not five and twenty years ago?"

"I do not know," he answered. "How should I know, who am but an ignorant old black man, who was born not much more than eighty years ago? Yet, Lady, tell me, for I seek your wisdom, where were you born from? Out of the earth, or out of the heavens? What? You shake your head, you who do not remember? Well, neither do I remember. Yet it is true that all circles meet somewhere, and it is true that the Portuguese maiden said she would come again; and lastly it is true that she was such an one as you are, for she haunts this place, and I, who have seen her sitting yonder in the moonlight, know her beauty well. Yet mayhap she comes no more in flesh, but still her spirit comes; for, Lady, out of those eyes of yours I see it gaze at me. Come," he added abruptly, "let us descend the wall, for as you cannot remember, there is more to show you. Have no fear—the steps are easy."

So they went down without much difficulty, since, from the accumulation of rubbish and other causes, the wall was a great deal lower on this side, and found themselves in the usual dense growth of vegetation and brushwood through which ran a little path. It led them past the ruins of buildings whereof the use and purpose were long since forgotten, for their roofs had fallen in hundreds or thousands of years ago, to the entrance of a cave which was placed almost at the foot of the monolithic cone, but thirty or forty yards further from the circle of the wall. Here the Molimo bade them stay while he lit the lamps within. Five minutes passed and he returned, saying that all was ready.

"Be not afraid of what you may see," he added, "for know, white people, that save my forefathers and myself, none have entered this place since the Portuguese perished here, nor have we, who do but come hither to pray and receive the word of the Munwali, ever ventured to disturb it. As it was, so it is. Come, Lady, come; she whose spirit goes with you was the last of your white race to pass this door. It is therefore fitting that your feet and her spirit should be the first to enter it again."

Benita hung back a little, for the adventure was eerie, then, determined that she would show no fear in the presence of this old priest, took the thin hand he stretched out to her, and walked forward with head erect. The two men began to follow her, but the Molimo stopped them, saying:

"Not so. The maiden enters first alone with me; it is her house, and should it please her to ask you to dwell therein, so be it. But first she must visit her house alone."

"Nonsense," said Mr. Clifford angrily. "I will not have it. It will frighten her."

"Lady, do you trust me?" asked the Molimo.

"Yes," she answered; adding, "Father, I think you had better let me go alone. I am not afraid now, and it may be wisest not to thwart him. This is a very strange business—not like anything else—and really I think that I had better go alone. If I do not come back presently, you can follow."

"Those who break in upon the sleep of the dead should walk gently, gently," piped the old Molimo in a sing-song voice. "The maiden's breath is pure; the maiden's foot is light; her breath will not offend the dead; her step will not disturb the dead. White men, white men, anger not the dead, for the dead are mighty, and will be revenged upon you when you are dead; soon, very soon, when you are dead—dead in your sorrows, dead in your sins, dead, gathered to that company of the dead who await us here."

And, still chanting his mystic song, he led Benita by the hand out of the light, onward into darkness, away from life, onward into the place of death.

CHAPTER 11

The Sleepers in the Cave

Like every other passage in this old fortress, the approach to the cave was narrow and winding; presumably the ancients had arranged them thus to facilitate their defence. After the third bend, however, Benita saw a light ahead which flowed from a native lamp lit in the arched entrance. At the side of this arch was a shell-shaped hollow, cut in the rock about three feet above the floor. Its appearance seemed familiar to her; why, she was soon to learn, although at the moment she did not connect it with anything in particular. The cave beyond was large, lofty, and not altogether natural, for its walls had evidently been shaped, or at any rate trimmed, by man. Probably here the old Priests had established their oracle, or place of offering.

At first Benita could not see much, since in that great cavern two lamps of hippopotamus oil gave but little light. Presently, however, her eyes became accustomed to the gloom, and as they advanced up its length she perceived that save for a skin rug upon which she guessed the Molimo sat at his solitary devotions, and some gourds and platters for water and food, all the front part of the place appeared to be empty. Beyond, in its centre, stood an object of some gleaming metal, that from its double handles and roller borne upon supports of rock she took to be some kind of winch, and rightly, for beneath it was the mouth of a great well, the water supply of the topmost fortification.

Beyond the well was a stone altar, shaped like a truncated cone or pyramid, and at some distance away against the far wall, as she dimly discovered by the lamp that stood upon the altar, cut in relief upon that wall indeed, a colossal cross to which, vigorously if rudely executed in white stone, hung the image of Christ crucified, the crown of thorns upon His drooping head. Now she understood. Whatever may have been the first worship to which this place was dedicated, Christians had usurped it, and set up here the sacred symbol of their faith, awful enough to look upon in such surroundings. Doubtless, also, the shell-shaped basin at the entrance had served the worshippers in this underground chapel as a stoup for holy water.

The Molimo lifted the lamp from the altar, and having adjusted its wick, held it up in front of the rood before which, although she was no Catholic, Benita bowed her head and crossed herself, while he watched her curiously. Then he lowered it, and she perceived that on the cemented floor lay great numbers of shrouded forms that at first looked to her like folk asleep. He stepped to one of them and touched it with his foot, whereon the cloth which with it was covered crumbled into dust, revealing beneath a white skeleton.

All those sleepers rested well indeed, for they had been dead at least two hundred years. There they lay—men, women, and children, though of the last but few. Some of them had ornaments on their bones, some were clad in armour, and by all the men were swords, or spears, or knives, and here and there what she took to be primitive fire-arms. Certain of them also had turned into mummies in that dry air—grotesque and dreadful objects from which she gladly averted her eyes.

The Molimo led her forward to the foot of the crucifix, where, upon its lowest step and upon the cemented floor immediately beneath it respectively, lay two shapes decorously covered with shawls of some heavy material interwoven with gold wire, for the manufacture of which the Makalanga were famous when first the Portuguese came into contact with them. The Molimo took hold of the cloths that seemed almost as good now as on the day when they were woven, and lifted them, revealing beneath the figures of a man and woman. The features were unrecognizable, although the hair, white in the man's case and raven black in that of the woman, remained perfect. They had been great people, for orders glittered upon the man's breast, and his sword was gold hilted, whilst the woman's bones were adorned with costly necklaces and jewels, and in her hand was still a book bound in sheets of silver. Benita took it up and looked at it. It was a missal beautifully illuminated, which doubtless the poor lady had been reading when at length she sank exhausted into the sleep of death.

"See the Lord Ferreira and his wife," said the Molimo, "whom their daughter laid thus before she went to join them." Then, at a motion from Benita, he covered them up again with their golden cloths.

"Here they sleep," he went on in his chanting voice, "a hundred and fifty and three of them—a hundred and fifty and three; and when I dream in this place at night, I have seen the ghosts of every one of them arise from beside their forms and come gliding down the cave—the husband with the wife, the child with the mother—to look at me, and ask when the maiden returns again to take her heritage and give them burial."

Benita shuddered; the solemn awfulness of the place and scene oppressed her. She began to think that she, too, saw those ghosts.

"It is enough," she said. "Let us be going."

So they went, and the pitiful, agonized Christ upon the cross, at which she glanced from time to time over her shoulder, faded to a white blot, then vanished away in the darkness, through which, from generation to generation, it kept its watch above the dead, those dead that in their despair once had cried to it for mercy, and bedewed its feet with tears.

Glad, oh! glad was she when she had left that haunted place behind her, and saw the wholesome light again.

"What have you seen?" asked her father and Meyer, in one breath, as they noted her white and frightened face.

She sank upon a stone seat at the entrance of the cave, and before she could open her lips the Molimo answered for her:

"The maiden has seen the dead. The Spirit who goes with her has given greeting to its dead that it left so long ago. The maiden has done reverence to the White One who hangs upon the cross, and asked a blessing and a pardon of Him, as she whose Spirit goes with her did reverence before the eyes of my forefathers, and asked a blessing and a pardon ere she cast herself away." And he pointed to the little golden crucifix which hung upon Benita's bosom, attached to the necklace which Tamas, the messenger, had given her at Rooi Krantz.

"Now," he went on, "now the spell is broken, and the sleepers must depart to sleep elsewhere. Enter, white men; enter, if you dare, and ask for pardon and for blessing if it may be found, and gather up the dry bones and take the treasure that was theirs, if it may be found, and conquer the curse that goes with the treasure for all save one, if you can, if you can, if you can! Rest you here, maiden, in the sweet sunshine, and follow me, white men; follow me into the dark of the dead to seek for that which the white men love." And once more he vanished down the passage, turning now and again to beckon to them, while they went after him as though drawn against their wish. For now, at the last moment, some superstitious fear spread from him to them, and showed itself in their eyes.

To Benita, half fainting upon the stone seat, for this experience had shaken her to the heart, it seemed but a few minutes, though really the best part of an hour had gone by, when her father reappeared as white-faced as she had been.

"Where is Mr. Meyer?" she asked.

"Oh!" he answered. "He is collecting all the golden ornaments off those poor bodies, and tumbling their bones together in a corner of the cave."

Benita uttered an exclamation of horror.

"I know what you mean," said her father. "But, curse the fellow! he has no reverence, although at first he seemed almost as scared as I was myself. He said that as we could not begin our search with all those corpses about, they had best be got out of the way as soon as possible. Or perhaps it was because he is really afraid of them, and wanted to prove to himself that they are nothing more than dust. Benita," went on the old man, "to tell you the truth, I wish heartily that we had left this business alone. I don't believe that any good will come of it, and certainly it has brought enough trouble already. That old prophet of a Molimo has the second sight, or something like it, and he does not hide his opinion, but keeps chuckling away in that dreadful place, and piping out his promises of ill to be."

"He promised me nothing but good," said Benita with a little smile. "Though I don't see how it can happen. But if you dislike the thing, father, why not give it up and try to escape?"

"It is too late, dear," he replied passionately. "Meyer would never come, and I can't in honour leave him. Also, I should laugh at myself for the rest of my life; and, after all, why should we not have the gold if it can be found? It belongs to nobody. We do not get it by robbery, or murder; nuggets are of no use to Portuguese who have been dead two hundred years, and whose heirs, if they have any, it is impossible to discover. Nor can it matter to them whether they lie about singly as they died or were placed after death, or piled together in a corner. Our fears were mere churchyard superstitions, which we have caught from that ghoul of a Molimo. Don't you agree with me?"

"Yes, I suppose so," answered Benita, "though a fate may cling to certain things or places, perhaps. At any rate, I think that it is of no use turning back now, even if we had anywhere to turn, so we may as well go through with the venture and await its end. Give me the water-bottle, please. I am thirsty."

A while later Jacob Meyer appeared, carrying a great bundle of precious objects wrapped in one of the gold *cere*-cloths, which bundle he hid away behind a stone.

"The cave is much tidier now," he said, as he flicked the thick dust which had collected on them during his unhallowed task from his hands, and hair, and garments. Then he drank greedily, and asked:

"Have you two made any plans for our future researches?"

They shook their heads.

"Well, then, I have. I thought them out while I was bone-carting, and here they are. It is no use our going down below again; for one thing, the journey is too dangerous, and takes too long; and for another, we are safer up above, where we have plenty to do."

"But," said Benita, "how about things to eat and sleep on, and the rest?"

"Simple enough, Miss Clifford; we must get them up. The Kaffirs will bring them to the foot of the third wall, and we will haul them to its top with a rope. Of water it seems there is plenty in that well, which is fed by a spring a hundred and fifty feet down, and the old chain is still on the roller, so we only need a couple of buckets from the wagon. Of wood for cooking there is plenty also, growing on the spot; and we can camp in the cave or outside of it, as we like, according to the state of the weather. Now, do you rest here while I go down. I will be back in an hour with some of the gear, and then you must help me."

So he went, and the end of it was that before nightfall they had enough things for their immediate needs, and by the second night, working very hard, were more or less comfortably established in their strange habitation. The canvas flap from the wagon was arranged as a tent for Benita, the men sleeping beneath a thick-leaved tree near by. Close at hand, under another tree, was their cooking place. The provisions of all sorts, including a couple of cases of square-face and a large supply of biltong from the slaughtered cattle, they stored with a quantity of ammunition in the mouth of the cave. Fresh meat also was brought to them daily, and hauled up in baskets—that is, until there was none to bring—and with it grain for bread, and green *mealies* to serve as vegetables. Therefore, as the water from the well proved to be excellent and quite accessible, they were soon set up in all things necessary, and to these they added from time to time as opportunity offered.

In all these preparations the old Molimo took a part, nor, when they were completed, did he show any inclination to leave them. In the morning he would descend to his people below, but before nightfall he always returned to the cave, where for many years it had been his custom to sleep—at any rate several times a week, in the gruesome company of the dead Portuguese. Jacob Meyer persuaded Mr. Clifford that his object was to spy upon them, and talked of turning him out; but Benita, between whom and the old man had sprung up a curious friendship and sympathy, prevented it, pointing out that they were much safer with the Molimo, as a kind of hostage, than they could be without him; also, that his knowledge of the place, and of other things, might prove of great help to them. So in the end he was allowed to remain, as indeed he had a perfect right to do.

All this while there was no sign of any attack by the Matabele. Indeed, the fear of such a thing was to some extent dying away, and Benita, watching from the top of the wall, could see that their nine remaining oxen, together with the two horses—for that belonging to Jacob Meyer had died—and the Makalanga goats and sheep, were daily driven out to graze; also, that the women were working in the crops upon the fertile soil around the lowest wall. Still, a strict watch was kept, and at night everyone slept within the fortifications; moreover, the drilling of the men and their instruction in the use of firearms went on continually under Tamas, who now, in his father's old age, was the virtual chief of the people.

It was on the fourth morning that at length, all their preparations being completed, the actual search for the treasure began. First, the Molimo was closely interrogated as to its whereabouts, since they thought that even if he did not know this exactly, some traditions of the fact might have descended to him from his ancestors. But he declared with earnestness that he knew nothing, save that the Portuguese maiden had said that it was hidden; nor, he added, had any dream or vision come to him concerning this matter, in which he took no interest. If it was there, it was there; if it was not there, it was not there—it remained for the white men to search and see.

For no very good reason Meyer had concluded that the gold must have been concealed in or about the cave, so here it was that they began their investigations.

First, they bethought them of the well into which it might possibly have been thrown, but the fact of this matter proved very difficult to ascertain. Tying a piece of metal—it was an old Portuguese sword-hilt—to a string, they let it down and found that it touched water at a depth of one hundred and twenty feet, and bottom at a depth of one hundred and forty-seven feet. Therefore there were twenty-seven feet of water. Weighting a bucket they sank it until it rested upon this bottom, then wound it up again several times. On the third occasion it brought up a human bone and a wire anklet of pure gold. But this proved nothing, except that some ancient, perhaps thousands of years ago, had been thrown, or had fallen, into the well.

Still unsatisfied, Jacob Meyer, who was a most intrepid person, determined to investigate the place himself, a task of no little difficulty and danger, since proper ladders were wanting, nor, had they existed, was there anything to stand them on. Therefore it came to this: a seat must be rigged on to the end of the old copper chain, and be lowered into the pit after the fashion of the bucket. But, as Benita pointed out, although they might let him down, it was possible that they would not be able to draw him up again, in which case his plight must prove unfortunate. So, when the seat had been prepared, an experiment was made with a stone weighing approximately as much as a man. This Benita and her father let down easily enough, but, as they anticipated, when it came to winding it up again, their strength was barely sufficient to the task. Three people could do it well, but with two the thing was risky. Now Meyer asked—or, rather, commanded—the Molimo to order some of his men to help him, but this the old chief refused point blank to do.

First, he made a number of excuses. They were all employed in drilling, and in watching for the Matabele; they were afraid to venture here, and so forth. At last Meyer grew furious; his eyes flashed, he ground his teeth, and began to threaten.

"White man," said the Molimo, when he had done, "it cannot be. I have fulfilled my bargain with you. Search for the gold; find it and take it away if you can. But this place is holy. None of my tribe, save he who holds the office of Molimo for the time, may set a foot therein. Kill me if you will—I care not; but so it is, and if you kill me, afterwards they will kill you."

Now Meyer, seeing that nothing was to be gained by violence, changed his tone, and asked if he himself would help them.

"I am old, my strength is small," he replied; "yet I will put my hand to the chain and do my best. But, if I were you, I would not descend that pit."

"Still, I will descend it, and tomorrow," said Meyer.

CHAPTER 12

The Beginning of the Search

Accordingly, on the next day the great experiment was made. The chain and ancient winding gear had been tested and proved to be amply sufficient to the strain. Therefore, nothing remained save for Meyer to place himself in the wooden seat with an oil-lamp, and in case this should be extinguished, matches and candles, of both of which they had a large supply.

He did so boldly enough, and swung out over the mouth of the pit, while the three of them clutched the handles of the winch. Then they began to lower, and slowly his white face disappeared into the black depth. At every few turns his descent was stopped that he might examine the walls of the well, and when he was about fifty feet down he called to them to hold on, which they did, listening while he struck at the rock with a hammer, for here it sounded very hollow.

At length he shouted to them to lower away again, and they obeyed, until nearly all the chain was out, and they knew he must be near the water. Now Benita, peeping over the edge, saw that the star of light had vanished. His lamp was out, nor did he appear to attempt to re-light it. They shouted down the well to him, but no answer coming, began to wind up as fast as they were able. It was all that their united strength could manage, and very exhausted were they when at length Jacob reappeared at the top. At first, from the look of him they thought that he was dead, and had he not tied himself to the chain, dead he certainly would have been, for evidently his senses had left him long ago. Indeed, he had fallen almost out of the seat, over which his legs hung limply, his weight being supported by the hide rope beneath his arms which was made fast to the chain.

They swung him in and dashed water over his face, till, to their relief, at last he began to gasp for breath, and revived sufficiently to enable them to half-lead and half-carry him out into the fresh air.

"What happened to you?" asked Clifford.

"Poisoned with gases, I suppose," Meyer answered with a groan, for his head was aching sadly. "The air is often bad at the bottom of deep wells, but I could smell or feel nothing until suddenly my senses left me. It was a near thing—a very near thing."

Afterwards, when he had recovered a little, he told them that at one spot deep down in the well, on the river side of it, he found a place where it looked as though the rock had been cut away for a space of about six feet by four, and afterwards built up again with another sort of stone set in hard mortar or cement. Immediately beneath, too, were socket-holes in which the ends of beams still remained, suggesting that here had been a floor or platform. It was while he was examining these rotted beams that insensibility overcame him. He added that he thought that this might be the entrance to the place where the gold was hidden.

"If so," said Mr. Clifford, "hidden it must remain, since it can have no better guardian than bad air. Also, floors like that are common in all wells to prevent rubbish from falling into the water, and the stone-work you saw probably was only put there by the ancients to mend a fault in the rock and prevent the wall from caving in."

"I hope so," said Meyer, "since unless that atmosphere purifies a good deal I don't think that even I dare go down again, and until one gets there, of that it is difficult to be sure, though of course a lantern on a string will tell one something."

This was the end of their first attempt. The search was not renewed until the following afternoon, when Meyer had recovered a little from the effects of the poisoning and the chafing of the hide ropes beneath his arms. Indeed, from the former he never did quite recover, since thenceforward Benita, who for her own reasons watched the man closely, discovered a marked and progressive change in his demeanour. Hitherto he had appeared to be a reserved man, one who kept tight hand upon himself, and, if she knew certain things about him, it was rather because she guessed, or deduced them, than because he allowed them to be seen. On two occasions only had he shown his heart before her—when they had spoken together by the shores of Lake Chrissie on the day of the arrival of the messengers, and he declared his ardent desire for wealth and power; and quite recently, when he killed the Matabele envoy. Yet she felt certain that this heart of his was very passionate and insurgent; that his calm was like the ice that hides the stream, beneath which its currents run fiercely, none can see whither. The fashion in which his dark eyes would flash, even when his pale countenance remained unmoved, told her so, as did other things.

For instance, when he was recovering from his swoon, the first words that passed his lips were in German, of which she understood a little, and she thought that they shaped themselves to her name, coupled with endearing epithets. From that time forward he became less guarded—or, rather, it seemed as though he were gradually losing power to control himself. He would grow excited without apparent cause, and begin to declaim as to what he would do when he had found the gold; how he would pay the world back all it had caused him to suffer—how he would become a "king."

"I am afraid that you will find that exalted position rather lonely," said Benita with a careless laugh, and next minute was sorry that she had spoken, for he answered, looking at her in a way that she did not like:

"Oh, no! There will be a queen—a beautiful queen, whom I shall endow with wealth, and deck with jewels, and surround with love and worship."

"What a fortunate lady!" she said, still laughing, but taking the opportunity to go away upon some errand.

At other times, especially after dark, he would walk up and down in front of the cave, muttering to himself, or singing wild old German songs in his rich voice. Also, he made a habit of ascending the granite pillar and seating himself there, and more than once called down to her to come up and share his "throne." Still, these outbreaks were so occasional that her father, whose perceptions appeared to Benita to be less keen than formerly, scarcely noticed them, and for the rest his demeanour was what it had always been.

Further researches into the well being out of the question, their next step was to make a thorough inspection of the chapel-cave itself. They examined the walls inch by inch, tapping them with a hammer to hear if they sounded hollow, but without result. They examined the altar, but it proved to be a solid mass of rock. By the help of a little ladder they had made, they examined the crucifix, and discovered that the white figure on the cross had evidently been fashioned out of some heathen statue of soft limestone, for at its back were the remains of draperies, and long hair which the artist had not thought it necessary to cut away. Also, they found that the arms had been added, and were of a slightly different stone, and that the weight of the figure was taken partly by an iron staple which supported the body, and partly by strong copper wire twisted to resemble cord, and painted white, which was passed round the wrists and supported the arms. This wire ran through loops of rock cut in the traverse of the cross, that itself was only raised in relief by chiselling away the solid stone behind.

Curiously enough, this part of the search was left to Mr. Clifford and Benita, since it was one that Jacob Meyer seemed reluctant to undertake. A Jew by birth, and a man who openly professed his want of belief in that or any other religion, he yet seemed to fear this symbol of the Christian faith, speaking of it as horrible and unlucky; yes, he who, without qualm or remorse, had robbed and desecrated the dead that lay about its feet. Well, the crucifix told them nothing; but as Mr. Clifford, lantern in hand, descended the ladder, which Benita held, Jacob Meyer, who was in front of the altar, called to them excitedly that he had found something.

"Then it is more than we have," said Mr. Clifford, as he laid down the ladder and hurried to him.

Meyer was sounding the floor with a staff of wood—an operation which he had only just began after the walls proved barren.

"Listen now," he said, letting the heavy staff drop a few paces to the right of the altar, where it produced the hard, metallic clang that comes from solid stone when struck. Then he moved to the front of the altar and dropped it again, but now the note was hollow and reverberant. Again and again he repeated the experiment, till they had exactly mapped out where the solid rock ended and that which seemed to be hollow began—a space of about eight feet square.

"We've got it," he said triumphantly. "That's the entrance to the place where the gold is," and the others were inclined to agree with him.

Now it remained to put their theory to the proof—a task of no small difficulty. Indeed, it took them three days of hard, continual work. It will be remembered that the floor of the cave was cemented over, and first of all this cement, which proved to be of excellent quality, being largely composed of powdered granite, must be broken up. By the help of a steel crowbar, which they had brought with them in the wagon, at length that part of their task was completed, revealing the rock beneath. By this time Benita was confident that, whatever might lie below, it was not the treasure, since it was evident that the poor, dying Portuguese would not have had the time or the strength to cement it over. When she told the others so, however, Meyer, convinced that he was on the right tack, answered that doubtless it was done by the Makalanga after the Portuguese days, as it was well known that they retained a knowledge of the building arts of their forefathers until quite a recent period, when the Matabele began to kill them out.

When at length the cement was cleared away and the area swept, they discovered—for there ran the line of it—that here a great stone was set into the floor; it must have weighed several tons. As it was set in cement, however, to lift it, even if they had the strength to work the necessary levers, proved quite impossible. There remained only one thing to be done—to cut a way through. When they had worked at this task for several hours, and only succeeded in making a hole six inches deep, Mr. Clifford, whose old bones ached and whose hands were very sore, suggested that perhaps they might break it up with gunpowder. Accordingly, a pound flask of that explosive was poured into the hole, which they closed over with wet clay and a heavy rock, leaving a quill through which ran an extemporized fuse of cotton wick. All being prepared, their fuse was lit, and they left the cave and waited.

Five minutes afterwards the dull sound of an explosion reached their ears, but more than an hour went by before the smoke and fumes would allow them to enter the place, and then it was to find that the results did not equal their expectations. To begin with, the slab was only cracked—not shattered, since the strength of the powder had been expended upwards, not downwards, as would have happened in the case of dynamite, of which they had none. Moreover, either the heavy stone which they had placed upon it, striking the roof of the cave, or the concussion of the air, had brought down many tons of rock, and caused wide and dangerous-looking cracks. Also, though she said nothing of it, it seemed to Benita that the great white statue on the cross was leaning a little further forward than it used to do. So the net result of the experiment was that they were obliged to drag away great fragments of the fallen roof that lay upon the stone, which remained almost as solid and obdurate as before.

So there was nothing for it but to go on working with the crowbar. At length, towards the evening of the third day of their labour, when the two men were utterly tired out, a hole was broken through, demonstrating the fact that beneath this cover lay a hollow of some sort. Mr. Clifford, to say nothing of Benita, who was heartily weary of the business, wished to postpone proceedings till the morrow, but Jacob Meyer would not. So they toiled on until about eleven o'clock at night, when at length the aperture was of sufficient size to admit a man. Now, as in the case of the well, they let down a stone tied to a string, to find that the place beneath was not more than eight feet deep. Then, to ascertain the condition of the air, a candle was lowered, which at first went out, but presently burnt well enough. This point settled, they brought their ladder, whereby Jacob descended with a lantern.

In another minute they heard the sound of guttural German oaths rising through the hole. Mr. Clifford asked what was the matter, and received the reply that the place was a tomb, with nothing in it but an accursed dead monk, information at which Benita could not help bursting into laughter.

The end of it was that both she and her father went down also, and there, sure enough, lay the remains of the old missionary in his cowl, with an ivory crucifix about his neck, and on his breast a scroll stating that he, Marco, born at Lisbon in 1438, had died at Bambatse in the year 1503, having laboured in the Empire of Monomotapa for seventeen years, and suffered great hardships and brought many souls to Christ. The scroll added that it was he, who before he entered into religion was a sculptor by trade, that had fashioned the figure on the cross in this chapel out of that of the heathen goddess which had stood in the same place from unknown antiquity. It ended with a request, addressed to all good Christians in Latin, that they who soon must be as he was would pray for his soul and not disturb his bones, which rested here in the hope of a blessed resurrection.

When this pious wish was translated to Jacob Meyer by Mr. Clifford, who still retained some recollection of the classics which he had painfully acquired at Eton and Oxford, the Jew could scarcely contain his wrath. Indeed, looking at his bleeding hands, instead of praying for the soul of that excellent missionary, to reach whose remains he had laboured with such arduous, incessant toil, he cursed it wherever it might be, and unceremoniously swept the bones, which the document asked him not to disturb, into a corner of the tomb, in order to ascertain whether there was not, perhaps, some stair beneath them.

"Really, Mr. Meyer," said Benita, who, in spite of the solemnity of the surroundings, could not control her sense of humour, "if you are not careful the ghosts of all these people will haunt you."

"Let them haunt me if they can," he answered furiously. "I don't believe in ghosts, and defy them all."

At this moment, looking up, Benita saw a figure gliding out of the darkness into the ring of light, so silently that she started, for it might well have been one of those ghosts in whom Jacob Meyer did not believe. In fact, however, it was the old Molimo, who had a habit of coming upon them thus.

"What says the white man?" he asked of Benita, while his dreamy eyes wandered over the three of them, and the hole in the violated tomb.

"He says that he does not believe in spirits, and that he defies them," she answered.

343

"The white gold-seeker does not believe in spirits, and he defies them," Mambo repeated in his sing-song voice. "He does not believe in the spirits that I see all around me now, the angry spirits of the dead, who speak together of where he shall lie and of what shall happen to him when he is dead, and of how they will welcome one who disturbs their rest and defies and curses them in his search for the riches which he loves. There is one standing by him now, dressed in a brown robe with a dead man cut in ivory like to that," and he pointed to the crucifix in Jacob's hands, "and he holds the ivory man above him and threatens him with sleepless centuries of sorrow, when he is also one of those spirits in which he does not believe."

Then Meyer's rage blazed out. He turned upon the Molimo and reviled him in his own tongue, saying that he knew well where the treasure was hidden, and that if he did not point it out he would kill him and send him to his friends, the spirits. So savage and evil did he look that Benita retreated a little way, while Mr. Clifford strove in vain to calm him. But although Meyer laid his hand upon the knife in his belt and advanced upon him, the old Molimo neither budged an inch nor showed the slightest fear.

"Let him rave on," he said, when at length Meyer paused exhausted. "Just so in a time of storm the lightnings flash and the thunder peals, and the water foams down the face of rock; but then comes the sun again, and the hill is as it has ever been, only the storm is spent and lost. I am the rock, he is but the wind, the fire, and the rain. It is not permitted that he should hurt me, and those spirits in whom he does not believe treasure up his curses, to let them fall again like stones upon his head."

Then, with a contemptuous glance at Jacob, the old man turned and glided back into the darkness out of which he had appeared.

CHAPTER 13

Benita Plans Escape

The next morning, while she was cooking breakfast, Benita saw Jacob Meyer seated upon a rock at a little distance, sullen and disconsolate. His chin was resting on his hand, and he watched her intently, never taking his eyes from her face. She felt that he was concentrating his will upon her; that some new idea concerning her had come into his mind; for it was one of her miseries that she possessed the power of interpreting the drift of this man's thoughts. Much as she detested him, there existed that curious link between them.

It may be remembered that, on the night when they first met at the crest of Leopard's Kloof, Jacob had called her a "thought-sender," and some knowledge of their mental intimacy had come home to Benita. From that day forward her chief desire had been to shut a door between their natures, to isolate herself from him and him from her. Yet the attempt was never entirely successful.

Fear and disgust took hold of her, bending there above the fire, all the while aware of the Jew's dark eyes that searched her through and through. Benita formed a sudden determination. She would implore her father to come away with her. Of course, such an attempt would be terribly dangerous. Of the Matabele nothing had been seen; but they might be about, and even if enough cattle could be collected to draw the wagon, it belonged to Meyer as much as to her father, and must therefore be left for him. Still, there remained the two horses, which the Molimo had told her were well and getting fat.

At this moment Meyer rose and began to speak to her.

"What are you thinking of, Miss Clifford?" he asked in his soft foreign voice.

She started, but answered readily enough:

"Of the wood which is green, and the kid cutlets which are getting smoked. Are you not tired of kid, Mr. Meyer?" she went on.

He waved the question aside. "You are so good—oh! I mean it—so really good that you should not tell stories even about small things. The wood is not green; I cut it myself from a dead tree; and the meat is not smoked; nor were you thinking of either. You were thinking of me, as I was thinking of you; but what exactly was in your mind, this time I do not know, and that is why I ask you to tell me."

"Really, Mr. Meyer," she answered flushing; "my mind is my own property."

"Ah! do you say so? Now I hold otherwise—that it is my property, as mine is yours, a gift that Nature has given to each of us."

"I seek no such gift," she answered; but even then, much as she would have wished to do so, she could not utter a falsehood, and deny this horrible and secret intimacy.

"I am sorry for that, as I think it very precious; more precious even than the gold which we cannot find; for Miss Clifford, it brings me nearer you."

She turned upon him, but he held up his hand, and went on:

"Oh! do not be angry with me, and do not fear that I am going to trouble you with soft speeches, for I shall not, unless a time should come, as I think that perhaps it will, when you may wish to listen to them. But I want to point out something to you, Miss Clifford. Is it not a wonderful thing that our minds should be so in tune, and is there not an object in all this? Did I believe as you do, I should say that it was Heaven working in us—no: do not answer that the working comes from lower down. I take no credit for reading that upon your lips; the retort is too easy and obvious. I am content to say, however, that the work is that of instinct and nature, or, if you will, of fate, pointing out a road by which together we might travel to great ends."

"I travel my road alone, Mr. Meyer."

"I know, I know, and that is the pity of it. The trouble between man and woman is that not in one case out of a million, even if they be lovers, do they understand each other. Their eyes may seek one another, their hands and lips may meet, and yet they remain distinct, apart, and often antagonistic. There is no communication of the soul. But when it chances to be hewn from the same rock as it were—oh! then what happiness may be theirs, and what opportunities!"

"Possibly, Mr. Meyer; but, to be frank, the question does not interest me."

"Not yet; but I am sure that one day it will. Meanwhile, I owe you an apology. I lost my temper before you last night. Well, do not

346

judge me hardly, for I was utterly worn out, and that old idiot vexed me with his talk about ghosts, in which I do not believe."

"Then why did it make you so angry? Surely you could have afforded to treat it with contempt, instead of doing—as you did."

"Upon my word! I don't know, but I suppose most of us are afraid lest we should be forced to accept that which we refuse. This ancient place gets upon the nerves, Miss Clifford; yours as well as mine. I can afford to be open about it, because I know that you know. Think of its associations: all the crime that has been committed here for ages and ages, all the suffering that has been endured here. Doubtless human sacrifices were offered in this cave or outside of it; that great burnt ring in the rock there may have been where they built the fires. And then those Portuguese starving to death, slowly starving to death while thousands of savages watched them die. Have you ever thought what it means? But of course you have, for like myself you are cursed with imagination. God in heaven! is it wonderful that it gets upon the nerves? especially when one cannot find what one is looking for, that vast treasure"—and his face became ecstatic—"that shall yet be yours and mine, and make us great and happy."

"But which at present only makes me a scullery-maid and most unhappy," replied Benita cheerfully, for she heard her father's footstep. "Don't talk any more of the treasure, Mr. Meyer, or we shall quarrel. We have enough of that during business hours, when we are hunting for it, you know. Give me the dish, will you? This meat is cooked at last."

Still Benita could not be rid of that treasure, since after breakfast the endless, unprofitable search began again. Once more the cave was sounded, and other hollow places were discovered upon which the two men got to work. With infinite labour three of them were broken into in as many days, and like the first, found to be graves, only this time of ancients who, perhaps, had died before Christ was born. There they lay upon their sides, their bones burnt by the hot cement that had been poured over them, their gold-headed and gold-ferruled rods of office in their hands, their gold-covered pillows of wood, such as the Egyptians used, beneath their skulls, gold bracelets upon their arms and ankles, cakes of gold beneath them which had fallen from the rotted pouches that once hung about their waists, vases of fine glazed pottery that had been filled with offerings, or in some cases with gold dust to pay the expenses of their journey in the other world, standing round them, and so forth.

In their way these discoveries were rich enough—from one tomb alone they took over a hundred and thirty ounces of gold—to say nothing of their surpassing archaeological interest. Still they were not what they sought: all that gathered wealth of Monomotapa which the fleeing Portuguese had brought with them and buried in this, their last stronghold.

Benita ceased to take the slightest interest in the matter; she would not even be at the pains to go to look at the third skeleton, although it was that of a man who had been almost a giant, and, to judge from the amount of bullion which he took to the tomb with him, a person of great importance in his day. She felt as though she wished never to see another human bone or ancient bead or bangle; the sight of a street in Bayswater in a London fog—yes, or a toy-shop window in Westbourne Grove—would have pleased her a hundred times better than these unique remains that, had they known of them in those days, would have sent half the learned societies of Europe crazy with delight. She wished to escape from Bambatse, its wondrous fortifications, its mysterious cone, its cave, its dead, and— from Jacob Meyer.

Benita stood upon the top of her prison wall and looked with longing at the wide, open lands below. She even dared to climb the stairs which ran up the mighty cone of granite, and seated herself in the cup-like depression on its crest, whence Jacob Meyer had called to her to come and share his throne. It was a dizzy place, for the pillar leaning outwards, its point stood almost clear of the water-scarped rock, so that beneath her was a sheer drop of about four hundred feet to the Zambesi bed. At first the great height made her feel faint. Her eyes swam, and unpleasant tremors crept along her spine, so that she was glad to sink to the floor, whence she knew she could not fall. By degrees, however, she recovered her nerve, and was able to study the glorious view of stream and marshes and hills beyond.

For she had come here with a purpose, to see whether it would not be possible to escape down the river in a canoe, or in native boats such as the Makalanga owned and used for fishing, or to cross from bank to bank. Apparently it was impossible, for although the river beneath and above them was still enough, about a mile below began a cataract that stretched as far as she could see, and was bordered on either side by rocky hills covered with forest, over which, even if they could obtain porters, a canoe could not be carried. This, indeed, she had already heard from the Molimo, but knowing his timid nature, she wished to judge of the matter for herself. It came to this then: if they were to go, it must be on the horses.

Descending the cone Benita went to find her father, to whom as yet she had said nothing of her plans. The opportunity was good, for she knew that he would be alone. As it chanced, on that afternoon Meyer had gone down the hill in order to try to persuade the Makalanga to give them ten or twenty men to help them in their excavations. In this, it will be remembered, he had already failed so far as the Molimo was concerned, but he was not a man easily turned from his purpose, and he thought that if he could see Tamas and some of the other captains he might be able by bribery, threats, or otherwise, to induce them to forget their superstitious fears, and help in the search. As a matter of fact, he was utterly unsuccessful, since one and all they declared that for them to enter that sacred place would mean their deaths, and that the vengeance of Heaven would fall upon their tribe and destroy it root and branch.

Mr. Clifford, on whom all this heavy labour had begun to tell, was taking advantage of the absence of his taskmaster, Jacob, to sleep awhile in the hut which they had now built for themselves beneath the shadow of the baobab-tree. As she reached it he came out yawning, and asked her where she had been. Benita told him.

"A giddy place," he said. "I have never ventured to try it myself. What did you go up there for, dear?"

"To look at the river while Mr. Meyer was away, father; for if he had seen me do so he would have guessed my reason; indeed, I dare say that he will guess it now."

"What reason, Benita?"

"To see whether it would not be possible to escape down it in a boat. But there is no chance. It is all rapids below, with hills and rocks and trees on either bank."

"What need have you to escape at present?" he asked eyeing her curiously.

"Every need," she answered with passion. "I hate this place; it is a prison, and I loathe the very name of treasure. Also," and she paused.

"Also what, dear?"

"Also," and her voice sank to a whisper, as though she feared that he should overhear her even at the bottom of the hill; "also, I am afraid of Mr. Meyer."

This confession did not seem to surprise her father, who merely nodded his head and said:

"Go on."

"Father, I think that he is going mad, and it is not pleasant for us to be cooped up here alone with a madman, especially when he has begun to speak to me as he does now."

"You don't mean that he has been impertinent to you," said the old man, flushing up, "for if so——"

"No, not impertinent—as yet," and she told him what had passed between Meyer and herself, adding, "You see, father, I detest this man; indeed, I want to have nothing to do with any man; for me all that is over and done with," and she gave a dry little sob which appeared to come from her very heart. "And yet, he seems to be getting some kind of power over me. He follows me about with his eyes, prying into my mind, and I feel that he is beginning to be able to read it. I can bear no more. Father, father, for God's sake, take me away from this hateful hill and its gold and its dead, and let us get out into the *veld* again together."

"I should be glad enough, dearest," he answered. "I have had plenty of this wild goose chase, which I was so mad as to be led into by the love of wealth. Indeed, I am beginning to believe that if it goes on much longer I shall leave my bones here."

"And if such a dreadful thing as that were to happen, what would become of me, alone with Jacob Meyer?" she asked quietly. "I might even be driven to the same fate as that poor girl two hundred years ago," and she pointed to the cone of rock behind her.

"For Heaven's sake, don't talk like that!" he broke in.

"Why not? One must face things, and it would be better than Jacob Meyer; for who would protect me here?"

Mr. Clifford walked up and down for a few minutes, while his daughter watched him anxiously.

"I can see no plan," he said, stopping opposite her. "We cannot take the wagon even if there are enough oxen left to draw it, for it is his as much as mine, and I am sure that he will never leave this treasure unless he is driven away."

"And I am sure I hope that he will not. But, father, the horses are our own; it was his that died, you remember. We can ride away on them."

He stared at her and answered:

"Yes, we could ride away to our deaths. Suppose they got sick or lame; suppose we meet the Matabele, or could find no game to shoot; suppose one of us fell ill—oh! and a hundred things. What then?"

"Why, then it is just as well to perish in the wilderness as here, where our risks are almost as great. We must take our chance, and trust to God. Perhaps He will be merciful and help us. Listen now, father. Tomorrow is Sunday, when you and I do no work that we can help. Mr. Meyer is a Jew, and he won't waste Sunday. Well now, I will say that I want to go down to the outer wall to fetch some clothes which I left in the wagon, and to take others for the native women to wash, and of course you will come with me. Perhaps he will be deceived, and stay behind, especially as he has been there today. Then we can get the horses and guns and ammunition, and anything else that we can carry in the way of food, and persuade the old Molimo to open the gate for us. You know, the little side gate that cannot be seen from up here, and before Mr. Meyer misses us and comes to look, we shall be twenty miles away, and—horses can't be overtaken by a man on foot."

"He will say that we have deserted him, and that will be true."

"You can leave a letter with the Molimo explaining that it was my fault, that I was getting ill and thought that I should die, and that you knew it would not be fair to ask him to come, and so to lose the treasure, to every halfpenny of which he is welcome when it is found. Oh! father, don't hesitate any longer; say that you will take me away from Mr. Meyer."

"So be it then," answered Mr. Clifford, and as he spoke, hearing a sound, they looked up and saw Jacob approaching them.

Luckily he was so occupied with his own thoughts that he never noted the guilty air upon their faces, and they had time to compose themselves a little. But even thus his suspicions were aroused.

"What are you talking of so earnestly?" he asked.

"We were wondering how you were getting on with the Makalanga," answered Benita, fibbing boldly, "and whether you would persuade them to face the ghosts. Did you?"

"Not I," he answered with a scowl. "Those ghosts are our worst enemies in this place; the cowards swore that they would rather die. I should have liked to take some of them at their word and make ghosts of them; but I remembered the situation and didn't. Don't be afraid, Miss Clifford, I never even lost my temper, outwardly at any rate. Well, there it is; if they won't help us, we must work the harder. I've got a new plan, and we'll begin on it tomorrow."

"Not tomorrow, Mr. Meyer," replied Benita with a smile. "It is Sunday, and we rest on Sunday, you know."

"Oh! I forgot. The Makalanga with their ghosts and you with your Sunday—really I do not know which is the worse. Well, then, I must do my own share and yours too, I suppose," and he turned with a shrug of his shoulders.

CHAPTER 14

The Flight

The next morning, Sunday, Meyer went to work on his new plan. What it was Benita did not trouble to inquire, but she gathered that it had something to do with the measuring out of the chapel cave into squares for the more systematic investigation of each area. At twelve o'clock he emerged for his midday meal, in the course of which he remarked that it was very dreary working in that place alone, and that he would be glad when it was Monday, and they could accompany him. His words evidently disturbed Mr. Clifford not a little, and even excited some compunction in the breast of Benita.

What would his feelings be, she wondered, when he found that they had run away, leaving him to deal with their joint undertaking single-handed! Almost was she minded to tell him the whole truth; yet—and this was a curious evidence of the man's ascendancy over her—she did not. Perhaps she felt that to do so would be to put an end to their scheme, since then by argument, blandishments, threats, force, or appeal to their sense of loyalty, it mattered not which, he would bring about its abandonment. But she wanted to fulfil that scheme, to be free of Bambatse, its immemorial ruins, its graveyard cave, and the ghoul, Jacob Meyer, who could delve among dead bones and in living hearts with equal skill and insight, and yet was unable to find the treasure that lay beneath either of them.

So they hid the truth, and talked with feverish activity about other things, such as the drilling of the Makalanga, and the chances of an attack by the Matabele, which happily now seemed to be growing small; also of the conditions of their cattle, and the prospect of obtaining more to replace those that had died. Indeed, Benita went farther; in her new-found zeal of deception she proceeded to act a lie, yes, even with her father's reproachful eyes fixed upon her. Incidentally she mentioned that they were going to have an outing, to climb down the ladder and visit the Makalanga camp between the first and second walls and mix with the great world for a few hours; also to carry their washing to be done there, and bring up some clean clothes and certain books which she had left below.

Jacob came out of his thoughts and calculations, and listened gloomily.

"I have half a mind to come with you," he said, words at which Benita shivered. "It certainly is most cursed lonesome in that cave, and I seem to hear things in it, as though those old bones were rattling, sounds like sighs and whispers too, which are made by the draught."

"Well, why don't you?" asked Benita.

It was a bold stroke, but it succeeded. If he had any doubts they vanished, and he answered at once:

"Because I have not the time. We have to get this business finished one way or another before the wet season comes on, and we are drowned out of the place with rain, or rotted by fever. Take your afternoon out, Miss Clifford; every maid of all work is entitled to as much, and I am afraid that is your billet here. Only," he added, with that care for her safety which he always showed in his more temperate moods, "pray be careful, Clifford, to get back before sundown. That wall is too risky for your daughter to climb in the dusk. Call me from the foot of it; you have the whistle, and I will come down to help her up. I think I'll go with you after all. No, I won't. I made myself so unpleasant to them yesterday that those Makalanga can't wish to see any more of me at present. I hope you will have a more agreeable afternoon than I shall. Why don't you take a ride outside the wall? Your horses are fat and want exercise, and I do not think that you need be afraid of the Matabele." Then without waiting for an answer, he rose and left them.

Mr. Clifford looked after him doubtfully.

"Oh, I know," said Benita, "it seems horribly mean, but one must do shabby things sometimes. Here are the bundles all ready, so let us be off."

Accordingly they went, and from the top of the wall Benita glanced back to bid goodbye to that place which she hoped never to see again. Yet she could not feel as though she looked her last upon it; to her it wore no air of farewell, and even as she descended the perilous stairs, she found herself making mental notes as to how they might best be climbed again. Also, she could not believe that she had done with Mr. Meyer. It seemed to her as though for a long while yet her future would be full of him.

They reached the outer fortifications in safety, and there were greeted with some surprise but with no displeasure by the Makalanga, whom they found still drilling with the rifles, in the use of which a certain number of them appeared to have become fairly proficient. Going to the hut in which the spare goods from the wagon had been stored, they quickly made their preparations. Here also, Mr. Clifford wrote a letter, one of the most unpleasant that he had ever been called upon to compose. It ran thus:

Dear Meyer,

I don't know what you will think of us, but we are escaping from this place. The truth is that I am not well, and my daughter can bear it no longer. She says that if she stops here, she will die, and that hunting for treasure in that ghastly grave-yard is shattering her nerves. I should have liked to tell you, but she begged me not, being convinced that if I did, you would over-persuade us or stop us in some way. As for the gold, if you can find it, take it all. I renounce my share. We are leaving you the wagon and the oxen, and starting down country on our horses. It is a perilous business, but less so than staying here, under the circumstances. If we never meet again we hope that you will forgive us, and wish you all good fortune.—Yours sincerely and with much regret,

T. Clifford

The letter written, they saddled the horses which had been brought up for their inspection, and were found to be in good case, and fastened their scanty belongings, and as many cartridges as they could carry in packs behind their saddles. Then, each of them armed with a rifle—for during their long journeyings Benita had learned to shoot—they mounted and made for the little side-entrance, as the main gate through which they had passed on their arrival was now built up. This side-entrance, a mere slit in the great wall, with a precipitous approach, was open, for now that their fear of the Matabele had to some extent passed off, the Makalanga used it to drive their sheep and goats in and out, since it was so constructed with several twists and turns in the thickness of the wall, that in a few minutes it could be effectually blocked by stones that lay at hand. Also, the ancient architect had arranged it in such a fashion that it was entirely commanded from the crest of the wall on either side.

The Makalanga, who had been watching their proceedings curiously, made no attempt to stop them, although they guessed that they might have a little trouble with the sentries who guarded the entrances all day, and even when it was closed at night, with whom also Mr. Clifford proposed to leave the letter. When they reached the place, however, and had dismounted to lead the horses down the winding passage and the steep ascent upon its further side, it was to find that the only guard visible proved to be the old Molimo himself, who sat there, apparently half asleep.

But as they came he showed himself to be very much awake, for without moving he asked them at once whither they were going.

"To take a ride," answered Mr. Clifford. "The lady, my daughter, is weary of being cooped up in this fortress, and wishes to breathe the air without. Let us pass, friend, or we shall not be back by sunset."

"If you be coming back at sunset, white man, why do you carry so many things upon your packs, and why are your saddle-bags filled with cartridges?" he asked. "Surely you do not speak the truth to me, and you hope that never more will you see the sun set upon Bambatse."

Now understanding that it was hopeless to deceive him, Benita exclaimed boldly:

"It is so; but oh! my Father, stay us not, for fear is behind us, and therefore we fly hence."

"And is there no fear before you, maiden? Fear of the wilderness, where none wander save perchance the Amandabele with their bloody spears; fear of wild beasts and of sickness that may overtake you so that, first one and then the other, you perish there?"

"There is plenty, my Father, but none of them so bad as the fear behind. Yonder place is haunted, and we give up our search and would dwell there no more."

"It is haunted truly, maiden, but its spirits will not harm you whom they welcome as one appointed, and we are ever ready to protect you because of their command that has come to me in dreams. Nor, indeed, is it the spirits whom you fear, but rather the white man, your companion, who would bend you to his will. Deny it not, for I have seen it all."

"Then knowing the truth, surely you will let us go," she pleaded, "for I swear to you that I dare not stay."

"Who am I that I should forbid you?" he asked. "Yet I tell you that you would do well to stay and save yourselves much terror. Maiden, have I not said it days and day ago, that here and here only you must accomplish your fate? Go now if you will, but you shall return again," and once more he seemed to begin to doze in the sun.

The two of them consulted hastily together.

"It is no use turning back now," said Benita, who was almost weeping with doubt and vexation. "I will not be frightened by his vague talk. What can he know of the future more than any of the rest of us? Besides, all he says is that we shall come back again, and if that does happen, at least we shall have been free for a little while. Come, father."

"As you wish," answered Mr. Clifford, who seemed too miserable and depressed to argue. Only he threw down the letter upon the Molimo's lap, and begged him to give it to Meyer when he came to look for them.

The old man took no notice; no, not even when Benita bade him farewell and thanked him for his kindness, praying that all good fortune might attend him and his tribe, did he answer a single word or even look up. So they led their horses down the narrow passage where there was scarcely room for them to pass, and up the steep path beyond. On the further side of the ancient ditch they remounted them while the Makalanga watched them from the walls, and cantered away along the same road by which they had come.

Now this road, or rather track, ran first through the gardens and then among the countless ruined houses that in bygone ages formed the great city whereof the mount Bambatse had been the citadel and sanctuary. The relics of a lost civilization extended for several miles, and were bounded by a steep and narrow neck or pass in the encircling hills, the same that Robert Seymour and his brother had found too difficult for their wagon at the season in which they visited the place some years before. This pass, or port as it is called in South Africa, had been strongly fortified, for on either side of it were the ruins of towers. Moreover, at its crest it was so narrow and steep-sided that a few men posted there, even if they were armed only with bows and arrows, could hold an attacking force in check for a considerable time. Beyond it, after the hill was descended, a bush-clad plain dotted with *kopjes* and isolated granite pillars formed of boulders piled one upon another, rolled away for many miles.

Mr. Clifford and Benita had started upon their mad journey about three o'clock in the afternoon, and when the sun began to set they found themselves upon this plain fifteen or sixteen miles from Bambatse, of which they had long lost sight, for it lay beyond the intervening hills. Near to them was a *kopje*, where they had outspanned by a spring of water when on their recent journey, and since they did not dare to travel in the dark, here they determined to off-saddle, for round this spring was good grass for the horses.

As it chanced, they came upon some hartebeest here which were trekking down to drink, but although they would have been glad of meat, they were afraid to shoot, fearing lest they should attract attention; nor for the same reason did they like to light a fire. So having knee-haltered the horses in such fashion that they could not wander far, and turned them loose to feed, they sat down under a tree, and made some sort of a meal off the biltong and cooked corn which they had brought with them. By the time this was finished darkness fell, for there was little moon, so that nothing remained to do except to sleep within a circle of a few dead thorn-boughs which they had drawn about their camp. This, then, they did, and so weary were they both, that notwithstanding all the emotions through which they had passed, and their fears lest lions should attack them—for of these brutes there were many in this *veld*—rested soundly and undisturbed till within half an hour of dawn.

Rising somewhat chilled, for though the air was warm a heavy dew had soaked their blankets, once more they ate and drank by starlight, while the horses, which they had tied up close to them during the night, filled themselves with grass. At the first break of day they saddled them, and before the sun rose were on their road again. At length up it came, and the sight and warmth of it put new heart into Benita. Her fears seemed to depart with the night, and she said to her father that this successful start was of good augury, to which he only answered that he hoped so.

All that day they rode forward in beautiful weather, not pressing their horses, for now they were sure that Jacob Meyer, who if he followed at all must do so on foot, would never be able to overtake them. At noon they halted, and having shot a small buck, Benita cooked some of it in the one pot that they had brought with them, and they ate a good meal of fresh meat.

Riding on again, towards sundown they came to another of their old camping-places, also a bush-covered *kopje*. Here the spring of water was more than halfway up the hill, so there they off-saddled in a green bower of a place that because of its ferns and mosses looked like a rock garden. Now, although they had enough cold meat for food, they thought themselves quite safe in lighting a fire. Indeed, this it seemed necessary to do, since they had struck the fresh spoor of lions, and even caught sight of one galloping away in the tall reeds on the marshy land at the foot of the hill.

That evening they fared sumptuously upon venison, and as on the previous day lay down to rest in a little "*boma*" or fence made of boughs. But they were not allowed to sleep well this night, for scarcely had they shut their eyes when a hyena began to howl about them. They shouted and the brute went away, but an hour or two later, they heard ominous grunting sounds, followed presently by a loud roar, which was answered by another roar, whereat the horses began to whinny in a frightened fashion.

"Lions!" said Mr. Clifford, jumping up and throwing dead wood on the fire till it burnt to a bright blaze.

After that all sleep became impossible, for although the lions did not attack them, having once winded the horses they would not go away, but continued wandering round the *kopje*, grunting and growling. This went on till abut three o'clock in the morning, when at last the beasts took their departure, for they heard them roaring in the distance. Now that they seemed safe, having first made up the fire, they tried to get some rest.

When, as it appeared to her, Benita had been asleep but a little while, she was awakened by a new noise. It was still dark, but the starlight showed her that the horses were quite quiet; indeed, one of them was lying down, and the other eating some green leaves from the branches of the tree to which it was tethered. Therefore that noise had not come from any wild animal of which they were afraid. She listened intently, and presently heard it again; it was a murmur like to that of people talking somewhere at the bottom of the hill. Then she woke her father and told him, but although once or twice they thought they heard the sound of footsteps, nothing else could be distinguished. Still they rose, and having saddled and bridled the horses as noiselessly as might be, waited for the dawn.

At last it came. Up on the side of the *kopje* they were in clear air, above which shone the red lights of morning, but under them lay billows of dense, pearl-hued mist. By degrees this thinned beneath the rays of the risen sun, and through it, looking gigantic in that light, Benita saw a savage wrapped in a *kaross*, who was walking up and down and yawning, a great spear in his hand.

"Look," she whispered, "look!" and Mr. Clifford stared down the line of her outstretched finger.

"The Matabele," he said. "My God! the Matabele!"

CHAPTER 15

The Chase

The Matabele it was, sure enough; there could be no doubt of it, for soon three other men joined the sentry and began to talk with him, pointing with their great spears at the side of the hill. Evidently they were arranging a surprise when there was sufficient light to carry it out.

"They have seen our fire," whispered her father to Benita; "now, if we wish to save our lives, there is only one thing to do—ride for it before they muster. The *impi* will be camped upon the other side of the hill, so we must take the road we came by."

"That runs back to Bambatse," faltered Benita.

"Bambatse is better than the grave," said her father. "Pray Heaven that we may get there."

To this argument there was no answer, so having drunk a sup of water, and swallowing a few mouthfuls of food as they went, they crept to the horses, mounted them, and as silently as possible began to ride down the hill.

The sentry was alone again, the other three men having departed. He stood with his back towards them. Presently when they were quite close on to him, he heard their horses' hoofs upon the grass, wheeled round at the sound, and saw them. Then with a great shout he lifted his spear and charged.

Mr. Clifford, who was leading, held out his rifle at arm's length—to raise it to his shoulder he had no time—and pulled the trigger. Benita heard the bullet clap upon the hide shield, and next instant saw the Matabele warrior lying on his back, beating the air with his hands and feet. Also, she saw beyond the shoulder of the *kopje*, which they were rounding, hundreds of men marching, and behind them a herd of cattle, the dim light gleaming upon the stabbing spears and on the horns of the oxen. She glanced to the right, and there were more men. The two wings of the *impi* were closing upon them. Only a little lane was left in the middle. They must get through before it shut.

"Come," she gasped, striking the horse with her heel and the butt of her gun, and jerking at its mouth.

Her father saw also, and did likewise, so that the beasts broke into a gallop. Now from the point of each wing sprang out thin lines of men, looking like great horns, or nippers, whose business it was to meet and cut them off. Could they pass between them before they did meet? That was the question, and upon its answer it depended whether or no they had another three minutes to live. To think of mercy at the hands of these bloodthirsty brutes, after they had just killed one of their number before their eyes, was absurd. It was true he had been shot in self-defence; but what count would savages take of that, or of the fact that they were but harmless travellers? White people were not very popular with the Matabele just then, as they knew well; also, their murder in this remote place, with not another of their race within a couple of hundred miles, would never even be reported, and much less avenged. It was as safe as any crime could possibly be.

All this passed through their minds as they galloped towards those closing points. Oh! the horror of it! But two hundred yards to cover, and their fate would be decided. Either they would have escaped at least for a while, or time would be done with them; or, a third alternative, they might be taken prisoners, in all probability a yet more dreadful doom. Even then Benita determined that if she could help it this should not befall her. She had the rifle and the revolver that Jacob Meyer had given her. Surely she would be able to find a moment to use one or the other upon herself. She clenched her teeth, and struck the horse again and again, so that now they flew along. The Matabele soldiers were running their best to catch them, and if these had been given but five seconds of start, caught they must have been. But that short five seconds saved their lives.

When they rushed through them the foremost men of the nippers were not more than twenty yards apart. Seeing that they had passed, these halted and hurled a shower of spears after them. One flashed by Benita's cheek, a line of light; she felt the wind of it. Another cut her dress, and a third struck her father's horse in the near hind leg just above the knee-joint, remaining fast there for a stride or two, and then falling to the ground. At first the beast did not seem to be incommoded by this wound; indeed, it only caused it to gallop quicker, and Benita rejoiced, thinking that it was but a scratch. Then she forgot about it, for some of the Matabele, who had guns, began to shoot them, and although their marksmanship was vile, one or two of the bullets went nearer than was pleasant. Lastly a man, the swiftest runner of them all, shouted after them in Zulu:

"The horse is wounded. We will catch you both before the sun sets."

Then they passed over the crest of a rise and lost sight of them for a while.

"Thank God!" gasped Benita when they were alone again in the silent *veld*; but Mr. Clifford shook his head.

"Do you think they will follow us?" she asked.

"You heard what the fellow said," he answered evasively. "Doubtless they are on their way to attack Bambatse, and have been round to destroy some other wretched tribe, and steal the cattle which we saw. Yes, I fear that they will follow. The question is, which of us can get to Bambatse first."

"Surely we ought to on the horses, father."

"Yes, if nothing happens to them," and as he spoke the words the mare which he was riding dropped sharply upon her hind leg, the same that had been struck with the spear; then recovered herself and galloped on.

"Did you see that?" he asked.

She nodded; then said:

"Shall we get off and look at the cut?"

"Certainly not," he answered. "Our only chance is to keep her moving; if once the wound stiffens, there's an end. The sinew cannot have been severed, or it would have come before now."

So they pushed on.

All that morning did they canter forward wherever the ground was smooth enough to allow them to do so, and notwithstanding the increasing lameness of Mr. Clifford's mare, made such good progress that by midday they reached the place where they had passed the first night after leaving Bambatse. Here sheer fatigue and want of water forced them to stop a little while. They dismounted and drank greedily from the spring, after which they allowed the horses to drink also; indeed it was impossible to keep them away from the water. Then they ate a little, not because they desired food, but to keep up their strength, and while they did so examined the mare. By now her hind leg was much swollen, and blood still ran from the gash made by the *assegai*. Moreover, the limb was drawn up so that the point of the hoof only rested on the ground.

"We must get on before it sets fast," said Mr. Clifford, and they mounted again.

Great heavens! what was this? The mare would not stir. In his despair Mr. Clifford beat it cruelly, whereupon the poor brute hobbled forward a few paces on three legs, and again came to a standstill. Either an injured sinew had given or the inflammation was now so intense that it could not bend its knee. Understanding what this meant to them, Benita's nerve gave out at last, and she burst into weeping.

"Don't cry, love," he said. "God's will be done. Perhaps they have given up the hunt by now; at any rate, my legs are left, and Bambatse is not more than sixteen miles away. Forward now," and holding to her saddle-strap they went up the long, long slope which led to the *poort* in the hills around Bambatse.

They would have liked to shoot the mare, but being afraid to fire a rifle, could not do so. So they left the unhappy beast to its fate, and with it everything it carried, except a few of the cartridges. Before they went, however, at Benita's prayer, her father devoted a few seconds to unbuckling the girths and pulling off the bridle, so that it might have a chance of life. For a little way it hobbled after them on three legs, then, the saddle still upon its back, stood whinnying piteously, till at last, to Benita's intense relief, a turn in their path hid it from their sight.

Half a mile further on she looked round in the faint hope that it might have recovered itself and followed. But no mare was to be seen. Something else was to be seen, however, for there, three or four miles away upon the plain behind them, easy to be distinguished in that dazzling air, were a number of black spots that occasionally seemed to sparkle.

"What are they?" she asked faintly, as one who feared the answer.

"The Matabele who follow us," answered her father, "or rather a company of their swiftest runners. It is their spears that glitter so. Now, my love, this is the position," he went on, as they struggled forward: "those men will catch us before ever we can get to Bambatse; they are trained to run like that, for fifty miles, if need be. But with this start they cannot catch your horse, you must go on and leave me to look after myself."

"Never, never!" she exclaimed.

"But you shall, and you must. I am your father and I order you. As for me, what does it matter? I may hide from them and escape, or— at least I am old, my life is done, whereas yours is before you. Now, goodbye, and go on," and he let go of the saddle-strap.

By way of answer Benita pulled up the horse.

"Not one yard," she said, setting her mouth.

Then he began to storm at her, calling her disobedient, and undutiful, and when this means failed to move her, to implore her almost with tears.

"Father, dear," she said, leaning down towards him as he walked, for now they were going on again, "I told you why I wanted to run away from Bambatse, didn't I?—because I would rather risk my life than stay. Well, do you think that I wish to return there and live in that place alone with Jacob Meyer? Also, I will tell you another thing. You remember about Mr. Seymour? Well, I can't get over that; I can't get over it at all, and therefore, although of course I am afraid, it is all one to me. No, we will escape together, or die together; the first if we can."

Then with a groan he gave up the argument, and as he found breath they discussed their chances. Their first idea was to hide, but save for a few trees all the country was open; there was no place to cover them. They thought of the banks of the Zambesi, but between them and the river rose a bare, rock-strewn hill with several miles of slope. Long before they could reach its crest, even if a horse were able to travel there, they must be overtaken. In short, there was nothing to do except to push for the *nek*, and if they were fortunate enough to reach it before the Matabele, to abandon the horse there and try to conceal themselves among the ruins of the houses beyond. This, perhaps, they might do when once the sun was down.

But they did not deceive themselves; the chances were at least fifty to one against them, unless indeed their pursuers grew weary and let them go.

At present, however, they were by no means weary, for having perceived them from far away, the long-legged runners put on the pace, and the distance between them and their quarry was lessening.

"Father," said Benita, "please understand one thing. I do not mean to be taken alive by those savages."

"Oh! how can I——" he faltered.

"I don't ask you," she answered. "I will see to that myself. Only, if I should make any mistake——" and she looked at him.

The old man was getting very tired. He panted up the steep hillside, and stumbled against the stones. Benita noted it, and slipping from the horse, made him mount while she ran alongside. Then when he was a little rested they changed places again, and so covered several miles of country. Subsequently, when both of them were nearly exhausted, they tried riding together—she in front and he behind, for their baggage had long since been thrown away. But the weary beast could not carry this double burden, and after a few hundred yards of it, stumbled, fell, struggled to its feet again, and stopped.

So once more they were obliged to ride and walk alternately.

Now there was not much more than an hour of daylight left, and the narrow pass lay about three miles ahead of them. That dreadful three miles; ever thereafter it was Benita's favourite nightmare! At the beginning of it the leading Matabele were about two thousand yards behind them; half-way, about a thousand; and at the commencement of the last mile, say five hundred.

Nature is a wonderful thing, and great are its resources in extremity. As the actual crisis approached, the weariness of these two seemed to depart, or at any rate it was forgotten. They no longer felt exhausted, nor, had they been fresh from their beds, could they have climbed or run better. Even the horse seemed to find new energy, and when it lagged Mr. Clifford dug the point of his hunting knife into its flank. Gasping, panting, now one mounted and now the other, they struggled on towards that crest of rock, while behind them came death in the shape of those sleuth-hounds of Matabele. The sun was going down, and against its flaming ball, when they glanced back they could see their dark forms outlined; the broad spears also looked red as though they had been dipped in blood. They could even hear their taunting shouts as they called to them to sit down and be killed, and save trouble.

Now they were not three hundred yards away, and the crest of the pass was still half a mile ahead. Five minutes passed, and here, where the track was very rough, the horse blundered upwards slowly. Mr. Clifford was riding at the time, and Benita running at his side, holding to the stirrup leather. She looked behind her. The savages, fearing that their victims might find shelter over the hill, were making a rush, and the horse could go no faster. One man, a great tall fellow, quite out-distanced his companions. Two minutes more and he was not over a hundred paces from them, a little nearer than they were to the top of the pass. Then the horse stopped and refused to stir any more.

Mr. Clifford jumped from the saddle, and Benita, who could not speak, pointed to the pursuing Matabele. He sat down upon a rock, cocked his rifle, took a deep breath, and aimed and fired at the soldier who was coming on carelessly in the open. Mr. Clifford was a good shot, and shaken though he was, at this supreme moment his skill did not fail him. The man was struck somewhere, for he staggered about and fell; then slowly picked himself up, and began to hobble back towards his companions, who, when they met him, stopped a minute to give him some kind of assistance.

That halt proved their salvation, for it gave them time to make one last despairing rush, and gain the brow of the *poort*. Not that this would have saved them, however, since where they could go the Matabele could follow, and there was still light by which the pursuers would have been able to see to catch them. Indeed, the savages, having laid down the wounded man, came on with a yell of rage, fifty or more of them.

Over the pass father and daughter struggled, Benita riding; after them, perhaps sixty yards away, ran the Matabele, gathered in a knot now upon the narrow, ancient road, bordered by steep hillsides.

Then suddenly from all about them, as it appeared to Benita, broke out the blaze and roar of rifles, rapid and continuous. Down went the Matabele by twos and threes, till at last it seemed as though but quite a few of them were left upon their feet, and those came on no more; they turned and fled from the neck of the narrow pass to the open slope beyond.

Benita sank to the ground, and the next thing that she could remember was hearing the soft voice of Jacob Meyer, who said:

"So you have returned from your ride, Miss Clifford, and perhaps it was as well that the thought came from you to me that you wished me to meet you here in this very place."

CHAPTER 16

Back at Bambatse

How they reached Bambatse Benita never could remember, but afterwards she was told that both she and her father were carried upon litters made of ox-hide shields. When she came to her own mind again, it was to find herself lying in her tent outside the mouth of the cave within the third enclosure of the temple-fortress. Her feet were sore and her bones ached, physical discomforts that brought back to her in a flash all the terrors through which she had passed.

Again she saw the fierce pursuing Matabele; again heard their cruel shouts and the answering crack of the rifles; again, amidst the din and the gathering darkness, distinguished the gentle, foreign voice of Meyer speaking his words of sarcastic greeting. Next oblivion fell upon her, and after it a dim memory of being helped up the hill with the sun pouring on her back and assisted to climb the steep steps of the wall by means of a rope placed around her. Then forgetfulness again.

The flap of her tent was drawn aside and she shrank back upon her bed, shutting her eyes for fear lest they should fall upon the face of Jacob Meyer. Feeling that it was not he, or learning it perhaps from the footfall, she opened them a little, peeping at her visitor from between her long lashes. He proved to be—not Jacob or her father, but the old Molimo, who stood beside her holding in his hand a gourd filled with goat's milk. Then she sat up and smiled at him, for Benita had grown very fond of this ancient man, who was so unlike anyone that she had ever met.

"Greeting, Lady," he said softly, smiling back at her with his lips and dreamy eyes, for his old face did not seem to move beneath its thousand wrinkles. "I bring you milk. Drink; it is fresh and you need food."

So she took the gourd and drank to the last drop, for it seemed to her that she had never tasted anything so delicious.

"Good, good," murmured the Molimo; "now you will be well again."

"Yes, I shall get well," she answered; "but oh! what of my father?"

"Fear not; he is still sick, but he will recover also. You shall see him soon."

"I have drunk all the milk," she broke out; "there is none left for him."

"Plenty, plenty," he answered, waving his thin hand. "There are two cups full—one for each. We have not many she-goats down below, but the best of their milk is saved for you."

"Tell me all that has happened, Father," and the old priest, who liked her to call him by that name, smiled again with his eyes, and squatted down in the corner of the tent.

"You went away, you remember that you would go, although I told you that you must come back. You refused my wisdom and you went, and I have learned all that befell you and how you two escaped the *impi*. Well, that night after sunset, when you did not return, came the Black One—yes, yes, I mean Meyer, whom we name so because of his beard, and," he added deliberately, "his heart. He came running down the hill asking for you, and I gave him the letter.

"He read it, and oh! then he went mad. He cursed in his own tongue; he threw himself about; he took a rifle and wished to shoot me, but I sat silent and looked at him till he grew quiet. Then he asked why I had played him this trick, but I answered that it was no trick of mine who had no right to keep you and your father prisoners against your will, and that I thought you had gone away because you were afraid of him, which was not wonderful if that was how he talked to you. I told him, too, I who am a doctor, that unless he was careful he would go mad; that already I saw madness in his eye; after which he became quiet, for my words frightened him. Then he asked what could be done, and I said—that night, nothing, since you must be far away, so that it would be useless to follow you, but better to go to meet you when you came back. He asked what I meant by your coming back, and I answered that I meant what I said, that you would come back in great haste and peril—although you would not believe me when I told you so—for I had it from the Munwali whose child you are.

"So I sent out my spies, and that night went by, and the next day and night went by, and we sat still and did nothing, though the Black One wished to wander out alone after you. But on the following morning, at the dawn, a messenger came in who reported that it had been called to him by his brethren who were hidden upon hilltops and in other places for miles and miles, that the Matabele *impi*, having destroyed another family of the Makalanga far down the Zambesi, was advancing to destroy us also. And in the afternoon came a second spy, who reported that you two had been surrounded by the *impi*, but had broken through them, and were riding hitherward for your lives. Then I took fifty of the best of our people and put them under the command of Tamas, my son, and sent them to ambush the pass, for against the Matabele warriors on the plain we, who are not warlike, do not dare to fight.

"The Black One went with them, and when he saw how sore was your strait, wished to run down to meet the Matabele, for he is a brave man. But I had said to Tamas—'No, do not try to fight them in the open, for there they will certainly kill you.' Moreover, Lady, I was sure that you would reach the top of the *poort*. Well, you reached it, though but by the breadth of a blade of grass, and my children shot with the new rifles, and the place being narrow so that they could not miss, killed many of those hyenas of Amandabele. But to kill Matabele is like catching fleas on a dog's back: there are always more. Still it served its turn, you and your father were brought away safely, and we lost no one."

"Where, then, are the Matabele now?" asked Benita.

"Outside our walls, a whole regiment of them: three thousand men or more, under the command of the Captain Maduna, he of the royal blood, whose life you begged, but who nevertheless hunted you like a buck."

"Perhaps he did not know who it was," suggested Benita.

"Perhaps not," the Molimo answered, rubbing his chin, "for in such matters even a Matabele generally keeps faith, and you may remember he promised you life for life. However, they are here ravening like lions round the walls, and that is why we carried you up to the top of the hill, that you might be safe from them."

"But are you safe, my Father?"

"I think so," he replied with a dry little chuckle in his throat. "Whoever built this fortress built it strong, and we have blocked the gates. Also, they caught no one outside; all are within the walls, together with the sheep and goats. Lastly, we have sent most of the women and children across the Zambesi in canoes, to hide in places we know of whither the Amandabele cannot follow, for they dare not swim a river. Therefore, for those of us that remain we have food for three months, and before then the rains will drive the *impi* out."

"Why did you not all go across the river, Father?"

"For two reasons, Lady. The first is, that if we once abandoned our stronghold, which we have held from the beginning, Lobengula would take it, and keep it, so that we could never re-enter into our heritage, which would be a shame to us and bring down the vengeance of the spirits of our ancestors upon our heads. The second is, that as you have returned to us we stay to protect you."

"You are very good to me," murmured Benita.

"Nay, nay, we brought you here, and we do what I am told to do from Above. Trouble may still come upon you; yes, I think that it will come, but once more I pray you, have no fear, for out of this evil root shall spring a flower of joy," and he rose to go.

"Stay," said Benita. "Has the chief Meyer found the gold?"

"No; he has found nothing; but he hunts and hunts like a hungry jackal digging for a bone. But that bone is not for him; it is for you, Lady, you and you only. Oh! I know, you do not seek, still you shall find. Only the next time that you want help, do not run away into the wilderness. Hear the word of Munwali given by his mouth, the Molimo of Bambatse!" And as he spoke, the old priest backed himself out of the tent, stopping now and again to bow to Benita.

A few minutes later her father entered, looking very weak and shaken, and supporting himself upon a stick. Happy was the greeting of these two who, with their arms about each other's neck, gave thanks for their escape from great peril.

"You see, Benita, we can't get away from this place," Mr. Clifford said presently. "We must find that gold."

"Bother the gold," she answered with energy; "I hate its very name. Who can think of gold with three thousand Matabele waiting to kill us?"

"Somehow I don't feel afraid of them any more," said her father; "they have had their chance and lost it, and the Makalanga swear that now they have guns to command the gates, the fortress cannot be stormed. Still, I am afraid of someone."

"Who?"

"Jacob Mayer. I have seen him several times, and I think that he is going mad."

"The Molimo said that too, but why?"

"From the look of him. He sits about muttering and glowing with those dark eyes of his, and sometimes groans, and sometimes bursts into shouts of laughter. That is when the fit is on him, for generally he seems right enough. But get up if you think you can, and you shall judge for yourself."

"I don't want to," said Benita feebly. "Father, I am more afraid of him now than ever. Oh! why did you not let me stop down below, among the Makalanga, instead of carrying me up here again, where we must live alone with that terrible Jew?"

"I wished to, dear, but the Molimo said we should be safer above, and ordered his people to carry you up. Also, Jacob swore that unless you were brought back he would kill me. Now you understand why I believe that he is mad."

"Why, why?" gasped Benita again.

"God knows," he answered with a groan; "but I think that he is sure that we shall never find the gold without you, since the Molimo has told him that it is for you and you alone, and he says the old man has second sight, or something of the sort. Well, he would have murdered me—I saw it in his eye—so I thought it better to give in rather than that you should be left here sick and alone. Of course there was one way——" and he paused.

She looked at him and asked:

"What way?"

"To shoot him before he shot me," he answered in a whisper, "for your sake, dear—but I could not bring myself to do it."

"No," she said with a shudder, "not that—not that. Better that we should die than that his blood should be upon our hands. Now I will get up and try to show no fear. I am sure that is best, and perhaps we shall be able to escape somehow. Meanwhile, let us humour him, and pretend to go on looking for this horrible treasure."

So Benita rose to discover that, save for her stiffness, she was but little the worse, and finding all things placed in readiness, set to work with her father's help to cook the evening meal as usual. Of Meyer, who doubtless had placed things in readiness, she saw nothing.

Before nightfall he came, however, as she knew he would. Indeed, although she heard no step and her back was towards him, she felt his presence; the sense of it fell upon her like a cold shadow. Turning round she beheld the man. He was standing close by, but above her, upon a big granite boulder, in climbing which his soft *veld schoons*, or hide shoes, had made no noise, for Meyer could move like a cat. The last rays from the sinking sun struck him full, outlining his agile, nervous shape against the sky, and in their intense red light, which flamed upon him, he appeared terrible. He looked like a panther about to spring; his eyes shone like a panther's, and Benita knew that she was the prey whom he desired. Still, remembering her resolution, she determined to show no fear, and addressed him:

"Good-evening, Mr. Meyer. Oh! I am so stiff that I cannot lift my neck to look at you," and she laughed.

He bounded softly from the rock, like a panther again, and stood in front of her.

"You should thank the God you believe in," he said, "that by now you are not stiff indeed—all that the jackals have left of you."

"I do, Mr. Meyer, and I thank you, too; it was brave of you to come out to save us. Father," she called, "come and tell Mr. Meyer how grateful we are to him."

Mr. Clifford hobbled out from his hut under the tree, saying:

"I have told him already, dear."

"Yes," answered Jacob, "you have told me; why repeat yourself? I see that supper is ready. Let us eat, for you must be hungry; afterwards I have something to tell you."

So they ate, with no great appetite, any of them—indeed Meyer touched but little food, though he drank a good deal, first of strong black coffee and afterwards of squareface and water. But on Benita he pressed the choicest morsels that he could find, eyeing her all the while, and saying that she must take plenty of nutriment or her beauty would suffer and her strength wane. Benita bethought her of the fairy tales of her childhood, in which the ogre fed up the princess whom he purposed to devour.

"You should think of your own strength, Mr. Meyer," she said; "you cannot live on coffee and squareface."

"It is all I need tonight. I am astonishingly well since you came back. I can never remember feeling so well, or so strong. I can do the work of three men, and not be tired; all this afternoon, for instance, I have been carrying provisions and other things up that steep wall, for we must prepare for a long siege together; yet I should never know that I had lifted a single basket. But while you were away—ah! then I felt tired."

Benita changed the subject, asking him if he had made any discoveries.

"Not yet, but now that you are back the discoveries will soon come. Do not be afraid; I have my plan which cannot fail. Also, it was lonely working in that cave without you, so I only looked about a little outside till it was time to go to meet you, and shoot some of those Matabele. Do you know?—I killed seven of them myself. When I was shooting for your sake I could not miss," and he smiled at her.

Benita shrank from him visibly, and Mr. Clifford said in an angry voice:

"Don't talk of those horrors before my daughter. It is bad enough to have to do such things, without speaking about them afterwards."

"You are right," he replied reflectively; "and I apologise, though personally I never enjoyed anything so much as shooting those Matabele. Well, they are gone, and there are plenty more outside. Listen! They are singing their evening hymn," and with his long finger he beat time to the volleying notes of the dreadful Matabele war-chant, which floated up from the plain below. "It sounds quite religious, doesn't it? only the words—no, I will not translate them. In our circumstances they are too personal.

"Now I have something to say to you. It was unkind of you to run away and leave me like that, not honourable either. Indeed," he added with a sudden outbreak of the panther ferocity, "had you alone been concerned, Clifford, I tell you frankly that when we met again, I should have shot you. Traitors deserve to be shot, don't they?"

"Please stop talking to my father like that," broke in Benita in a stern voice, for her anger had overcome her fear. "Also it is I whom you should blame."

"It is a pleasure to obey you," he answered bowing; "I will never mention the subject any more. Nor do I blame you—who could?— not Jacob Meyer. I quite understand that you found it very dull up here, and ladies must be allowed their fancies. Also you have come back; so why talk of the matter? But listen: on one point I have made up my mind; for your own sake you shall not go away any more until we leave this together. When I had finished carrying up the food I made sure of that. If you go to look tomorrow morning you will find that no one can come up that wall—and, what is more, no one can go down it. Moreover, that I may be quite certain, in future I shall sleep near the stair myself."

Benita and her father stared at each other.

"The Molimo has a right to come," she said; "it is his sanctuary."

"Then he must celebrate his worship down below for a little while. The old fool pretends to know everything, but he never guessed what I was going to do. Besides, we don't want him breaking in upon our privacy, do we? He might see the gold when we find it, and rob us of it afterwards."

CHAPTER 17

The First Experiment

Again Benita and her father stared at each other blankly, almost with despair. They were trapped, cut off from all help; in the power of a man who was going mad. Mr. Clifford said nothing. He was old and growing feeble; for years, although he did not know it, Meyer had dominated him, and never more so than in this hour of stress and bewilderment. Moreover, the man had threatened to murder him, and he was afraid, not so much for himself as for his daughter. If he were to die now, what would happen to her, left alone with Jacob Meyer? The knowledge of his own folly, understood too late, filled him with shame. How could he have been so wicked as to bring a girl upon such a quest in the company of an unprincipled Jew, of whose past he knew nothing except that it was murky and dubious? He had committed a great crime, led on by a love of lucre, and the weight of it pressed upon his tongue and closed his lips; he knew not what to say.

For a little while Benita was silent also; hope died within her. But she was a bold-spirited woman, and by degrees her courage re-asserted itself. Indignation filled her breast and shone through her dark eyes. Suddenly she turned upon Jacob, who sat before them smoking his pipe and enjoying their discomfiture.

"How dare you?" she asked in a low, concentrated voice. "How dare you, you coward?"

He shrank a little beneath her scorn and anger; then seemed to recover and brace himself, as one does who feels that a great struggle is at hand, upon the issue of which everything depends.

"Do not be angry with me," he answered. "I cannot bear it. It hurts—ah! you don't know how it hurts. Well, I will tell you, and before your father, for that is more honourable. I dare—for your sake."

"For my sake? How can it benefit me to be cooped up in this

horrible place with you? I would rather trust myself with the Maka-langa, or even," she added with bitter scorn, "even with those bloody-minded Matabele."

"You ran away from them very fast a little while ago, Miss Clifford. But you do not understand me. When I said for your sake, I meant for my own. See, now. You tried to leave me the other day and did not succeed. Another time you might succeed, and then—what would happen to me?"

"I do not know, Mr. Meyer," and her eyes added—"I do not care."

"Ah! but I know. Last time it drove me nearly mad; next time I should go quite mad."

"Because you believe that through me you will find this treasure of which you dream day and night, Mr. Meyer——"

"Yes," he interrupted quickly. "Because I believe that in you I shall find the treasure of which I dream day and night, and because that treasure has become necessary to my life."

Benita turned quickly towards her father, who was puzzling over the words, but before either of them could speak Jacob passed his hand across his brow in a bewildered way and said:

"What was I talking of? The treasure, yes, the uncountable treas-ure of pure gold, that lies hid so deep, that is so hard to discover and to possess; the useless, buried treasure that would bring such joy and glory to us both, if only it could be come at and reckoned out, piece by piece, coin by coin, through the long, long years of life."

Again he paused; then went on.

"Well, Miss Clifford, you are quite right; that is why I have dared to make you a prisoner, because, as the old Molimo said, the treasure is yours and I wish to share it. Now, about this treasure, it seems that it can't be found, can it, although I have worked so hard?" and he looked at his delicate, scarred hands.

"Quite so, Mr. Meyer, it can't be found, so you had better let us go down to the Makalanga."

"But there is a way, Miss Clifford, there is a way. You know where it lies, and you can show me."

"If I knew I would show you soon enough, Mr. Meyer, for then you could take the stuff and our partnership would be at an end."

"Not until it is divided ounce by ounce and coin by coin. But first—first you must show me, as you say you will, and as you can."

"How, Mr. Meyer? I am not a magician."

"Ah! but you are. I will tell you how, having your promise. Listen now, both of you. I have studied. I know a great many secret things, and I read in your face that you have the gift—let me look in your eyes a while, Miss Clifford, and you will go to sleep quite gently, and then in your sleep, which shall not harm you at all, you will see where that gold lies hidden, and you will tell us."

"What do you mean?" asked Benita, bewildered.

"I know what he means," broke in Mr. Clifford. "You mean that you want to mesmerize her as you did the Zulu chief."

Benita opened her lips to speak, but Meyer said quickly:

"No, no; hear me first before you refuse. You have the gift, the precious gift of clairvoyance, that is so rare."

"How do you know that, Mr. Meyer? I have never been mesmerized in my life."

"It does not matter how. I do know it; I have been sure of it from the moment when first we met, that night by the *kloof*. Although, perhaps, you felt nothing then, it was that gift of yours working upon a mind in tune, my mind, which led me there in time to save you, as it was that gift of yours which warned you of the disaster about to happen to the ship—oh! I have heard the story from your own lips. Your spirit can loose itself from the body: it can see the past and the future; it can discover the hidden things."

"I do not believe it," answered Benita; "but at least it shall not be loosed by you."

"It shall, it shall," he cried with passion, his eyes blazing on her as he spoke. "Oh! I foresaw all this, and that is why I was determined you should come with us, so that, should other means fail, we might have your power to fall back upon. Well, they have failed; I have been patient, I have said nothing, but now there is no other way. Will you be so selfish, so cruel, as to deny me, you who can make us all rich in an hour, and take no hurt at all, no more than if you had slept awhile?"

"Yes," answered Benita. "I refuse to deliver my will into the keeping of any living man, and least of all into yours, Mr. Meyer."

He turned to her father with a gesture of despair.

"Cannot you persuade her, Clifford? She is your daughter, she will obey you."

"Not in that," said Benita.

"No," answered Mr. Clifford. "I cannot, and I wouldn't if I could. My daughter is quite right. Moreover, I hate this supernatural kind of thing. If we can't find this gold without it, then we must let it alone, that is all."

Meyer turned aside to hide his face, and presently looked up again, and spoke quite softly.

"I suppose that I must accept my answer, but when you talked of any living man just now, Miss Clifford, did you include your father?"

She shook her head.

"Then will you allow him to try to mesmerize you?"

Benita laughed.

"Oh, yes, if he likes," she said. "But I do not think that the operation will be very successful."

"Good, we will see tomorrow. Now, like you, I am tired. I am going to bed in my new camp by the wall," he added significantly.

****

"Why are you so dead set against this business?" asked her father, when he had gone.

"Oh, father!" she answered, "can't you see, don't you understand? Then it is hard to have to tell you, but I must. In the beginning Mr. Meyer only wanted the gold. Now he wants more, me as well as the gold. I hate him! You know that is why I ran away. But I have read a good deal about this mesmerism, and seen it once or twice, and who knows? If once I allow his mind to master my mind, although I hate him so much, I might become his slave."

"I understand now," said Mr. Clifford. "Oh, why did I ever bring you here? It would have been better if I had never seen your face again."

On the morrow the experiment was made. Mr. Clifford attempted to mesmerize his daughter. All the morning Jacob, who, it now appeared, had practical knowledge of this doubtful art, tried to instruct him therein. In the course of the lesson he informed him that for a short period in the past, having great natural powers in that direction, he had made use of them professionally, only giving up the business because he found it wrecked his health. Mr. Clifford remarked that he had never told him that before.

"There are lots of things in my life that I have never told you," replied Jacob with a little secret smile. "For instance, once I mesmerized you, although you did not know it, and that is why you always have to do what I want you to, except when your daughter is near you, for her influence is stronger than mine."

Mr. Clifford stared at him.

"No wonder Benita won't let you mesmerize her," he said shortly.

Then Jacob saw his mistake.

"You are more foolish than I thought," he said. "How could I mesmerize you without your knowing it? I was only laughing at you."

"I didn't see the laugh," replied Mr. Clifford uneasily, and they went on with the lesson.

That afternoon it was put to proof—in the cave itself, where Meyer seemed to think that the influences would be propitious. Benita, who found some amusement in the performance, was seated upon the stone steps underneath the crucifix, one lamp on the altar and others one each side of her.

In front stood her father, staring at her and waving his hands mysteriously in obedience to Jacob's directions. So ridiculous did he look indeed while thus engaged that Benita had the greatest difficulty in preventing herself from bursting into laughter. This was the only effect which his grimaces and gesticulations produced upon her, although outwardly she kept a solemn appearance, and even from time to time shut her eyes to encourage him. Once, when she opened them again, it was to perceive that he was becoming very hot and exhausted, and that Jacob was watching him with such an unpleasant intentness that she re-closed her eyes that she might not see his face.

It was shortly after this that of a sudden Benita did feel something, a kind of penetrating power flowing upon her, something soft and subtle that seemed to creep into her brain like the sound of her mother's lullaby in the dim years ago. She began to think that she was a lost traveller among alpine snows wrapped round by snow, falling, falling in ten myriad flakes, every one of them with a little heart of fire. Then it came to her that she had heard this snow-sleep was dangerous, the last of all sleeps, and that its victims must rouse themselves, or die.

Benita roused herself just in time—only just, for now she was being borne over the edge of a precipice upon the wings of swans, and beneath her was darkness wherein dim figures walked with lamps where their hearts should be. Oh, how heavy were her eyelids! Surely a weight hung to each of them, a golden weight. There, there, they were open, and she saw. Her father had ceased his efforts; he was rubbing his brow with a red pocket-handkerchief, but behind him, with rigid arms outstretched, his glowing eyes fastened on her face, stood Jacob Meyer. By an effort she sprang to her feet, shaking her head as a dog does.

"Have done with this nonsense," she said. "It tires me," and snatching one of the lamps she ran swiftly down the place.

Benita expected that Jacob Meyer would be very angry with her, and braced herself for a scene. But nothing of the sort happened. A while afterwards she saw the two of them approaching, engaged apparently in amicable talk.

"Mr. Meyer says that I am no mesmerist, love," said her father, "and I can quite believe him. But for all that it is a weary job. I am as tired as I was after our escape from the Matabele."

She laughed and answered:

"To judge by results I agree with you. The occult is not in your line, father. You had better give it up."

"Did you, then, feel nothing?" asked Meyer.

"Nothing at all," she answered, looking him in the eyes. "No, that's wrong, I felt extremely bored and sorry to see my father making himself ridiculous. Grey hairs and nonsense of that sort don't go well together."

"No," he answered. "I agree with you—not of that sort," and the subject dropped.

For the next few days, to her intense relief, Benita heard no more of mesmerism. To begin with, there was something else to occupy their minds. The Matabele, tired of marching round the fortress and singing endless war-songs, had determined upon an assault. From their point of vantage on the topmost wall the three could watch the preparations which they made. Trees were cut down and brought in from a great distance that rude ladders might be fashioned out of them; also spies wandered round reconnoitring for a weak place in the defences. When they came too near the Makalanga fired on them, killing some, so that they retreated to the camp, which they had made in a fold of ground at a little distance. Suddenly it occurred to Meyer that although here the Matabele were safe from the Makalanga bullets, it was commanded from the greater eminence, and by way of recreation he set himself to harass them. His rifle was a sporting Martini, and he had an ample supply of ammunition. Moreover, he was a beautiful marksman, with sight like that of a hawk.

A few trial shots gave him the range; it was a shade under seven hundred yards, and then he began operations. Lying on the top of the wall and resting his rifle upon a stone, he waited until the man who was superintending the manufacture of the ladders came out into the open, when, aiming carefully, he fired. The soldier, a white-bearded savage, sprang into the air, and fell backwards, while his companions stared upwards, wondering whence the bullet had come.

"Pretty, wasn't it?" said Meyer to Benita, who was watching through a pair of field-glasses.

"I dare say," she answered. "But I don't want to see any more," and giving the glasses to her father, she climbed down the wall.

But Meyer stayed there, and from time to time she heard the report of his rifle. In the evening he told her that he had killed six men and wounded ten more, adding that it was the best day's shooting which he could remember.

"What is the use when there are so many?" she asked.

"Not much," he answered. "But it annoys them and amuses me. Also, it was part of our bargain that we should help the Makalanga if they were attacked."

"I believe that you like killing people," she said.

"I don't mind it, Miss Clifford, especially as they tried to kill you."

CHAPTER 18

The Other Benita

At irregular times, when he had nothing else to do, Jacob went on with his man-shooting, in which Mr. Clifford joined him, though with less effect. Soon it became evident that the Matabele were very much annoyed by the fatal accuracy of this fire. Loss of life they did not mind in the abstract, but when none of them knew but that their own turn might come next to perish beneath these downward plunging bullets, the matter wore a different face to them. To leave their camp was not easy, since they had made a thorn *boma* round it, to protect them in case the Makalanga should make a night sally; also they could find no other convenient spot. The upshot of it all was to hurry their assault, which they delivered before they had prepared sufficient ladders to make it effective.

At the first break of dawn on the third day after Mr. Clifford's attempt at mesmerism, Benita was awakened by the sounds of shouts and firing. Having dressed herself hastily, she hurried in the growing light towards that part of the wall from below which the noise seemed to come, and climbing it, found her father and Jacob already seated there, their rifles in hand.

"The fools are attacking the small gate through which you went out riding, Miss Clifford, the very worst place that they could have chosen, although the wall looks very weak there," said the latter. "If those Makalanga have any pluck they ought to teach them a lesson."

Then the sun rose and they saw companies of Matabele, who carried ladders in their hands, rushing onwards through the morning mist till their sight of them was obstructed by the swell of the hill. On these companies the two white men opened fire, with what result they could not see in that light. Presently a great shout announced that the enemy had gained the fosse and were setting up the ladders. Up to this time the Makalanga appeared to have done nothing, but now they began to fire rapidly from the ancient bastions which commanded the entrance the *impi* was striving to storm, and soon through the thinning fog they perceived wounded Matabele staggering and crawling back towards their camp. Of these, the light now better, Jacob did not neglect to take his toll.

Meanwhile, the ancient fortress rang with the hideous tumult of the attack. It was evident that again and again, as their fierce war-shouts proclaimed, the Matabele were striving to scale the wall, and again and again were beaten back by the raking rifle fire. Once a triumphant yell seemed to announce their success. The fire slackened and Benita grew pale with fear.

"The Makalanga cowards are bolting," muttered Mr. Clifford, listening with terrible anxiety.

But if so their courage came back to them, for presently the guns cracked louder and more incessant than before, and the savage cries of "Kill! Kill! Kill!" dwindled and died away. Another five minutes and the Matabele were in full retreat, bearing with them many dead and wounded men upon their backs or stretched out on the ladders.

"Our Makalanga friends should be grateful to us for those hundred rifles," said Jacob as he loaded and fired rapidly, sending his bullets wherever the clusters were thickest. "Had it not been for them their throats would have been cut by now," he added, "for they could never have stopped those savages with the spear."

"Yes, and ours too before nightfall," said Benita with a shudder, for the sight of this desperate fray and fear of how it might end had sickened her. "Thank Heaven, it is over! Perhaps they will give up the siege and go away."

But, notwithstanding their costly defeat, for they had lost over a hundred men, the Matabele, who were afraid to return to Buluwayo except as victors, did nothing of the sort. They only cut down a quantity of reeds and scrub, and moved their camp nearly to the banks of the river, placing it in such a position that it could no longer be searched by the fire of the two white men. Here they sat themselves down sullenly, hoping to starve out the garrison or to find some other way of entering the fortress.

Now Meyer's shooting having come to an end for lack of men to shoot at, since the enemy exposed themselves no more, he was again able to give his full attention to the matter of the treasure hunt.

As nothing could be found in the cave he devoted himself to the outside enclosure which, it may be remembered, was grown over with grass and trees and crowded with ruins. In the most important of these ruins they began to dig somewhat aimlessly, and were rewarded by finding a certain amount of gold in the shape of beads and ornaments, and a few more skeletons of ancients. But of the Portuguese hoard there was no sign. Thus it came about that they grew gloomier day by day, till at last they scarcely spoke to each other. Jacob's angry disappointment was written on his face, and Benita was filled with despair, since to escape from their gaoler above and the Matabele below seemed impossible. Moreover, she had another cause for anxiety.

The ill-health which had been threatening her father for a long while now fell upon him in earnest, so that of a sudden he became a very old man. His strength and energy left him, and his mind was so filled with remorse for what he held to be his crime in bringing his daughter to this awful place, and with terror for the fate that threatened her, that he could think of nothing else. In vain did she try to comfort him. He would only wring his hands and groan, praying that God and she would forgive him. Now, too, Meyer's mastery over him became continually more evident. Mr. Clifford implored the man, almost with tears, to unblock the wall and allow them to go down to the Makalanga. He even tried to bribe him with the offer of all his share of the treasure, if it were found, and when that failed, of his property in the Transvaal.

But Jacob only told him roughly not to be a fool, as they had to see the thing through together. Then he would go again and brood by himself, and Benita noticed that he always took his rifle or a pistol with him. Evidently he feared lest her father should catch him unprepared, and take the law into his own hands by means of a sudden bullet.

One comfort she had, however: although he watched her closely, the Jew never tried to molest her in any way, not even with more of his enigmatic and amorous speeches. By degrees, indeed, she came to believe that all this was gone from his mind, or that he had abandoned his advances as hopeless.

A week passed since the Matabele attack, and nothing had happened. The Makalanga took no notice of them, and so far as she was aware the old Molimo never attempted to climb the blocked wall or otherwise to communicate with them, a thing so strange that, knowing his affection for her, Benita came to the conclusion that he must be dead, killed perhaps in the attack. Even Jacob Meyer had abandoned his digging, and sat about all day doing nothing but think.

Their meal that night was a miserable affair, since in the first place provisions were running short and there was little to eat, and in the second no one spoke a word. Benita could swallow no food; she was weary of that sun-dried trek-ox, for since Meyer had blocked the wall they had little else. But by good fortune there remained plenty of coffee, and of this she drank two cups, which Jacob prepared and handed to her with much politeness. It tasted very bitter to her, but this, Benita reflected, was because they lacked milk and sugar. Supper ended, Meyer rose and bowed to her, muttering that he was going to bed, and a few minutes later Mr. Clifford followed his example. She went with her father to the hut beneath the tree, and having helped him to remove his coat, which now he seemed to find difficulty in doing for himself, bade him good-night and returned to the fire.

It was very lonely there in the silence, for no sound came from either the Matabele or the Makalanga camps, and the bright moonlight seemed to people the place with fantastic shadows that looked alive. Benita cried a little now that her father could not see her, and then also sought refuge in bed. Evidently the end, whatever it might be, was near, and of it she could not bear to think. Moreover, her eyes were strangely heavy, so much so that before she had finished saying her prayers sleep fell upon her, and she knew no more.

Had she remained as wakeful as it was often her fate to be during those fearful days, towards midnight she might have heard some light-footed creature creeping to her tent, and seen that the moonrays which flowed through the gaping and ill-closed flap were cut off by the figure of a man with glowing eyes, whose projected arms waved over her mysteriously. But Benita neither heard nor saw. In her drugged rest she did not know that her sleep turned gradually to a magic swoon. She had no knowledge of her rising, or of how she threw her thick cloak about her, lit her lamp, and, in obedience to that beckoning finger, glided from the tent. She never heard her father stumble from his hut, disturbed by the sound of footsteps, or the words that passed between him and Jacob Meyer, while, lamp in hand, she stood near them like a strengthless ghost.

"If you dare to wake her," hissed Jacob, "I tell you that she will die, and afterwards you shall die," and he fingered the pistol at his belt. "No harm shall come to her—I swear it! Follow and see. Man, man, be silent; our fortunes hang on it."

Then, overcome also by the strange fierceness of that voice and gaze, he followed.

On they go to the winding neck of the cavern, first Jacob walking backwards like the herald of majesty; then majesty itself in the shape of this long-haired, death-like woman, cloaked and bearing in her hand the light; and last, behind, the old, white-bearded man, like Time following Beauty to the grave. Now they were in the great cavern, and now, avoiding the open tombs, the well mouth and the altar, they stood beneath the crucifix.

"Be seated," said Meyer, and the entranced Benita sat herself down upon the steps at the foot of the cross, placing the lamp on the rock pavement before her, and bowing her head till her hair fell upon her naked feet and hid them. He held his hands above her for a while, then asked:

"Do you sleep?"

"I sleep," came the strange, slow answer.

"Is your spirit awake?"

"It is awake."

"Command it to travel backwards through the ages to the beginning, and tell me what you see here."

"I see a rugged cave and wild folk dwelling in it; an old man is dying yonder," and she pointed to the right; "and a black woman with a babe at her breast tends him. A man, it is her husband, enters the cave. He holds a torch in one hand, and with the other drags a buck."

"Cease," said Meyer. "How long is this ago?"

"Thirty-three thousand two hundred and one years," came the answer, spoken without any hesitation.

"Pass on," he said, "pass on thirty thousand years, and tell me what you see."

For a long while there was silence.

"Why do you not speak?" he asked.

"Be patient; I am living through those thirty thousand years; many a life, many an age, but none may be missed."

Again there was silence for a long while, till at length she spoke:

"They are done, all of them, and now three thousand years ago I see this place changed and smoothly fashioned, peopled by a throng of worshippers clad in strange garments with clasps upon them. Behind me stands the graven statue of a goddess with a calm and cruel face, in front of the altar burns a fire, and on the altar white-robed priests are sacrificing an infant which cries aloud."

"Pass on, pass on," Meyer said hurriedly, as though the horror of that scene had leapt to his eyes. "Pass on two thousand seven hundred years and tell me what you see."

Again there was a pause, while the spirit he had evoked in the body of Benita lived through those ages. Then slowly she answered:

"Nothing, the place is black and desolate, only the dead sleep beneath its floor."

"Wait till the living come again," he commanded; "then speak."

"They are here," she replied presently. "Tonsured monks, one of whom fashions this crucifix, and their followers who bow before the Host upon the altar. They come, they go—of whom shall I tell you?"

"Tell me of the Portuguese; of those who were driven here to die."

"I see them all," she answered, after a pause. "Two hundred and three of them. They are ragged and way-worn and hungry. Among them is a beautiful woman, a girl. She draws near to me, she enters into me. You must ask her,"—this was spoken in a very faint voice—"I am I no more."

Mr. Clifford attempted to interrupt, but fiercely Meyer bade him to be silent.

"Speak," he commanded, but the crouching figure shook her head.

"Speak," he said again, whereon another voice, not that of Benita, answered in another tongue:

"I hear; but I do not understand your language."

"Great Heaven!" said Meyer, "it is Portuguese," and for a while the terror of the thing struck him dumb, for he was aware that Benita knew no Portuguese. He knew it, however, who had lived at Lorenço Marquez.

"Who are you?" he asked in that tongue.

"I am Benita da Ferreira. I am the daughter of the Captain da Ferreira and of his wife, the lady Christinha, who stand by you now. Turn, and you will see them."

Jacob started and looked about him uneasily.

"What did she say? I did not catch it all," asked Mr. Clifford.

He translated her words.

"But this is black magic," exclaimed the old man. "Benita knows no Portuguese, so how comes she to speak it?"

"Because she is no longer our Benita; she is another Benita, Benita da Ferreira. The Molimo was right when he said that the spirit of the dead woman went with her, as it seems the name has gone," he added.

"Have done," said Mr. Clifford; "the thing is unholy. Wake her up, or I will."

"And bring about her death. Touch or disturb her, and I tell you she will die," and he pointed to Benita, who crouched before them so white and motionless that indeed it seemed as though already she were dead. "Be quiet," he went on. "I swear to you that no hurt shall come to her, also that I will translate everything to you. Promise, or I will tell you nothing, and her blood be on your head."

Then Mr. Clifford groaned and said:

"I promise."

"Tell me your story, Benita da Ferreira. How came you and your people here?"

"The tribes of Monomotapa rose against our rule. They killed many of us in the lower land, yes, they killed my brother and him to whom I was affianced. The rest of us fled north to this ancient fortress, hoping thence to escape by the river, the Zambesi. The Mambo, our vassal, gave us shelter here, but the tribes besieged the walls in thousands, and burnt all the boats so that we could not fly by the water. Many times we beat them back from the wall; the ditch was full of their dead, and at last they dared to attack no more.

"Then we began to starve and they won the first wall. We went on starving and they won the second wall, but the third wall they could not climb. So we died; one by one we laid ourselves down in this cave and died, till I alone was left, for while our people had food they gave it to me who was the daughter of their captain. Yes, alone I knelt at the foot of this crucifix by the body of my father, praying to the blessed Son of Mary for the death that would not come, and kneeling there I swooned. When I awoke again the Mambo and his men stood about me, for now, knowing us to be dead, the tribes had gone, and those who were in hiding across the river had returned and knew how to climb the wall. They bore me from among the dead, they gave me food so that my strength came back; but in the night I, who in my wickedness would not live, escaped from them and climbed the pillar of black rock, so that when the sun rose they saw me standing there. They begged of me to come down, promising to protect me, but I said 'No,' who in the evil of my heart only desired to die, that I might join my father and my brother, and one who was dearer to me than all. They asked of me where the great treasure was hidden."

At these words Jacob gasped, then rapidly translated them, while the figure before them became silent, as though it felt that for the moment the power of his will was withdrawn.

"Speak on, I bid you," he said, and she continued, the rich, slow voice dropping word after word from the lips of Benita in the alien speech that this Benita never knew.

"I answered that it was where it was, and that if they gave it up to any save the one appointed, then that fate which had befallen my people would befall theirs also. Yes, I gave it into their keeping until I came again, since with his dying breath my father had commanded me to reveal it to none, and I believed that I who was about to die should never come again.

386

"Then I made my last prayer, I kissed the golden crucifix that now hangs upon this breast wherein I dwell," and the hand of the living Benita was lifted, and moving like the hand of a dead thing, slowly drew out the symbol from beneath the cloak, held it for a moment in the lamplight, and let it fall to its place again. "I put my hands before my eyes that I might not see, and I hurled myself from the pinnacle."

Now the voice ceased, but from the lips came a dreadful sound, such as might be uttered by one whose bones are shattered upon rocks, followed by other sounds like those of one who chokes in water. They were so horrible to hear that Mr. Clifford nearly fainted, and even Jacob Meyer staggered and turned white as the white face of Benita.

"Wake her! For God's sake, wake her!" said her father. "She is dying, as that woman died hundreds of years ago."

"Not till she has told us where the gold is. Be quiet, you fool. She does not feel or suffer. It is the spirit within her that lives through the past again."

Once more there was silence. It seemed as though the story were all told and the teller had departed.

"Benita da Ferreira," said Meyer at length, "I command you, tell me, are you dead?"

"Oh! would that I were dead, as my body is dead!" wailed the lips of Benita. "Alas! I cannot die who suffer this purgatory, and must dwell on here alone until the destined day. Yes, yes, the spirit of her who was Benita da Ferreira must haunt this place in solitude. This is her doom, to be the guardian of that accursed gold which was wrung from the earth by cruelty and paid for with the lives of men."

"Is it still safe?" whispered Jacob.

"I will look;" then after a pause, "I have looked. It is there, every grain of it, in ox-hide bags; only one of them has fallen and burst, that which is black and red."

"Where is it?" he said again.

"I may not tell you; never, never."

"Is there anyone whom you may tell?"

"Yes."

"Whom?"

"Her in whose breast I lie."

"Tell her then."

"I have told her; she knows."

"And may she tell me?"

"Let her guard the secret as she will. O my Guardian, I thank thee. My burden is departed; my sin of self-murder is atoned."

"Benita da Ferreira, are you gone?"

No answer.

"Benita Clifford, do you hear me?"

"I hear you," said the voice of Benita, speaking in English, although Jacob, forgetting, had addressed her in Portuguese.

"Where is the gold?"

"In my keeping."

"Tell me, I command you."

But no words came; though he questioned her many times no words came, till at last her head sank forward upon her knees, and in a faint voice she murmured:

"Loose me, or I die."

CHAPTER 19

The Awaking

Still Jacob Meyer hesitated. The great secret was unlearned, and, if this occasion passed, might never be learned. But if he hesitated, Mr. Clifford did not. The knowledge of his child's danger, the sense that her life was mysteriously slipping away from her under pressure of the ghastly spell in which she lay enthralled, stirred him to madness. His strength and manhood came back to him. He sprang straight at Meyer's throat, gripped it with one hand, and with the other drew the knife he wore.

"You devil!" he gasped. "Wake her or you shall go with her!" and he lifted the knife.

Then Jacob gave in. Shaking off his assailant he stepped to Benita, and while her father stood behind him with the lifted blade, began to make strange upward passes over her, and to mutter words of command. For a long while they took no effect; indeed, both of them were almost sure that she was gone. Despair gripped her father, and Meyer worked at his black art so furiously that the sweat burst out upon his forehead and fell in great drops to the floor.

Oh, at last, at last she stirred! Her head lifted itself a little, her breast heaved.

"Lord in Heaven, I have saved her!" muttered Jacob in German, and worked on.

Now the eyes of Benita opened, and now she stood up and sighed. But she said nothing; only like a person walking in her sleep, she began to move towards the entrance of the cave, her father going before her with the lamp. On she went, and out of it straight to her tent, where instantly she cast herself upon her bed and sank into deep slumber. It was as though the power of the drug-induced oblivion, which for a while was over-mastered by that other stronger power invoked by Jacob, had reasserted itself.

Meyer watched her for awhile; then said to Mr. Clifford:

"Don't be afraid and don't attempt to disturb her. She will wake naturally in the morning."

"I hope so for both our sakes," he answered, glaring at him, "for if not, you or I, or the two of us, will never see another."

Meyer took no notice of his threats; indeed the man seemed so exhausted that he could scarcely stand.

"I am done," he said. "Now, as she is safe, I don't care what happens to me. I must rest," and he staggered from the tent, like a drunken man.

Outside, at the place where they ate, Mr. Clifford heard him gulping down raw gin from the bottle. Then he heard no more.

All the rest of the night, and for some hours of the early morning, did her father watch by the bed of Benita, although, lightly clad as he was, the cold of dawn struck to his bones. At length, when the sun was well up, she rose in her bed, and her eyes opened.

"What are you doing here, father?" she said.

"I have come to see where you were, dear. You are generally out by now."

"I suppose that I must have overslept myself then," she replied wearily. "But it does not seem to have refreshed me much, and my head aches. Oh! I remember," she added with a start. "I have had such a horrid dream."

"What about?" he asked as carelessly as he could.

"I can't recall it quite, but it had to do with Mr. Meyer," and she shivered. "It seemed as though I had passed into his power, as though he had taken possession of me, body and soul, and forced me to tell him all the secret things."

"What secret things, Benita?"

She shook her head.

"I don't know now, but we went away among dead people, and I told him there. Oh! father, I am afraid of that man—terribly afraid! Protect me from him," and she began to cry a little.

"Of course I will protect you, dear. Something has upset your nerves. Come, dress yourself and you'll soon forget it all. I'll light the fire."

A quarter of an hour later Benita joined him, looking pale and shaken, but otherwise much as usual. She was ravenously hungry, and ate of the biscuits and dried meat with eagerness.

"The coffee tastes quite different from that which I drank last night," she said. "I think there must have been something in it which gave me those bad dreams. Where is Mr. Meyer? Oh, I know!" and again she put her hand to her head. "He is still asleep by the wall."

"Who told you that?"

"I can't say, but it is so. He will not come here till one o'clock. There, I feel much better now. What shall we do, father?"

"Sit in the sun and rest, I think, dear."

"Yes, let us do that, on the top of the wall. We can see the Makalanga from there, and it will be a comfort to be sure that there are other human beings left in the world besides ourselves and Jacob Meyer."

So presently they went, and from the spot whence Meyer used to shoot at the Matabele camp, looked down upon the Makalanga moving about the first enclosure far below. By the aid of the glasses Benita even thought that she recognised Tamas, although of this it was difficult to be sure, for they were all very much alike. Still, the discovery quite excited her.

"I am sure it is Tamas," she said. "And oh! how I wish that we were down there with him, although it is true that then we should be nearer to the Matabele. But they are better than Mr. Meyer, much better."

Now for a while they were silent, till at length she said suddenly:

"Father, you are keeping something back from me, and things begin to come back. Tell me; did I go anywhere last night with Mr. Meyer—you and he and I together?"

He hesitated and looked guilty; Mr. Clifford was not a good actor.

"I see that we did; I am sure that we did. Father, tell me. I must know, I will know."

Then he gave way.

"I didn't want to speak, dear, but perhaps it is best. It is a very strange story. Will you promise not to be upset?"

"I will promise not to be more upset than I am at present," she answered, with a sad little laugh. "Go on."

"You remember that Jacob Meyer wanted to mesmerize you?"

"I am not likely to forget it," she answered.

"Well, last night he did mesmerize you."

"What?" she said. "*What?* Oh! how dreadful! Now I understand it all. But when?"

"When you were sound asleep, I suppose. At least, the first I knew of it was that some noise woke me, and I came out of the hut to see you following him like a dead woman, with a lamp in your hand."

Then he told her all the story, while she listened aghast.

"How dared he!" she gasped, when her father had finished the long tale. "I hate him; I almost wish that you had killed him," and she clenched her little hands and shook them in the air.

"That is not very Christian of you, Miss Clifford," said a voice behind her. "But it is past one o'clock, and as I am still alive I have come to tell you that it is time for luncheon."

Benita wheeled round upon the stone on which she sat, and there, standing amidst the bushes a little way from the foot of the wall, was Jacob Meyer. Their eyes met; hers were full of defiance, and his of conscious power.

"I do not want any luncheon, Mr. Meyer," she said.

"But I am sure that you do. Please come down and have some. Please come down."

The words were spoken humbly, almost pleadingly, yet to Benita they seemed as a command. At any rate, with slow reluctance she climbed down the shattered wall, followed by her father, and without speaking they went back to their camping place, all three of them, Jacob leading the way.

When they had eaten, or made pretence to eat, he spoke.

"I see that your father has told you everything, Miss Clifford, and of that I am glad. As for me, it would have been awkward, who must ask your forgiveness for so much. But what could I do? I knew, as I have always known, that it was only possible to find this treasure by your help. So I gave you something to make you sleep, and then in your sleep I hypnotized you, and—you know the rest. I have great experience in this art, but I have never seen or heard of anything like what happened, and I hope I never shall again."

Hitherto Benita had sat silent, but now her burning indignation and curiosity overcame her shame and hatred.

"Mr. Meyer," she said, "you have done a shameful and a wicked thing, and I tell you at once that I can never forgive you."

"Don't say that. Please don't say that," he interrupted in tones of real grief. "Make allowances for me. I had to learn, and there was no other way. You are a born clairvoyant, one among ten thousand, my art told me so, and you know all that is at stake."

"By which you mean so many ounces of gold, Mr. Meyer."

"By which I mean the greatness that gold can give, Miss Clifford."

"Such greatness, Mr. Meyer, as a week of fever, or a Matabele spear, or God's will can rob you of. But the thing is done, and soon or late the sin must be paid for. Now I want to ask you a question. You believe in nothing; you have told me so several times. You say that there is no such thing as a spirit, that when we die, we die, and there's an end. Do you not?"

"Yes, I do."

"Then tell me, what was it that spoke out of my lips last night, and how came it that I, who know no Portuguese, talked to you in that tongue?"

He shrugged his shoulders.

"You have put a difficult question, but one I think that can be answered. There is no such thing as a spirit, an identity that survives death. But there is such a thing as the subconscious self, which is part of the animating principle of the universe, and, if only its knowledge can be unsealed, knows all that has passed and all that is passing in that universe. One day perhaps you will read the works of my compatriot, Hegel, and there you will find it spoken of."

"You explain nothing."

"I am about to explain, Miss Clifford. Last night I gave to your sub-conscious self—that which knows all—the strength of liberty, so that it saw the past as it happened in this place. Already you knew the story of the dead girl, Benita da Ferreira, and that story you re-enacted, talking the tongue she used as you would have talked Greek or any other tongue, had it been hers. It was not her spirit that animated you, although at the time I called it so for shortness, but your own buried knowledge, tricked out and furnished by the effort of your human imagination. That her name, Benita, should have been yours also is no doubt a strange coincidence, but no more. Also we have no proof that it was so; only what you said in your trance."

"Perhaps," said Benita, who was in no mood for philosophical argument. "Perhaps also one day you will see a spirit, Mr. Meyer, and think otherwise."

"When I see a spirit and know that it is a spirit, then doubtless I shall believe in spirits. But what is the good of talking of such things? I do not seek spirits; I seek Portuguese gold. Now, I am sure you can tell where that gold lies. You would have told us last night, had not your nervous strength failed you, who are unaccustomed to the state of trance. Speaking as Benita da Ferreira, you said that you saw it and described its condition. Then you could, or would, say no more, and it became necessary to waken you. Miss Clifford, you must let me mesmerize you once again for a few minutes only, for then we will waste no time on past histories, and we shall find the gold. Unless, indeed," he added by an afterthought, and looking at her sharply, "you know already where it is; in which case I need not trouble you."

"I do not know, Mr. Meyer. I remember nothing about the gold."

"Which proves my theory. What purported to be the spirit of Benita da Ferreira said that it had passed the secret on to you, but in your waking state you do not know that secret. In fact, she did not pass it on because she had no existence. But in your sub-conscious state you will know. Therefore I must mesmerize you again. Not at once, but in a few days' time, when you have quite recovered. Let us say next Wednesday, three days hence."

"You shall never mesmerize me again, Mr. Meyer."

"No, not while I live," broke in her father, who had been listening to this discussion in silence.

Jacob bowed his head meekly.

"You think so now, but I think otherwise. What I did last night I did against your will, and that I can do again, only much more easily. But I had rather do it with your will, who work not for my own sake only, but for the sake of all of us. And now let us talk no more of the matter, lest we should grow angry." Then he rose and went away.

The next three days were passed by Benita in a state of constant dread. She knew in herself that Jacob Meyer had acquired a certain command over her; that an invincible intimacy had sprung up between them. She was acquainted with his thoughts; thus, before he asked for it, she would find herself passing him some article at table or elsewhere, or answering a question that he was only about to ask. Moreover, he could bring her to him from a little distance. Thus, on two or three occasions when she was wandering about their prison enclosure, as she was wont to do for the sake of exercise, she found her feet draw to some spot—now one place and now another—and when she reached it there before her was Jacob Meyer.

"Forgive me for bringing you here," he would say, smiling after his crooked fashion, and lifting his hat politely, "but I wish to ask you if you have not changed your mind as to being mesmerized?"

Then for a while he would hold her with his eyes, so that her feet seemed rooted to the ground, till at length it was as though he cut a rope by some action of his will and set her free, and, choked with wrath and blind with tears, Benita would turn and run from him as from a wild beast.

But if her days were evil, oh! what were her nights? She lived in constant terror lest he should again drug her food or drink, and, while she slept, throw his magic spell upon her. To protect herself from the first danger she would swallow nothing that had been near him. Now also she slept in the hut with her father, who lay near its door, a loaded rifle at his side, for he had told Jacob outright that if he caught him at his practices he would shoot him, a threat at which the younger man laughed aloud, for he had no fear of Mr. Clifford.

Throughout the long hours of darkness they kept watch alternately, one of them lying down to rest while the other peered and listened. Nor did Benita always listen in vain, for twice at least she heard stealthy footsteps creeping about the hut, and felt that soft and dreadful influence flowing in upon her. Then she would wake her father, whispering, "He is there, I can feel that he is there." But by the time that the old man had painfully dragged himself to his feet—for now he was becoming very feeble and acute rheumatism or some such illness had got hold of him—and crept from the hut, there was no one to be seen. Only through the darkness he would hear the sound of a retreating step, and of low, mocking laughter.

Thus those miserable days went by, and the third morning came, that dreaded Wednesday. Before it was dawn Benita and her father, neither of whom had closed their eyes that night, talked over their strait long and earnestly, and they knew that its crisis was approaching.

"I think that I had better try to kill him, Benita," he said. "I am growing dreadfully weak, and if I put it off I may find no strength, and you will be at his mercy. I can easily shoot him when his back is turned, and though I hate the thought of such a deed, surely I shall be forgiven. Or if not, I cannot help it. I must think of my duty to you, not of myself."

"No, no," she answered. "I will not have it. It would be murder, although he has threatened you. After all, father, I believe that the man is half mad, and not responsible. We must take our chance and trust to God to save us. If He does not," she added, "at the worst I can always save myself," and she touched the pistol which now she wore day and night.

"So be it," said Mr. Clifford, with a groan. "Let us pray for deliverance from this hell and keep our hands clean of blood."

CHAPTER 20

Jacob Meyer Sees a Spirit

For a while they were silent, then Benita said:

"Father, is it not possible that we might escape, after all? Perhaps that stair on the rampart is not so completely blocked that we could not climb over it."

Mr. Clifford, thinking of his stiff limbs and aching back, shook his head and answered:

"I don't know; Meyer has never let me near enough to see."

"Well, why do you not go to look? You know he sleeps till late now, because he is up all night. Take the glasses and examine the top of the wall from inside that old house near by. He will not see or hear you, but if I came near, he would know and wake up."

"If you like, love, I can try, but what are you going to do while I am away?"

"I shall climb the pillar."

"You don't mean——" and he stopped.

"No, no, nothing of that sort. I shall not follow the example of Benita da Ferreira unless I am driven to it; I want to look, that is all. One can see far from that place, if there is anything to see. Perhaps the Matabele are gone now, we have heard nothing of them lately."

So they dressed themselves, and as soon as the light was sufficiently strong, came out of the hut and parted, Mr. Clifford, rifle in hand, limping off towards the wall, and Benita going towards the great cone. She climbed it easily enough, and stood in the little cup-like depression on its dizzy peak, waiting for the sun to rise and disperse the mists which hung over the river and its banks.

Now whatever may have been the exact ceremonial use to which the ancients put this pinnacle, without doubt it had something to do with sun-worship. This, indeed, was proved by the fact that, at any rate at this season of the year, the first rays of the risen orb struck full upon its point. Thus it came about that, as she stood there waiting, Benita of a sudden found herself suffused in light so vivid and intense that, clothed as she was in a dress which had once been white, it must have caused her to shine like a silver image. For several minutes, indeed, this golden spear of fire blinded her so that she could see nothing, but stood quite still, afraid to move, and waiting until, as the sun grew higher, its level rays passed over her. This they did presently, and plunging into the valley, began to drive away the fog. Now she looked down, along the line of the river.

The Matabele camp was invisible, for it lay in a hollow almost at the foot of the fortress. Beyond it, however, was a rising swell of ground; it may have been half a mile from where she stood, and on the crest of it she perceived what looked like a wagon tent with figures moving round it. They were shouting also, for through the silence of the African morn the sound of their voices floated up to her.

As the mist cleared off Benita saw that without doubt it was a wagon, for there stood the long row of oxen, also it had just been captured by the Matabele, for these were about it in numbers. At the moment, however, they appeared to be otherwise occupied, for they were pointing with their spears to the pillar on Bambatse.

Then it occurred to Benita that, placed as she was in that fierce light with only the sky for background, she must be perfectly visible from the plain below, and that it might be her figure perched like an eagle between heaven and earth which excited their interest. Yes, and not theirs only, for now a white man appeared, who lifted what might have been a gun, or a telescope, towards her. She was sure from the red flannel shirt and the broad hat which he wore that he must be a white man, and oh! how her heart yearned towards him, whoever he might be! The sight of an angel from heaven could scarcely have been more welcome to Benita in her wretchedness.

Yet surely she must be dreaming. What should a white man and a wagon be doing in that place? And why had not the Matabele killed him at once? She could not tell, yet they appeared to have no murderous intentions, since they continued to gesticulate and talk whilst he stared upwards with the telescope, if it were a telescope. So things went on for a long time, for meanwhile the oxen were outspanned, until, indeed, more Matabele arrived, who led off the white man, apparently against his will, towards their camp, where he disappeared. Then there was nothing more to be seen. Benita descended the column.

At its foot she met her father, who had come to seek her.

"What is the matter?" he asked, noting her excited face.

"Oh!" she said or rather sobbed, "there is a wagon with a white man below. I saw the Matabele capture him."

"Then I am sorry for the poor devil," answered the father, "for he is dead by now. But what could a white man have been doing here? Some hunter, I suppose, who has walked into a trap."

The face of Benita fell.

"I hoped," she said, "that he might help us."

"As well might he hope that we could help him. He is gone, and there is an end. Well, peace to his soul, and we have our own troubles to think of. I have been to look at that wall, and it is useless to think of climbing it. If he had been a professional mason, Meyer could not have built it up better; no wonder that we have seen nothing more of the Molimo, for only a bird could reach us."

"Where was Mr. Meyer," asked Benita.

"Asleep in a blanket under a little shelter of boughs by the stair. At least, I thought so, though it was rather difficult to make him out in the shadow; at any rate, I saw his rifle set against a tree. Come, let us go to breakfast. No doubt he will turn up soon enough."

So they went, and for the first time since the Sunday Benita ate a hearty meal of biscuits soaked in coffee. Although her father was so sure that by now he must have perished on the Matabele spears, the sight of the white man and his wagon had put new life into her, bringing her into touch with the world again. After all, might it not chance that he had escaped?

All this while there had been no sign of Jacob Meyer. This, however, did not surprise them, for now he ate his meals alone, taking his food from a little general store, and cooking it over his own fire. When they had finished their breakfast Mr. Clifford remarked that they had no more drinking water left, and Benita said that she would go to fetch a pailful from the well in the cave. Her father suggested that he should accompany her, but she answered that it was not necessary as she was quite able to wind the chain by herself. So she went, carrying the bucket in one hand and a lamp in the other.

As she walked down the last of the zigzags leading to the cave, Benita stopped a moment thinking that she saw a light, and then went on, since on turning the corner there was nothing but darkness before her. Evidently she had been mistaken. She reached the well and hung the pail on to the great copper hook, wondering as she did so how many folk had done likewise in the far, far past, for the massive metal of that hook was worn quite thin with use. Then she let the roller run, and the sound of the travelling chain clanked dismally in that vaulted, empty place. At length the pail struck the water, and she began to wind up again, pausing at times to rest, for the distance was long and the chain heavy. The bucket appeared. Benita drew it to the side of the well, and lifted it from the hook, then took up her lamp to be gone.

Feeling or seeing something, which she was not sure, she held the lamp above her head, and by its light perceived a figure standing between her and the entrance to the cave.

"Who are you?" she asked, whereon a soft voice answered out of the darkness, the voice of Jacob Meyer.

"Do you mind standing still for a few minutes, Miss Clifford? I have some paper here and I wish to make a sketch. You do not know how beautiful you look with that light above your head illuminating the shadows and the thorn-crowned crucifix beyond. You know, whatever paths fortune may have led me into, by nature I am an artist, and never in my life have I seen such a picture. One day it will make me famous.

'How statue-like I see thee stand! The agate lamp within thy hand.'

That's what I should put under it; you know the lines, don't you?"

"Yes, Mr. Meyer, but I am afraid you will have to paint your picture from memory, as I cannot hold up this lamp any longer; my arm is aching already. I do not know how you came here, but as you have followed me perhaps you will be so kind as to carry this water."

"I did not follow you, Miss Clifford. Although you never saw me I entered the cave before you to take measurements."

"How can you take measurements in the dark?"

"I was not in the dark. I put out my light when I caught sight of you, knowing that otherwise you would run away, and fate stood me in good stead. You came on, as I willed that you should do. Now let us talk. Miss Clifford, have you changed your mind? You know the time is up."

"I shall never change my mind. Let me pass you, Mr. Meyer."

"No, no, not until you have listened. You are very cruel to me, very cruel indeed. You do not understand that, rather than do you the slightest harm, I would die a hundred times."

"I do not ask you to die; I ask you to leave me alone—a much easier matter."

"But how can I leave you alone when you are a part of me, when—I love you? There, the truth is out, and now say what you will."

Benita lifted the bucket of water; its weight seemed to steady her. Then she put it down again, since escape was impracticable; she must face the situation.

"I have nothing to say, Mr. Meyer, except that *I* do not love *you* or any living man, and I never shall. I thank you for the compliment you have paid me, and there is an end."

"Any living man," he repeated after her. "That means you love a dead man—Seymour, he who was drowned. No wonder that I hated him when first my eyes fell on him years ago, long before you had come into our lives. Prescience, the sub-conscious self again. Well, what is the use of loving the dead, those who no longer have any existence, who have gone back into the clay out of which they were formed and are not, nor evermore shall be? You have but one life; turn, turn to the living, and make it happy."

"I do not agree with you, Mr. Meyer. To me the dead are still living; one day I shall find them. Now let me go."

"I will not let you go. I will plead and wrestle with you as in the old fable my namesake of my own race wrestled with the angel, until at length you bless me. You despise me because I am a Jew, because I have had many adventures and not succeeded; because you think me mad. But I tell you that there is the seed of greatness in me. Give yourself to me and I will make you great, for now I know that it was you whom I needed to supply what is lacking in my nature. We will win the wealth, and together we will rule——"

"Until a few days hence we starve or the Matabele make an end of us. No, Mr. Meyer, no," and she tried to push past him.

He stretched out his arms and stopped her.

"Listen," he said, "I have pleaded with you as man with woman. Now, as you refuse me and as you alone stand between me and madness, I will take another course. I am your master, your will is servant to my will; I bid you obey me."

He fixed his eyes upon hers, and Benita felt her strength begin to fail.

"Ah!" he said, "you are my servant now, and to show it I shall kiss you on the lips; then I shall throw the sleep upon you, and you will tell me what I want to know. Afterwards we can be wed when it pleases me. Oh! do not think that your father will defend you, for if he interferes I shall kill that foolish old man, whom until now I have only spared for your sake. Remember that if you make me angry, I shall certainly kill him, and your father's blood will be on your head. Now I am going to kiss you."

Benita lifted her hand to find the pistol at her waist. It fell back again; she had no strength; it was as though she were paralysed as a bird is paralysed by a snake so that it cannot open its wings and fly away, but sits there awaiting death. She was given over into the hands of this man whom she hated. Could Heaven allow such a thing? she wondered dimly, and all the while his lips drew nearer to her face.

They touched her own, and then, why or wherefore Benita never understood, the spell broke. All his power was gone, she was as she had been, a free woman, mistress of herself. Contemptuously she thrust the man aside, and, not even troubling to run, lifted her pail of water and walked away.

Soon she saw the light again, and joyfully extinguished her lamp. Indeed, the breast of Benita, which should have been so troubled after the scene through which she had passed, strangely enough was filled with happiness and peace. As that glorious sunlight had broken on her eyes, so had another light of freedom arisen in her soul. She was no longer afraid of Jacob Meyer; that coward kiss of his had struck off the shackles which bound her to him. Her mind had been subject to his mind, but now that his physical nature was brought into the play, his mental part had lost its hold upon her.

As she approached the hut she saw her father seated on a stone outside it, since the poor old man was now so weak and full of pain that he could not stand for very long, and seeing, remembered Meyer's threats against him. At the thought all her new-found happiness departed.

She might be safe; she felt sure that she was safe, but how about her father? If Meyer could not get his way probably he would be as good as his word, and kill him. She shivered at the thought, then, recovering herself, walked forward steadily with her bucket of water.

"You have been a long while gone, my love," said Mr. Clifford.

"Yes, father, Mr. Meyer was in the cave, and kept me."

"How did he get there, and what did he want?"

"I don't know how he got there—crept in when we were not looking, I suppose. But as for what he wanted—listen, dear," and word for word she told him what had passed.

Before she had finished, her father was almost choking with wrath.

"The dirty Jew! The villain!" he gasped. "I never dreamed that he would dare to attempt such an outrage. Well, thank Heaven! I can still hold a rifle, and when he comes out——"

"Father," she said gently, "that man is mad. He is not responsible for his actions, and therefore, except in self-defence, you must not think of such a thing. As for what he said about you, I believe it was only an empty threat, and for me you need have no fear, his power over me is gone; it went like a flash when his lips touched me," and she rubbed her own as though to wipe away some stain. "I am afraid of nothing more. I believe—yes, I believe the old Molimo was right, and that all will end well——"

As she was speaking Benita heard a shuffling sound behind her, and turned to learn its cause. Then she saw a strange sight. Jacob Meyer was staggering towards them, dragging one foot after the other through the grass and stones. His face was ghastly pale, his jaw had dropped like that of a dead man, and his eyes were set wide open and full of horror.

"What is the matter with you, man?" asked Mr. Clifford.

"I—I—have seen a ghost," he whispered. "You did not come back into the cave, did you?" he added, pointing at Benita, who shook her head.

"What ghost?" asked Mr. Clifford.

"I don't know, but my lamp went out, and then a light began to shine behind me. I turned, and on the steps of that crucifix I saw a woman kneeling. Her arms clasped the feet of the figure, her forehead rested upon the feet, her long black hair flowed down, she was dressed in white, and the light came from her body and her head. Very slowly she turned and looked at me, and oh, Heaven! that face——" and he put his hand before his eyes and groaned. "It was beautiful; yes, yes, but fearful to see, like an avenging angel. I fled, and the light—only the light—came with me down the cave, even at the mouth of it there was a little. I have seen a spirit, I who did not believe in spirits, I have seen a spirit, and I tell you that not for all the gold in the world will I enter that place again."

Then before they could answer, suddenly as though his fear had got some fresh hold of him, Jacob sprang forward and fled away, crashing through the bushes and leaping from rock to rock like a frightened buck.

Chapter 21

The Message From the Dead

"Meyer always said that he did not believe in spirits," remarked Mr. Clifford reflectively.

"Well, he believes in them now," answered Benita with a little laugh. "But, father, the poor man is mad, that is the fact of it, and we must pay no attention to what he says."

"The old Molimo and some of his people—Tamas, for instance—declared that they have seen the ghost of Benita da Ferreira. Are they mad also, Benita?"

"I don't know, father. Who can say? All these things are a mystery. All I do know is that I have never seen a ghost, and I doubt if I ever shall."

"No, but when you were in that trance something that was not you spoke out of your mouth, which something said that it was your namesake, the other Benita. Well, as you say, we can't fathom these things, especially in a haunted kind of place like this, but the upshot of it is that I don't think we have much more to fear from Jacob."

"I am not so sure, father. Mad people change their moods very suddenly."

As it happened Benita was quite right. Towards suppertime Jacob Meyer reappeared, looking pale and shaken, but otherwise much as usual.

"I had a kind of fit this morning," he explained, "the result of an hallucination which seized me when my light went out in that cave. I remember that I thought I had seen a ghost, whereas I know very well that no such thing exists. I was the victim of disappointment, anxieties, and other still stronger emotions," and he looked at Benita. "Therefore, please forget anything I said or did, and—would you give me some supper?"

Benita did so, and he ate in silence, with some heartiness. When he had finished his food, and swallowed two or three tots of squareface, he spoke again:

"I have come here, where I know I am not welcome, upon business," he said in a calm, matter-of-fact voice. "I am tired of this place, and I think it is time that we attained the object of our journey here, namely, to find the hidden gold. That, as we all know, can only be done in a certain way, through the clairvoyant powers of one of us and the hypnotic powers of another. Miss Clifford, I request that you will allow me to throw you into a state of trance. You have told us everything else, but you have not yet told us where the treasure is hidden, and this it is necessary that we should know."

"And if I refuse, Mr. Meyer?"

"Then I am sorry, but I must take means to compel your obedience. Under those circumstances, much against my will, I shall be obliged"—here his eye blazed out wildly—"to execute your father, whose obstinacy and influence stand between us and splendid fortunes. No, Clifford," he added, "don't stretch out your hand towards that rifle, for I am already covering you with the pistol in my pocket, and the moment your hand touches it I shall fire. You poor old man, do you imagine for a single second that, sick as you are, and with your stiff limbs, you can hope to match yourself against my agility, intellect, and strength? Why, I could kill you in a dozen ways before you could lift a finger against me, and by the God I do not believe in, unless your daughter is more compliant, kill you I will!"

"That remains to be seen, my friend," said Mr. Clifford with a laugh, for he was a brave old man. "I am not certain that the God—whom you do not believe in—will not kill you first."

Now Benita, who had been taking counsel with herself, looked up and said suddenly:

"Very well, Mr. Meyer, I consent—because I must. Tomorrow morning you shall try to mesmerize me, if you can, in the same place, before the crucifix in the cave."

"No," he answered quickly. "It was not there, it was here, and here it shall be again. The spot you mention is unpropitious to me; the attempt would fail."

"It is the spot that I have chosen," answered Benita stubbornly.

"And this is the spot that I have chosen, Miss Clifford, and my will must prevail over yours."

"Because you who do not believe in spirits are afraid to re-enter the cave, Mr. Meyer, lest you should chance——"

"Never mind what I am or am not afraid of," he replied with fury. "Make your choice between doing my will and your father's life. Tomorrow morning I shall come for your answer, and if you are still obstinate, within half an hour he will be dead, leaving you and me alone together. Oh! you may call me wicked and a villain, but it is you who are wicked, you, you, *you* who force me to this deed of justice."

Then without another word he sprang up and walked away from them backwards, as he went covering Mr. Clifford with the pistol which he had drawn from his pocket. The last that they saw of him were his eyes, which glowered at them through the darkness like those of a lion.

"Father," said Benita, when she was sure that he had gone, "that madman really means to murder you; there is no doubt of it."

"None whatever, dear; if I am alive tomorrow night I shall be lucky, unless I can kill him first or get out of his way."

"Well," she said hurriedly, "I think you can. I have an idea. He is afraid to go into that cave, I am sure. Let us hide ourselves there. We can take food and shall have plenty of water, whereas, unless rain falls, he can get nothing to drink."

"But what then, Benita? We can't stop in the dark for ever."

"No, but we can wait there until something happens. Something must and will happen. His disease won't stand still. He may go raving mad and kill himself. Or he may attempt to attack us, though that is not likely, and then we must do what we can in self defence. Or help may reach us from somewhere. At the worst we shall only die as we should have died outside. Come, let us be quick, lest he should change his mind, and creep back upon us."

So Mr. Clifford gave way, knowing that even if he could steel himself to do the deed of attempting to kill Jacob, he would have little chance against that strong and agile man. Such a struggle would only end in his own death, and Benita must then be left alone with Meyer and his insane passions.

Hurriedly they carried their few belongings into the cave. First they took most of the little store of food that remained, the three hand-lamps and all the paraffin; there was but one tin. Then returning they fetched the bucket, the ammunition, and their clothes. Afterwards, as there was still no sign of Meyer, they even dared to drag in the wagon tent to make a shelter for Benita, and all the wood that they had collected for firing. This proved a wearisome business, for the logs were heavy, and in his crippled state Mr. Clifford could carry no great burden. Indeed, towards the end Benita was forced to complete the task alone, while he limped beside her with his rifle, lest Jacob should surprise them.

When at length everything was done it was long past midnight, and so exhausted were they that, notwithstanding their danger, they flung themselves down upon the canvas tent, which lay in a heap at the end of the cave near the crucifix, and fell asleep.

When Benita woke the lamp had gone out, and it was pitch dark. Fortunately, however, she remembered where she had put the matches and the lantern with a candle in it. She lit the candle and looked at her watch. It was nearly six o'clock. The dawn must be breaking outside, within an hour or two Jacob Meyer would find that they had gone. Suppose that his rage should overcome his fear and that he should creep upon them. They would know nothing of it until his face appeared in the faint ring of light. Or he might even shoot her father out of the darkness. What could she do that would give them warning? A thought came to her.

Taking one of the tent ropes and the lantern, for her father still slept heavily, she went down to the entrance of the cave, and at the end of the last zigzag where once a door had been, managed to make it fast to a stone hinge about eighteen inches above the floor, and on the other side to an eye opposite that was cut in the solid rock to receive a bolt of wood or iron. Meyer, she knew, had no lamps or oil, only matches and perhaps a few candles. Therefore if he tried to enter the cave it was probable that he would trip over the rope and thus give them warning. Then she went back, washed her face and hands with some water that they had drawn on the previous night to satisfy their thirst, and tidied herself as best she could. This done, as her father still slept, she filled the lamps, lit one of them, and looked about her, for she was loth to wake him.

Truly it was an awful place in which to dwell. There above them towered the great white crucifix; there in the corner were piled the remains of the Portuguese. A skull with long hair still hanging to it grinned at her, a withered hand was thrust forward as though to clutch her. Oh, no wonder that in such a spot Jacob Meyer had seen ghosts! In front, too, was the yawning grave where they had found the monk; indeed, his bones wrapped in dark robes still lay within, for Jacob had tumbled them back again. Then beyond and all around deep, dark, and utter silence.

At last her father woke, and glad enough was she of his human company. They breakfasted upon some biscuits and water, and afterwards, while Mr. Clifford watched near the entrance with his rifle, Benita set to work to arrange their belongings. The tent she managed to prop up against the wall of the cave by help of some of the wood which they had carried in. Beneath it she spread their blankets, that it might serve as a sleeping place for them both, and outside placed the food and other things.

While she was thus engaged she heard a sound at the mouth of the cave—Jacob Meyer was entering and had fallen over her rope. Down it she ran, lantern in hand, to her father, who, with his rifle raised, was shouting:

"If you come in here, I put a bullet through you!"

Then came the answer in Jacob's voice, which rang hollow in that vaulted place:

"I do not want to come in; I shall wait for you to come out. You cannot live long in there; the horror of the dark will kill you. I have only to sit in the sunlight and wait."

Then he laughed, and they heard the sound of his footsteps retreating down the passage.

"What are we to do?" asked Mr. Clifford despairingly. "We cannot live without light, and if we have light he will certainly creep to the entrance and shoot us. He is quite mad now; I am sure of it from his voice."

Benita thought a minute, then she answered:

"We must build up the passage. Look," and she pointed to the lumps of rock that the explosion of their mine had shaken down from the roof, and the slabs of cement that they had broken from the floor with the crowbar. "At once, at once," she went on; "he will not come back for some hours, probably not till night."

So they set to work, and never did Benita labour as it was her lot to do that day. Such of the fragments as they could lift they carried between them, others they rolled along by help of the crowbar. For hour after hour they toiled at their task. Luckily for them, the passage was not more than three feet wide by six feet six high, and their material was ample. Before the evening they had blocked it completely with a wall several feet in thickness, which wall they supported on the inside with lengths of the firewood lashed across to the old hinges and bolt-holes, or set obliquely against its face.

It was done, and they regarded their work with pride, although it seemed probable that they were building up their own tomb. Because of its position at an angle of the passage, they knew that Meyer could not get to it with a pole to batter it down. Also, there was no loose powder left, so his only chance would be to pull it to pieces with his hands, and this, they thought, might be beyond his power. At least, should he attempt it, they would have ample warning. Yet that day was not to pass without another trouble.

Just as they had rolled up and levered into place a long fragment of rock designed to prevent the ends of their supporting pieces of wood from slipping on the cement floor, Mr. Clifford uttered an exclamation, then said:

"I have wrung my back badly. Help me to the tent. I must lie down."

Slowly and with great pain they staggered up the cave, Mr. Clifford leaning on Benita and a stick, till, reaching the tent at last, he almost fell on to the blankets and remained there practically crippled.

Now began Benita's terrible time, the worst of all her life. Every hour her father became more ill. Even before they took refuge in the cave he was completely broken down, and now after this accident he began to suffer very much. His rheumatism or sciatica, or whatever it was, seemed to settle upon the hurt muscles of his back, causing him so much pain that he could scarcely sleep for ten minutes at a stretch. Moreover, he would swallow but little of the rough food which was all Benita was able to prepare for him; nothing, indeed, except biscuit soaked in black coffee, which she boiled over a small fire made of wood that they had brought with them, and occasionally a little broth, tasteless stuff enough, for it was only the essence of biltong, or sun-dried flesh, flavoured with some salt.

Then there were two other terrors against she must fight, the darkness and the dread of Jacob Meyer. Perhaps the darkness was the worse of them. To live in that hideous gloom in which their single lamp, for she dared burn no more lest the oil should give out, seemed but as one star to the whole night, ah! who that had not endured it could know what it meant? There the sick man, yonder the grinning skeletons, around the blackness and the silence, and beyond these again a miserable death, or Jacob Meyer. But of him Benita saw nothing, though once or twice she thought that she heard his voice raving outside the wall which they had built. If so, either he did not try to pull it down, or he failed in the attempt, or perhaps he feared that should he succeed, he would be greeted by a bullet. So at last she gave up thinking about him. Should he force his way into the cave she must deal with the situation as best she could. Meanwhile, her father's strength was sinking fast.

Three awful days went by in this fashion, and the end drew near. Although she tried to force herself to it, Benita could not swallow enough food to keep up her strength. Now that the passage was closed the atmosphere of this old vault, for it was nothing more, thickened by the smoke of the fire which she was obliged to burn, grew poisonous and choked her. Want of sleep exhausted her, dread of what the morrow might bring forth crushed her strong spirit. She began to break down, knowing that the hour was near when she and her father must die together.

Once, as she slept awhile at his side, being wakened by his groaning, Benita looked at her watch. It was midnight. She rose, and going to the embers of the little fire, warmed up some of her biltong broth which she poured into a tin pannikin. With difficulty she forced him to swallow a few mouthfuls of it, then, feeling a sudden weakness, drank the rest herself. It gave her power to think, and her father dozed off into an uneasy sleep.

Alas! thinking was of no use, nothing could be done. There was no hope save in prayer. Restlessness seized Benita, and taking the lantern she wandered round the cave. The wall that they had built remained intact, and oh! to think that beyond it flowed the free air and shone the blessed stars! Back she came again, skirting the pits that Jacob Meyer had dug, and the grave of the old monk, till she reached the steps of the crucifix, and holding up her candle, looked at the thorn-crowned brow of the Christ above.

It was wonderfully carved; that dying face was full of pity. Would not He Whom it represented pity her? She knelt down on the topmost step, and clasping the pierced feet with her arms, began to pray earnestly, not for herself but that she might save her father. She prayed as she had never prayed before, and so praying, sank into a torpor or a swoon.

It seemed to Benita that this sleep of hers suddenly became alive; in it she saw many things. For instance, she saw herself seated in a state of trance upon that very step where now she knelt, while before her stood her father and Jacob Meyer. Moreover, something spoke in her; she could not hear a voice, but she seemed to see the words written in the air before her. These were the words:—

"*Clasp the feet of the Christ and draw them to the left. The passage beneath leads to the chamber where the gold is hid, and thence to the river bank. That is the secret which ere I depart, I the dead Benita, pass on to you, the living Benita, as I am commanded. In life and death peace be to your soul.*"

Thrice did this message appear to repeat itself in the consciousness of Benita. Then, suddenly as she had slept, she woke again with every letter of it imprinted on her mind. Doubtless it was a dream, nothing but a dream bred by the fact that her arms were clasping the feet of the crucifix. What did it say? "Draw them to the left."

She did so, but nothing stirred. Again she tried, and still nothing stirred. Of course it was a dream. Why had such been sent to mock her? In a kind of mad irritation she put out all her remaining strength and wrestled with those stony feet. *They moved a little*—then of a sudden, without any further effort on her part, swung round as high as the knees where drapery hung, concealing the join in them. Yes, they swung round, revealing the head of a stair, up which blew a cold wind that it was sweet to breathe.

Benita rose, gasping. Then she seized her lantern and ran to the little tent where her father lay.

CHAPTER 22

The Voice of the Living

Mr. Clifford was awake again now.

"Where have you been?" he asked querulously in a thin voice. "I wanted you."

Then as the light from the candle shone upon it, he noted the change that had come over her pale face, and added:

"What has happened? Is Meyer dead? Are we free?"

Benita shook her head. "He was alive a few hours ago, for I could hear him raving and shouting outside the wall we built. But, father, it has all come back to me; I believe that I have found it."

"What has come back? What have you found? Are you mad, too, like Jacob?"

"What something told me when I was in the trance which afterwards I forgot, but now remember. And I have found the passage which leads to where they hid the gold. It begins behind the crucifix, where no one ever thought of looking."

This matter of the gold did not seem to interest Mr. Clifford. In his state all the wealth beneath the soil of Africa would not have appealed to him. Moreover, he hated the name of that accursed treasure, which was bringing them to such a miserable end.

"Where does the passage run? Have you looked?" he asked.

"Not yet, but the voice in me said—I mean, I dreamed—that it goes down to the river-side. If you leant on me do you think that you could walk?"

"Not one inch," he answered. "Here where I am I shall die."

"No, no, don't talk like that. We may be saved now that I have found a way. Oh, if only you could—if only you could walk, or if I had the strength to carry you!" and she wrung her hands and began to weep, so weak was she.

Her father looked at her searchingly. Then he said:

411

"Well, love, I cannot, so there's an end. But you can, and you had better go."

"What! And leave you? Never."

"Yes, and leave me. Look, there is but a little oil left and only a few candles. The biscuits are done and neither of us can swallow that biltong any more. I suppose that I am dying, and your health and strength are failing you quickly in this darkness; if you stop here you must soon follow me. And what is the alternative? The madman outside—that is, if you could find strength to pull down the wall, which I doubt. You had best go, Benita."

But still she said she would not.

"Do you not see," he added, "that it is my only chance of life? If you go you may be able to bring me help before the end comes. Should there be a passage the probability is that, although they know nothing of it, it finishes somewhere by the wall of the first enclosure where the Makalanga are. If so, you may find the Molimo, or if he is dead, Tamas or one of the others, and they will help us. Go, Benita, go at once."

"I never thought of that," she answered in a changed voice. "Of course, it may be so, if the passage goes down at all. Well, at least I can look and come back to tell you."

Then Benita placed the remainder of the oil close by her father's side, so that he could refill the lamp, for the use of his hands still remained to him. Also, she set there such crumbs of biscuit as were left, some of the biltong, a flask of Hollands, and a pail of water. This done, she put on her long cloak, filled one of its pockets with biltong, and the other with matches and three of the four remaining candles. The fourth she insisted on leaving beside her father's bed. When everything was ready she knelt down at his side, kissed him, and from her heart put up a prayer that they might both live to meet again, although she knew well that this they could scarcely hope to do.

Had two people ever been in a more dreadful situation, she wondered, as she looked at her father lying there, whom she must leave to fight with Death alone in that awful place, while she went forth to meet him in the unknown bowels of the earth!

Mr. Clifford read her thoughts. "Yes," he said, "it is a strange parting and a wild errand. But who knows? It may please Providence to take you through, and if not—why, our troubles will soon be over."

Then once more they kissed, and not daring to try to speak, Benita tore herself away. Passing into the passage whereof the lower half of the crucifix formed the door, she paused for a moment to examine it and to place a fragment of rock in such fashion that it could not shut again behind her. Her idea was that it worked by aid of some spring, but now she saw that this was not so, as the whole mass hung upon three stone hinges beautifully concealed. The dust and corrosion of ages which had made this door so hard to open, by filling up the tiny spaces between it and its framework, had also rendered these cracks utterly imperceptible to the eye. So accurately was it fashioned, indeed, that no one who did not know its secret would have discovered it if they searched for months or years.

Though at the time Benita took little note of such details, the passage beyond and the stair descending from it showed the same perfect workmanship. Evidently this secret way dated not from the Portuguese period, but from that of the Phoenicians or other ancients, to whose treasure-chamber it was the approach, opening as it did from their holy of holies, to which none were admitted save the head priests. The passage, which was about seven feet high by four wide, had been hewn out of the live rock of the mountain, for thousands of little marks left by the workmen's chisels were still discernible upon its walls. So it was with the stair, that had been but little used, and remained fresh as the day when it was finished.

Down the steps, candle in hand, flitted Benita, counting them as she went. The thirtieth brought her to a landing. Here it was that she saw the first traces of that treasure which they had suffered so much to find. Something glittered at her feet. She picked it up. It was a little bar of gold weighing two or three ounces that doubtless had been dropped there. Throwing it down again she looked in front of her, and to her dismay saw a door of wood with iron bolts. But the bolts had never been shot, and when she pulled at it the door creaked upon its rusty hinges and opened. She was on the threshold of the treasure-chamber!

It was square and of the size of a small room, packed on either side almost to the low, vaulted roof with small bags of raw hide, carelessly arranged. Quite near to the door one of these bags had slipped down and burst open. It was filled with gold, some in ingots and some in raw nuggets, for there they lay in a shining, scattered heap. As she stooped to look it came into the mind of Benita that her father had said that in her trance she had told them that one of the bags of treasure was burst, and that the skin of which it had been made was black and red. Behold! before her lay the burst bag, and the colour of the hide was black and red.

She shivered. The thing was uncanny, terrible. Uncanny was it also to see in the thick dust, which in the course of twenty or more of centuries had gathered on the floor, the mark of footprints, those of the last persons who had visited this place. There had been two of them, a man and a woman, and they were no savages, for they wore shoes. Benita placed her foot in the print left by that dead woman. It filled it exactly, it might have been her own. Perhaps, she thought to herself, that other Benita had descended here with her father, after the Portuguese had hidden away their wealth, that she might be shown where it was, and of what it consisted.

One more glance at all this priceless, misery-working gold, and on she went, she who was seeking the gold of life and liberty for herself and him who lay above. Supposing that the stairway ended there? She stopped, she looked round, but could see no other door. To see the better she halted and opened the glass of her lantern. Still she could perceive nothing, and her heart sank. Yet why did the candle flicker so fiercely? And why was the air in this deep place so fresh? She walked forward a pace or two, then noticed suddenly that those footprints of the dead that she was following disappeared immediately in front of her, and she stopped.

It was but just in time. One step more and she would have fallen down the mouth of a deep pit. Once it had been covered with a stone, but this stone was removed, and had never been replaced. Look! there it stood against the wall of the chamber. Well was this for Benita, since her frail strength would not have sufficed to stir that massive block, even if she had discovered its existence beneath the dust.

Now she saw that down the pit ran another ladderlike stair of stone, very narrow and precipitous. Without hesitation she began its descent. Down she went and down—one hundred steps, two hundred steps, two hundred and seventy-five steps, and all the way wherever the dust had gathered the man's and the woman's footprints ran before her. There was a double line of them, one line going down and the other line returning. Those that returned were the last, for often they appeared over those that descended. Why had these dead people returned, Benita wondered.

The stair had ended; now she was in a kind of natural cave, for its sides and roof were rugged; moreover, water trickled and dripped from them. It was not very large, and it smelt horribly of mud and other things. Again she searched by the feeble light of her candle, but could see no exit. Suddenly she saw something else, however, for stepping on what she took to be a rock, to her horror it moved beneath her. She heard a snap as of jaws, a violent blow upon the leg nearly knocked her off her feet, and as she staggered backwards she saw a huge and loathsome shape rushing away into the darkness. The rock that she had trodden on was a crocodile which had its den here! With a little scream she retreated to her stair. Death she had expected—but to be eaten by crocodiles!

Yet as Benita stood there panting a blessed hope rose in her breast. If a crocodile came in there it must also get out, and where such a great creature could go, a woman would be able to follow. Also, she must be near the water, since otherwise it could never have chosen this hole for its habitation. She collected her courage, and having clapped her hands and waved the lantern about to scare any alligators that might still be lurking there, hearing and seeing nothing more, she descended to where she had trodden upon the reptile. Evidently this was its bed, for its long body had left an impress upon the mud, and all about lay the remains of creatures that it had brought in for food. Moreover, a path ran outwards, its well-worn trail distinct even in that light.

She followed this path, which ended apparently in a blank wall. Then it was that Benita guessed why those dead folks' footprints had returned, for here had been a doorway which in some past age those who used it built up with blocks of stone and cement. How, then, did the crocodile get out? Stooping down she searched, and perceived, a few yards to the right of the door, a hole that looked as though it were water-worn. Now Benita thought that she understood. The rock was softer here, and centuries of flood had eaten it away, leaving a crack in the stratum which the crocodiles had found out and enlarged. Down she went on her hands and knees, and thrusting the lantern in front of her, crept along that noisome drain, for this was what it resembled. And now—oh! now she felt air blowing in her face, and heard the sound of reeds whispering, and water running, and saw hanging like a lamp in the blue sky, a star—the morning star! Benita could have wept, she could have worshipped it, yet she pushed on between rocks till she found herself among tall reeds, and standing in water. She had gained the banks of the Zambesi.

Instantly, by instinct as it were, Benita extinguished her candle, fearing lest it should betray her, for constant danger had made her very cunning. The dawn had not yet broken, but the waning moon and the stars gave a good light. She paused to look. There above her towered the outermost wall of Bambatse, against which the river washed, except at such times as the present, when it was very low.

So she was not in the fortress as she had hoped, but without it, and oh! what should she do? Go back again? How would that serve her father or herself? Go on? Then she might fall into the hands of the Matabele whose camp was a little lower down, as from her perch upon the top of the cone she had seen that poor white man do. Ah! the white man! If only he lived and she could reach him! Perhaps they had not killed him after all. It was madness, yet she would try to discover; something impelled her to take the risk. If she failed and escaped, perhaps then she might call to the Makalanga, and they would let down a rope and draw her up the wall before the Matabele caught her. She would not go back empty-handed, to die in that dreadful place with her poor father. Better perish here in the sweet air and beneath the stars, even if it were upon a Matabele spear, or by a bullet from her own pistol.

She looked about her to take her bearings in case it should ever be necessary for her to return to the entrance of the cave. This proved easy, for a hundred or so feet above her—where the sheer face of the cliff jutted out a little, at that very spot indeed on which tradition said that the body of the Señora da Ferreira had struck in its fall, and the necklace Benita wore today was torn from her—a stunted mimosa grew in some cleft of the rock. To mark the crocodile run itself she bent down a bunch of reeds, and having first lit a few Tandstickor brimstone matches and thrown them about inside of it, that the smell of them might scare the beast should it wish to return, she set her lantern behind a stone near to the mouth of the hole.

Then Benita began her journey which, when the river was high, it would not have been possible for her to make except by swimming. As it was, a margin of marsh was left between her and the steep, rocky side of the mount from which the great wall rose, and through this she made her way. Never was she likely to forget that walk. The tall reeds dripped their dew upon her until she was soaked; long, black-tailed finches—*saccaboolas* the natives call them—flew up undisturbed, and lobbed away across the river; owls flitted past and bitterns boomed at the coming of the dawn. Great fish splashed also in the shallows, or were they crocodiles? Benita hoped not—for one day she had seen enough of crocodiles.

It was all very strange. Could she be the same woman, she wondered, who not a year before had been walking with her cousins down Westbourne Grove, and studying Whiteley's windows? What would these cousins say now if they could see her, white-faced, large-eyed, desperate, splashing through the mud upon the unknown banks of the Zambesi, flying from death to death!

On she struggled, above her the pearly sky in which the stars were fading, around her the wet reeds, and pervading all the heavy low-lying mists of dawn. She was past the round of the walls, and at length stood upon dry ground where the Matabele had made their camp. But in that fog she saw no Matabele; probably their fires were out, and she chanced to pass between the sentries. Instinctively, more than by reason, she headed for that hillock upon which she had seen the white man's wagon, in the vague hope that it might still be there. On she struggled, still on, till at length she blundered against something soft and warm, and perceived that it was an ox tied to a trek-tow, beyond which were other oxen and a white wagon-cap.

So it *was* still there! But the white man, where was he? Through the dense mist Benita crept to the *disselboom*. Then, seeing and hearing nothing, she climbed to the *voorkissie* and kneeling on it, separated the tent flaps and peered into the wagon. Still she could see nothing because of the mist, yet she heard something, a man breathing in his sleep. Somehow she thought that it was a white man; a Kaffir did not breathe like that. She did not know what to do, so remained kneeling there. It seemed as though the man who was asleep began to feel her presence, for he muttered to himself—surely the words were English! Then quite suddenly he struck a match and lit a candle which stood in a beer bottle by his side. She could not see his face while he lit the match, for his arm hid it, and the candle burned up slowly. Then the first thing she saw was the barrel of a revolver pointing straight at her.

"Now, my black friend," said a pleasant voice, "down you go or I shoot. One, two! Oh, my God!"

The candle burned up, its light fell upon the white, elfish face of Benita, whose long dark hair streamed about her; it shone in her great eyes. Still she could see nothing, for it dazzled her.

"Oh, my God!" said the voice again. "Benita! Benita! Have you come to tell me that I must join you? Well, I am ready, my sweet, my sweet! Now I shall hear your answer."

"Yes," she whispered, and crawling forward down the cartel Benita fell upon his breast.

For she knew him at last—dead or living she cared not—she knew him, and out of hell crept to him, her heaven and her home!

CHAPTER 23

Benita Gives Her Answer

"Your answer, Benita," Robert said dreamily, for to him this thing seemed a dream.

"Have I not given it, months ago? Oh, I remember, it was only in my heart, not on my lips, when that blow fell on me! Then afterwards I heard what you had done and I nearly died. I wished that I might die to be with you, but I could not. I was too strong; now I understand the reason. Well, it seems that we are both living, and whatever happens, here is my answer, if it is worth anything to you. Once and for all, I love you. I am not ashamed to say it, because very soon we may be separated for the last time. But I cannot talk now, I have come here to save my father."

"Where is he, Benita?"

"Dying in a cave up at the top of that fortress. I got down by a secret way. Are the Matabele still here?"

"Very much so," he answered. "But something has happened. My guard woke me an hour ago to say that a messenger had arrived from their king, Lobengula, and now they are talking over the message. That is how you came to get through, otherwise the sentries would have *assegaied* you, the brutes," and he drew her to him and kissed her passionately for the first time; then, as though ashamed of himself, let her go.

"Have you anything to eat?" she asked. "I—I—am starving. I didn't feel it before, but now———"

"Starving, you starving, while I—look, here is some cold meat which I could not get down last night, and put by for the Kaffirs. Great Heavens! that I should feed you with Kaffirs' leavings! But it is good—eat it."

Benita took the stuff in her fingers and swallowed it greedily; she who for days had lived on nothing but a little biscuit and biltong. It tasted delicious to her—never had she eaten anything so good. And all the while he watched her with glowing eyes.

"How can you look at me?" she said at length. "I must be horrible; I have been living in the dark and crawling through mud. I trod upon a crocodile!" and she shuddered.

"Whatever you are I never want to see you different," he answered slowly. "To me you are most beautiful."

Even then, wreck as she was, the poor girl flushed, and there was a mist in her eyes as she looked up and said:

"Thank you. I don't care now what happens to me, and what has happened doesn't matter at all. But can we get away?"

"I don't know," he answered; "but I doubt it. Go and sit on the wagon-box for a few minutes while I dress, and we will see."

Benita went. The mist was thinning now, and through it she saw a sight at which her heart sank, for between her and the mount Bambatse Matabele were pouring towards their camp on the river's edge. They were cut off. A couple of minutes later Robert joined her, and as he came she looked at him anxiously in the growing light. He seemed older than when they had parted on the *Zanzibar,* changed, too, for now his face was serious, and he had grown a beard; also, he appeared to limp.

"I am afraid there is an end," she said, pointing to the Matabele below.

"Yes, it looks like it. But like you, I say, what does it matter now?" and he took her hand in his, adding: "let us be happy while we can if only for a few minutes. They will be here presently."

"What are you?" she asked. "A prisoner?"

"That's it. I was following you when they captured me; for I have been here before and knew the way. They were going to kill me on general principles, only it occurred to one of them who was more intelligent than the rest that I, being a white man, might be able to show them how to storm the place. Now I was sure that you were there, for I saw you standing on that point, though they thought you were the Spirit of Bambatse. So I wasn't anxious to help them, for then—you know what happens when the Matabele are the stormers! But—as you still lived—I wasn't anxious to die either. So I set them to work to dig a hole with their *assegais* and sharp axes, through granite. They have completed exactly twenty feet of it, and I reckon that there are one hundred and forty to go. Last night they got tired of that tunnel and talked of killing me again, unless I could show them a better plan. Now all the fat is in the fire, and I don't know what is to happen. Hullo! here they come. Hide in the wagon, quick!"

Benita obeyed, and from under cover of the tent where the Matabele could not see her, watched and listened. The party that approached consisted of a chief and about twenty men, who marched behind him as a guard. Benita knew that chief. He was the captain Maduna, he of the royal blood whose life she had saved. By his side was a Natal Zulu, Robert Seymour's driver, who could speak English and acted as interpreter.

"White man," said Maduna, "a message has reached us from our king. Lobengula makes a great war and has need of us. He summons us back from this petty fray, this fight against cowards who hide behind walls, whom otherwise we would have killed, everyone, yes, if we sat here till we grew old. So for this time we leave them alone."

Robert answered politely that he was glad to hear it, and wished them a good journey.

"Wish yourself a good journey, white man," was the stern reply.

"Why? Do you desire that I should accompany you to Lobengula?"

"No, you go before us to the *kraal* of the Black One who is even greater than the child of Moselikatse, to that king who is called Death."

Robert crossed his arms and said: "Say on."

"White man, I promised you life if you would show us how to pierce or climb those walls. But you have made fools of us—you have set us to cut through rock with spears and axes. Yes, to hoe at rock as though it were soil—you who with the wisdom of your people could have taught us some better way. Therefore we must go back to our king disgraced, having failed in his service, and therefore you who have mocked us shall die. Come down now, that we may kill you quietly, and learn whether or no you are a brave man."

Then it was, while her lover's hand was moving towards the pistol hidden beneath his coat, that Benita, with a quick movement, emerged from the wagon in which she crouched, and stood up at his side upon the driving box.

"*Ow!*" said the Captain. "It is the White Maiden. Now how came she here? Surely this is great magic. Can a woman fly like a bird?" and they stared at her amazed.

"What does it matter how I came, chief Maduna?" she answered in Zulu. "Yet I will tell you why I came. It was to save you from dipping your spear in the innocent blood, and bringing on your head the curse of the innocent blood. Answer me now. Who gave you and your brother yonder your lives within that wall when the Makalanga would have torn you limb from limb, as hyenas tear a buck? Was it I or another?"

"*Inkosikaas*—Chieftainess," replied the great Captain, raising his broad spear in salute. "It was you and no other."

"And what did you promise me then, Prince Maduna?"

"Maiden of high birth, I promised you your life and your goods, should you ever fall into my power."

"Does a leader of the Amandabele, one of the royal blood, lie like a Mashona or a Makalanga slave? Does he do worse—tell half the truth only, like a cheat who buys and keeps back half the price?" she asked contemptuously. "Maduna, you promised me not one life, but two, two lives and the goods that belong to both. Ask of your brother there, who was witness of the words."

"Great Heavens!" muttered Robert Seymour to himself, as he looked at Benita standing with outstretched hand and flashing eyes. "Who would have thought that a starved woman could play such a part with death on the hazard?"

"It is as this daughter of white chiefs says," answered the man to whom she had appealed. "When she freed us from the fangs of those dogs, you promised her two lives, my brother, one for yours and one for mine."

"Hear him," went on Benita. "He promised me two lives, and how did this prince of the royal blood keep his promise? When I and the old man, my father, rode hence in peace, he loosed his spears upon us; he hunted us. Yet it was the hunters who fell into the trap, not the hunted."

"Maiden," replied Maduna, in a shamed voice, "that was your fault, not mine. If you had appealed to me I would have let you go. But you killed my sentry, and then the chase began, and ere I knew who you were my runners were out of call."

"Little time had I to ask your mercy; but so be it," said Benita. "I accept your word, and I forgive you that offence. Now fulfil your oath. Begone and leave us in peace."

Still Maduna hesitated.

"I must make report to the king," he said. "What is this white man to you that I should spare him? I give you your life and your father's life, not that of this white man who has tricked us. If he were your father, or your brother, it would be otherwise. But he is a stranger, and belongs to me, not to you."

"Maduna," she asked, "do women such as I am share the wagon of a stranger? This man is more to me than father or brother. He is my husband, and I claim his life."

"Ow!" said the spokesman of the audience, "we understand now. She is his wife, and has a right to him. If she were not his wife she would not be in his wagon. It is plain that she speaks the truth, though how she came here we do not know, unless, as we think, she is a witch," and he smiled at his own cleverness.

"*Inkosikaas*," said Maduna, "you have persuaded me. I give you the life of that white fox, your husband, and I hope that he will not trick you as he has tricked us, and set you to hoe rock instead of soil," and he looked at Robert wrathfully. "I give him to you and all his belongings. Now, is there anything else that you would ask?"

"Yes," replied Benita coolly, "you have many oxen there which you took from the other Makalanga. Mine are eaten and I need cattle to draw my wagon. I ask a present of twenty of them, and," she added by an afterthought, "two cows with young calves, for my father is sick yonder, and must have milk."

"Oh! give them to her. Give them to her," said Maduna, with a tragic gesture that in any other circumstances would have made Benita laugh. "Give them to her and see that they are good ones, before she asks our shields and spears also—for after all she saved my life."

So men departed to fetch those cows and oxen, which presently were driven in.

While this talk was in progress the great *impi* of the Matabele was massing for the march, on the flat ground a little to the right of them. Now they began to come past in companies, preceded by the lads who carried the mats and cooking-pots and drove the captured sheep and cattle. By this time the story of Benita, the witch-woman whom they could not kill, and who had mysteriously flown from the top of the peak into their prisoner's wagon, had spread among them. They knew also that it was she who had saved their general from the Makalanga, and those who had heard her admired the wit and courage with which she had pleaded and won her cause. Therefore, as they marched past in their companies, singing a song of abuse and defiance of the Makalanga who peered at them from the top of the wall, they lifted their great spears in salutation to Benita standing upon the wagon-box.

Indeed, they were a wondrous and imposing spectacle, such a one as few white women have ever seen.

At length all were gone except Maduna and a body-guard of two hundred men. He walked to the front of the wagon and addressed Robert Seymour.

"Listen, you fox who set us to hoe granite," he said indignantly. "You have outwitted us this time, but if ever I meet you again, then you die. Now I have given you your life, but," he added, almost pleadingly, "if you are really brave as white men are said to be, will you not come down and fight me man to man for honour's sake?"

"I think not," answered Robert, when he understood this challenge, "for what chance should I have against so brave a warrior? Also this lady—my wife—needs my help on her journey home."

Maduna turned from him contemptuously to Benita.

"I go," he said, "and fear not; you will meet no Matabele on that journey. Have you more words for me, O Beautiful One, with a tongue of oil and a wit that cuts like steel?"

"Yes," answered Benita. "You have dealt well with me, and in reward I give you of my good luck. Bear this message to your king from the White Witch of Bambatse, for I am she and no other. That he leave these Makalanga, my servants, to dwell unharmed in their ancient home, and that he lift no spear against the White Men, lest that evil which the Molimo foretold to you, should fall upon him."

"Ah!" said Maduna, "now I understand how you flew from the mountain top into this man's wagon. You are not a white woman, you are the ancient Witch of Bambatse herself. You have said it, and with such it is not well to war. Great lady of Magic, Spirit from of old, I salute you, and I thank you for your gifts of life and fortune. Farewell."

Then he, too, stalked away at the head of his guard, so that presently, save for the three Zulu servants and the herd of cattle, Robert and Benita were left utterly alone.

Now, her part played and the victory won, Benita burst into tears and fell upon her lover's breast.

Presently she remembered, and freed herself from his arms.

"I am a selfish wretch," she said. "How dare I be so happy when my father is dead or dying? We must go at once."

"Go where?" asked the bewildered Robert.

"To the top of the mountain, of course, whence I came. Oh! please don't stop to question me, I'll tell you as we walk. Stay," and she called to the Zulu driver, who with an air of utter amazement was engaged in milking one of the gift cows, to fill two bottles with the milk.

"Had we not better shout to the Makalanga to let us in?" suggested Robert, while this was being done, and Benita wrapped some cooked meat in a cloth.

"No, no. They will think I am what I said I was—the Witch of Bambatse, whose appearance heralds misfortune, and fear a trap. Besides, we could not climb the top wall. You must follow my road, and if you can trust them, bring two of those men with you with lanterns. The lad can stop to herd the cattle."

Three minutes later, followed by the two Zulus, they were walking—or rather, running—along the banks of the Zambesi.

"Why do you not come quicker?" she asked impatiently. "Oh, I beg your pardon, you are lame. Robert, what made you lame, and oh! why are you not dead, as they all swore you were, you, you—hero, for I know that part of the story?"

"For a very simple reason, Benita: because I didn't die. When that Kaffir took the watch from me I was insensible, that's all. The sun brought me to life afterwards. Then some natives turned up, good people in their way, although I could not understand a word they said. They made a stretcher of boughs and carried me for some miles to their *kraal* inland. It hurt awfully, for my thigh was broken, but I arrived at last. There a Kaffir doctor set my leg in his own fashion; it has left it an inch shorter than the other, but that's better than nothing.

"In that place I lay for two solid months, for there was no white man within a hundred miles, and if there had been I could not have communicated with him. Afterwards I spent another month limping up towards Natal, until I could buy a horse. The rest is very short. Hearing of my reported death, I came as fast as I could to your father's farm, Rooi Krantz, where I learned from the old *vrouw* Sally that you had taken to treasure-hunting, the same treasure that I told you of on the *Zanzibar*.

"So I followed your spoor, met the servants whom you had sent back, who told me all about you, and in due course, after many adventures, as they say in a book, walked into the camp of our friends, the Matabele.

"They were going to kill me at once, when suddenly you appeared upon that point of rock, glittering like—like the angel of the dawn. I knew that it must be you, for I had found out about your attempted escape, and how you were hunted back to this place. But the Matabele all thought that it was the Spirit of Bambatse, who has a great reputation in these parts. Well, that took off their attention, and afterwards, as I told you, it occurred to them that I might be an engineer. You know the rest, don't you?"

"Yes," answered Benita softly. "I know the rest."

Then they plunged into the reeds and were obliged to stop talking, since they must walk in single file. Presently Benita looked up and saw that she was under the thorn which grew in the cleft of the rock. Also, with some trouble she found the bunch of reeds that she had bent down, to mark the inconspicuous hole through which she had crept, and by it her lantern. It seemed weeks since she had left it there.

"Now," she said, "light your candles, and if you see a crocodile, please shoot."

CHAPTER 24

The True Gold

"Let me go first," said Robert.

"No," answered Benita. "I know the way; but please do watch for that horrible crocodile."

Then she knelt down and crept into the hole, while after her came Robert, and after him the two Zulus, who protested that they were not ant-bears to burrow under ground. Lifting the lantern she searched the cave, and as she could see no signs of the crocodile, walked on boldly to where the stair began.

"Be quick," she whispered to Robert, for in that place it seemed natural to speak low. "My father is above and near his death. I am dreadfully afraid lest we should be too late."

So they toiled up the endless steps, a very strange procession, for the two Zulus, bold men enough outside, were shaking with fright, till at length Benita clambered out of the trap door on to the floor of the treasure chamber, and turned to help Robert, whose lameness made him somewhat slow and awkward.

"What's all that?" he asked, pointing to the hide sacks, while they waited for the two scared Kaffirs to join them.

"Oh!" she answered indifferently, "gold, I believe. Look, there is some of it on the floor, over Benita da Ferreira's footsteps."

"Gold! Why, it must be worth——! And who on earth is Benita da Ferreira?"

"I will tell you afterwards. She has been dead two or three hundred years; it was her gold, or her people's, and those are her footprints in the dust. How stupid you are not to understand! Never mind the hateful stuff; come on quickly."

So they passed the door which she had opened that morning, and clambered up the remaining stairway. So full was Benita of terrors that she could never remember how she climbed them. Suppose that the foot of the crucifix had swung to; suppose that her father were dead; suppose that Jacob Meyer had broken into the cave? Well for herself she was no longer afraid of Jacob Meyer. Oh, they were there! The heavy door *had* begun to close, but mercifully her bit of rock kept it ajar.

"Father! Father!" she cried, running towards the tent.

No answer came. She threw aside the flap, held down the lantern and looked. There he lay, white and still. She was too late!

"He is dead, he is dead!" she wailed. Robert knelt down at her side, and examined the old man, while she waited in an agony.

"He ought to be," he said slowly; "but, Benita, I don't think he is. I can feel his heart stir. No, don't stop to talk. Pour out some of that squareface, and here, mix it with this milk."

She obeyed, and while he held up her father's head, with a trembling hand emptied a little of the drink into his mouth. At first it ran out again, then almost automatically he swallowed some, and they knew that he was alive, and thanked Heaven. Ten minutes later Mr. Clifford was sitting up staring at them with dull and wondering eyes, while outside the two Zulus, whose nerves had now utterly broken down, were contemplating the pile of skeletons in the corner and the white towering crucifix, and loudly lamenting that they should have been brought to perish in this place of bones and ghosts.

"Is it Jacob Meyer who makes that noise?" asked Mr. Clifford faintly. "And, Benita, where have you been so long, and—who is this gentleman with you? I seem to remember his face."

"He is the white man who was in the wagon, father, an old friend come to life again. Robert, can't you stop the howling of those Kaffirs? Though I am sure I don't wonder that they howl; I should have liked to do so for days. Oh! father, father, don't you understand me? We are saved, yes, snatched out of hell and the jaws of death."

"Is Jacob Meyer dead, then?" he asked.

"I don't know where he is or what has happened to him, and I don't care, but perhaps we had better find out. Robert, there is a madman outside. Make the Kaffirs pull down that wall, would you? and catch him."

"What wall? What madman?" he asked, staring at her.

"Oh, of course you don't know that, either. You know nothing. I'll show you, and you must be prepared, for probably he will shoot at us."

"It all sounds a little risky, doesn't it?" asked Robert doubtfully.

"Yes, but we must take the risk. We cannot carry my father down that place, and unless we can get him into light and air soon, he will certainly die. The man outside is Jacob Meyer, his partner—you remember him. All these weeks of hardship and treasure-hunting have sent him off his head, and he wanted to mesmerize me and——"

"And what? Make love to you?"

She nodded, then went on:

"So when he could not get his way about the mesmerism and so forth, he threatened to murder my father, and that is why we had to hide in this cave and build ourselves up, till at last I found the way out."

"Amiable gentleman, Mr. Jacob Meyer, now as always," said Robert flushing. "To think that you should have been in the power of a scoundrel like that! Well, I hope to come square with him."

"Don't hurt him, dear, unless you are obliged. Remember he is not responsible. He thought he saw a ghost here the other day."

"Unless he behaves himself he is likely to see a good many soon," muttered Robert.

Then they went down the cave, and as silently as possible began to work at the wall, destroying in a few minutes what had been built up with so much labour. When it was nearly down the Zulus were told that there was an enemy outside, and that they must help to catch him if necessary, but were not to harm him. They assented gladly enough; indeed, to get out of that cave they would have faced half a dozen enemies.

Now there was a hole right through the wall, and Robert bade Benita stand to one side. Then as soon as his eyes became accustomed to the little light that penetrated there, he drew his revolver and beckoned the Kaffirs to follow. Down the passage they crept, slowly, lest they should be blinded when they came to the glare of the sunshine, while Benita waited with a beating heart.

A little time went by, she never knew how long, till suddenly a rifle shot rang through the stillness. Benita was able to bear no more. She rushed down the winding passage, and presently, just beyond its mouth, in a blurred and indistinct fashion saw that the two white men were rolling together on the ground, while the Kaffirs sprang round watching for an opportunity to seize one of them. At that moment they succeeded, and Robert rose, dusting his hands and knees.

"Amiable gentleman, Mr. Jacob Meyer," he repeated. "I could have killed him as his back was towards me, but didn't because you asked me not. Then I stumbled with my lame leg, and he whipped round and let drive with his rifle. Look," and he showed her where the bullet had cut his ear. "Luckily I got hold of him before he could loose off another."

Benita could find no words, her heart was too full of thankfulness. Only she seized Robert's hand and kissed it. Then she looked at Jacob.

He was lying upon the broad of his back, the two big Zulus holding his arms and legs; his lips were cracked, blue and swollen; his face was almost black, but his eyes still shone bright with insanity and hate.

"I know you," he screamed hoarsely to Robert. "You are another ghost, the ghost of that man who was drowned. Otherwise my bullet would have killed you."

"Yes, Mr. Meyer," Seymour answered, "I am a ghost. Now, you boys, here's a bit of rope. Tie his hands behind his back and search him. There is a pistol in that pocket."

They obeyed, and presently Meyer was disarmed and bound fast to a tree.

"Water," he moaned. "For days I have had nothing but the dew I could lick off the leaves."

Pitying his plight, Benita ran into the cave and returned presently with a tin of water. One of the Kaffirs held it to his lips, and he drank greedily. Then, leaving one Zulu to watch him, Robert, Benita, and the other Zulu went back, and as gently as they could carried out Mr. Clifford on his mattress, placing him in the shade of a rock, where he lay blessing them feebly, because they had brought him into the light again. At the sight of the old man Meyer's rage blazed up afresh.

"Ah," he screamed, "if only I had killed you long ago, she would be mine now, not that fellow's. It was you who stood between us."

"Look here, my friend," broke in Robert. "I forgive you every-thing else, but, mad or sane, be good enough to keep Miss Clifford's name off your lips, or I will hand you over to those Kaffirs to be dealt with as you deserve."

Then Jacob understood, and was silent. They gave him more water and food to eat, some of the meat that they had brought with them, which he devoured ravenously.

"Are you sensible now?" asked Robert when he had done. "Then listen to me; I have some good news for you. That treasure you have been hunting for has been found. We are going to give you half of it, one of the wagons and some oxen, and clear you out of this place. Then if I set eyes on you again before we get to a civilized country, I shoot you like a dog."

"You lie!" said Meyer sullenly. "You want to turn me out into the wilderness to be murdered by the Makalanga or the Matabele."

"Very well," said Robert. "Untie him, boys, and bring him along. I will show him whether I lie."

"Where are they taking me to?" asked Meyer. "Not into the cave? I won't go into the cave; it is haunted. If it hadn't been for the ghost there I would have broken down their wall long ago, and killed that old snake before her eyes. Whenever I went near that wall I saw it watching me."

"First time I ever heard of a ghost being useful," remarked Robert. "Bring him along. No, Benita, he shall see whether I am a liar."

So the lights were lit, and the two stalwart Zulus hauled Jacob forward, Robert and Benita following. At first he struggled violently, then, on finding that he could not escape, went on, his teeth chattering with fear.

"It is cruel," remonstrated Benita.

"A little cruelty will not do him any harm," Robert answered. "He has plenty to spare for other people. Besides, he is going to get what he has been looking for so long."

They led Jacob to the foot of the crucifix, where a paroxysm seemed to seize him, then pushed him through the swinging doorway beneath, and down the steep stairs, till once more they all stood in the treasure-chamber.

"Look," said Robert, and, drawing his hunting-knife, he slashed one of the hide bags, whereon instantly there flowed out a stream of beads and nuggets. "Now, my friend, am I a liar?" he asked.

At this wondrous sight Jacob's terror seemed to depart from him, and he grew cunning.

"Beautiful, beautiful!" he said, "more than I thought—sacks and sacks of gold. I shall be a king indeed. No, no, it is all a dream—like the rest. I don't believe it's there. Loose my arms and let me feel it."

"Untie him," said Robert, at the same time drawing his pistol and covering the man; "he can't do us any hurt."

The Kaffirs obeyed, and Jacob, springing at the slashed bag, plunged his thin hands into it.

"No lie," he screamed, "no lie," as he dragged the stuff out and smelt at it. "Gold, gold, gold! Hundreds of thousands of pounds' worth of gold! Let's make a bargain, Englishman, and I won't kill you as I meant to do. You take the girl and give me all the gold," and in his ecstasy he began to pour the glittering ingots over his head and body.

"A new version of the tale of Danaë," began Robert in a sarcastic voice, then suddenly paused, for a change had come over Jacob's face, a terrible change.

It turned ashen beneath the tan, his eyes grew large and round, he put up his hands as though to thrust something from him, his whole frame shivered, and his hair seemed to erect itself. Slowly he retreated backwards, and would have fallen down the unclosed trap-hole had not one of the Kaffirs pushed him away. Back he went, still back, till he struck the further wall and stood there, perhaps for half a minute. He lifted his hand and pointed first to those ancient footprints, some of which still remained in the dust of the floor, and next, as they thought, at Benita. His lips moved fast, he seemed to be pleading, remonstrating, yet—and this was the ghastliest part of it— from them there came no sound. Lastly, his eyes rolled up until only the whites of them were visible, his face became wet as though water had been poured over it, and, still without a sound, he fell forward and moved no more.

So terrible was the scene that with a howl of fear the two Kaffirs turned and fled up the stairway. Robert sprang to the Jew, dragged him over on to his back, put his hand upon his breast and lifted his eyelids.

"Dead," he said. "Stone dead. Privation, brain excitement, heart failure—that's the story."

"Perhaps," answered Benita faintly; "but really I think that I begin to believe in ghosts also. Look, I never noticed them before, and I didn't walk there, but those footsteps seem to lead right up to him." Then she turned too and fled.

Another week had gone by. The wagons were laden with a burden more precious perhaps than wagons have often borne before. In one of them, on a veritable bed of gold, slept Mr. Clifford, still very weak and ill, but somewhat better than he had been, and with a good prospect of recovery, at any rate for a while. They were to trek a little after dawn, and already Robert and Benita were up and waiting. She touched his arm and said to him:

"Come with me. I have a fancy to see that place once more, for the last time."

So they climbed the hill and the steep steps in the topmost wall that Meyer had blocked—re-opened now—and reaching the mouth of the cave, lit the lamps which they had brought with them, and entered. There were the fragments of the barricade that Benita had built with desperate hands, there was the altar of sacrifice standing cold and grey as it had stood for perhaps three thousand years. There was the tomb of the old monk who had a companion now, for in it Jacob Meyer lay with him, his bones covered by the debris that he himself had dug out in his mad search for wealth; and there the white Christ hung awful on His cross. Only the skeletons of the Portuguese were gone, for with the help of his Kaffirs Robert had moved them every one into the empty treasure-chamber, closing the trap beneath, and building up the door above, so that there they might lie in peace at last.

In this melancholy place they tarried but a little while, then, turning their backs upon it for ever, went out and climbed the granite cone to watch the sun rise over the broad Zambesi. Up it came in glory, that same sun which had shone upon the despairing Benita da Ferreira, and upon the English Benita when she had stood there in utter hopelessness, and seen the white man captured by the Matabele.

Now, different was their state indeed, and there in that high place, whence perhaps many a wretched creature had been cast to death, whence certainly the Portuguese maiden had sought her death, these two happy beings were not ashamed to give thanks to Heaven for the joy which it had vouchsafed to them, and for their hopes of life full and long to be travelled hand in hand. Behind them was the terror of the cave, beneath them were the mists of the valley, but above them the light shone and rolled and sparkled, and above them stretched the eternal sky!

They descended the pillar, and near the foot of it saw an old man sitting. It was Mambo, the Molimo of the Makalanga: even when they were still far away from him they knew his snow-white head and thin, ascetic face. As they drew near Benita perceived that his eyes were closed, and whispered to Robert that he was asleep. Yet he had heard them coming, and even guessed her thought.

"Maiden," he said in his gentle voice, "maiden who soon shall be a wife, I do not sleep, although I dream of you as I have dreamt before. What did I say to you that day when first we met? That for you I had good tidings; that though death was all about you, you need not fear; that in this place you who had known great sorrow should find happiness and rest. Yet, maiden, you would not believe the words of the Munwali, spoken by his prophet's lips, as he at your side, who shall be your husband, would not believe me in years past when I told him that we should meet again."

"Father," she answered, "I thought your rest was that which we find only in the grave."

"You would not believe," he went on without heeding her, "and therefore you tried to fly, and therefore your heart was torn with terror and with agony, when it should have waited for the end in confidence and peace."

"Father, my trial was very sore."

"Maiden, I know it, and because it was so sore that patient Spirit of Bambatse bore with you, and through it all guided your feet aright.

Yes, with you has that Spirit gone, by day, by night, in the morning and in the evening. Who was it that smote the man who lies dead yonder with horror and with madness when he would have bent your will to his and made you a wife to him? Who was it that told you the secret of the treasure-pit, and what footsteps went before you down its stair? Who was it that led you past the sentries of the Amandabele and gave you wit and power to snatch your lord's life from Maduna's bloody hand? Yes, with you it has gone and with you it will go. No more shall the White Witch stand upon the pillar point at the rising of the sun, or in the shining of the moon."

"Father, I have never understood you, and I do not understand you now," said Benita. "What has this spirit to do with me?"

He smiled a little, then answered slowly:

"That I may not tell you; that you shall learn one day, but never here. When you also have entered into silence, then you shall learn. But I say to you that this shall not be till your hair is as white as mine, and your years are as many. Ah! you thought that I had deserted you, when fearing for your father's life you wept and prayed in the darkness of the cave. Yet it was not so, for I did but suffer the doom which I had read to fulfil itself as it must do."

He rose to his feet and, resting on his staff, laid one withered hand upon the head of Benita.

"Maiden," he said, "we meet no more beneath the sun. Yet because you have brought deliverance to my people, because you are sweet and pure and true, take with you the blessing of Munwali, spoken by the mouth of his servant Mambo, the old Molimo of Bambatse. Though from time to time you must know tears and walk in the shade of sorrows, long and happy shall be your days with him whom you have chosen. Children shall spring up about you, and children's children, and with them also shall the blessing go. The gold you white folk love is yours, and it shall multiply and give food to the hungry and raiment to those that are a-cold. Yet in your own heart lies a richer store that cannot melt away, the countless treasure of mercy and of love. When you sleep and when you wake Love shall take you by the hand, till at length he leads you through life's dark cave to that eternal house of purest gold which soon or late those that seek it shall inherit," and with his staff he pointed to the glowing morning sky wherein one by one little rosy clouds floated upwards and were lost.

To Robert and to Benita's misty eyes they looked like bright-winged angels throwing wide the black doors of night, and heralding that conquering glory at whose advent despair and darkness flee away.

ALSO FROM LEONAUR
AVAILABLE IN SOFTCOVER OR HARDCOVER WITH DUST JACKET

TROS OF SAMOTHRACE 1: WOLVES OF THE TIBER *by Talbot Mundy*—When his ship is taken and his crew slaughtered Tros of Samothrace is captured by Imperial Rome.

TROS OF SAMOTHRACE 2: DRAGONS OF THE NORTH *by Talbot Mundy*—Tros of Samothrace burns for vengeance and has declared himself the implacable enemy of Rome.

TROS OF SAMOTHRACE 3: SERPENT OF THE WAVES *by Talbot Mundy*—Tros, his allies and the forces of Rome have drawn apart to prepare for the conflict to come.

TROS OF SAMOTHRACE 4: CITY OF THE EAGLES *by Talbot Mundy*—As Tros of Samothrace continues in his attempts to confound Caesar's plans for the invasion of Britain, he journeys to the Eternal City to seek the aid of its great leaders—and Caesar's opponents—Cato, Pompey and the Vestal Virgins themselves!

TROS OF SAMOTHRACE 5: CLEOPATRA *by Talbot Mundy*—Cleopatra—Queen of Egypt—is a formidable character ever ready to play the game of intrigue, betrayal and shifting loyalties to suit her own objectives. Blood will surely be spilt and once again Tros finds himself inexorably caught up in monumental events that threaten his life and those he loves.

TROS OF SAMOTHRACE 6: THE PURPLE PIRATE *by Talbot Mundy*—The epic saga of the ancient world—Tros of Samothrace—draws to a conclusion in this sixth—and final—volume. Julius Caesar has been assassinated and Queen Cleopatra of Egypt finds herself in a perilous position and desperate for allies to secure her power.

THE ILLUSTRATED & COMPLETE BRIGADIER GERARD *by Sir Arthur Conan Doyle*—These are the adventures of Conan Doyle's incomparable French hero-the finest swordsman in the Light Cavalry-Etienne Gerard. Arranged for the first time in historical chronological order, his many enthusiasts can now properly appreciate his colourful career as he fights, loves and blunders his way through the Napoleonic epoch-from his earliest adventure as a young blade determined to reach his lady love despite the unwelcome attention of her fathers bull-through many campaigns and special missions-to the bloody field of Waterloo, the downfall of his beloved Emperor and beyond. This is the complete collection of these classic stories. What makes this edition exceptional is the inclusion of nearly 140 illustrations-mostly by the famed military artist William Barnes Wollen-which accurately portray the spirit of the stories and the uniforms and scenes of the events they portray.

LEONAUR

ALSO FROM LEONAUR

AVAILABLE IN SOFTCOVER OR HARDCOVER WITH DUST JACKET

GARRETT P. SERVISS' SCIENCE FICTION by *Garrett P. Serviss*—Three Interplanetary Adventures including the unauthorised sequel to H. G. Wells' *War of the Worlds*--*Edison's Conquest of Mars, A Columbus of Space, The Moon Metal*.

JUNK DAY by *Arthur Sellings*—". . . . his finest novel was his last, *Junk Day*, a post-holocaust tale set in the ruins of his native London and peopled with engrossing character types . . . . perhaps grimmer than his previous work but pointedly more energetic." *The Encyclopedia of Science Fiction*.

KIPLING'S SCIENCE FICTION by *Rudyard Kipling*—Science Fiction & Fantasy stories by a Master Storyteller including 'As East As A,B,C' 'With The Night Mail'.

THE COLLECTED SCIENCE FICTION AND FANTASY OF STANLEY G. WEINBAUM: THE BLACK HEART by *Stanley G. Weinbaum*—Classic Strange Tales Including: the Complete Novel The Dark Other, Plus Proteus Island and Others Stories included in this Volume The Dark Other (novel) Proteus Island The Adaptive Ultimate Pymalion's Spectacles.

THE COLLECTED SCIENCE FICTION AND FANTASY OF STANLEY G. WEINBAUM: STRANGE GENIUS by *Stanley G. Weinbaum*—Classic Tales of the Human Mind at Work Including the Complete Novel The New Adam, the 'van Manderpootz' Stories and Others Stories included in this Volume The New Adam (novel) The Brink of Infinity The Circle of Zero Graph The Worlds of If The Ideal The Point of View.

THE COLLECTED SCIENCE FICTION AND FANTASY OF STANLEY G. WEINBAUM OTHER EARTHS by *Stanley G. Weinbaum*—Classic Futuristic Tales Including: Dawn of Flame & its Sequel The Black Flame, plus The Revolution of 1960 & Others.

THE COLLECTED SCIENCE FICTION AND FANTASY OF STANLEY G. WEINBAUM INTERPLANETARY ODYSSEYS by *Stanley G. Weinbaum*— Classic Tales of Interplanetary Adventure Including: A Martian Odyssey, its Sequel Valley of Dreams, the Complete 'Ham' Hammond Stories and Others Stories included in this Volume Mars A Martian Odyssey Valley of Dreams Venus Parasite Planet The Lotus Eaters Uranus The Planet of Doubt Titan Flight on Titan Pluto The Red Peri Io The Mad Moon Europa Redemption Cairn Ganymede Tidal Moon.

SUPERNATURAL BUCHAN by *John Buchan*—Stories of Ancient Spirits, Uncanny Places & Strange Creatures.